I0829500

The Art of Sherlock Holmes

West Palm Beach

Conceived And Curated By

Phil Growick

Special Edition ISBN 978-1-78705-403-5
Standard Edition ISBN 978-1-78705-411-0

Published in the UK by MX Publishing
335 Princess Park Manor, Royal Drive,
London, N11 3GX
www.mxpublishing.co.uk

Conceived and Curated by Phil Growick

A share of the net proceeds from the sales of merchandising and licensing of The Art of Sherlock Holmes will be donated to the following charities:

The Mandel Public Library of West Palm Beach (www.wpb.org/mycitylibrary)

Happy Life Children's Home, Nairobi, Kenya (www.happylifechildrenshome.com)

Stepping Stones School, Hindhead, UK (www.steppingstones.org.uk)

Contents

To the artists and the authors who inspire them.

And to Maiju, always Maiju.

Introduction

The Art of Sherlock Holmes is truly unique.

While there have been literally hundreds of Holmes pastiches written (even a few of mine), there never has been a volume where Holmes short stories are interpreted by some of the most accomplished artists in the world.

In this first local edition, fifteen artists who live or create in West Palm Beach have each had a story assigned to them – specifically dependent on the particular talent of each artist.

Whether the interpretations be from the forms of abstract, contemporary, realist, minimalist, symbolism, or an amalgam of various forms, each piece of art created is unique, hypnotic, mesmerizing and unforgettable. Each created specifically to express the essence of each incredible Holmes story.

The fifteen stories herein range from the impossibly baffling (except for Holmes) to the humorous, paranormal, or simply intellectually intricate. You're presented with murder, theft, treason, betrayal, love, loss and greed. All the ingredients to make a delicious Holmes meal of mystery.

But please remember, art is in the eye of the beholder. So, we hope you'll appreciate each creation for what it is: an inimitable interpretation of a truly unique Holmes story.

Phil Growick

The Tale of the
First Adventure

by Derrick Belanger

This story first appeared in the MX Book of New Sherlock Holmes Stories Volume IV.

Derrick Belanger is an author, publisher, and educator most noted for his books and lectures on Sherlock Holmes and Sir Arthur Conan Doyle. A number of his books have been #1 bestsellers in their categories on Amazon.com including Sherlock Holmes: The Adventure of the Peculiar Provenance, Sherlock Holmes: The Adventure of the Primal Man, MacDougall Twins with Sherlock Holmes: Attack of the Violet Vampire!, and both volumes of his two volume anthology A Study in Terror: Sir Arthur Conan Doyle's Revolutionary Stories of Fear and the Supernatural. Mr. Belanger is co-owner of the publishing company Belanger Books which has reissued new editions of the August Derleth Solar Pons books as well as publishing new Solar Pons story collections. His academic work has been published in The Colorado Reading Journal and Gifted Child Today. A former instructor at Washington State University, and a current middle school Special Education teacher at Century Middle School in the Adams 12 School District, Derrick lives in Broomfield, Colorado with his wife Abigail Gosselin and their two daughters, Rhea and Phoebe. Find him at www.belangerbooks.com and http://belangerbooks-sherlockholmes.blogspot.com/.

Anthony Hernandez was born in Havana, Cuba on October 16, 1972. His love and passion for art influenced his life as a young child. Anthony was fascinated by works of artists from his birthplace including Amelia Peláez, Mario Carreño and Rene' Portocarrero. At the age of 12 he immigrated to Chicago and now resides in Florida. His work is predominantly in the medium of acrylic paintings on canvas and murals.Anthony is a firm believer that everything is somehow connected: *"Our actions and our intentions, whether good or bad, create a chain reaction. Each work or piece in any medium I use will carry that message of connection. I always emphasize that art and life go hand in hand; it is about decisions not conditions"*.

www.anthonyhernandezart.com

Artwork size: 36 x 48

Medium: Acrylic on canvas

It was with exciting news that I hurried to 221b Baker Street one late autumn afternoon. I had just received an unexpected patient, and the man came with information about my dear friend Sherlock Holmes. The man, a Mr. Zenas Cooper, had arrived at my doorstep supporting his back with a well-worn wooden cane. He had injured himself in the process of lifting a large trunk of clothing, and was afraid he had caused serious damage. His brother, Tobias Cooper, a regular patient of mine, had recommended Zenas see me before his long ride back to Devon. After a few tests, I could see that my initial diagnosis, that Mr. Cooper had strained his lumbar, was accurate. I assured the man that while the pain and discomfort were debilitating, if he rested and stayed off of his feet, he would be healed within a week's time.

Mr. Cooper was a good twenty years my senior. A large man with ruddy cheeks, wispy white hair, emerald eyes, and a jolly laugh, he was in good spirits despite his situation and said he felt blessed that his wife had packed his cane on his London sojourn to visit his brother. Just as he completed his visit and I assisted the man to the front door, he paused and asked in his booming voice, "Say . . . I think . . . no, no, I'm sure it is a coincidence."

I inquired as to what the gentleman was puzzling about.

"You wouldn't happen to be the same Dr. Watson who wrote that story in Lippincott's? . . . *The Sign of the Four*, I believe it was called."

I assured him that I was, and the man let out such a bellowing laugh that for a moment I thought he had become Dickens' Ghost of Christmas Present. "My good man," he started, "you tell Master Holmes, for he will always be Master Holmes to me, that Mr. Cooper still remembers the good turn he did for me, and that I am and will eternally be grateful."

I asked the man whatever Holmes had done for him, and his face brightened to an even warmer shade of red. "Why, Master Holmes saved my marriage, the lad did. Bright boy. Exceptional, really. The top student I ever taught in my first year class. Suppose with Master Holmes, it's hard to say how much I taught him and how much he taught me. I could tell you more, but I am afraid I have a train to catch. Please do give Master Holmes my kind regards, and ask him about the good turn he did for Mr. Cooper. You're Dr. Watson, after all. You'd want his telling of the events if you see fit to turn the tale into one of your publications. I'm sure I'd miss some of the important details for it was so long ago, but that Master Holmes, with that brain of his, even though he was just eleven at the time, I'm sure he remembers every detail." And with a wink, he hobbled off down the steps to his awaiting taxi. I assisted the man into the cab, and no sooner had his left then I hailed one myself, for with this information, curiosity had seized me. Mr. Cooper had been my final patient for the day, and I knew Mrs. Watson was visiting a friend for the afternoon and wouldn't return until early in the evening. I just had to see Holmes, had to know about this mystery he'd puzzled out at such a young age.

As the hansom pulled up in front of 221b Baker Street, I nearly leaped out of the cab. I found the door to my friend's residence unlocked and practically flung it open. Fortunately, Mrs. Hudson was not at home, for I'm sure she would have scolded me for not knocking before entering. Not tarrying a moment, I bounded up the seventeen steps to Holmes's sitting room as fast as my legs could carry me. When I was almost at the top of the stairs, a sharp jolt of pain shot through my left leg, which still suffered from a wound I'd received from a Jezail bullet in the Afghan War. I gave out a holler, winced, and cursed myself for my over-ambition. Using the railing of the stairs, I supported myself and limped up to the door of the first floor rooms. I didn't bother knocking, but with a swift turn of the knob swung the door wide and found Holmes in his armchair, reading over several papers with a magnifying glass.

"Watson," he said, barely taking his eyes off of the document he was inspecting, "it appears that the ransom letter to the Australian businessman Robert Steele was not written by his daughter, but rather by his wife. The curl of the q and the curve of the g are quite definitely the same." He lowered the papers and motioned for me to sit down. "Now then, please have a seat, get off of your foot, and tell me about this patient who had knowledge about my past."

"Really, Holmes," I groaned, collapsing into my favorite chair. I pulled the hassock to me and raised my injured leg upon it. I could tell the pain would go away with the passage of time and rest. "How, even with your powers of observation, could you have known about the gentleman who visited me this afternoon?"

"None of my so called powers is beyond those contained by every person in this fair city. I simply observe, analyze, make logical connections, and draw my conclusions based on the evidence presented," Holmes stated matter-of-factly. "Now, if you'll excuse me for just a moment." He gathered the papers he had been examining, stood, and took them to his desk. With a quick stride, he then went to his spirit case and returned to his seat carrying two glasses of brandy. He handed one to me, for which I thanked him.

"We need to make sure my Boswell does not overexert himself. Now, my dear Watson, tell me about this unexpected patient of yours."

"Not quite yet, Holmes. First you must tell me how you knew my patient was connected to your childhood."

"Really, Watson, that is quite elementary," he said and took another sip of his brandy. "Look at the time of day. You practically sprinted up the steps to tell me some exciting news. Me, not your wife, for clearly you did not have enough time to see Mrs. Watson after your hours ended and then come to Baker Street. You must have left your practice in great haste, for you did not notice you still wore the stethoscope around your neck. Indeed, you still do."

Here, I paused and checked myself. The stethoscope was indeed upon my person. In my hurry and excitement, I did not even notice. With a look of embarrassment, I took off the device and placed it in my coat pocket.

"You see," Holmes chuckled. "So, what would cause my good friend to dash off to visit me? Was it something negative, a warning perhaps? Certainly not with the high spirits you exuded, even with your reinjured wound. So, therefore, it had to be something exciting. But what did you discover that could not wait until this evening or even the weekend to tell me? It had to be something particularly extraordinary, and the conclusion, from the time of day of your visit along with your garb, is that it was a patient who brought you such information. Since only yesterday you were asking again about my past, particularly my childhood, the logical conclusion is that you met someone from then who revealed some part of my history from before we met. Am I correct?"

"You are, Holmes, in every aspect." But here it was my turn to crack a wicked smile. "But, you do not know who it is that visited me."

Holmes let out one of his odd silent laughs and held up his lanky right arm, *tsking* me with his pointer finger. "There is only so much I can deduce with the data provided. But tell me, my good man, who was this unexpected patient?"

"His name," I said through gritted teeth for my injury flared up again, "is Mr. Zenas Cooper."

At the mention of Mr. Cooper's name, a strange change came over my companion. His eyes bulged and gaunt face drooped. Holmes turned away from me for a moment, contemplating, his skin turning a sickly ashen hue.

I let a silent moment pass, then I quietly said, "I have upset you."

He kept his lips closed, his eyes not quite in the present, then the glow returned to his silver orbs, and he stated soberly, "You caught me unawares. I did not expect to ever hear the name of my old instructor again. I consider my work for the man one of the greatest failures of my entire life."

"Failures!" I stammered. "Why Holmes, the man raved about you. Said you saved his marriage."

At these words, Holmes mouth turned downward into a deep frown. "Pray tell, what exactly did Mr. Cooper tell you?"

I recounted my patient's story to Holmes in every detail, though there were not many details to share. Still, as I told Holmes Cooper's deep praise for the detective, my friend kept scoffing and slowly shaking his head.

"Well, Holmes," I concluded, "if I may be so bold as to say that even I can deduce your version of events is quite different from that of Mr. Cooper. What happened while you were one of Mr. Cooper's pupils? And how did you, at such a young age, save the man's marriage?"

"That, Watson," Holmes said, bluntly cutting me off and raising his long right pointer finger in my face, "is a rather unique way of explaining the events." Holmes paused, settled into his chair, and finished off his brandy. He let out a long sigh, and I could tell this was not a story he wished to relate; yet my good friend did continue. "I will tell you the exact details of my time with Mr. Cooper, Watson, with none of my former instructor's biases; however, I believe you will find this story not fit for the general public. Even with your romanticizing of events, there is not much of a tale to flesh out for your readership. But perhaps, it is a tale worth telling, but first – "

Holmes took a moment to refill our brandy glasses and get his clay pipe and tobacco. He handed me my glass, for which I thanked him, lit his pipe, took a few puffs, and allowed the plumes of smoke to waft in the air before settling into his velvet lined chair and beginning his tale.

"At the age of eleven, I began attending a day school in Kennington. My father had come to the conclusion that his son should be properly educated, not just learning letters and arithmetic from Mother, but a true, formal education. We relocated to a villa in the London suburb, and I attended classes.

"I was a first year and found my school aesthetically displeasing. The rooms were particularly dank and drab. We had no athletic fields, just a small square of asphalt surrounded by towering brick buildings, all as equally run down as the building which contained my classes."

"But why did your father send you to a school in such squalid conditions?" I inquired.

"Because, my dear Watson, like myself, my father knew quality over prestige. The school had an excellent faculty, even though they had to teach in less-than-becoming circumstances. The Chemistry teacher was particularly noted, as was the instructor in Mathematics. Mr. Cooper was my instructor in Letters, a rather large blowhard who thought more of his capabilities than his abilities warranted.

"Of course in this environment, despite its lack of amenities, I flourished. It was my first taste of formal schooling, Watson, and I thrived."

"I am sure you were an apt student, the type all instructors dream of having in their classes," I said.

Here Holmes began to chuckle, but his laughter choked on some of his drifting pipe smoke. After a few good hacks, Holmes caught himself and explained, "My word, no, no, no, nothing could be further from the truth. Often those in positions of authority do not like having their ideas and certainly their position challenged, and as you are aware, Watson, I have no issue letting anyone, no matter their stature in life, know of their inefficiencies. When I would explain to one of my instructors an error that he made, no matter how miniscule, I was met with scorn and derision. For who was I, a mere first year, to question their scholarly integrity? I was surprised by this reaction, for my parents always encouraged my questioning and were quick to admit to their mistakes. This was the first time I was exposed to those who wore their title on their sleeve and felt that the best students kept their tongues stilled.

"A similar reaction came from my fellow classmates. This may surprise you, Watson, but at the age of eleven, I had a sharp mind, yet I lacked my current social skills."

Here, I bit my tongue and tried not to burst out into loud guffaws. Holmes had many things, a brilliant mind, an encyclopedic knowledge of London, and a strong sense of justice. His social skills, though, were still definitely lacking. Holmes either did not notice my contained outburst or chose to ignore me as he continued on with his story.

"I did not understand the rules of the school yard, nor how to navigate the difficulties of making and maintaining friends. I was not afraid to correct either the teachers or my fellow students, and I was quickly shunned by most of the other boys. Trying to help out a student who was making the most rudimentary errors on translating a passage in Latin was met with fisticuffs on the gravel schoolyard. I swiftly learned to keep to myself, stay quiet, and take in as much knowledge as I could without being noticed by the students or faculty."

"It must have been a rather lonely time in your life," I imagined.

"Ah, it actually was not. There were two dear friends which I made during my first year of schooling. One was Mr. Sherman who, as you know is the keeper of Toby, the finest canine tracker whose paws have ever walked the streets of London. I had heard Mr. Lemming, my science instructor, talk of a wonderful shop in Lower Lambeth, in Pinchin Lane, whose owner was an extraordinary naturalist and bird stuffer. One day, I made my way to his shop, and though he was just as suspicious of outsiders then as he is now, I spoke to him of the belief that the ancestors of fowl were prehistoric lizards, and this piqued his curiosity. He let my knowledgeable boyhood self into his rooms, and we began a friendship which, as you know, continues to this day.

"The other friend was a lad by the name of Percival Stevenson, a scrawny, sickly boy who, like me, found himself shunned by the other pupils. He was not a particularly bright boy, though he did have some artistic talent, particularly with watercolors. When I assisted Percival on his assignments, he enjoyed the attention. Indeed, he may not have passed his classes without my assistance.

"Due to Percival's artistic capabilities, the headmaster had taken an interest in him, as had his daughter, a capable artist who often came to the school to visit her father. It is with the headmaster's daughter where Mr. Cooper's case begins.

"Over the course of the school year, Mr. Cooper became enamored with Miss Davis. She was a rather petite and attractive lady in her early thirties, much in contrast to her gnarled and balding father. Miss Davis was a frequent visitor to the school, and she and Cooper were often seen walking the halls together on Mr. Cooper's off-hours. Had it not been for the fact that Miss Davis was also visiting her father, who clearly approved of their friendship, gossip would have spread throughout the school and into the homes of my classmates. Since it was believed nothing illicit was occurring at the school, for Headmaster Davis would surely put an end to any rumors that cast a shadow upon himself or his school, the romance was allowed to develop in plain sight.

"You may recall, Watson, that in the winter of that year, I became gravely ill with a lingering case of pneumonia. I was frequently absent from my classes, and if it wasn't for my intellect, would have surely failed. The few times I was able to attend classes, Percival explained what I had missed, and I gleaned the material I skipped during my stays at home. Unexpectedly, over the course of the winter months, Percy blossomed into a striking lad. As I became sick, he seemed to become stronger. His personality changed as his body filled out, and he became more participatory in class and more brazen in his approach towards others. Percy still remained an outcast among our peers, mainly due to a development of condescension towards others he deemed less mentally capable than himself. Yet, despite the changes in the boy as is so common of one of that age, our friendship did not sever; in fact, due to my own intellectual superiority, the bonds tightened, and we became stronger. Percy would derisively discuss the other classmates, how he couldn't believe their common errors – errors, I reminded him, which he so easily made himself at the beginning of the school year. He also confided in me about his life at home, girls who lived in his neighborhood who had caught his eye and he theirs, and aspirations he had for his future.

"'Just think, Sherlock, would it not be exciting to be a constable of the law? Arresting criminals and bringing them to justice? I bet that would impress Marcy Wilson!'

"'Who?' I inquired.

"'Why, Marcy Wilson. She lives in my neighborhood and is a true diamond in the rough.'

"'Ah, yes,' I said coyly to my friend and then let out a few good hacks from my still lingering cough. 'With all the girls you are smitten with, it is difficult for me to keep track. Wasn't it Julia Moreau last week? And . . . let's see . . . Eva Walker the week prior to that?'

"Percy let out a hearty laugh. 'They were mere flirtations compared to Marcy, a true Helen of Troy.'

"He sounds like a good man to me," I said, interrupting Holmes, and noting how much young Percival sounded like a young John Watson.

"Yes, Watson, he definitely had your eye when it came to the fairer sex. But as I said, he was not popular with the lads in the classroom. While I was away much of that winter, Percy became outspoken in the classroom, and unlike me, he knew how to follow the social norms with the teachers, though as far as other students were concerned, Percy was willful and, as I explained, would criticize not only their mistakes but their mental facilities. This caused him to raise the ire of one boy in particular, Willie Muggins, a pig-nosed bulldog of a lad much more suited to the fields of a battle than the seat of a classroom. Muggins struggled in all of his classes, but mostly in Literature, where he could never read below the surface of a story. Percy would ridicule Willie in the classroom, and at first, Willie responded with blows on the schoolyard.

"One early spring day when I was absent, the headmaster caught Willie attacking Percival. Headmaster Davis stormed over to the two boys, holding up his form to its tallest height. Willie was too busy jabbing his fists at Percy who, as I understand it, was doing a sufficient job blocking the blows and getting in a few good punches of his own. At one point, while Willie had his fist pulled back and was ready to take a good lunge in at Percy, Headmaster Davis, who was now directly behind the boy, swiftly reached over and with a strong yank, grabbed Willie by his left ear and twisted. Willie howled in pain as the headmaster kept the ear firmly in his grip and hauled Willie out to the center of the schoolyard. He threw the lad to the ground in front of all the students and then paddled him mercilessly. After Headmaster Davis had sufficiently beaten the boy in public, he ended with an announcement that if a student lay a finger on another student in the schoolyard, they would immediately be met with an expulsion.

"A week after this incident, I returned to classes, still rather weak but definitely on the mend. One morning in Literature class, we were discussing the *Morte d'Arthur*. Mr. Cooper was leading a discussion on the 'Tale of the Sankgreal', and he had asked Willie why, on several occasions in the story, Galahad boards a rudderless boat.

"'Why would Galahad board a boat with no captain?' Cooper boomed. 'Come now Master Muggins, surely even you can find meaning between the lines of text and answer this rather elementary question.'

"Willie just sat in his seat, red faced and fuming. But the lad did try to answer the question. 'Because he was brave,' he tried.

"'There is nothing brave about sailing off in a ship you can't steer,' scolded Cooper. 'That's the surest way to commit suicide. Come on, you can do better than that,' Cooper encouraged. 'You do like this story, don't you lad?'

"'Yes, sir,' confirmed Willie.

"'Do you really understand it, though?' inquired Mr. Cooper as he spoke slowly to Willie, making sure the boy heard the question.

"'I'm not sure, sir. I'm trying my best.'

"'You're trying your best, aye. Come now, think. They are searching for the Holy Grail. Now think my boy, if they are searching for the Grail, why would Galahad board a rudderless boat?'

"Willie scowled at the question. He hemmed and hawed a bit and was probably going to say some off-the-mark response when Percival blurted, 'Isn't it obvious! He's boarding a rudderless boat because it is steered by the divine hand of God.'

"'Why, yes, excellent answer Master Stevenson. The implication is in fact that God is the captain of the ship.'

"The discussion moved on, but I caught the look of pure spite that crossed the visage of Willie Muggins as he glowered at both Cooper and Percival.

"My next class for that day was Science where, if I recall, we were beginning to study the differences between alkalines and acids. You can imagine how dreadfully bored I was in that class, Watson. As Mr. Lemming lengthily explained something which should have been stated in a mere matter of seconds, I was overtaken with a coughing fit. I asked permission to leave to go to the latrine and recompose myself.

"'Really, Master Holmes,' scoffed Lemming, 'if you are not well enough to attend my class then you should not be at this school. But, I'd rather you were sick outside of the confines of my classroom. Away with you, boy, and when you return, I expect you to take down any notes you missed.' And with a dismissive wave of his hand, he sent me out of the room.

"To get to the privy, I had to walk down a long corridor containing the Headmaster and teachers' offices. I walked at a rather slow pace, still feeling weak from my sickness, and I was thinking about how Lemming should be the one sitting in the classroom and I standing at the lectern, when I approached the entryway to the headmaster's room. The door to his office was ajar, and I heard shouting from within. I instantly recognized the voices as that of Headmaster Davis and Mr. Cooper.

"'Why would I do such a thing?' harrumphed Davis. 'I have already given you my blessing.'

"'Bah!' scowled Cooper. 'Why should I believe you? It would be just like you, Davis, to offer your blessing and then sneak behind my back. You've never liked me, which is why I have never been offered the position of Department Chair.'

"'Ridiculous,' scoffed Davis. 'I don't care a bit if the ring is missing. You still have my blessing to marry my daughter. And as for department head, you have time on your side, my friend. Patience is all you need. Now, wait . . . who's there?'

"I had burst out into another coughing fit while standing outside the office. When the door flung wide, I had recomposed myself.

"'Why, Master Holmes? What are you doing here?' the headmaster asked, and then his eyes became slits and his teeth clenched. 'Were you spying on us?'

"I explained to the headmaster that I was going to the privy because I was feeling ill. I was overtaken by a coughing fit and leaned against the wall. When pressed if I heard any of their conversation, I looked puzzled and asked, 'What conversation?'

"The headmaster was satisfied with my answer and Cooper offered to escort me to ensure that I returned to class safely. Afterwards, I returned with Cooper, but on the way to class, he stopped me and brought me into his office.

"'I'm no fool, Master Holmes, and neither are you,' he stated gruffly.

"'What do you mean, sir?' I asked innocently.

"'Don't play games with me, boy. You're the smartest of the lot and a fine actor. If I didn't know you better, I'd have been just as fooled as that imbecile, Davis. But the man is right, as I'm sure you noted. He did not take the ring from my coat pocket.'

"'What ring, sir?'

"'Come now, Master Holmes, surely you can puzzle it out.'

"I nodded as the answer was obvious. 'It is the engagement ring you wish to use to propose to Miss Davis, sir. You kept it in the right breast pocket of your coat. Am I right, sir?'

"'How did you know that?' questioned Cooper, who suddenly looked at me with a suspicious eye.

"'Simple, sir. All through class this morning, you kept inserting your hand into your right breast pocket and fidgeting with an object. It is clear to me that it was an item of great importance, as you kept checking to ensure it was still there.'

"Cooper let out a joyful laugh. 'Indeed you are correct, my dear Master Holmes, and this morning I showed the ring to Headmaster Davis and asked his blessing to propose to his daughter, which he heartily granted. During your class, I kept checking up on the ring, mulling over my word choice for when I proposed to the fair Miss Davis. But after your class, I noted that the ring had gone missing.'

"'And you believe it was a student who took your ring, sir.'

"'Yes, Master Holmes, and I believe you are the man who can get me my ring back.'

"'Me, sir?' I questioned, truly surprised at the turn in this conversation.

"'Yes, Master Holmes. You are the cleverest man in this school, and that includes both teachers and pupils, and I don't mind saying so. I need your help, boy. Can you return the ring to my possession by the end of the school day?'

"'How would I do that, sir?'

"'Why, Master Holmes, I have given you a challenge, a fitting challenge for your intellect. I would betray you if I gave you any ideas about how to solve this mystery.'

"'May I ask a few questions, sir?'

"'Be my guest, Master Holmes.'

"'When was the last time you remember having the ring in your possession?'

"'Well, let's see, it was before the end of class. Then, after you were dismissed, I spoke to Master Muggins about his efforts, then I noticed the ring was missing. Why, you don't suppose . . . ?'

"'I don't suppose anything, sir,' I answered, 'but I do believe you will have the ring in your possession by the end of the day.'

"And with that, Watson, I left Cooper's office, excited for this opportunity to prove myself, for it was a true opportunity. For the first time since I entered that school, I felt that an instructor took a wholehearted interest in me, saw me as an intellectual equal, superior even, and was challenging me. It was my duty to rise to the occasion."

I was taken aback by the turns in Holmes's narrative. How could a grown man turn to a mere child, even one of Holmes's intellect, to solve such a personal matter? My friend, who had paused to take a few puffs from his pipe, read the expression upon my face and answered my unstated question.

"Watson, I can see that you disapprove of Cooper asking a pupil to solve his personal dilemma. The man should not be faulted; he should be recognized. I still find it one of his more positive attributes that he was able to note my intellectual prowess and not let age or position in life interfere with the most logical person to solve the case of his missing ring."

"And you solved the case, Holmes?" I inquired.

"Of course, Watson. Today, I would dismiss such a case as not being intellectually stimulating; however, at the age of twelve – yes Watson, twelve, my birthday was that January – I found the case to be somewhat of a thrill."

"A thrill, Holmes! Really!" I stated bluntly, for it was obvious to me that Willie Muggins was at fault. The lad had sought revenge for his embarrassment by Cooper in his classroom.

Holmes nodded silently. "A case, even one as simple as this, held my attention. I knew who was at fault, yet I still had the problem of actually retrieving the ring. Where would the ring be hidden? The answer, of course, was obvious. The best hiding spot for the ring would be in a coat pocket, such as it was the best place for Cooper to conceal the ring. Fortunately, it was a particularly warm afternoon, and when we were released for time in the courtyard, all of us removed our coats and stored them on the coat rack in the hallway before disappearing outside and enjoying the balmy spring day.

"With all the first years away from the coats which were hanging in our designated rack inside, I knew I had the perfect opportunity to retrieve the ring.

"I sought the aid of my dear friend Percy in executing my plan for the ring's retrieval. Percy listened intently to my story, and when I finished explaining, he stiffened up and said, 'I am at your service, Sherlock.'

"The plan was simple. Mr. Henderson, the burly History teacher, was outside, keeping an eye on the students, making sure that no fights broke out in the yard, especially after the headmaster's thrashing of Willie and his threat to the students. As Percy and I were walking by the man, I started another of my coughing fits and actually fell on the ground in front of the instructor. After a few harsh hacks, Percy helped me to my feet, and I asked if Percy could take me inside to get a glass of water. The teacher agreed to my request.

"Once inside the school, I went to the coat rack, found Willie's jacket, and when I returned to the schoolyard, I had Cooper's ring safely in my possession."

"Well done, Holmes," I commended my friend. "Even at such a young age, you were extraordinary at puzzling out a dilemma."

But at this congratulations, my friend's lips turned into a deep slit of a frown and his skin took on a grey pallor. "I puzzled out this simple problem, but I still ended up making what I fear was one of the gravest errors of my life."

"I don't understand, Holmes," I said, completely perplexed. He kept referring to the case as a failure, and yet it was a rather straightforward success. In fact, I found the case so routine as to be too dull to share with my readers.

Holmes leaned back in his chair, his fingers steepled and eyes stared off to the memory of his youth. He spoke softly with a touch of melancholia in his voice which I had only heard on a rare occasion. "At the end of the day, I reported to Cooper's office. I could see the greedy anticipation in his eyes as he sat in his chair fidgeting, his fingers tapping each other in such a way as to appear that they were fighting amongst themselves. When his emerald eyes fell on me, I gave him a boastful smile, and he knew I had completed my mission.

"'You've done it Holmes! You have the ring!' exploded the ruddy-faced man.

"I shrugged my shoulders and held out my left fist, palm up. I uncurled my fingers and there, resting in the center of my hand was Cooper's ring.

"As quick as a hawk pouncing on a mouse, the man snatched the ring from me and held it up towards the lamplight, inspecting it to make sure it was not damaged.

"'Good show, lad!' he said through jolly chuckles. 'Good show. You were able to get it away from Muggins. I'd love to see the look on that boy's face when he realizes he doesn't have the ring anymore. I will get to see his expression when he sees my dear Miss Davis with the ring upon her finger. It will be perfect. But tell me something, Master Holmes. In the afternoon, just an hour ago, I came up with an excuse and had Master Muggins called to my office. I had him turn out his pockets, and the boy had nothing but a dull pencil. I thought he would know why I sent for him, but the lad was a fine actor, pretended he knew nothing about any missing ring.'

"'That's because,' I bragged, ''twas not Muggins who took your ring, sir. You had it all wrong, sir.'

"Cooper's face plummeted at this news. His eyes bulged, and he looked as though I had struck him across the cheek. 'Not Muggins,' he stammered. Then, he burst out into one of his hearty laughs. 'You are one of a kind, Master Holmes. One of a kind. So, indulge me, my boy. Who, pray tell, took the ring from my pocket?'

"'The answer is quite simple, sir. 'Twas Percival Stevenson who snatched your ring.'

"Percival!" I admit, just as Mr. Cooper must have done, I sputtered at this declaration. I thought Holmes would chastise me for being surprised that his childhood friend was a common thief. But he did not comment nor even acknowledge my reaction. He kept telling his tale in that same, somber tone of voice.

"I explained everything to Cooper, Watson. I told of how I saw Percy palm the ring from Cooper's pocket when he was distracted at the end of class and chastising Muggins. I said how I had told Percy when we were in the schoolyard that we could get revenge on Muggins by sneaking inside and stealing several sovereigns I said he had in his coat pocket. Of course, that was a complete ruse. When I had my fake coughing fit on the schoolyard and Percy helped me inside, I was able to snatch the ring from his pants pocket where he kept it, and replaced it with a stone I discovered of about the same size and shape. When we went to the coat rack, I used my own money which I had in my pocket, and I showed it to Percy after we returned outdoors. He assumed that I had stolen the money from Muggins when I had it in my possession all the time."

"Astonishing Holmes," I said, impressed with his youthful skills. Then, I inquired, "But I do not understand why your friend would take the ring? Had his family fallen on hard times? Did he have a vendetta against Cooper, or was it just a bit of a lark?"

Holmes lowered his eyes and shook his head. "Your questions are almost identical to those asked by Cooper, and I was such a braggart, so proud of myself, that I told Cooper everything without thinking of the consequences.

"'It all has to do with Miss Davis, sir. I'm surprised you haven't seen it yourself,' I stated to Mr. Cooper.

"Here Cooper eyed me most suspiciously. 'Seen . . . what . . . ?' he inquired with a drawn out drawl, as if he was not sure if the answer should be obvious, if he wanted to hear it, or if he should even trust me.

"'As you like to say, sir, the answer is rather elementary. I've noticed when Miss Davis is with Master Stevenson how much alike their visages are. I've also noted that both walk with a slightly odd gait, one where the right foot turns out and the toes curl at each step. With the interest which Miss Davis shows towards Master Stevenson and their physical similarities, I quickly deduced that Miss Davis – '

"'Is Master Stevenson's mother,' concluded Mr. Cooper. His face had turned sickly and his lower lip quivered at this information.

"'That's right, sir. I believe Percy stole your ring so that you would not be able to marry his mother. I do believe he likes you. He's just being protective of his mum.'

"The man composed himself enough to thank me for this news, and he sent me on my way. Fool that I was."

"Why, Holmes, you are being far too harsh towards yourself. I believe you did Mr. Cooper a good turn," I said reassuringly.

"A good turn," Holmes spat. "And what do you think happened after I told Cooper all that I had learned?"

"Why, of course the gentleman did not marry Miss Davis," I stated matter-of-factly. "I assume that the child was illegitimate, since Miss Davis was never presented as a widow, and therefore, that Miss Davis was not a suitable choice for Mr. Cooper. Also, I hope the boy was harshly punished for his crime."

"Not a suitable choice," Holmes said sadly with a slow shake of his head. "You hope the boy was harshly punished! Oh Watson, you are a traditionalist to the point where you don't see the harm it can do."

"Really, Holmes. I don't see – "

"No, you don't," Holmes snapped, and I could tell that I had raised the ire of my dear friend. "Rest assured that young Percy did get punished, but it is my belief it was unwarranted. Indeed, the guilt that I feel – " Holmes caught himself. He was shaking slightly, feeling a mix of sadness and rage. Finally, he took a swig of brandy, let out a long sigh, and recomposed, continued in his soft, melancholy tone of voice. "Had I just returned the ring to Cooper and not revealed where I had gotten it, he would have been none the wiser, would have married Miss Davis, and I'm sure, in good time, would have learned the truth, and instead of turning away, he would have adopted Master Stevenson, whom he would have grown to love. Percival would have found himself in a joyful family situation.

"Instead, Mr. Cooper did not only reject Miss Davis. He also, after sending me away that afternoon, went straight to the headmaster and threatened to expose the secret of his illegitimate grandson unless he made Cooper the department chair."

"My goodness, Holmes. Did he really?"

"He was furious, Watson. He thought the headmaster was trying to trick him into marrying Miss Davis. Percival never returned to school. I never saw my friend again.

"You see, Watson, one of the tricks of being a true detective is that one must solve a case, but one must know how much information is proper to reveal in doing so. I was right to take the case, but I was wrong to identify the guilty party. It is why, as you've noted, sometimes my tactics are quite different than those of Scotland Yard. I wish I could wind the clock back, knowing what I know now and put that knowledge into the young version of myself. I solved the case, Watson. I suppose it was my first true case, yet in the end, I failed my friend, and that is unforgivable."

"You were just a boy," I started.

Holmes dismissed me with a wave of his lanky arm. He did not want to hear my excuses for his conduct.

"Now, Watson, the hour is getting late, and you should return to your home, to your wife. If you'll excuse me, there is a 'Concerto in D Major' which I would like to practice. It is a rather fitting piece on this somber afternoon."

As I limped down the steps that late afternoon, I heard the piercing wail of the detective's violin while he began to play his lament for his childhood friend. Those haunting notes stayed with me all through my cab drive home and into my dinner with my wife, Mary. I found myself feeling a sense of guilt and despair, for while my friend mentioned his failure to young Percival, I realized that in many ways I had failed Holmes as well. In my two published recounts of his adventures, I had presented the man as a cold, calculating machine. Nothing could be further from the truth. Holmes had a strong sense of justice and fairness. He preferred to help the downtrodden than the elite, and he would let a crook go free if he knew the criminal would right his wrongs and never commit a crime again. It was better to do that than send a man to jail where he would harden and seek a life of lawlessness. That appreciation for the human condition was lacking in my characterization of Holmes, and this was a wrong that I had to right.

I had been toying with an idea of focusing on shorter narratives and writing a series about the greatest adventures which I had shared with my friend. But where would I start? There were so many tales to choose from. Perhaps I would start with a case where Holmes was *not* triumphant. Perhaps a narrative where Holmes shows disdain towards the aristocracy, maybe even royalty, displaying a sense of respect towards someone like a child, or a woman. That was it! A woman! *The* Woman! I thought of the portrait on Holmes's mantel, put pen to paper, and began to write.

The Tranquility
of the Morning
by Mike Hogan

This story first appeared in The MX Book of New Sherlock Holmes Stories Volume VII.

Mike Hogan studied English literature and spent many years in business. He writes novels, plays and screenplays, and is a Sherlock Holmes, Monty Python and Frasier fan. He divides his time between the UK and Asia, rides the Amtrak rails in America at least twice a year, and somehow always ends up in New Orleans. www.kaleidoscopeproductions.co.uk

Haitian-American artist **Tracy Guiteau** headed for Providence Rhode Island to attend the renowned Rhode Island School Design where she received a BFA degree in Fashion Design in 2007. During her training at RISD, she traveled internationally to learn and broaden her artistic experience at the University of Westminster in London. At an early age, Guiteau had made a discovery that takes most of us all our lives to stumble on. She had found her purpose. Constantly putting the hours into her craft and her dreams with a positive sense of exuberance, her presence is undoubtedly heavy on the scene. Exhibiting internationally, all over the country and scoring countless mentions and write-ups from publications.

There are five words hidden in the art. Can you find them?

www.TracyGuiteau.com

Artwork size: 40 x 30

Medium: Acrylic on canvas

Tracy Guiteau '18

I stood at the open window of our sitting room in Baker Street one crisp, clear Sunday morning, smoking a fine cigar and sipping an excellent cup of pre-breakfast coffee. The street below me was busy in the dry, chill weather that had followed days of rain, and pedestrians strolled under streetlamps that were still draped with the remains of the victor's laurels that had honoured the exploits of our victorious Army. Even in the wan sunlight, Baker Street presented a busy, festive appearance. The strains of a military band playing martial airs wafted from the Park in the intervals between sprightly music hall tunes played by a hugely bearded hurdy-gurdy man who had made his pitch outside our door. A flock of children in their Sunday clothes surrounded him, petting his monkey companion and clamouring for their favourite tunes.

I leaned out of the window, called for "Abdul Abulbul Amir", and threw down a penny, which the monkey caught with an athletic leap in the air.

The door of Holmes's bedroom opened, and he strode across the room, reached past me and slammed the window shut.

"Do have a care, my dear fellow. The sash pulleys are original," I said, somewhat sharply.

Holmes grabbed his *Times* from the table, slumped into his chair before the fireplace, wrapped himself in his disreputable shawl, and jabbed tobacco into his morning cherry-wood pipe with his thumb. "How can I *think* with this cacophony?"

I went to the door and called down to Billy, skulking in the hall as usual, for fresh coffee. I turned back to Holmes. "Shall I order breakfast now, or do you want your coffee first?"

Holmes flapped his newspaper and grunted a reply which long exposure to early-morning under-employed Holmes allowed me to interpret, and I called again to Billy to bring breakfast immediately.

"I will be glad when this ridiculous fuss is over and we can settle down to pleasant, quiet mornings again," Holmes remarked from behind his paper. "Our so-called war with the Kingdom of Burma was a purely commercial venture, a military excess akin to a rampaging elephant stamping on a delicate flower. It was accompanied by assurances of Burmese independence that were were outright lies."

My companion had been cranky and argumentative during the Christmas and New Year festivities, doubtless due to the paucity of clients over the holidays and what he considered the vacant, simple-minded merriment of the populace, and I had no intention of provoking another row over the Army's victories in Upper Burma. I changed the subject. "Celebrations in the street are less noisy, and far less destructive than riots," I suggested. "I am astonished at reports that the agitator, John Burns, has been aquitted."

Holmes flicked down a corner of his paper and frowned a quizzical frown.

"The man who led the mob along Pall Mall, smashing the windows of the gentlemen's clubs, attacking members and passers-by, and shouting Socialist slogans. Disgraceful behaviour."

"He with the red flag? I did not know his name." Holmes went back to his newspaper, and I threw a shovelful of coal into the grate, poking our recalcitrant fire into a semblance of flickering life. "The chimney's still blocked. We'll have to get the sweeps in, like it or lump it. We could spend a day and night at my club to avoid the mess, or better yet, have a refreshing week-end in Torquay."

Holmes did not deign to answer my suggestion. Our chimney had long been due for a cleaning, but Holmes detestation of the inevitable disruption – tidying of papers, covering furniture, soot everywhere – was so profound that in his tetchy mood he had refused to countenance the sweep. My holiday cheer had been dampened by the chill and sooty atmosphere, and as my bedroom fireplace connected to the same blocked flue, I had been obliged to sleep under a mound of blankets, shivering in my dressing gown, balaclava, and mittens.

The arrival of the second post and breakfast coincided, and Holmes and I set to our kippers and bacon and eggs in silence as we read our mail, in my case a wad of end-of-year bills, club and magazine subscription demands, and reminders from tradesmen of essential services that might be provided to a discerning customer at a discount and with payment spread across the calendar. I tipped most of my post into our kindling box.

Holmes shared the last of the coffee between our cups, then he waved a telegram flimsy at me.

"Not a client, Holmes," I said, wearily. "Not on a Sunday. I had hoped for a quiet day catching up on my reading. I have the last two weeks' *Lancets* yet unread."

"He will be here at eleven: A gentlemanly hour to start the business of the day." Holmes passed me the telegram.

"*Beg leave report strange phenomenon stop 11 a.m. stop Coulteney.*" I raised my eyebrows.

"Short and sweet," said Holmes. 'A military gentleman, I suggest, with his '*beg leave report*' and admirably succinct style. Note the carefully chosen term, '*phenomenon*'." Holmes stood and felt along the mantel for his pipe while I anticipated his request and took down the '*C*' volume of his scrapbook index. I flicked through it to no avail.

"'*Coulteney, Admiral Sir Arthur, retired, and Lady Alice of Coulteney Hall, Berkshire and Curzon Street in London*'," Holmes said, consulting *Who's Who*. "He commanded the China station in the sixties. Interests include china (with a small '*c*'), fishing etc., etc. The admiral sired a son, Major Albert Coulteney, Indian Army, unmarried." Holmes dropped the volume on his desk.

"Your client could be the admiral or the major," I said.

"Undoubtedly the son."

I frowned at the telegram. "Is there some clue in the phrasing that I have missed?"

The doorbell rang downstairs, and Billy showed our visitor up to our sitting room. Major Coulteney, as Holmes had somehow deduced, proved to be a handsome, tanned, square-faced man in his mid-forties in a plain black frock-coat and matching top hat. His only adornments were a gold watch chain across his waistcoat and a very fine gold cravat-pin in the shape of an elongated '*S*', set with a two gleaming, green gems. He wore wide mourning bands around his hat and sleeve.

Having introduced himself and shaken my hand, the major laid his gloves, hat, and stick on our sideboard, and after a few preparatory remarks about the weather, sat on the sofa I indicated. Holmes had busied himself with his newspaper and pipe as our guest arrived, but at last he laid his paper aside, steepled his fingers in a characteristic gesture, and regarded our visitor with the intensity of a mongoose glaring at a python, or perhaps the other way around. Major Coulteney did not appear disconcerted by my friend's unsociable behaviour.

"Do I have the honour of addressing Mr. Sherlock Holmes?" he asked mildly.

"Oh, I do apologise," I said. "May I introduce Mr. Holmes? Holmes, this is Major Coulteney."

"I see from the newspapers that the erstwhile Kingdom of Burma has been annexed by the British Crown," Holmes said in an admonishing tone, "despite assurances that the current king would be replaced by a dynastic successor. I predict arid years of thuggery and warlordism. The Burmese are a pugnacious race, when aroused."

I readied myself for a most inhospitable row, but fortuitously the sitting-room door opened and Mrs. Hudson entered with a tray of coffee. I stood. "Perhaps Major Coulteney would prefer a whisky?"

He shook his head. "Coffee would be most acceptable. It is a little early for me. I have an occasional twinge of gout that I supress by daytime abstinence."

Mrs. Hudson smiled an approving smile, handed cups of coffee, and offered seed cake. She accepted the major's thanks, suggesting that nothing was too good for our heroes of the Burma campaign.

The door closed behind her, and Major Coulteney smiled at me. "I wonder how that lady knew I soldiered in Burma."

"Mrs. Hudson has been our landlady for several years, and I have no doubt that she, like me, has picked up one or two of Mr. Holmes's sleuthhound tricks."

"Tricks?" snarled Holmes.

I ignored him. "You did not achieve such a deep suntan any time recently in this country, Major. It has been a dark and dismal winter. Your bearing is military, of course, suggesting that you are an officer recently returned from a long posting, probably in India or the North-West frontier. A senior officer in a line regiment, I might suggest. And, according to the papers, our troops in Burma are mostly drawn from the Indian Army." I turned to Holmes and raised my eyebrows, willing him to be civil, but he merely smiled his Buddha smile.

"You have suffered a recent bereavement," I continued, indicating the mourning band around the major's arm. "Was your regiment closely engaged in the fighting?"

"We suffered several casualties, but I wear these mourning favours for my father, Admiral Coulteney. You may have seen the notice in *The Times* last month."

I gave Holmes a disdainful look. So much for sleuthhounding, I thought. He had seen the admiral's death notice in the paper.

"I am adjutant of the Third Madras Light Infantry," Major Coulteney continued. "The regiment was heavily engaged on the Irrawaddy, and then took part in an expedition up-country from Toungou."

"I read of that," I exclaimed. "A very creditable operation, particularly with regard to the difficult terrain and your lack of cavalry support."

Major Coulteney bowed. "After King Thibaw's surrender, I was released to return home on leave. Word of my father's death was cabled to the regimental barracks in India while I was aboard a steamer heading for home, and I did not receive the sad news until I had settled into my club, the Travellers."

"You did not stay at your townhouse in Curzon Street?" I asked.

He smiled. "I see you have done your homework, Doctor. No, I had booked rooms at the Travellers by cable, and when I disembarked I did not yet know of my father's death. He and I did not see eye-to-eye on a number of matters, and I had thought it prudent to make my London base in Pall Mall. We always observed an informal truce while my mother was present, but we could rarely get through a day, and certainly not a dinner, without an argument erupting."

"You are now in residence in Curzon Street with your mother?"

"I stay there, but Lady Coulteney, who is in poor health, is in Lourdes, where she hopes to recover her vitality at the shrine of Saint Bernadette. We are a Catholic family."

"Nothing serious, I hope?"

"Her maid *de chambre* recently resigned, and the shock brought on a migraine. She was extremely fortunate in acquiring a replacement at very short notice."

I blinked at Holmes, willing him to make a contribution to our conversation, and at last he stirred himself out of his sulk. "Might I know the matter?" he asked, yawning and stretching. "What can I do for you, Major?"

Major Coulteney seemed to gird himself before he replied. "You must understand, Mr. Holmes, that I am a military man, a gunner by training, and thus steeped in the empirical: Trajectories, windage, rifled bores, and ballistics are my creed, and apart from a residual adherence to the tenets of the Roman Catholic Church, I have no truck with spirits, demons, and the like."

Holmes flicked his eyes to me then back to our visitor. "But?"

"I am embarrassed to admit that our house on Curzon Street is infested by at least one, and perhaps several ghosts." Major Coulteney shook his head. "If I might trespass on your time and indulgence, it might be simpler if were to show you the phenomenon rather than attempt a description?" He stood and handed me a pair of calling cards. "If you gentlemen would be so kind as to visit me in Curzon Street, perhaps this afternoon if that is not too inconvenient, then I need trespass on Mr. Holmes's valuable time no further."

I avoided my friend's eyes as I saw the major to the door.

"Major Coulteney," Holmes called from his place by our smoky fire, "you were last home on leave about eight years ago, is that correct?"

The major blinked at Holmes. "That is so."

"You wear a most interesting tiepin. Jade of course, and depicting a letter of the Burmese alphabet."

Major Coulteney fingered the jewel. "The letter '*N*'."

Holmes bowed farewell, and the major turned to me with a quizzical look, but I could offer no gloss on Holmes's questions. I saw him to out to his cab.

"Oh, dear," I said as I returned to the sitting room. "I thought we were done with ghosts and ghouls. We are approaching the end of a rational century." I frowned at Holmes. "Was it necessary to be quite so insufferable? I know we disagree on the Burma question, and you are one of your moods, but – "

"What do you make of Major Coulteney?" Holmes asked, stretching up to the mantel and scrabbling for his pipe.

I filled my own morning pipe as I considered. "He told his tale in a straightforward manner, admitting his poor relationship with his papa. That accords with his long spell of duty abroad. I am sure he would have been allowed home leave earlier, had he applied."

"His clothes have obviously been in storage for some time. His jacket was full around the shoulders: He has lost some weight. And there was the smell."

I frowned.

"Mothballs."

"Is that how you knew that he had been away for eight years?" I asked.

"No, no, surely you noticed his cravat? That lamentable style of bright paisley came into fashion for a mercifully brief period about nine years ago. No valet who knows his business would let his master out in public wearing it now. The rage is all for plain, dark hues. The major's cravat also clashed violently with his jade tiepin. I imagine his soldier servant knows only red, white, and blue."

"Major Coulteney talked of the loss of his mother's maid as having more effect on her than her husband's death!" I said.

"To lose a husband is unfortunate; to lose a *femme de chambre* may be a far more climacteric event for a woman of mature years, dependent on Beatrice or Sofia as the only person who understands her hair, and perhaps as a confidant. If the maid dies (the Queen is notoriously wearing on hers, and they expire with inevitable frequency) that is inconvenient. If the girl is so disloyal as to give notice and obtain employment in another house, taking her mistress's secrets with her – that is a catastrophe."

"You sound like one of those clever, epigrammatic writers, Holmes."

"Thank you."

"I intended the comparison as a criticism." I stood. "I'll inform Mrs. Hudson that we may be late for dinner."

"Liver and bacon," Holmes replied, and I stiffened.

"Pagani's?" I suggested *sotto voce*, glancing towards the closed sitting-room door, "although our funds are much depleted after the holiday season. Or the public house opposite the station does veal pie, boiled potato, and a pudding at eightpence farthing."

Holmes smiled a reptilian smile.

Our cab stopped outside an imposing mansion in Curzon Street with a black front door, reached by a flight of gleaming stone steps and adorned with a silver lion's head doorknocker. The door opened wide as I paid the cabby, revealing an upper servant dressed in a pale blue robe, bound with a gold sash, and wearing a strange hat, something between a military forage cap and a fez, surmounted by a huge deep-yellow blossom – an orchid. He bowed deeply, introduced himself as the butler, and welcomed Holmes and me by name in unaccented English as footmen took our coats, hats, and canes.

The butler led us across a marble-floored hall from which a magnificent double staircase led to upper floors and into a drawing room in which a very welcome fire blazed. We were offered cigars and cigarettes before he left us to inform his master of our arrival, trailing a faint scent of patchouli.

I warmed my coattails at the fire and gave Holmes a reproachful look. "We must do something about our chimney – "

"*Ming Chenghua*," Holmes said, lifting a blue-and-white Chinese vase from the mantel. "A very fine example."

Major Coulteney strode in, beaming, with the butler behind him. "I can't thank you gentlemen enough for coming. I am at my wits' end." He offered drinks, which the oddly-dressed butler dispensed with impeccable grace, leaving Holmes and me settled in chairs in front of the fire.

"I see you noticed the china," Major Coulteney continued as the door closed behind the servant. "In his later years, my father was an invalid, hardly going out except occasionally to his club to dine. He amused himself with his china collection, and that is part of the problem. It is my understanding that the collection includes pieces of great antiquity and value. The vase on the mantel is one, according to Cheng."

"Cheng is an expert in chinaware? A dealer?" Holmes asked.

"Cheng is our butler."

Holmes smiled and rubbed his hands together. "How very interesting." He turned to me. "You will have noticed Cheng's slightly slanted eyes, the mark of the Oriental."

"He has strong, forward projecting zygomatic arches and relatively large epicanthic folds," I answered, "but his nasal bridge is not particularly low-rooted." I sipped my whisky, not without a certain inner satisfaction, as Holmes and the major digested my remarks.

"Cheng was a boy of mixed parentage," Major Coulteney continued, "who ran from an orphanage and sneaked aboard my father's ship when it was docked in Kowloon, China, oh, forty or more years ago. The sailors hid him from the authorities and he became a kind of ship's mascot. Father took the boy under his wing and put him in the care of the ship's schoolmaster with the midshipmen and cadets. He evidently thrived. Father often commented that, had he been able to regularise Cheng' position in the Navy, he would have risen through the ranks and retired as an admiral."

The major pursed his lips. "As it was, Cheng sailed with my father for a number of years, first as his cabin boy, then as confidential secretary. When the admiral retired, he took over the running of this London house and our country estate. I returned home last month, and I found that he had acquired certain airs above his station, as servants with indulgent masters are wont to do over time." Major Coulteney fingered his paisley cravat. "Even having the presumption to proffer unwelcome advice on matters of gentlemanly attire."

I stifled a smile. "Is Cheng connected with your problem?"

"Yes. Well, no, not exactly. With certain exceptions, Cheng is an admirable butler. The house runs like clockwork. My mother's friends, who spend much of their time exchanging anecdotes on the iniquity of servants, look upon him as the very model of perfection, despite his sartorial proclivities (which my father and mother found charming) and his pretentions."

Major Coulteney sniffed. "As my father's health declined, he relied more and more on Cheng to help him prepare a catalogue of the china collection that was his obsession. When his sight began to fade, Cheng read to him from the large collection of reference books my father had amassed, thus acquiring a considerable knowledge of Chinese pottery. He was allowed to bid for my father at auctions."

"Close to, your tiepin is very fine," Holmes remarked. The major and I frowned at him in confusion.

"Thank you." Major Coulteney fingered the gleaming jewel at his neck. "I was with my regiment in India for a few months when the British Resident at Mandalay requested an augmentation to his military guard and I transferred there. The jewel was a gift from a friend."

"Mandalay!" I exclaimed. "A city of golden temples and yellow-clad monks – "

"Gamboge-clad," Holmes corrected.

I took an irritated gulp of my whisky as the major continued his story.

"On my return home after my father's death, I proposed to my mother that we sell the china and give Cheng his notice, but she is convinced that Cheng is indispensable. My mother is somewhat delicate, and I fear that any disturbance in her domestic arrangements (coming so soon after the replacement of her *femme de chambre*) would have a profound effect on her well-being."

"And her husband's death," I suggested.

"Yes, that too, of course. The hurt of my father's recent death is upon her, and she will suffer no change whatever in the house. And that brings us to the problem." Major Coulteney stood. "Perhaps you gentlemen would follow me?"

The major led us outside into the hall, where Cheng waited with a footman, and ushered us past the grand staircase and into a room opposite.

"I believe I know your butler from somewhere," I murmured as we entered a dim reception room. "Could I have seen his image in the papers?"

Major Coulteney answered me with a significant look, which I interpreted as a request not to pursue that topic.

We found ourselves in a charming, bow-windowed room with a row of three crystal chandeliers hanging from the ceiling and numerous crystal and gold wall sconces, but lit only by the flickering flames of the fire in the grate. Glass-fronted cabinets alternated with mirrors along the walls. Cheng manipulated a device by the door and the gloom of winter late-afternoon was dispersed by a blaze of light that revealed rows of Chinese blue-and-white porcelain on glass shelves in the cabinets, gleaming in the bright lights, and more tall vases on the mantel shelf on either side of a glittering jade ornament.

"My father had electric lights installed as his sight began to fade, but our parlour maids refuse to enter this room even in daylight. Luckily, another maid –" Major Coulteney frowned and turned to Cheng.

"Maggie, sir."

"Just so, Maggie is unperturbed by the phenomenon."

"Our skivvy is Irish, but entirely pragmatical," Cheng explained. He offered a drinks tray, but Holmes ignored him, loped across the room to the fireplace, and snatched a blue-and-white vase from the mantel.

"Do you mind if my colleague examines the china a little more closely?" I asked superfluously as Holmes held the vase to an electric wall sconce, muttering to himself. He turned to Major Coulteney. "This is a magnificent example of *Ming Xuande* from the fifteenth century – pity you do not have the pair."

"Actually, we do." Major Coulteney said in a light tone. He nodded to Cheng, who went through a green-baize-covered side-door and returned with an elderly maid in a grey uniform holding a brush and pan. She grinned a gap-toothed grin at us and displayed the contents of the pan, a heap of broken blue-and-white china. She mimed a sort-of sliding wiggle and a crash to the floor, and grinned again. I stifled a chuckle, and Holmes grabbed the dustpan from her and sifted through the shards.

"A hundred guineas the pair," the major said.

"And with one vase gone, the balance of the room is even more disturbed," said Cheng.

I frowned. "Balance?"

"*Qi*," said Holmes. "Cheng is referring to the *feng shui* of the room: Its orientation according to the principles of celestial harmony."

Cheng bowed. "Precisely, sir. The room tilts to the East, and naturally, things slide with it."

"Thank you, Cheng," Major Coulteney said coldly.

The butler bowed again and led the other servants from the room. Major Coulteney ushered Holmes and me to over-stuffed sofas. Holmes sat with the dustpan on his knees, stirring the shards.

"Our housekeeper, Mrs. Mason, swears that she and the maids have seen vases and even the candlesticks on the mantel jerk and dance on many occasions recently." Major Coulteney took a gulp of whisky and turned to me, his fierce eyes belying his previous equanimity. "You see what I am beset with, Doctor? A kitchen skivvy is dusting the parlour, with a king's ransom in blue-and-white china on display that I cannot dispose of. What next? The boot boy answering the door to visitors and Cook polishing the silver?"

"Heaven forfend," I said sympathetically.

"The phenomenon manifests itself only in this room?" Holmes asked.

"It does."

"In which direction do the objects dance?"

"East to west," the major answered, "towards the windows." He stood and took a palm-sized jade ornament from the collection of *objets d'art* on the mantel. "According to Cheng, this green dragon guards the east, and he is the key to the problem."

Holmes took the dragon and peered at through his magnifying glass. "Carved from a single piece of jadeite of the very finest quality. He is a new addition to the collection? I see no other jade items."

"My father collected only porcelain. I bought the dragon in the Burmese capital, brought it home, and placed it on the mantel a fortnight or so ago. The manifestation began the following day."

Holmes leapt up, crossed to the windows, and scanned the frames. "No signs of forced entry." He turned to Major Coulteney. "You saw this latest incident?"

"I did. As I have said, I am no spiritualist, but what I saw was uncanny. The vase wobbled along the shelf past the candlestick and crashed to the floor."

"Cheng was present?"

"He came instantly at my call." The major frowned. "You have a theory, Mr. Holmes? A solution to the problem?"

Holmes tapped his finger to his lip as he considered, then he shrugged. "The affair may be perfectly simple, or it may be exquisitely convoluted."

"I am afraid my companion is a connoisseur of convolution," I admitted.

"As for solutions," Holmes said with a smile, "I am sure Cheng could find you a *feng shui* master who would re-orient the room. He might only require that the dragon be placed elsewhere, and tranquillity may be re-established."

Major Coulteney stiffened. "I hardly think that would suit, Mr. Holmes. It is a question of authority, of who is master and who is man. With my father passed on, I am the head of this household." He fingered the jade ornament at his throat. "I intend to marry shortly, and I have no intention of bringing my wife into a household in which she might feel the slightest awkwardness with the staff." The major's tone hardened further. "Cheng made his objection to my placing the jade dragon on the mantel abundantly clear, but I will not allow my authority to be gainsaid by him or any shaman or witch doctor he may set against me."

Major Coulteney looked from Holmes to me, breathing heavily, his expression betraying his embarrassment as he continued. "I am sorry, gentlemen, I spoke a little intemperately. The thing is, my mother is due to return from Lourdes tomorrow, and it is imperative that this matter be resolved before then." He blinked at Holmes. "I know it is an awful imposition, but would you gentlemen be prepared to stay a little longer and give the phenomenon a chance to expose itself? I can offer you a fair dinner, a curry, if that suits? Cook has mastered the art of the real Madras curry. Cheng obtains the proper ingredients from a ships' chandler in Limehouse."

Holmes took out his watch and regarded it with a doubtful expression.

"We did not think to bring evening clothes," I said.

"We are not fashionable," the major answered. "My father kept naval hours and dined at three in his afternoon attire. I follow Army ways and dine at seven in my undress uniform or even a frock coat."

Holmes raised his eyebrows at me, and, thinking of the liver and bacon that awaited us at home, I instantly nodded agreement. "Very well, Major. Doctor Watson and I are at your disposal," Holmes answered.

We were assigned a large and well-appointed bedroom in which to perform our ablutions, with a lavatory at the end of the hall. A footman saw to our needs in the matter of towels, soap, and hot water with admirable efficiency.

"Mr. Cheng's rooms are on the top floor, I imagine?" Holmes asked him.

"Yes, sir. First on the left."

Dinner was excellent, a choice of a joint of beef or the chicken curry Major Coulteney had promised. I accepted both with a little urging from our host. The wines too were of the very best quality. Cheng stood behind his new master making sure we were well served. He wore a dark blue, sari-like garment, and his cap was adorned with a matching, deep blue orchid.

Although I had served in Afghanistan and India, I knew very little of farther east, and I requested Major Coulteney to give me a succinct account of the recent war with the Burmese, which he did, sketching the line of the Irrawaddy in wine on the table after the cloth was drawn and positioning condiment dispensers and fruit from the bowl to represent our gunboats and the Burmese forts.

He explained that, after King Thibaw had exhibited disdain for our mercantile interests in Burma and threatened British property, Naval gunboats besieged his capital, Ava. Seeing the strength of the forces arrayed against him, the king had soon surrendered. The war was over within a fortnight.

"The palace was looted," Major Coulteney said with a slight moue of distaste. "Jewels, silks, china, and gold were shipped to Britain and presented to the royal family and other notables. A Prize

Committee was instituted at Mandalay to auction off the lesser items, mostly to Army and Navy officers and civil servants. Objects of high religious importance, including eleven gold idols of Lord Buddha, were shipped to Calcutta to be distributed to museums."

"Is that where you acquired your jade dragon?" I asked.

The major shifted in his seat in obvious discomfort. "I bought it at an informal auction in King Thibaw's bedroom in Ava. One of my sepoys had liberated it from a heathen shrine. I got him to show me the place he'd found it – a most magnificent altar with a scroll in Chinese script hanging beside it. The altar itself was jade-and-gold encrusted, depicting dragons in flight, and of such a weight that a Naval party with a hoist was required to remove it."

"The Jade Dragon Disturbs the Tranquillity of the Morning," Cheng said from his place behind the major.

"It is a fine piece," said Holmes.

"From the reign of the Qianlong Emperor of China," Cheng continued. "The jade is a representation of *Ao Guang*, the Dragon King of the Eastern Sea, who brought chaos to the world by creating droughts, storms, and other disasters. The dragon's baneful influence, particularly during the full moon period, may be mitigated by surrounding the beast with images of the other eight dragons, or placing a cloth-of-gold cover over the image."

"Like a tea cosy?" I suggested, "or a cloth over a budgie cage?"

"Thank you, Cheng, that will be all," Major Coulteney said sharply

"I *know* I have seen Cheng somewhere before," I said softly as the door closed behind the butler.

"He is something of a hero, I suppose," the major said slowly, swirling his port in the light from a candelabrum. "He was at the Travellers picking up my sea trunks for transport here last month when a mob filled the street outside shouting Democratic slogans and calling for the downfall of the rich. They'd been pushed out of Trafalgar Square by the police, and a man with a red flag was leading them down Pall Mall. Members from the Travellers and several other clubs along Pall Mall returned their taunts with interest, and there was some violence – stone throwing and fisticuffs for the most part. The mob surged forward, intending to invade the Travellers, but they were stopped cold by Cheng at the head of a phalanx of Club footmen. Cheng planted himself in the doorway and held the pass wielding a Zulu knobkerrie from a display on the wall of the Smoking Room.

"He might have been overwhelmed, but a determined charge by members of the Diogenes Club cleared a path for a file of police constables to reach the doors and set up a defensive line. The man with the red flag – "

"John Burns," I said.

" – led the mob on towards the Park and they vandalized the windows of the Carlton Club on the way. I am astonished that the wretch has been released uncharged. Various newspapers featured sketches of Cheng facing down the mob, some showing him as a Roman centurion chastising barbarians. *The Daily Mail* likened him to General Gordon of Khartoum confronting the mad Mahdists."

"Good Lord," I exclaimed. "He does not strike one as such a feisty fellow."

Major Coulteney shrugged. "The press obviously sensationalised the incident." The major regarded the glowing end of his cigar for a moment before he continued. "It is of no relevance to the matter in hand, but I should not like you to have the impression that Cheng is some sort of warrior saint. I know for a fact that he has had at least two assignations in Rupert Street with an unknown woman, heavily veiled."

"You had him dogged?" Holmes asked.

"Of course not," Major Coulteney answered, reddening. "The boot boy happened to be passing."

The port circled the table for the last time, untouched, and Major Coulteney looked down at the table, still ill at ease. "I am happy that our dinner was undisturbed, but might I prevail on you gentlemen to stay the night? I'm sure Cheng has made the necessary arrangements – he is a mind reader. We might yet have a manifestation, and I should not like you to miss it."

Holmes nodded acquiescence and, having thanked the major for a fine dinner, we smoked final cigars and said our goodnights. As his master had intimated, Cheng had made the necessary provisions for our comfort, and he led us up to our room with a pair of nightlights.

I stopped at a display case at the top of the stairs that I had not noticed on the way down. "I say, what splendid fishing flies."

"Thank you, sir."

"You made these?"

"Indeed, sir, from instructions in an angling magazine and a little imagination. The author of the article suggested that it was essential to think like a trout while assembling the fly. Admiral Coulteney was pleased with the results, as were the trout."

"I see," I answered doubtfully.

"The final piece of the jigsaw," Holmes murmured.

I slept very well. The sheets had been well-aired, the fire burned merrily, and I had curled my feet around a welcome hot water bottle. I woke up refreshed, and after our toilette, Holmes and I made our way downstairs to the breakfast room. He stopped on the landing, tapped his pocket and, having forgotten his magnifying glass, bid me go on as he darted back upstairs.

We breakfasted together in a pleasant room looking out over a lawn bordered by evergreens, both of us with our heads in our newspapers. Cheng supervised the service, wearing a bright yellow garment and with a matching pale yellow flower entwined in his hair. Our host joined us as the table was cleared, explaining that he had breakfasted earlier and just returned from a brisk walk. "I hope you slept well?" he enquired.

"Magnificently," I answered.

"We are done," said Holmes.

Major Coulteney and I gaped at him. "You've solved the case?" the major asked.

"At five-fifty-three yesterday afternoon," Holmes replied. "Since then I have been tidying up, assembling the shards as it were. We might continue our discussion in the lair of the Jade Dragon." He turned to Cheng. "I would be grateful if you would join us."

Cheng bowed and led the way out and across the hall.

Holmes stopped. "I left my magnifying glass on the dresser in our room. Excuse me." I frowned at him, and he winked back before he again loped upstairs!

He joined the major, Cheng, and me in the China room. "Have there been any recent changes in the household," he asked. "You mentioned a new *femme de chambre.*"

"Ethel, but I hardly think she has a hand in this affair. She is with my mother in Lourdes."

"The previous maid?"

"Carried off by the postman and wed at Gretna Green. My mother made strong representations to the postal authorities, but they will admit no responsibility."

I heard a faint scraping sound and my head snapped around. One of the Chinese vases on the mantelpiece seemed to jiggle, then it flew through the air and crashed onto the parquet floor by the window, shattering into shards.

Cheng staggered to the wall, his face ashen as Holmes strode across the room, pulled out his magnifying glass and closely examined the floor, window frames, and the shards of porcelain. He stood. "Would you allow me to deal with this, Major? I believe that I will be able to rid you of this expensive nuisance in short order, given a free hand and with the help of Doctor Watson and Cheng."

Major Coulteney coloured and he seemed about to remonstrate, but Holmes pre-empted him. "I must ask you to remain outside and whatever noises you may hear, however strange, you must not open the door. That is of the first importance. The *Qi* must not be allowed to dissipate until I have mastered the Jade Dragon."

"Very well," The major answered in a stiff tone. He talked out, closing the door behind him.

I blinked at Holmes. "I say, old man, should we not ask for a Bible?"

He rubbed his hands together, "Let us begin."

"I think Cheng had better take a seat," I suggested. "He is in shock."

I settled the butler on a sofa and turned to face Holmes. He stood before the fireplace looking very much like a magician at the Alhambra about to pull a rabbit from an unlikely place.

"Would you mind passing me that Chinese vase?" he requested, directing me to one of the display cases. I gently removed a foot-tall, blue-and-white vase from its glass shelf and handed it carefully to Holmes. Cheng watched us white-faced and wide-eyed. "Do have a care, sir, that is an Imperial vase of Emperor Kangxi of the Qing Dynasty! It is priceless."

Holmes lifted the blue-and-white vase above his head. "The solution to our problem is simple enough. We must convince the wraith to depart by showing our indifference to its destructive conduct."

"Noooo!" Cheng cried, darting up from his seat, arms outstretched.

 Holmes dashed the vase onto the grate where it shattered into a thousand pieces. "There, that might get the attention of the Jade Dragon."

Cheng hands flew to his mouth. "Oh, sir, how could you!" He collapsed back onto the sofa with his head in his hands.

Holmes smiled at him. "The game – "

"Is afoot?" I suggested.

Holmes sighed. "I was about to say to Cheng that the game is up. I think he could do with a reviving glass of brandy."

"I was distressed beyond words by my master's death," Cheng said, holding a glass of brandy in both hands as if deriving warmth from it. Holmes and I sat on the sofa opposite him. "The admiral was, if I may be excused the liberty, like a father to me. When he died, and I heard that the young master was returning home, I was doubly distraught. I made an attempt at madness, gentlemen. For several days, I fancied myself a Ming Dynasty tea caddy, then a police constable on patrol, and finally a Mandalay river steamer: Toot, toot! But nobody seemed to notice."

 Holmes sniffed. "Might I suggest that your somewhat outlandish dress and manner made it difficult for your master and colleagues to give sufficient weight to any further peculiarities you accumulated?"

"Just so, sir. Then I attempted to convince myself that the very ideas I was coming up with – the poltergeist, the constable, tea caddy, and so on – were in themselves evidence of derangement. But I am a hard person to convince." Cheng shook his head. "I had a rough childhood, but a varied and full life since, by grace of Admiral Coulteney. I owed him life, gentlemen, for his Lordship picked me up from the gutters of Kowloon and made a man of me, and I had promised him that I would never abandon the family. No, I could not in conscience leave Her Ladyship, but how could I stay? What was I to do?"

"And Ethel's role in the matter," Holmes asked.

"I see you know it all, sir. Ethel and I met at the Upper Servant's Christmas Ball in Blackfriars last November, and a mutual understanding was reached between us. She agreed to leave her employment with Lady Kennedy and replace my mistress's maid, who'd run off with the postman."

I frowned. "I must admit that I am confused. Was your relationship with Major Coulteney so uncomfortable that you could not endure continuing in employment with his family after the admiral's death?"

Cheng nodded. "We never got on, Doctor. Nor did he and his father, which was a cause of sadness for my mistress, his mother. I formed the impression that (forgive my forwardness, gentlemen) that young Master Albert blamed me for the coldness between him and his father."

"He considered that you had replaced him in his father's affections?" I asked.

"I hardly like to speculate, Doctor. Young Albert did not excel at school, and he was unable to follow in the admiral's footsteps into the Navy due to the new scholastic provisions. He did not meet the requirements for Sandhurst, and it was only through a connection on Lady Alice's side of the family that he found a place in the Indian Army."

"He evidently did not share his father's interest in porcelain," I suggested.

"Nor angling," Cheng added. "There were few topics on which father and son could converse, and those inevitably led to a row." A malevolent gleam appeared in Cheng's eyes for a moment, before he resumed his usual benign expression. "And then the cable came from Mandalay. Albert was coming home and bringing with him a wife." Cheng's lips curled, "And such a wife! I was at my wits' end. The news sped the admiral to his grave, and nearly killed Her Ladyship."

I frowned, utterly at a loss. "Not Ethel, surely!"

"A Burmese lady whose name begins with '*N*'," Holmes said, smiling at me.

Cheng crossed himself. "Nanda, a heathen princess, so we are told. She is staying at Benson's Private Hotel, in the ladies' wing. She is a witch. She has entranced Lord Albert with the power of the Jade Dragon."

Holmes beamed at me. "*Cherchez la femme.*"

"If I may, Holmes." I turned to Cheng. "You must forget this nonsense of tea caddies and vases and poltergeists. And dragon ornaments and witches, for that matter. I say nothing of any Roman Catholic beliefs and observances, except to offer a medical opinion that excess in spiritual matters can have unfortunate consequences similar to abuse of drugs or alcohol. You must think of your sanity, old chap. Many a stout fellow has gone East and returned a mental wreck. Think on that. And you were born out there, which must be a heavy burden. Do not subject your mental faculties to excessive strain. You might consider transferring your allegiance to a religious body with a less effusive doctrine, one not quite so cluttered with saints and devils and so on – "

"The Salvation Army?" Holmes suggested.

"I was thinking of the Church of England, Holmes, and speaking only as a medical man."

"I take no offence, Doctor," Cheng said.

"And I would advise you to resign your position here. If the antagonism between you and your new master is to be augmented by his marriage, you will do your new mistress and Her Ladyship no good by remaining. Is there nobody on His Lordship's staff who might take your place?"

Cheng considered. "A hard question, sir. William (his real name is Kenneth, but the admiral always insisted that his senior footman was a William) is competent. He could be trained. I could nurture him farther along the road to adequacy in a year or so. Yes, a year might be possible; I believe I could bring William up in that time, or a little more.”

“What will you do after you leave the family?”

“I have a sum put away, sir, and I had thought to take the lease on a public house in a pleasant village, Devon perhaps.”

“Very well.” I frowned at Cheng. “The poltergeist or whatever. That was your work?”

He blanched. “The wiggling of objects on the mantel sir, yes, and I must admit to the destruction of the first vase.” He gazed in melancholy at the heap of broken porcelain by the window. “But the second vase was the dragon, and then Mr. Holmes – ” He sobbed into his cupped hands.

I turned to Holmes. “No one could fault your bravura, old man, but it was a rather expensive way to make a point.”

Holmes smiled. “Was it? You saw the debris of the first broken vase brought to us by the skivvy. Have you no observations to make?”

I sniffed. “I expect I saw, but I did not observe.”

“Exactly. You did not notice that the chips were granular in texture and far too thick to be fine Chinese porcelain, totally unlike the traditional hard-paste translucence of the true *Ming Chenghua*. It was plaster of Paris.”

“A fake!”

“The vase, together with five other blanks, was the product of the Gelder and Co., of Stepney, as indicated by the name branded into the wooden crate under Cheng’s bed upstairs.”

I glared at Cheng, who hung his head even further. “I had blank replicas made of some of the finer pieces, so that I could practice painting them, sir. I wanted to put myself in the mind of their creator to further understand the process.”

“As you did with the trout flies,” I said, and instantly a lamp was lit in my mind. I turned to Holmes. “I have it! You said yesterday that the fishing flies were the last piece of the jigsaw! I have it! Fishing line!”

Holmes smiled. “The rod room is at the back of the house, directly behind us. It was there that I stationed Maggie with one of Admiral Coulteney’s split bamboo rods, the line running outside the house, in through the window pulley, and attached to a handle of the vase on the mantle.” He held up a shard of blue-and-white. “Plaster of Paris,” and tossed it to the floor. “I hope she hasn’t damaged the rod. As you saw, the gentle, teasing pull I had suborned her with a sixpence to make on the line at exactly ten this morning was more of fearful yank. Cheng played his vase along the mantel like a trout in a pond. The skivvy’s previous experience of fishing may have been from a coracle, but what she lacked in finesse was made up for in raw power.”

Holmes ushered me to the window by the fireplace, pulled a curtain aside and indicated the window pulley in the sash frame. “You see? There is very slightly more wear on the inner side of the pulley, where the fishing line ran.”

"Or perhaps the Coulteneys do not take as much care with their sash windows as we do," I said. "All three vases were fakes? The Jade Dragon and *Qi* and so on were so much nonsense?"

"The originals are in Cheng's wardrobe, wrapped in tissue." Holmes turned to Cheng. "You suggested that Major Coulteney contact me and request that I investigate the phenomenon. Why?"

"I thought your presence might bring matters to a head, Mr. Holmes. Your name is well-known among the higher servants, in the best houses of course, and well respected."

Holmes rubbed his hands together. "Let us report our successful vanquishing of the baleful dragon to our client.

Major Coulteney shook Holmes's hand. "I say, old man, I owe you a thankee."

"Not at all. Cheng is quite back to his old self, and as long as the dragon is moved to a new home, it will be de-fused, as it were, and you will have no more visitations."

"Not the faintest taint of negative *Qi* remains," I suggested, giving Holmes an admonishing look. "And as you can see, the vases have miraculously reassembled themselves."

The major took the jade dragon from the mantel and held it out to Holmes. "Then you won't mind if I give you this. Do with it what you will. I think it's best out of this house before my mother returns."

Holmes slipped the figurine into his coat pocket. "You mentioned your impending marriage, Major. Has a date been set?"

Major Coulteney flushed, and his hand went to his tiepin. "Not yet. Arrangements in such cases take a very long time. The embroidery alone might take months."

"Just so. Then might I suggest that you make an agreement with your butler for him to give a year's notice? That would enable him to train a successor, and give time for your mother to become used to the new circumstances."

Holmes and I said our goodbyes and left Major Coulteney to ponder on Holmes suggestion.

Cheng showed us to the door. "You do not credit the Jade Dragon with any role in the affair, Mr. Holmes?" he murmured. "Despite his facing west and off the line of *Qi*? You do not think he disturbed the tranquillity of the morning?"

"I do not. And since he is now in my custody, a more congenial member of the *Kowloon* may take his place."

Cheng nodded. "If you have a mind to put the Dragon to auction, gentlemen, I should advise a reserve of not less than twenty guineas."

Holmes took the ornament from his pocket and smiled. "Really? I would have thought a jade of this excellence might fetch substantially more. I thought fifty at the very least."

"Dragons are a drug on the market, sir. I doubt you would find a buyer at more than thirty."

Holmes held out the figurine. "Thirty-five."

Cheng bowed, took the figurine and slipped it into a fold in his robes. He took an envelope from his cuff, passed it to Holmes, bowed again and showed us out to a waiting hansom. "A very good day to you, gentlemen."

I frowned at Holmes as we settled on the bench.

"The envelope contains a cheque on the London and Counties bank for thirty-five guineas. Cheng has an account with them with more than two hundred pounds on deposit, and he will receive a further five hundred from Admiral Coulteney's will. He intends to make an offer, through intermediaries, for his master's china, proposing to sell the items over a period of years and thus fund his ambition to own a public house. He will call it the *Kowloon*, the Nine Dragons Inn." Holmes tapped on the roof of the cab and gave him a further instruction, and we stopped at a townhouse a hundred yards or so along Curzon Street.

Holmes indicated that I should accompany him, and we stepped down into the street. "Follow my lead," he said. "And gird your loins. Her Ladyship is an American."

The front door was opened by a footman, who on learning who we had come to see, ushered us into an ornately furnished drawing room where we waited, warming our coattails in front of a splendid fire. The door opened and a fine-featured lady of a certain age swept in wearing an afternoon dress.

She peered through gold *pinz-nes* at the calling card Holmes had given the servant. "You wish to see me, Mr. Holmes?" she said in a cold tone faintly tinged with an American accent.

"Lady Kennedy, it will not do," said Holmes. "I understand your irritation at the loss of Ethel, who I am sure is the only person on earth who understood your hair, but consider, my dear madam, a butler is not a *maid de chamber*. They are entirely different orders of creation. It is as though Lady Coulteney pinched your comb, and you demanded her first-born in reparation. Ladies' maids may be trained. A competent butler is born, not made, and a butler of Cheng's excellence is a gift from a benevolent deity."

Lady Kennedy pouted and made to turn away.

"You should also know that he intends to tender his resignation from the household of Lady Coulteney and take the lease on a public house in Torquay."

"Torquay!" Lady Kennedy's hands flew to her face in horror.

"I am afraid so. And not one of the more salubrious parts of the town."

The footman showed us out, and we climbed back aboard the hansom.

"Lady Kennedy tried to suborn Cheng in retaliation for the loss of her maid, Ethel," I said as we set off for Baker Street."

Holmes nodded. "She stalked the poor man in the street, entreating him to defect. She pressed money on him, threatening to denounce him to Lady Coulteney unless he took it."

"An odd form of blackmail," I suggested. "No wonder he was so worn down, poor chap."

Holmes took out the envelope and waved it. "Pagani's tonight. Or would you prefer a roast at the Criterion?"

I considered. "The roast." We sat in silence for a while as the cab jogged by the Park.

"A Burmese princess," Holmes said with a smile. "They are accounted fetching by those who appreciate the glories of Oriental womanhood. Lady Nanda Coulteney has a nice ring to it."

"A Catholic family, Holmes," I reminded him. "Cheng advised his new master to call you in, expecting you to find him a way out of his dilemma. I believe we have been played, old man."

"Do you?" Holmes answered, "Oh, by the way, before we left home yesterday afternoon, I instructed Mrs. Hudson to get the chimney sweep in, so all should be spick and span for our return to Baker Street after a most comfortable night away." He yawned. "I must ask Cheng to send us the recipe for that curry."

Two Plus Two
by Phil Growick

First appeared in the MX Book of New Sherlock Holmes Stories Volume III.

Phil Growick, who conceived and curated *The Art of Sherlock Holmes*, is also the author of two Sherlock Holmes novels: *The Secret Journal of Dr. Watson*, and its sequel, *The Revenge of Sherlock Holmes*. One of his short stories, Two Plus Two, also appears here. Though retired from his previous career in the happy world of advertising, he currently serves as the Chairman of Art In Public Places for the City of West Palm Beach and serves in an advisory capacity for several of the city's departments. He is especially involved with the city's Homeless Task Force.

Vicki Siegel is an America contemporary artist known for her mixed media works that unite painting and photography together. By combining these mediums, she creates images that merge her fascination with humanity, nature, and the environment, with the physicality of paint. Vicki Siegel grew up in both New York City and Chicago, attending the University of Illinois, Urbana, (BFA), and continued with Master of Fine Art course work, focusing on photography, at Tyler School of Art, Rome. She worked as an art director and later creative director in advertising in Milan, Chicago, and S. Florida. Siegel's work is widely exhibited and collected. She is a fulltime working artist, with a studio in Delray Beach, Florida. Along with her studio practice, she instructs painting, conducts painting workshops, speaks to art groups and juries shows.

www.vickisiegelart.com

Artwork size: 40 x 30

Medium: Acrylic and archival pigment inks

TWO PLUS
ABCD
EFGH
IJKLM

"Watson, how much is two plus two"

The question was so odd and abruptly put that for the moment, I, stammered.

Holmes and I had been sitting quite comfortably that morning, the eleventh of June, in our rooms, I, reading the morning *Times*, and Holmes lying on his sofa, in his usual state of morning dishevelment, just staring at the ceiling.

"Pardon me," I was finally able to utter, "could you please repeat that?"

"Certainly. How much is two plus two?"

Knowing Holmes, as much as any person could know Sherlock Holmes, I immediately judged this question to be one of some impenetrable import.

Why would Holmes, with his Olympian intellect, ask such a seemingly foolish question? No, therefore it could not be foolish, and if not foolish, then it must have some profound meaning.

The silence in the room began to weigh heavily, as a hostile humidity in a tropical clime, only abated by Holmes's soft puffs of his pipe.

As my mind spun the possible permutations of a solution to this riddle, Holmes turned his head just so to glance at me, gauge my predicament, and returned it to its former position, transfixed at the ceiling.

If I answered the obvious, "Why, four, of course," I might be the recipient of one of Holmes's more biting barbs, such as, "Oh, really? Are you quite positive, Watson? Have you delved into your Hippocratic method to deduce that answer?"

But if I said nothing, I would appear even more trivial to Holmes. A man of my profession and standing in the community not able to answer a question that a child of six could exclaim most readily? I had to say something, so I did.

"Oh, no, Holmes; you shall not dally with me in such manner."

"Dally? Dally?" He had turned his head full round to my direction, his eyes though soft, still intense in their waiting for my explanation. "In what manner do I dally with you, Watson? Please explain yourself." His head went back to studying the ceiling.

"Holmes, you have given me the simplest of questions which only leads me to suspect a conundrum."

"A conundrum?" He chuckled. "Why, Watson, if I were to make present of a conundrum to you, it would be one of such an intricate nature that I, myself, would find it difficult to puzzle through, for were I to present you with such a conundrum, it would merely be me only listening to myself to hear me through my seminal solution."

Even for Holmes, that last statement was a conundrum in itself. The logic of his utterance was lost to me completely, which left me, once again, being coerced into giving him some sort of an answer.

"All right, Holmes; all right. The answer to your question of how much is two plus two, is, plainly, four." I found that I had raised myself from my chair with my arms pushing unknowingly against the arm-rests and upon the expulsion of my answer, I fell, somewhat heavily, back into my seat. He looked at me once more.

"Four. Are you absolutely positive, Watson? Is there not an iota of apprehension in your posit?"

"No; not one. Two plus two is most certainly four. It has always been four and it shall, until the end of time, be four."

And then I paused for a moment as I heard myself say, "What other possible response could there be?"

Holmes leapt to his feet as suddenly as if he had been stung by a bee in his buttocks, pointed a nicotine-stained index finger at me and shouted, "You see? Watson, you've just opened your mind to the possibility of there being another answer."

"I did no such thing."

He advanced towards me with a self-satisfied grin that recalled a child who had eaten forbidden treats without his parents' suspicion.

"Did you not, just a moment ago, ask if there might be some other possible answer?"

I stammered.

Holmes twirled round in so graceful a manner that would do a ballet dancer proud and reclined himself once again on his sofa, eyes once again studying the celling for perhaps some hidden and eternal truths.

"You stammer, Watson, yet you will not admit that you suspect that somewhere in the cosmos there may be another solution to this very simple question."

"It was merely a figure of speech, Holmes. I did not mean to suggest that there could be any other possible answer. Two plus two must be four."

"Must it?"

"Of course, it must. I'll prove it to you."

With that, I begged him turn his head in my direction as I borrowed some matchsticks from the area in which he kept his pipes and their attendant accessories and proceeded to put two matches down, then another two, counting as I went till I had come to the number four.

"There, Holmes. I have taken two matchsticks and added two more matchsticks and by carefully counting, the sum I have arrived at is four."

"Bravo, Watson. You have just, in your most scientific manner, demonstrated empirical proof that your answer must be correct."

"Precisely."

"However, you are wrong."

"Wrong?"

"Precisely."

I stood erect and stiff as I said, "What do you mean, wrong, Holmes? How can I possibly be wrong?" I believe my voice was rising in such a manner as to make one blush, should one have been in the company of several gentlemen.

"Oh, it is quite possible, Watson, quite possible."

"How can it possibly be possible? Two plus two is four. How can it not be four?"

"When it is not two plus two?"

"What on earth do you mean by that, Holmes? When it is not two plus two? For the last hour or so all you have done is bludgeon me with this ridiculous proposition."

"Watson, I have not bludgeoned you in any manner. Although to you, in so relaxed a disposition, a mental exercise may seem like someone has taken a truncheon to your brain."

"That is unkind, Holmes; even for you."

"I meant no insult, Watson, only that you have been led astray by your own ears and your own powers of total linguistic recall."

"I have not the foggiest notion of what you are talking about."

"Of course, not. Therefore, I will explain. Now, if you would be good enough to reseat yourself and try to return to that relaxed state from which you, yourself, escaped."

Reluctantly, I did as he asked; and when he was quite satisfied that my blood pressure had retreated from the volcanic heights of Vesuvius, he quietly and methodically began his explanation.

"Watson, first, the questioned I posed was a trap."

"Ah, hah!" I exclaimed. "Just as I thought."

"Well, not really; for the trap was such that you could never see it coming. You could only hear it coming."

"Hear it coming? What can that possibly mean?"

"Dare I say, elementary, Watson? Dare I say it?"

I said nothing, which said everything.

"Now, you heard me ask you how much is two plus two? Correct?"

"Correct."

He leapt for exclamation and, it seemed, from the sheer joy of what was next to come, stayed in mid-air for an untenable amount of time.

"Not so. Spell two plus two."

"*T-w-o, p-l-u-s, t-w-o*." As I spelled it out, I took extra care in my reckoning.

"All right and very good."

I smiled broadly.

"But Watson, what if I did not mean *t-w-o, p-l-u-s, t-w-o*?"

"What do you mean, Holmes?

"Watson, how many words in the English language are there for the word '*two*'?"

I had to think quickly now, and came back with an answer and a question at the same time, "Three?"

"Yes. Perfect. There is the number *two*, the 'also' *too*, *t-o-o*, and the adverb, *t-o*. So yes, there are three twos."

"But how could you ask me to add *t-o* to *t-o*?"

"You see, Watson? *To to to.*"

"Yes, well, to to to. But what about *too* to *too*?"

"The same. *Too to too.*"

"I believe I'm getting a headache," said I.

"Closer to an earache, Watson. We can go around for days with *two*'s and *to*'s and *too*'s, but that would only lead us to four."

"But that is what I have been saying all along. Two plus two is four."

"Is it really, Watson? Are you forgetting *fore*?"

"The number four?"

"No, how many *four*'s are there?"

"What do you mean how many *four*'s are there?"

"Exactly, just that. How many *four*'s are there in the English language?"

I slapped myself on the forehead and dejectedly came up with the same answer that I'd come up with before.

"Three."

"Precisely. We're back at three from the *two*'s and the *four*'s."

I was shaking my head from side to side in resigned assignation.

"Yes, Holmes: *f-o-u-r*, *f-o-r*, and *f-o-r-e*. Four for fore."

"Astonishing, is it not, Watson? And let us now dismiss *one*."

"One what?"

"How many *one*'s are there in the English language?"

"I would say three but that would be pressing my good fortune. So let me think, and I have it, two."

"So you are saying there are two *one*'s?"

"I think I am. Yes, I am. There is the number one, *o-n-e*, and when you win a battle or game, you won, *w-o-n*."

"Marvelous. We're making wonderful progress, Watson, wonderful progress."

"Progress to what?" My head was truly spinning and as it spun it was draining my energy and threatening to assume to rotation of our Earth.

"Progress to the numbers, and the numbers, whether arithmetic or linguistic, are everything. So, tell me, Watson, how many *eight*'s are there in the English language?"

"Please, Holmes, I beg of you. No more of these semantic gymnastics."

"What a marvelous phrase, Watson. Semantic gymnastics. No wonder you have had such success with your chronicles of our adventures. But I beg you to prolong your stated agony for only two more examples, Watson, only two. Which leads us to the conclusion that no matter what number you choose to study, there are only two or three homonyms."

"And for this, you have wasted a perfectly good morning?"

"Not wasted, at all. I did this to show you that what you hear may not be what is truly meant. And that when you assume what is said by someone to be what that someone says, it may not be what that someone has said, at all. Do you see?"

"See? I do not even seem to hear. Holmes, I am adrift. When this bizarre exercise of yours commenced I, as a physician, was quite positive that I was in the best of health. Now, after these numbers and words and arithmetic and not understanding what perfect strangers are saying to me, I am not sure of what you are saying to me. And you are most certainly not a stranger."

As I sank once more into my seat, Holmes slapped his right knee with his left hand, I suppose for some demonstrative emphasis, and gave a dindle of a laugh.

Oh, please, forgive me here, for there is no such word as *dindle*. In fact, I believe I have just coined it. However, it seems eminently appropriate in this case, as the sound emitting from Holmes was not a full blown laugh, nor a snort, nor snicker, nor chortle, nor most certainly not a guffaw. It was the faintest of sounds of gleeful satisfaction; therefore, it must be considered in the diminutive, and therefore I christen the utterance a *dindle*. You may take the word or discard it, the choice is yours.

"Watson, you still fail to grasp the importance of what we have been doing."

"I suppose so, Holmes; I will give you that."

"What if, Watson, I was paving the way for you and me to solve one of our newest riddles?"

"And which one is that, if I dare ask?"

"I am sure you will most certainly remember the young woman who sat precisely where you now sit, not more than two weeks passed. Miss Emily Kent."

"Of course, of course. She was quite young, very attractive, and she wanted to engage you to find some missing amulet, if I recall."

"Quite right. But the amulet gone missing was not just some amulet. It was the Amulet of Anubis."

"Yes," I was still puzzling over whatever import Holmes seemed to hold so dear, at the moment.

"The Amulet of Anubis was discovered by no one less than Miss Kent's renowned father, the noted Egyptologist, Sir Lionel Kent. And though he perished shortly after that discovery, and many attributed it to an ancient Egyptian curse of some sort, that amulet is the only one found bearing the likeness of Anubis and is considered priceless.

"Miss Kent stated that the amulet lay under lock and key in the home of Mrs. Annabel Brookfield, her grandmother. That only her grandmother, who was quite elderly now, I believe the dark side of ninety, kept that key secreted where only she knew its whereabouts.

"Miss Kent further stated that it was she and her grandmother together who had discovered the amulet missing, and that she had immediately notified the police. After two desultory weeks of police work without success, she came to me to see if I could do what the police could not."

"Yes. But from what I recall, you accepted the challenge without your usual enthusiasm. It would seem to me that finding such a treasure would have given spark to your powers of deduction and elucidation."

"On point, Watson. But it was not any lack of interest. It was that I was in the middle of a coincidence, and as you are well aware, to me, there is no such thing as a coincidence."

"I do not follow."

"Then follow this. Do you ever peruse the *Times* for any retail news of substance?"

"I feel I am falling further behind," I conceded glumly.

"It was approximately two weeks prior to the amulet's theft that Brently & Crafton, perhaps London's supreme fine arts and antiquities auction house, held an auction of the rarest Egyptian treasures and artifacts."

"No, I never bother with such information."

"Well, then, perhaps you should. For the coincidence of the Amulet of Anubis being stolen in so short a span after that auction, is too much of a transparent coincidence."

Once Sherlock Holmes had his mind onto a theory, it is best likened to a snapping turtle's jaws snapping shut.

"You see, Watson, with ancient Egyptian auction fever at high pitch, the Amulet of Anubis would fetch a much loftier price; especially to someone who had not been able to outbid others for specific pieces. And finally, there would be no seller's premium fastened onto the item's sale price."

"Yes, I see that now."

"Good. And now that you are in step, let us take this step by step.

"Do you remember what Miss Kent said specifically about how she and her grandmother found the amulet missing?"

After a moment of sorting through my mental file, I did remember.

"I believe she said that she had asked to borrow the amulet, as she had in the past, to wear at a charity ball. When her grandmother went to retrieve the amulet, she found it missing, and would have fallen to the ground in a dead faint, had not Miss Kent been there to bear her up."

"Indeed. I am most happy to see your memory so facile."

I smiled. "I, as well."

"Now, another question to test that impressive memory. How did Miss Kent get to her grandmother's home?"

"She said she rode to her grandmother's home."

"Watson, please repeat what you just said."

"I said she told us that she rode to her grandmother's home."

"Rode or *rowed*?"

"Pardon me?"

"Words, Watson, words. *R-o-d-e* or *r-o-w-e-d*?"

The import of the question hit me as hard as if Holmes had slapped a brick to the side of my head, and I believe my mouth opened to a width in which a hansom cab could easily have run through.

"There is a rivulet that parallels the vehicular thoroughfare that leads from Miss Kent's home to that of her grandmother. It is a rivulet quite narrow and because of its lack of girth it is not much travelled by boatmen or by the athletic among us who crew.

"Now, do you further remember her answer when I asked her to be precise in the amount of time it took to get from her home to her grandmother's home?"

"Yes. She said it took her one hour."

"Don't you see, Watson? If she had used the thoroughfare and gone by cab, it would have taken her, at most, only half that time. If, however, she needed stealth to sheath a nefarious design, she would have *r-o-w-e-d*, not *r-o-d-e*, and in the darkness would have easily needed that heavy hour. Her statement about the time was a casual remark, but a mistake which led, in part, to her undoing."

"But what led you to the contention of the words?"

"If you remember, it was an unusually hot and humid day for London at this time of year."

"Of course I remember. I had even removed my waistcoat."

"And in such a situation, would not the average person remove any article of clothing adding to the discomfort caused by that heat?"

"Yes, I believe so."

"But did you notice that she did not remove her gloves and that she winced upon me taking her hand in greeting, even in so ginger a manner?"

"I recall that now, but at the time it meant nothing to me."

"In addition, as she was leaving, you touched her lightly on her shoulder as a gentleman would in guiding a woman through a doorway. She gave an almost imperceptible shudder."

"Now that you remark on that, I did notice it but gave it no consequence."

"Ah, but you most certainly should have. Just why would she not remove her gloves? Why was her hand in so delicate a condition that the gentle pressure of my own hand caused her pain which he tried so adroitly to disguise?

"After listening to her description of her travel to her grandmother's home and with all that I have just revealed, I began to wonder about that particular word. From that, I could discern that Miss Kent, while appearing to be a young woman in great distress, was, in fact, the very cause of that seeming distress. Yet how she accomplished that act I, as yet, have not deduced; though I'm in the felicitous process of doing so."

"But the gloves, Holmes, and the shuddering of her back."

"Oh, well, quite easily realized when weighing those words previously mentioned. Because if she *rowed*," and Holmes made the gesture of rowing a boat, "it would be an occupation completely unsuited to her station as a young lady of some stature, and therefore would have not only caused great welts and raw flesh upon her hands from the rowing, but pain in the musculature of the back from such an unaccustomed activity.

"Furthermore, I found her attitude much too easy and flippant. It did not take me long to come to the conclusion that, whatever fee I proposed, unless it was in the vicinity of purchasing the Taj Mahal, would find favour. For she only wanted me as further proof for the insurance company. I am sure you can see that."

"What an astute plan. Holmes. That woman has a criminal mind of the first order."

"Hardly, Watson. Had she a more supple and subtle intelligence, it would have taken me far longer to discern her machinations."

"But would not the insurance be in her grandmother's name? It would seem likely."

"It would under normal circumstances, but as Miss Kent is the sole beneficiary of her grandmother's insurance policy, the monetary restitution falls to her. Then, after a suitable amount of time would pass, I should expect Miss Kent to sell the Amulet of Anubis to any number of discreet purchasers."

"But how did you learn of the particulars of the insurance?"

"It is fairly well known in our upper classes that most great articles of consequential value would be insured by one of only two such companies chartered especially to provide such guarantees. It was easy enough for the police to obtain the appropriate information, once I had suggested they do so."

"Then tell me, how do you propose to reveal to her your knowledge of her theft and plans for the amulet?"

"That you shall see for yourself presently, as I am expecting her to call at any moment."

As if she had been eavesdropping at our keyhole, a gentle rap on our door announced Miss Kent's timely arrival.

She entered and Holmes closed the door behind her.

She was still wearing the gloves and breezed in with such studied insouciance that I saw a very self-satisfied smile on the face of Sherlock Holmes.

"Miss Kent," he said, extending his hand in the usual hand-shaking gesture, yet she simply nodded her assent and sat once more in the chair she had occupied on her previous visit. She used her handbag almost as a buffer between us, so tightly was it clutched and set in her lap. Holmes nodded to me to be sure I had just witnessed the process.

"So, Mr. Holmes, you have called me here, I gather, to give me great news. You have discovered the whereabouts of the Amulet of Anubis, and you possess the knowledge of who took it and how it was done."

"You are partially correct in that assumption, yes."

"I do not understand," said she; and for the first time, there was the wrinkling of her brow in unforeseen consternation.

"Permit me to explain. I most certainly know the identity of the thief."

At that word, I could gauge an audible, but stifled, gasp from Miss Kent. I must make note here of her remarkable self-control. Though he was no better than a common thief, her presence under fire, so to speak, would have recommended her to be at my side in Afghanistan. I also believed she would have behaved so cool under the attack of Zulus. The woman was cold as an Eskimo's igloo.

"Oh, yes, I have the thief's identity. In point of fact, I have already notified the very officers to whom you reported the crime. They were quite intrigued."

"Intrigued? That is an unusual word to be used such a manner," she said. It was here she began to display only the faintest hint of growing discomfort.

"True, Miss Kent, quite true. But it is not often that the police are presented with the fact that the criminal and the victim are one in the same."

At this she stood, ignoring me fully but fixing her gaze on Holmes, and as she spoke she began to slowly glide towards the door.

"I am not certain what you mean, Mr. Holmes, but I am beginning to feel that you intimate that I am the one in possession of the amulet."

"Bravo, Miss Kent. You have hit the nail on the proverbial head."

Holmes was positively jovial at the exchange, and as he moved to place himself between Miss Kent and the door, he motioned her to sit once more, which she did with some small amount of agitation.

"Mr. Holmes, I am not accustomed to being addressed in such a manner, and I voice my disproval of your insinuation. You forget that I am your benefactress, that I retained you to discover the true criminal, and to return the amulet to my grandmother."

"Of course, you retained me to do so, and as I have just demonstrated, done so. If you would be so kind as to remove your gloves, please."

"I shall do no such thing." She had stood again, in a stance of feminine defiance.

"Come, come, Miss Kent. Enough of the charade."

Holmes then lowered the tone of his voice and all semblance of cheer was gone. "I say once again, please remove your gloves."

"I shall not and you cannot force me to do so. Unless you resort to animal brute force."

"On the contrary, Miss Kent. Watson, would you be so kind as to open the door?

"Of course, Holmes," said I and when I did so, Inspector Michaels and Officer Willets entered the room. At their sight, Miss Kent blushed crimson.

"Gentlemen," said Holmes, "would you please kindly instruct Miss Kent to remove her gloves."

"You heard Mr. Holmes, Miss Kent," said the Inspector, "please do as you are told."

"I must protest this in the strongest terms. I shall speak with your superiors as soon as I am able."

"Well, miss, I can guarantee that you will be speaking with my superiors at the station and then with the magistrates, as well. But this is a serious police investigation, and I must insist that you remove your gloves."

She began muttering to herself, but slowly, very slowly, she placed her handbag between her feet, then removed one glove. It was immediate to all that her hand was still partially bandaged and that part of her hand free was worn and calloused. The same was revealed as she removed the other glove.

Though we all took in the unfortunate sight of her hands, it was Sherlock Holmes who nodded for me, as a medical man, to look more closely at the wounds. This I did, and after concurring nods to me and the police, it was Holmes who spoke.

"Pray tell, Miss Kent, how your hands came to be in so deplorable and painful a state?"

"It is from gardening."

At that, a reflexive laugh let loose from all of us, save Miss Kent.

"From gardening, you say? Miss Kent, for gardening to take such a toll on your hands, I should expect that you were using them in place of trowel and shovel. No, Miss Kent, I propose that your hands suffer from, shall we say, an unaccustomed rowing endeavor."

"I am sure I have no idea what you mean."

"I mean simply that under cover of night you rowed to your grandmother's home so no one could see you on the road, gained access with no great difficulty, since you already possess a key to the premises, and that while your grandmother slept safely and unknowingly in her bed, you took the key from its hidden location, secreted the amulet on your person, replaced the key, locked the front door as you left, and returned home by the same mode of transport."

"That is foolish. Only my grandmother knew where the key was hidden."

"That is true to a point. However, being so advanced in age, she would not have heard you surreptitiously watch as she retrieved the key to fetch the amulet for that charity ball for which you requested its use. However, there still is one part of my fee which I have not, as yet, earned." Here, Holmes paused for great impact.

"While I have identified the thief, I have not returned the amulet to its proper owner, your grandmother. I shall do that presently."

With that, Holmes so swiftly grabbed her handbag that the movement could well be compared to the speed and grace of a cheetah. Miss Kent could do nothing to retain hold of the item.

Holmes held the handbag aloft for all to see, then reached in and like a master magician, he pulled out the amulet with a grand, "*Voila!*"

It was Inspector Michaels who now spoke.

"But how did you know that she would have the amulet, Mr. Holmes?"

"Quite simple. With the help of my Baker Street Irregulars, whose noses are always close to the ground, it was child's play to learn that a certain party wishing to purchase the amulet would be meeting Miss Kent this very afternoon in London. Therefore, she must have the amulet with her. She just could not wait to obtain the funds which she would derive from the illegal sale."

"Well, Mr. Holmes, I must hand it to you. And please, sir, you must hand the amulet to me so I can return it to Mrs. Brookfield," said Michaels.

"Now, Miss Kent," he continued, "if you would be so kind as to go with Constable Willets, here. We have a much better mode of transport waiting for you outside. Our own lovely police wagon."

Miss Kent stood, holding herself erect, as Willets took her arm and led her out to the wagon.

"Thank you again, Mr. Holmes, for all of your help. I am not happy to admit that we would never have suspected Miss Kent. We were questioning gardeners, and delivery men, and the help, and, as you have shown me, everyone but the true felon."

With that, he gave a crisp finger to his forehead and was off.

"Good show, Holmes. For it was a show, you know."

"Of course I do, Watson."

With that, he was back to reclining on his sofa, his face once more scanning the ceiling for heaven knows what.

"Now, Watson, might you be more receptive for some more semantic gymnastics? For instance, when someone describes a ghastly sight, are they commenting on a *s-i-g-h-t* or a *s-i-t-e*, as one might find in so many of our historic castle ruins?

"Or let me advance this enticing notion," he proffered, "let us say that we have another female felon, a genuine criminal genius of the first order. And let us suppose that her name was Terry. Would she not then be a true *Miss Terry*?"

"Oh, my word." And with that, I left Sherlock Holmes to ponder the ceiling as I removed myself to a more convivial locale.

The Stolen Relic

by David Marcum

This story first appeared in the MX Book of New Sherlock Holmes Stories Volume V.

David Marcum plays The Game with deadly seriousness. He first discovered Sherlock Holmes at age ten in 1975. Since then he has collected, read, and chronicled literally thousands of Canonical Holmes adventures. In 2008 he began writing them and has since produced over forty well-regarded short stories and novels, as well as a number of essays about the world's greatest detective. In 2015, he conceived the idea of *The MX Book of New Sherlock Holmes Stories*, now at twelve massive volumes and still going strong. Counting these books, he has now edited over two-dozen anthologies, as well as re-issues of the Solar Pons and Dr. Thorndyke books, while continuing to write new Holmes stories. He is a licensed civil engineer living in Tennessee with his wife and son. His blog can be found at http://17stepprogram.blogspot.com/

https://www.amazon.com/David-Marcum/e/B00K1IKA92

Terre Rybovich A third-generation native of West Palm Beach, Florida, Terre is a daughter of Tommie Rybovich, the noted sports-fishing boat designer and builder. Like her father did, Terre chooses to explore the terrain that lies just beyond what's known. Her drawing technique first came to her years ago, while delirious with the flu. "Drawing backwards" was the initial idea, i.e., removing charcoal to create an image instead of adding charcoal to a white sheet of paper. Because her focus was on figurative work, she used her body to remove the charcoal. One unexpected outcome was how her mind reacted—and still reacts—when confronted with creative input that it didn't generate. Every new drawing requires a period of acquiescing before the mind accepts the body's imprint and its influence on how the drawing is finished. The result is that Terre creates artwork that her mind couldn't have imagined. It means she works in perpetual wonder. Terre's education is in politics and economics. Her first career was in grassroots activism and grant-making. The activist experience forged an enduring commitment to this world. It also instilled a courageous drive that she now channels into art-making. Her drawings have been exhibited widely in South Florida, and she is grateful for a growing circle of collectors. Terre's drawings have been part of the Viewing Program of the Drawing Center in New York City since 2004.

www.terrerybovich.com

Artwork size: 39 x 30

Medium: Charcoal, pastel, oil paint and graphite on paper

Terrie
Rybovich

I paused in the doorway of 221 Baker Street, anxious to make my way inside and out of the bitter wind, but held in place by the sound of the approaching carolers. They were singing "The Moon Shines Bright", a song I remembered from my youth, and the lilting refrain brought bittersweet memories to mind, despite the cheery major key. It recalled times long gone when, as a child, our family had traveled south to visit my mother's people during the Christmas season. It was only then that I was able to see a traditional English celebration, and with it all that I missed during those other years while being raised in Scotland, where Christmas is not celebrated as such.

As the carollers came closer, I heard the words more clearly: *The moon shines bright and the stars give a light, little before it is day; Our Lord our God he called on us, and bids us awake and pray.*

I took another step into the building, but caught myself as they began the next verse, which I also recalled and which seemed to reflect my thoughts from this seemingly grim December: *The life of a man it is but a span, it's like a mourning flower; We're here today, to-morrow we are gone, we are dead all in one hour.* Shaking my head at this decidedly dark sentiment, and trying to imagine how it could possibly fit into a Dickensian holiday, I went inside and shut the door.

I had not intended to return home so early that Christmas Eve, having meant to spend the morning at Barts, followed perhaps by a rare afternoon at some theatrical entertainment, and then possibly a meal. I was feeling distinctly antisocial, and sought solitude. However, I was not needed at the hospital, and I found that I wasn't in the mood for the rest of my plans. With nowhere left to go, I glumly returned home.

While hanging my coat, I could see light shining at the top of the stairs, indicating that the sitting room door was open. But even as I watched, the stairwell darkened when the door closed with a solid thud, followed immediately by Mrs. Hudson's determined descent. I had only known our landlady for slightly less than a year, but I recognized this as the tread she made when irritated.

Seeing me standing there, she said, "Doctor Watson, I am *so* sorry. I've tried to do what I could to make your sitting room more festive, but *he* will have none of it." And with that, she cast an angry look back over her shoulder.

"It's quite all right," I said. "As you know yourself from being raised in the north, all of this Christmas merriment is, even now, still occasionally somewhat foreign to me."

"I felt that way as well, when I was younger," Mrs. Hudson replied. "But I've grown to love it. The decorations and the songs. The food and the tree. It's certainly better than how we did it when I was growing up in Scotland, where Christmas was just another day."

"I suppose," I agreed halfheartedly and, with a nod to her, started up the stairs. The truth was that I had enjoyed the British version of the holiday at times in the past. But this year, I was finding it more difficult to embrace any celebratory feelings whatsoever.

When I was a child, my parents' marriage had never set well with my maternal English grandfather, and in spite of his widely read experience and knowledge, he simply could not understand why Christmas wasn't observed in Scotland. My father would attempt to explain how the Church of Scotland, strictly Presbyterian as it was, had no use for Christmas, or *Christ's Mass*. Long before, it had been decided to be a Catholic affair, and thus anything remotely "Popish" was abolished in Scotland in the 16th century. And so it has remained.

But my mother was English through and through, and she had made sure that in our home, at least, some sort of Christmas was acknowledged. It was nothing like that which we saw on those few occasions celebrated at Grandfather's, and her efforts did little to otherwise alleviate the dour northern winter that held the rest of our town in its grip every December.

After I came to London to study medicine, I truly found myself in the midst of the seasonal excitement. In my student days, while living in Bloomsbury, there was no happier celebrant than myself, though perhaps for all the wrong reasons. I was in the thick of every party, and it was said by many that no one kept Christmas better than John Watson. But then came the army, and Afghanistan.

Now, in that late December of 1881, I found myself at the end of a difficult year. In July of '80, I was wounded at Maiwand, and then sent back to England, my health irretrievably shattered. I was set ashore on the Portsmouth jetty during a wet snow, with neither kith nor kin left in England. After that rather miserable Christmas had passed, I was acknowledging Hogmanay with a drink at the Criterion, and sourly contemplating the need to find cheaper lodgings to reflect my limited half-pay, when I was hailed by an old acquaintance, Stamford. What followed was an introduction to Sherlock Holmes, and the amazing series of events that had come over the past year.

Amazing they had been, but some had also been disappointing. Just months earlier, following a great portion of the year spent enduring a painful recovery, I had been notified that the army officially had no further need for my services. Each day that had passed since then reminded me in some way that I was marking time, and not going forward with my life. I had made myself useful, filling in as a *locum*, or assisting at Barts and a few of the other hospitals. But I knew that I should be devoting myself to something more permanent. The thought would not leave me.

And now, standing in the doorway of the sitting room, I felt the same thing. I was too happy to return here, when I should be looking for a more effective and prosperous alternative.

I only paused in the doorway for an instant before propelling myself forward. My friend was there, lounging in his chair by the fire and puffing on his cherry-wood pipe, and scowling at a veritable mound of holly and ivy lying across the mantelpiece.

"Ah, Watson. Come warm yourself by the fire. You'll see that Mrs. Hudson just brought tea, along with this pestiferous sampling of *Ilex Aquifoliaceae* and *Hedera Araliaceae*, detritus from some forest that has been killed before its time to rot above our fireplace."

"*We're here today, to-morrow we are gone, we are dead all in one hour,*" I muttered to myself.

"What was that?"

"Nothing," I replied. "Nothing at all."

"My dear fellow," said Holmes, rising suddenly. "You're freezing. Sit down, while I pour you some tea." And he moved to the table, showing that hidden compassion of his that appeared in the most unexpected moments.

Soon I was thawing out, and my mood increased exponentially. I was even able to look with appreciation at the difference made by having the decoration draped in front of Holmes's criminal relics that still rested, now hidden, upon the mantel.

We sat in companionable silence for a while, both looking into the fire with our own thoughts. Therefore, it was with some surprise when the bell rang. Holmes glanced at me. "Rather late in the day for the usual clients who help me earn my bread and cheese."

"Perhaps it is a crony of Mrs. Hudson's, here to wish her the compliments of the Season."

"True enough. We shall soon see."

It quickly became apparent that the caller was not there to visit our landlady, as we heard steady footsteps ascending the stairs. In a moment there was a knock, and Holmes called for the visitor to enter.

As we stood, the door opened, revealing a man in his mid-thirties, dressed in the habiliments of a plain priest's cassock. He wore no coat, paying no deference to the British cold, and he was clearly a stranger to our shores.

"Mr. Holmes?" he said, looking from one to the other of us, and speaking in an accent that betrayed his Italian origins. Holmes nodded, and gestured the man towards the basket chair facing the fire.

"May we offer you some refreshment?" I asked.

"Nothing, thank you."

"This is my friend, Dr. Watson. You may speak freely before him."

The man greeted me with a friendly and open countenance. I revised my opinion of his age. Upon closer inspection before the light from the fire, I could see that he was in his early forties.

"My name," said the priest, "is Father Abele. I am of the order located at the *Basilica di San Nicola*, in Bari."

Holmes nodded and stood. "One moment if you please, Father." As he walked over to the shelf where he kept his indexes, the Father smiled patiently, glancing my way in a friendly manner before turning his eyes to the fire. As he warmed, I could see him visibly relax.

Returning to his chair, Holmes sat and began to leaf through the volume. "Hmm. Interesting indeed," he murmured. Then, looking back at the priest, he said, "And how can we help you?"

"You were recommended to me, Mr. Holmes, by a man to whom you provided a previous service, Father Gregor, of the Orthodox Church, regarding the recovery of some stolen icons."

Holmes nodded. "I remember the case." Glancing my way, he said, "Quite before your time, Watson."

Father Abele continued. "I hold a unique position within the *basilica*. It is my duty there to be something of a roving agent, tasked to deal with those issues which might have cause to require a more substantial . . . interaction with the outside world." He looked from one to the other of us. "In short, I am here because a relic from the church has been stolen."

Holmes's eyes brightened, and he tapped his finger on the index. "Indeed. Might I ask – ? But no, let me not anticipate your story. Please tell it in order, from the beginning."

The priest nodded. "As I said, I represent the church of *San Nicola*, or as you would call him, Saint Nicholas."

My eyes widened. "Saint Nicholas. *The* Saint Nicholas? As in Father Christmas?"

Father Abele smiled. "There is that connection, of course," he said. "Even as the Americans have corrupted his name into the garbled appellation of *Santa Claus*."

"The Americans are not completely to blame," added Holmes. "The Dutch called him *Sinterklaas*, and carried that name with them when they immigrated to the United States."

The priest nodded. "As you can imagine, we are quite aware of the different iterations and adaptations of our patron's name throughout the world. But you are correct, Dr. Watson. I am referring to the *true* Saint Nicholas, of historical fact, and so canonized by the Church.

"Quite odd," I said, "the way a man who lived and breathed can, over time, come to be perceived as a make-believe character."

"Indeed," the man continued. "If I may, I would share a bit of history with you. I assure you that it is relevant, and I will not waste too much of your time." With a nod from Holmes, Father Abele continued.

"In case you were not previously aware, Saint Nicholas was born in the year 270 A.D. in Myra, an Asian part of what is now Turkey, and in what was then the Roman Empire. From an early age, he was quite religious, and entered the church while still a boy. Throughout his life, his kindness for both children and sailors was highly recognized, and it was through stories spread across the known world at that time by these very sailors that his fame grew.

"Throughout his life, he performed a number of miracles, including resurrecting the dead, feeding the hungry from food stores that did not decrease as they were used, no matter how much was used, and performing acts of great kindness and then directing the gratitude to God. An example of this was when he provided the dowries for a man's three daughters when the man could not provide it himself. The story goes that the Saint did so," continued the priest, looking at us significantly, "by dropping gold coins down the man's chimney and so into the daughters' stockings, hanging there to dry – hence, the variant form of receiving gifts now credited to Santa Claus.

"When the Saint was in his mid-fifties, he was quite respected within the church, and was invited by Emperor Constantine himself to attend the first Council of Nicaea, where he was one of the signers of the Nicene Creed. He died in 343, and within a few hundred years from his death, he was recognized as one of the Saints of the Church.

"At the time of his death, his body was entombed in Myra, where – for over six-hundred years – his grave was a destination of pilgrims and worshipers from all over the world.

"But in 1087, following several decades of unrest, sailors from Italy, fearing that access to Nicholas's tomb would become unreachable for pilgrims, seized a number of the bones from his tomb in Myra and brought them back to Bari, where the *Basilica di San Nicola* was constructed, and where pilgrims have journeyed ever since."

"A number of the bones, you say," interrupted Holmes. "But not all of them, I believe."

"That is correct. The others, initially left behind in Myra, were later seized by Crusaders and taken to Venice, where they are also kept in a church dedicated to the Saint."

Holmes nodded. "And you mentioned that a relic from the church has been stolen. Are we to assume then that one or more of the bones of St. Nicholas has been taken?"

"One bone," replied our visitor.

"And you need our assistance to locate it."

"That," said Father Abele, "is somewhat accurate. I know who took the relic. But I have not yet located where he is in London, and as a stranger in your country, I do not have the authority to retrieve it from him."

"I'm afraid that you're mistaken, sir, if you believe that I have any such authority."

The priest nodded. "That is understood, Mr. Holmes. But your involvement in helping me to locate him will go a long way toward clearing the matter up, and will prevent me from blundering in and making a bad situation worse by my ignorance of your customs."

"So," I interrupted, "you simply wish to retrieve the relic, then? And by not involving the police, as you clearly do not wish to do, you do not intend to prosecute?"

Father Abele nodded. "My only interest is in retrieving the object. The thief's punishment is beyond my influence."

"And you are certain the thief is in London?"

"Yes. I believe that you will be able to help me determine his location."

"And this relic?" said Holmes. "You said it is a single bone?"

"Yes. A *distal phalange*, as I think you would call it, from the Saint's left hand."

"The tip of a finger, then," I said.

The priest inclined his head. "More specifically, that of his left thumb. It was stolen more than a week ago. We must retrieve it as soon as possible, before any of the *manna* is lost."

I raised my eyebrows, but Holmes's lips tightened. "My index mentions this phenomenon. I will be happy to help you reacquire the object, but I'm afraid that I cannot give any credence to this supposed miracle."

"Miracle?" I asked. "*Manna?*"

Holmes gestured toward the priest, indicating that he should elaborate upon the matter. "Following the Saint's death, his tomb in Myra was always said to have a sweet smell resembling roses. And it has excreted a liquid, known as *manna* or *myrrh*, which has healing powers."

"I'm afraid that – " interrupted Holmes, but the priest continued.

"I understand your disbelief, Mr. Holmes. It is difficult sometimes to have faith in the manifestation of God's miracles. But I have often seen this for myself. After the bones were brought to the *basilica* in Bari, the smell of roses from the tomb has continued, as well as the appearance of the liquid, to the present day. And I have watched how it has been used to perform many miracles."

"And the tomb with the other bones in Venice? Does it also produce this *manna*?"

"I have not been there myself, but it is my understanding that they also have vials of the liquid."

"But surely," said Holmes, "there is another explanation. Seepage of groundwater into the tomb, perhaps? Or condensation?"

The priest shook his head, a tolerant smile dancing upon his lips. "No, Mr. Holmes. The tomb has been verified to be watertight, and no water is entering through the stones. The bones themselves ooze the liquid, much more than could be accounted for by simple condensation. Enough, as a matter of fact, that it is bottled in vials for use, along with Holy Water, in the performance of miracles."

Holmes frowned, as if looking for another argument. Finally, he shook his head. "That is all neither here nor there," he said, "in terms of recovering the bone. As you say, it is important to you to do so sooner, rather than later, but the idea of this *manna's* existence in and of itself has no impact on the actual recovery. What were the circumstances of the theft?"

The priest nodded, as if some sort of accord had been reached, and there was now enough to be going on with. "A little over a week ago, a British ship was docked in Bari. St. Nicholas always had a special relationship with sailors, so it is not unusual for them to visit the *basilica* in order to honor the tomb. Many are simply curious, but a few are genuine pilgrims who wish to worship.

"On the day in question, a group of sailors were there, including one who was recognized as having been there before on several occasions. On previous visits, he was always reverent and respectful, and had asked a number of intelligent questions. This time, however, he did something unusual.

"One of the novitiates noticed that this sailor, a Russian who had previously introduced himself on an earlier visit as Grigori Golov, had stayed behind when his compatriots departed. No other visitors in the *basilica* were present at the time. The novitiate thought nothing of it until, a few minutes later, he returned from an errand to discover that the stone cover of the tomb had been shifted. He called for help, and a number of priests, including myself, quickly determined that the thumb bone had been removed. It was obvious that only Golov could had taken it. There was no damage to the tomb itself, and no other relics were moved.

"As I indicated, it is my position within the church to act in matters relating to the outside world. I quickly made my way to the docks, only to determine that the ship upon which Golov served, *The Good Catherine*, had just left port for England. Obviously, Golov had planned his theft to the minute, allowing for a successful escape.

"Not wanting to involve the police, I decided to follow Golov on my own to retrieve the relic. There were no ships leaving immediately, and I did not want to take the time to follow in so leisurely a manner in any case. Therefore, upon returning to the *basilica*, I arranged to travel by rail, setting foot here three days ago.

"I had just missed the arrival of *The Good Catherine*, but I was able to determine that Golov had disembarked from the ship. It is scheduled to sail again in two days. I have been unable to locate him, although I suspect that he lives in the East End of London. The officials at the shipping office became decidedly uncommunicative when I pressed my questions, and rather than wait for him to reappear at his ship, I decided to see if someone else could help me locate him sooner. I had been given your name, Mr. Holmes, and here we are."

Holmes patted his hand twice upon his index, and then stood abruptly, as he was wont to do upon making a decision. "I believe that I can assist you." He walked around the two of us, replacing the scrapbook. "If you will come back in three hours, I should have the information that you need."

If the priest was surprised at this sudden burst of activity or the promise of a quick solution, he did not show it. He rose from his chair, and I did so as well. With a nod and a small bow, the priest agreed to return, and walked from the room.

Holmes moved into his room, removing his dressing gown as he did so. "Watson, I shall be back in time to meet our client. Do continue to warm yourself in front of the fire." And then, reappearing and wearing clothing suitable for the cold, he departed.

Rather than reseating myself, I stepped over to the shelf holding Holmes's scrapbooks, pulling out the one that he had recently replaced. I found the entry on the Saint, but it gave no more additional information than that which had been recently provided by Father Abele. Unsatisfied, I returned to my seat.

Growing up, I had been exposed to the stories of St. Andrew, that Galilean fisherman who accompanied Christ during his lifetime, and who later carried on the work of the church. I knew about the story of the miracle associated with his name, in which King Angus had seen a vision of St. Andrew's Saltire Cross in the rising sun, and it had inspired him and his men to win a decisive victory over the opposing Saxons, thus leading to the adoption of that Cross as the Scottish symbol. But, in spite of this tale, stories of miracles like the healing fluid produced from the bones of St. Nicholas were not regularly part of the strict Church of Scotland Presbyterian fabric of my boyhood.

I was still brooding upon these questions nearly three hours later when Holmes reappeared, followed almost immediately by the priest. "I have found your sailor," said Holmes as we stepped outside.

"I had no doubts," said Father Abele.

Soon, we were in a four-wheeler, making our way to the south and east. Looking at the priest, sitting across from me in the bitter cold, and without a coat but seemingly indifferent to the fact, I began. "This *manna . . . ."*

The man nodded. "I understand, Doctor. You are curious about the healing properties. You perhaps believe that there is not a true power within the liquid, but rather that the ills are cured by the power of suggestion, and the patient's own desperate desire to be well once again."

"Such things are not unknown," I said. "I could tell you stories of men on the battlefield, during times when we had completely exhausted our supplies. They were given water and told that it was, in fact, morphine. Their belief was enough to convince them that their pain, sometimes from horrible wounds, had been reduced or even eliminated."

Father Abele nodded, and with a kind smile stated, "God has blessed us with minds that have great powers indeed. After all, these minds are created in His own image. One does not realize what the mind is capable of, whether in terms of great reasoning, or the expression of beautiful art or music, or even in terms of healing. But," he added, his face now quite serious, "none of that negates in any way the actual power of a true miracle, which is a separate and distinct thing from that which is conceived of within the mind. A miracle is a gift, granted to us by the Grace of God." And he settled back with finality.

Holmes had a slightly troubled look upon his face, and he was silent throughout this conversation, remaining so throughout the journey. I wondered what he was thinking, although I could imagine. The priest and I also sat quietly, and soon we were at our destination.

We stepped down from our cab, and Holmes led us to a dark arch, from which we signaled for our cabbie to wait. We passed through a tunnel-like passage into a tiny court, and inside were several doors. Holmes stopped in front of the second on the left. It was part of a mean cluster of dark brick buildings, yet surprisingly well kept, considering the neighborhood in which it had been built. "Golov lives on the third floor," said Holmes as we entered the building and climbed the stairs.

Inside, the air was somewhat warmer, although not much, and there was the stale smell of cooked cabbage that is so often found in buildings in that part of London. The stairwell was quite dark, but the treads appeared to be solidly placed, and there was an absence of the refuse that clutters buildings of this sort.

Stopping at the door indicated by Holmes, we caught our breath. From beyond it, we heard quiet conversation. Then the priest knocked solidly, and the voices stopped immediately. After a very short wait, there were heavy footsteps, and the door opened.

We were faced by a tall man, wrapped in a pea coat to ward off the chill. Behind him, we could see a woman with a sad face, standing beside a table where she had apparently been sitting. The man, undoubtedly the sailor Grigori Golov, looked from one to the other of us before settling on Father Abele. A look of sadness crossed his face as he identified the priest's cassock, and he said, with only a trace of accent, "So. You have come, then."

"Was there ever a doubt?" asked the priest, not unkindly. "You did nothing to hide your tracks, my son. We knew your name from when you visited the *basilica* on previous occasions. You waited until no one was there before you opened the tomb, so that it was unavoidably certain that you would be the one identified as the taker of the relic. You made no effort to hide your return to the ship, and your action was apparently planned so as to be able to leave with the vessel at its planned departure time."

Golov nodded. "As you say. But you must understand. I had no choice."

"May we come in?" asked Holmes. "Then, you can explain your reasons."

Golov stepped back, gesturing for us to pass by him. Shutting the door, he said, "This is my wife, Maria."

We nodded at the woman, who simply looked at us, a fearful expression upon her face, pinched with a kind of dread and terror.

"Are these policemen, then?" asked Golov of the priest, looking from Holmes to me. "Are you here to arrest me?"

"No, my son. These men are from here in London. I requested them to help me find you, as I do not know this city very well." He looked around. "Do you still have it? The relic?"

Golov nodded. "I do. And you must believe me that, after I had used it, I intended to return it. I would not have taken it for anything. But, you see, I had no choice."

Holmes nodded. "Is it your child?"

Golov nodded, while the priest looked to his side at my friend. "Child? What do you mean, Mr. Holmes?"

Pointing to several items that I had also spotted on the table in the center of the room, Holmes stated, "Surely it is obvious, from the medical accoutrements placed here and there, that there is illness in the home. There is indication of a child's presence from some of the objects in the room, but he or she – yes, a girl, I believe – is not present. Based upon the various icons placed on the walls, this is a family of deep faith. No doubt Mr. Golov intended to use the power of the relic to heal someone who is ill. Neither Mr. nor Mrs. Golov appears to be sick, so the relic was taken to aid someone else, most likely the child."

Father Abele looked back at the sailor. "Is that so?"

Golov nodded, and his wife began to cry softly.

"And did it help?" asked the priest. "Has your child been healed?"

"No," said Golov sadly. "She has been too ill to even be aware that the Saint's bone is now here."

"Surely," said Father Abele, "she does not need to know it is here for its healing power to make itself manifest."

"That may be," said the big sailor. "And yet, from the time that I returned with it, she has been asleep, suffering from a fever, and unaware that I brought it, as she had asked. I believed that she would know of its power if she recognized that it was here."

"Your daughter requested for you to bring the relic?"

"She did. Many has been the time that I've told her of my visits to the tomb of the Saint, when I've had the opportunity to travel to Bari. When she was scratched several weeks ago, the wound quickly became much worse than one would expect. The doctor came and speculated that the scratch might have simply brought to light some other illness that might prove to be incurable. When it did not seem to get any better, and it appeared as if the doctor could be proven right, our daughter mentioned that perhaps one of the bones of the Saint could be used to heal what the doctor could not.

"I do not know if she really meant for me to bring it, but I resolved that I would do so. Thus, on my last journey, I made my way to the tomb, and as you know, removed the bone." He swallowed, and continued. "I swear, Father, that I was as respectful and as careful as I could be. I would not have desecrated the tomb under any other circumstance, but . . . but . . . ." He broke off with a sob and hung his head. His wife took a step closer and pulled him to her.

"We are afraid," she said, speaking for the first time, "that she will die."

"I am a doctor," I said, stepping forward. "May I see her?"

At the same time, the priest also said, "The relic? Is it with your daughter?"

Golov looked up, from one to the other of us, and nodded. "In here."

He led us into the other room of the tiny flat, a dark chamber with most of the space taken by a small bed. Lying in the middle of it was a wee girl, probably about seven or eight, but appearing more insignificant due to a likely lack of nutrition during the early years of her life. She was huddled under several blankets, her breathing raspy and labored while she shifted from side to side, moaning lightly with each exhalation. Asking "May I?" and receiving a nod from both her parents, I leaned down and felt of her forehead. She was burning.

While I began to examine the girl, I heard the others talking softly behind me. "The relic?" asked the priest. "Where is it?"

"Here," said Golov, reaching for a small tin on a shabby table beside the bed. "I have not opened it since taking it," he said. "I wanted to keep it safe in transit, as you will understand, and there was no need to see it once I arrived, as Alina was too ill to take note of it."

"Then surely there may be enough . . ." said the priest softly to himself.

I glanced over my shoulder to see the Russian handing the tin to the priest. Father Abele took it and carefully raised the lid. Then he turned it slightly from side to side, in order to catch the faint light from the single-paned window. He stopped turning it when he found the angle he wished, and then he simply looked at it for a long moment. I continued to watch him, curious as to the apparent mesmerization that the object seemed to hold over him.

Finally, he looked up at Holmes, and then toward me. "Gentlemen? Would you like to see?"

He held it out, and I rose, even as Holmes took a step forward. Leaning in, we both saw inside the tin. It contained a small whitish nub, undoubtedly the bone from the tip of a thumb. It rested in the corner of the tin, nearly covered by an oily looking liquid. Even as I realized it, the scent of roses seemed to fill the room.

The priest smiled. "Mr. Golov," he said. "Did you also take any of the liquid that was in the tomb when you removed the relic?"

The sailor shook his head emphatically. "No, Father. I was careful to reach in and retrieve only the bone. I was praying as I did so, in order to be as respectful as possible. Some of the liquid lying around the bones in the bottom of the tomb got on my fingers as I picked out the bone, but I shook it off before I put it in the container. It was damp, but that was all." Suddenly, with a realization crossing his face, he asked, "Why?"

Turning slightly, the priest showed the girl's parents what Holmes and I had just seen, the fragment of St. Nicholas, nearly covered with a fluid that it had apparently excreted between the time it was taken in Bari and now. If one believed that sort of thing.

"But surely, Mr. Golov," said Holmes, stubbornly trying to make sense of what he had seen, "you added the liquid at some point. Or your wife."

"We did not!" cried the Russian, while his wife shook her head emphatically.

"Then someone on the ship from Bari," said Holmes. "Some other sailor who knew what you carried, and got at it at some point."

"No one knew that I had it. I did not tell anyone. I did not want to take the chance that it might be taken from me before I could return with it to Alina."

"A miracle, Mr. Holmes," said the priest simply. "A miracle."

Turning away from the frowning expression on my friend's face, I returned to my examination of the girl. She had a long scratch on her leg, quite infected, and suppurating. Around it, her leg was swollen, with streaks stretching above and below. I had seen this before, and knew that there was more going on beneath the skin than was easily seen.

"She fell," said her mother. "Outside. She said that as she did so, her leg dragged itself across a broken board."

I nodded. "No doubt there are splinters buried in the wound, adding to the injury. This and the fever are the body's way of fighting back. How long has she been like this?"

"She became ill about two weeks ago, not long after the injury. The doctor gave us this." She reached behind to a cabinet affixed to the wall and turned back with a brown bottle. I examined it with disgust, seeing that it was among the worst of the patent medicines available to the ignorant, prescribed by charlatans.

"Which doctor gave you this?"

"Doctor Anglesey," replied the girl's mother.

I snorted. I was aware of the man. In the year that I had been back in London, while volunteering my services at Barts, I had more than once come across the victims of this mountebank's practice.

"This concoction will not help her," I said, shaking the bottle and then handing it back. "She is in danger." I saw no reason to keep them from knowing the truth. "The treatment she received from your Doctor Anglesey did not help. In fact, letting her go for so long without true medical attention has only made the problem worse. She has blood poisoning, and . . . and there is a danger that she might lose her leg."

Golov's eyes widened, while his wife gave forth a sob. "Will she die?" asked the women quietly.

I shook my head. "It is not too late. She can be treated, but we must get her to hospital immediately."

I leaned down and began to wrap her tightly in the thin blankets. But as I was doing so, Father Abele spoke. "Doctor? If I may?"

I turned to see him holding the tin, a questioning look in his eyes. I knew what he was asking.

"Father, I simply cannot. We do not know what is in that liquid."

"We do not know what is in it, but we do not need to. We know from whence it comes."

"It may do more harm than good," I answered with exasperation. "It has been in contact with a bone, for goodness' sake."

"Exactly," said the priest. "For goodness' sake."

I hesitated, uncertain as to whether to allow it. I noticed the girl's father staring intently at me. He nodded. "Let him, Doctor," he said. "Please."

I straightened and glanced at Holmes. His eyes were in a frown, but, sensing my uncertainty, he nodded. With a sigh, I stepped back, allowing the priest access.

He sat himself on the edge of the bed and, laying a hand across the girl's brow, began to pray in low, even tones. Mr. and Mrs. Golov bowed their heads, silently mouthing the words to the prayer as well. Meanwhile, Holmes watched intently.

Father Abele took his open palm from the girl and brought it to the tin, held in his other hand. Placing a finger carefully inside, he brought it back out, now damp from the liquid *manna* within. Moving carefully, so that none of it would drop off, he extended his hand back to Alina's forehead, where he traced the figure of a cross, lengthwise and then side to side, still praying as he did so. Suddenly, almost the instant that he had finished and lifted away his fingertip, the girl gave a gasp and flickered her eyes, but then settled back into the same condition in which she had been when we found her.

Pulling aside the blankets, he then repeated his actions, carefully tracing the length of the girl's wound with the oily substance from the tin. This time, the girl gave no reaction, and the liquid simply shone in the dim light from the window before gradually losing its sheen as it dried.

With a solemn "Amen," the priest arose and made room for me. Not wanting to disturb the fluid, still faintly outlined on the girl's forehead, I placed a hand against her cheek. Was her fever already lessened? Surely not. And yet, I could not be sure in that cold room, and I did not want to take time to find out otherwise. Bundling her up, I rose and carried her out of the bedroom, and so on until we reached the street, where our four-wheeler was waiting.

Talking to our cabbie was another driver, apparently a friend of his, who had tarried for a while during the time that we were inside. The two were talking and smoking, while the second driver's hansom was parked nearby. "*How fortunate to find a second cab in this neighborhood,*" I thought to myself as I climbed with the girl into the four-wheeler. "*Almost a miracle,*" my mind added as I settled back on the seat, carefully holding my patient. I was joined by the girl's parents, while Holmes engaged the hansom for him and the priest to follow.

"The Royal London Hospital, Whitechapel Road," I called to our driver. "And hurry!"

"Right away," the man answered, gigging his horse. Within minutes we were in transit, and not long after, I was carrying the girl inside, explaining the situation, and being directed to a room in order to begin treatment.

Even as we had traveled, the girl had inexplicably and impossibly begun to show signs of recovery. I would like to believe that it was due to the uncomfortable shock of being taken from the womb-like atmosphere of the bedroom and out into the cold December day. How could she not react in some way? But a part of my mind could not help but wonder if the priest's ministrations had not had something to do with it.

Within an hour of our arrival at the hospital, the girl's wound had been debrided and treatment was being given for the fever. Careful probing had revealed a long nasty splinter, black and slick, invisible from the surface and resisting to the end as it was pulled from the girl's wound. The streaks of blood poisoning had already unexplainably commenced to recede back toward the puncture. And, in all honesty, the fever had already started to abate well before the efforts at the hospital began. Within a short while, it was with a great feeling of satisfaction that I was able to call in the sailor and his wife, who joyfully reunited with the now conscious and smiling girl at her bedside.

Some time later, in the hallway outside, Holmes and I stood with the priest.

"She will be fine," I said. "They will be able to take her home within a few hours."

"And now, Doctor? Mr. Holmes?" asked Father Abele. "Now do you see the power of the miracle?"

I wanted to answer, but my response was torn. As a doctor, I could credit the effect of the mind in letting the body cure itself. As a man of science, I wanted to reject the moonshine associated with a miracle. In the end, I said nothing, looking toward my friend.

With a tight smile, Holmes simply said, "There are all sorts of miracles, Father."

Seeing that this was the best that he was going to get, the priest nodded. "Your fee, Mr. Holmes?" He reached within his cassock, pulling out a worn leather purse that jingled with heavy coins. Holmes waved his hand.

"Not necessary, Father. My assistance was minimal."

"Nevertheless," said Father Abele. "I insist."

"If you must," said my friend, "then use it to assist the poor. Perhaps the Golov's could benefit from it. Anonymously, of course."

"Of course. And Doctor? May I compensate you for your troubles?"

"Not at all," I said. "Add my portion to Holmes's. For the Golov family."

"Very good," he replied. He replaced the purse and patted his chest, where the container holding the relic of the Saint now rested. "Then I must get this back to where it belongs. May you both go with God."

"And you, Father," I replied, while Holmes simply nodded.

Later, as we were leaving Whitechapel behind, I turned to Holmes, sitting beside me in the hansom. "Father Abele," I said with a false heartiness, as I attempted to place these events in some sort of container in which they could be examined and understood, "certainly believes in the power of this supposed miracle."

"Indeed. He has dedicated his life to such an idea."

I was silent for a moment, before I felt the need to say, "I must confess, Holmes, that the girl's response following the touch of the liquid, and the subsequent and unexpectedly immediate improvement in her condition, is unheard of. It seems to give some validity to the Father's argument."

"There are all sorts of miracles," said my friend, repeating his comment of a few minutes earlier.

I smiled. "I'm surprised, Holmes. You are the ultimate defender of the scientific and rational explanation over that of superstition. What credence do you give to miracles?"

Holmes was silent for so long that I thought he had chosen not to answer. The sound of the horse's steady tread went on for quite a while before he spoke. And then, finally, "Ah, Watson, how can I explain it? I seek rational explanations to questions, because if I cannot define a mystery within the known rules and laws by which we exist on a daily basis, what hope do I have? No ghosts need apply. If the possibility for a supernatural explanation *does* exist, then when do we choose to carry on and find the truth if a human agency is responsible, and when do we abandon our efforts and throw up our hands, declaring that the problem has no solution, for it is the fault of a spirit or god beyond our understanding, and therefore the solution cannot be perceived by our mere mortal minds?

"If I am to function within my chosen field, I have to believe that there is a rational and worldly explanation for every action. There have to be some defined parameters within which I can work. If a person believes himself to be haunted, I must determine who is doing whatever is being done to make him *think* that, and then relieve him of the problem. I cannot simply assume that the possibilities are endless. You, as a doctor, must do the same thing. You must seek the cause of a disease, and treat it with the best defined methods in order to achieve real results, rather than stepping back and simply counting on the effort of a prayer, hoping that some magical culmination to the situation will be achieved."

I started to reply, but Holmes added, "But, as I said, Watson, there are all sorts of miracles."

"That," I said, "is contradictory, and does not seem to fit with your previous statement."

"But it does. I cannot refuse to make an effort to find a solution, simply on the surrendering assumption that it is beyond my powers. Nevertheless, as a scientist, I must also be aware of the smallness of man in the great scheme of the Universe, and how little we truly know. We have so much more understanding of the physical world than we did even a hundred years ago, but it would be foolish to think that we now understand all of it, and that all the mysteries of existence are now solved. There are so many things that we think we know with certainty that we probably have wrong, and so much more that we do not even *know* that we do not know. Our understanding of the actual world is like that of an ant's knowledge of the workings of a steam engine."

"You astound me, Holmes. I was certain that you would have had a much different point of view."

"I'm happy that, even after a year, Watson, I can still surprise you. Would it also astonish you to learn that I believe in the human soul?"

"Frankly, yes it would."

"And yet, given my statement that we really know nothing about the Universe around us, how could I not? For what is it that gives us a self-awareness? What is it that takes all of the various separate substances that make up our bodies, each a miniscule dead piece of matter that has never been alive and will never be alive as we understand it, and brings it all together into a unit that functions together for a while as a cohesive unit, with thought and action and purpose, before separating again into dead pieces, each one going its own way. And for that matter, what is it that allows us to change the world around us, with or without a plan, in violation of all the natural laws of the Universe?"

I found myself fascinated as this conversation spiraled from the discussion of a sick girl to the laws of the Universe. "What do you mean by that?"

"Simply that the Universe works by following a defined set, as we understand them, of natural entropic laws. Heat disperses into coolness. Higher energy decreases into levels of lower energy. The force of gravity pulls a smaller object towards a heavier one, but with a mutual attraction always existing between both of them. Any random particle in the Universe will follow these natural laws governing its motion and behavior.

"But this," he said, raising a hand in front of us, "this simple action of raising my hand and holding it there because I *choose* to do so, defies all the laws of the Universe. The Law of Gravity states that I should not be able to voluntarily and decisively raise my hand, going against the pull of the entire planet. Everything in the Universe says no. And yet . . . I choose to do so, and then I so accomplish it.

"What is it that makes me decide to do this, to take this random collection of dead substances held together for a while as *me*, and place them in opposition to the will of the Universe? As a scientist, I see this action accomplished. It has happened, and happens everywhere, every day, whether raising a hand or a pyramid. It must be achieved by something. For lack of anything else better to call it, it must be a *soul*."

"But animals choose to move independently," I countered. "Plants grow in opposition to gravity. Are you saying that they have souls as well?"

He shrugged. "Who is to say? Perhaps we all have a fragment or spark of the Divine within each of us, to a greater or lesser degree. I know as little about it as an ant knows of a steam engine.

"But let me give you another example: If I choose to roll a boulder up to the top of a hill, something that would never happen naturally in this entropic universe, gravity immediately wants to pull it back down to the bottom. Suppose then that I brace it, where it cannot roll away. My action has thus defied one of the basic natural laws of the Universe. Wind and weather – both caused, by the way, by convection currents and other phenomena related to natural laws – will wear at the boulder and the earth beneath it for countless ages. They may do so for so long that the hillside itself erodes away, thus allowing the boulder to be freed again from its support, whereupon it will follow the natural laws and again roll back to the bottom. But in the meantime, during all those years, the boulder has been sitting where *my* own will and *my* energy and *my* choice placed it, where it never would have been located before, according to every natural law in the Universe. The same is true for a statue or a building made up of bricks and alloys and other materials that never would have been combined or formed together in that particular way or shape if someone had not intentionally done so, defying the laws and will and intent of the Universe.

"Knowing all of that, and additionally realizing how small we are in the great scheme of things, how can I doubt that there must be different sorts of miracles?"

I was quiet for a moment, contemplating the vast scope of his statement. Finally, I said, not knowing how else to reply, "I never knew that you felt this way."

"It has never come up. But how can we ignore it? When trying to determine that which is greater than us, there is nothing so necessary as deduction. And if we believe that existence is essentially good, as I do – in spite of much that I have seen – then the greatest assurance of that goodness seems to rest in the extras that we are given, such as flowers, for instance. Their beauty is an extra, an embellishment of life, and not a condition, and one that I am thankful for.

"But, even if I am thankful for this extra, I must conduct my work with a degree of separation from it, so that I do not end up counting on miracles. Yet, I do believe them, and the events of today convince me of that even more."

"How so? In what way?"

"We may or may not believe in the power of the *manna* from the St. Nicholas relic, although *'there are more things in heaven and earth, Watson, than are dreamt of in your philosophy'*, to paraphrase the Bard. The relic's liquid could have contributed to the girl Alina's recovery, or not. But I do believe that your unexpected return today, allowing you to be present in order to participate in our trip to Stepney, was part of a bigger plan. For you, a doctor, were with us when we visited this girl who needed medical attention. You had, I believe, intended to spend the day at Barts, and then at other pursuits. What if you hadn't been at home when Father Abele arrived? I would have found the Golovs, but would we have known to seek immediate additional treatment for the girl? Would we have recognized the seriousness of her illness? Or that her wound was much graver than it appeared from the surface? Perhaps the anointment of the *manna* would have healed the girl, but I have to believe that she needed the immediate attention of a physician as well – and you were there."

"The second cab," I said softly. Holmes raised his eyebrows. "I thought at the time that it was unusually fortunate that a second cab was waiting in that neighborhood when we carried the girl outside."

He nodded. "Another minor miracle, perhaps?" Then, lowering his voice, he continued. "And then there is the other occurrence, which might also be something of a miracle."

A silence fell as he ruminated for a moment, until I prodded him to continue. "I didn't tell you about how I located the Golovs," he said.

"I had assumed it was a straightforward investigation."

"I should have been. I was able to speak to my various contacts near the docks, and I was quickly given the man's address. But then . . . then I *couldn't find it.* Watson, you know that I have an encyclopedic knowledge of London, but in this case, it failed me. And everyone that I asked was uncertain as well as to the location of the little court where the sailor and his family lived.

"Time was passing, and soon I would need to return to Baker Street to meet the priest. Just when I was feeling most frustrated, I heard a soft voice behind me. Turning, I discovered a tall old man, with a white beard and a high forehead, smiling at me with a most warming expression. He spoke with an unusual accent that I couldn't quite place, clearly foreign, and with something of the Mediterranean about it. 'The house you seek is there, my son.' And he raised his arm, pointing toward that same dark passage, previously unnoticed by me up to that moment, where I later returned with you and Father Abele. Then he lowered his hand, his smile becoming possibly even more filled with pure joy than before. I wanted to speak, to ask a question, to thank him, but I found that I could not. And as he turned and walked away into the gloom, I was aware of his eyes, Watson. They were perhaps the kindest eyes that I have ever seen . . . ."

His voice faded, and I knew the unspoken thought between us. Who could the man have been who knew just where to direct Holmes in his moment of desperation? Someone from that neighborhood, perhaps, who had heard Holmes's attempts to locate the address, and had simply offered assistance. *Or could it have been . . . ?* But no – for that would be impossible. Still, one somehow knows that at Christmas, above all other times of the year, the possibility of miracles might somehow truly exist.

I raised my eyes to find Holmes smiling at me, obviously reading my thoughts. "So there are different sorts of miracles, Watson, and I think that today's events count. Most fittingly, they were Christmas miracles."

And as we rode in silence, I found, with further examination, that I agreed with him. I recalled my feelings of just a few hours before, as I had looked about me with a sore lack of appreciation for the season. In fact, considering the circumstances in which I might have found myself at this point in my life, had I not met my friend when I did, I was very fortunate indeed. If, in fact, there is an overall plan, as Holmes espoused, one that is greater than our understanding, I could only be thankful that I could dimly recognize and appreciate my place in it, and thus count my many blessings.

"Merry Christmas, Holmes," I was moved to say.

"Indeed, my friend. Indeed it is."

The Jet Brooch

By Denis O. Smith

This story first appeared in the MX Book of New Sherlock Holmes Stories Volume V.

Denis O Smith's first Sherlock Holmes story, *The Purple Hand*, was published in 1982. Since then he has written more than forty stories, recording previously unknown cases of the world's most famous detective. These have appeared in numerous magazines and anthologies, and in collections of his own, most recently *The Lost Chronicles of Sherlock Holmes*, *The New Chronicles of Sherlock Holmes* and *The Further Chronicles of Sherlock Holmes*. Born in Sheffield, in the north of England, Mr Smith now lives in the rural county of Norfolk. His interests, other than the career of Sherlock Holmes, include old maps, historical mysteries of all kinds, the history of London, and the railways of Britain.

David Teal is a figurative artist whose work emphasizes color, shape, and the use of space to suggest images and ideas. David Teal is a painter who also works in mixed media and three-dimensional forms. David Teal draws inspiration for his paintings from old family photos and reinterprets those images to reflect on today's world. Street scenes and news footage prompt mixed media and sculptural projects. David Teal's artistic influences range from contemporary realists Hockney, Katz, and Fischl to the exuberant colors, patterns, and lines of Matisse. Teal's work has been chosen for exhibitions in the Northeast and in South Florida by curators from prestigious museums and galleries including the Guggenheim, the Whitney, the Museum of Modern Art, Steven Harvey Fine Arts Projects, and the Frederic Snitzer Gallery. During his tenure at the Yale School of Art, Robert Storr chose three of David Teal's paintings for an exhibit. Dean Storr awarded these works honorable mention. Other influential jurors including Carter Foster, Marshall Price, Paulina Pobocha, Lauren Hinkson, and Rujeko Hockley have selected David Teal's paintings for various shows. David Teal resides in South Florida, between the beach and the swamp.

www.davidtealart.com

Artwork size: 20 x 30

Medium: Acrylic on Canvas

During the years I shared chambers with Mr. Sherlock Holmes, the well-known criminal investigator, he handled many cases which involved the intimate private concerns of families whose names would be recognized by most readers of the daily Press. I have included but few of these in this series of records I have laid before the public, for obvious reasons. I would be guilty of gross indiscretion and a very great breach of confidence were I to even hint at the nature of some of these adventures, let alone provide a detailed account. Occasionally, however, when some time has elapsed since the events in question, and when I am able with a few little changes to disguise the identities of those involved, it is possible for me to give an account of one or two of these narratives, if I judge that the facts of the matter are of sufficient interest to warrant it. Such a tale is the one I shall now recount, an odd little tangle with a mysterious package at one end and a well-known song at the other.

It was the week before Christmas. The weather was cold, and I had awoken that morning to the rapid rat-a-tat-tat of hail against my bedroom window. Our breakfast finished, Sherlock Holmes had pulled the sofa a little nearer to the fire, and now lounged there in his old mouse-coloured dressing-gown, examining a small, flat package, about an inch in depth and three or four inches square, which had been delivered that morning.

"I wonder what this can be?" he remarked, turning it over in his hand, as I sat down on the other side of the fireplace. "I was not expecting anything today, so it is probably from a stranger."

"Why do you not open it and see?" I suggested.

"All in good time," said he. "I prefer to examine the outside first. It is easier to extract any information that may be there while the package is still intact. What do you make of it, Watson?" he asked, tossing it across to me.

"It is a little lighter than I had expected," I said, weighing it in my hand. "I thought it might have been a tin of tobacco, but I don't think it is heavy enough for that. It is wrapped in rather dull brown paper. This is not gummed in any way; it is simply fastened with string. It feels as if there is a small cardboard box inside the wrapping," I added, as I gave the package a gently squeeze.

"Anything else?"

"Not that I can see."

"The address?"

I looked again at the address. "Why," I said in surprise, "the house number has been missed off. It simply says 'Mr. Sherlock Holmes, Baker Street, London'."

"Precisely. We benefit from the fact that the postman has delivered so many letters to me in the year we have been living here that he knows where to find me, even when the address is incomplete. Now, I can't imagine that anyone who knew it would forget to include the house number in the address. It therefore seems likely that it was not known by the sender, who just trusted to luck that the parcel would find me. This supports my initial supposition that it is from a stranger, and someone, moreover, who was not in a position to find out my full address. Are there any more clues in the wrapping?"

"I don't think so," I replied after a moment.

"What about the string?"

"It is just a commonplace piece of thin twine," I said as I examined it.

"Not quite," said Holmes with a shake of the head. "It is certainly commonplace, but it is not one piece but three, which have been knotted together to make a suitable length."

"That is true, but is that of any significance?"

"Well, it suggests either someone who is very parsimonious with his string – using short pieces that most people would probably have thrown away – or perhaps a servant or other employee who has used discarded string – perhaps rescued from a waste-paper basket – to avoid being accused of using his employer's property for his own purposes."

"It is possible."

"Next we come to the handwriting itself, which, as you see, is in pencil. It seems to me it is a woman's hand. Why the handwriting of men and women should differ in so distinctive a way, I do not know – it is a mystery I have not yet solved – but that they do so differ is undeniable. Of course, each hand has its own idiosyncrasies and not all women write in this way, but I have never yet encountered a single man whose hand was like this. Therefore, we are probably justified in saying it is the hand of a woman. It is clear enough, but not very regularly formed, so it may be the hand of a young person, although that inference cannot be drawn with the same degree of confidence. As to what you describe as dull brown paper, I think it is simply ordinary brown paper turned back to front, with the shiny side on the inside and the dull side on the outside. This suggests someone using old paper, and accords with the inferences we drew from the knotted string. Let us now open the package and see what it contains!"

He took a small pen-knife from the little table by his elbow, neatly cut the string, and slipped it from the packet. Then he unwrapped the brown paper and examined it closely for a moment. "This piece has been cut – rather hurriedly to judge from the irregular shape – from a larger sheet. It is indeed a used piece of paper, for on the other side there is another address, written in ink, in a different hand. I rather fancy that my mysterious correspondent has used this ingenious method to indicate where the package has come from."

He passed me the paper and I saw that the address on the back of it was "*Sir George Datchett, 8 Cumberland Gardens, Kensington*", although the name on the first line had been crossed through with a pencil. Holmes, meanwhile, was carefully lifting the lid from the cardboard box which had been wrapped in the paper. As he did so, he let out a cry of surprise, and I saw that the box was full to the brim with some white powder. He licked his finger, pushed it into the powder and tasted it.

"It is flour," said he, "perfectly ordinary flour. If you would pass me a piece of paper from the desk, Watson, I will tip it out and see if there is anything else beneath the flour."

I laid the sheet of paper on the hearth-rug and watched as my companion carefully tipped the flour onto it. All at once, a small, dark object fell out onto the little heap of flour. He picked it up, blew off the loose flour, then rubbed it on the sleeve of his dressing-gown. As he held it up, I saw that it was an ornate brooch. In the centre was a circular black disc, the size of a large coin, its surface faceted so that it caught the light with each slight movement, and around the edge was a golden rim in which the metal was teased into fantastic little twirls and curls.

"The stone in the middle looks like jet," I said.

My friend nodded his head. "Yes, and the setting is gold. It looks quite a valuable piece of jewellery." He passed me the brooch, and lifted the lid of the box to his nose. "There is a distinctive smell to this box," he said.

"Of what?"

"Soap. Scented soap. Quite expensive, I should say, as might be used in a fairly well-to-do household. Now, why should anyone send me a jet brooch without explanation, packed in flour in an old soap-box? Ah!"

He leaned over and extracted a tiny scrap of paper from the little heap of flour on the floor. The paper was of a rough, irregular shape and appeared to have been torn from the edge of a sheet of newspaper.

"Perhaps this will make things clearer," said my companion, but his face remained impassive as he examined it, and, with a frown, he passed it to me.

Upon the scrap of paper, just three words were written in pencil: "*Please help me*".

"That does not tell us much," I remarked.

"No," said Holmes. "It is written in the same hand as the address, and with the same pencil, but that is no more than one would expect."

"I wonder why the box has been filled with flour."

"Presumably to prevent the brooch from rattling about. The use of flour suggests someone who has access to a kitchen, or, to look at it another way, someone who does not have access to any more usual packing material, such as cotton wool. To sum up, then, our mysterious correspondent is probably female, probably young, and probably a domestic servant in a well-to-do household, who has read or heard my name somewhere and believes I may be able to help her. In what way she requires help we cannot say. It may have something to do with this brooch, but that is not certain. The brooch may be simply a deposit to secure my services – although it seems an unlikely piece of jewellery for a young housemaid to have in her possession."

"I was just thinking the same," I remarked. "It looks like something an older woman might wear."

As I was speaking there came a ring at the front-door bell. A few moments later, our landlady appeared in the doorway to inform us that a lady had called to see Mr. Sherlock Holmes, but had declined to give her name.

"One moment, Mrs. Hudson," said Holmes, springing to his feet. "I shall just restore a little order, and then you can show her up." Carefully, he picked up from the floor the sheet of paper on which lay the little heap of flour and carried it over to his desk. I gathered together the brown paper, string and cardboard box and handed them to him. These, together with the brooch and scrap of paper, he also placed on his desk and closed the lid. "Now," said he, as he pulled the sofa back from the fire, "I think we are ready to receive our visitor."

The woman who was shown into our room a few moments later was tall and stately in her bearing. Although of middle age, she had retained the figure and posture of a younger woman. She was wearing a very smart dark blue costume with yellow piping on the edges.

"Pray, take a seat," said Holmes, indicating the chair beside the hearth, "and let us know what we can do for you."

"No, thank you," returned our visitor in a firm tone. "I shall not be here for more than a few moments. I have simply called to collect something."

"Oh?" said Holmes in surprise. "And what might that be?"

"A brooch," said she. "My brooch. It has been sent here in error. The wrong address was written on the package."

"Did you address it yourself?"

"No. Someone else did."

"To whom should it have been sent?"

"To the jeweller. The clasp needs repairing."

"Well," said Holmes, "so far as I am aware, we have received no misaddressed parcels here."

"You must have; it was posted yesterday."

Holmes shook his head. "It is but a few days to Christmas, madam," said he, "and you must know what that means for postal deliveries. The sorting-offices have mailbags piled up to the ceiling, and everything takes longer than usual. If you would give me your name and address," he continued, taking up his note-book and pencil from the table, "I shall let you know if any misaddressed parcel arrives here."

The woman hesitated. "No," said she. "I shall call again tomorrow."

She had turned to leave us, but stopped as Holmes spoke again.

"It seems strange to me," said he, "that you should have my address at all. Do you – or anyone in your household – wish me to look into some problem for you?"

"Absolutely not," she returned sharply. "It is no concern of yours how the mistake was made. I simply wish you to return to me the package when I call again. Do you understand?"

"Understanding is not the issue here, madam," returned Holmes in an urbane tone. "Rather, it is a matter of proof. You will call again and expect me to hand over to you something I have received in the post. But how do I know you have any right to the object in question? For all I know, the brooch may have been stolen – possibly by you. If so, the rightful owner would scarcely thank me for handing it over to someone I have never met before and who refuses to give me her name."

Our visitor's face blanched perceptibly. "How dare you make such an impertinent remark!" she cried in a sharp tone. She appeared about to say more, but bit her lip and was silent for a moment, breathing very heavily. "I shall return tomorrow," she said at length, scarcely able to get the words out as her breast rose and fell with emotion, "and shall bring a pair of ear-rings with me that you will see exactly match the brooch." With that, she turned on her heel and left the room, slamming the door as she did so.

"What a very entertaining interview!" said Holmes after a moment.

"She appeared to be one used to having her instructions obeyed," I remarked, "but she also seemed very emotional about something."

Holmes nodded his head. "More than that," said he; "she is in a state of extreme anxiety. About what, I do not know – but I intend to find out. Of course, what she told us is a tissue of lies: there is nothing wrong with the clasp on the brooch, as I could see when I examined it."

"Will you follow her, to see where she goes?" I asked.

Holmes shook his head. "I am confident that the address on the reverse of that brown paper is pertinent to the matter. That is where I shall go."

He disappeared into his bedroom and did not emerge again for fifteen minutes. I looked up from the newspaper I was reading as he did so and received a shock. In the place of the neatly turned out fellow-lodger I had expected to see, there stood a disreputable-looking figure with a tangled beard, wearing an old, threadbare jacket and cap and a pair of ill-fitting corduroy trousers. The appearance was completed by a bright check muffler that was knotted round his neck.

"Is that you, Holmes?" I queried, not entirely in jest.

"Yes, Watson, it is I," returned he. "It is not only villains who can adopt disguises in order to pursue their ends. I am off to do a little research, and have adopted the character of Jack Brown, itinerant knife-grinder, which I believe will serve me the best."

"Knife-grinder?" I cried with a chuckle. "But you haven't got a grinding-wheel!"

"True, but that is not an insuperable obstacle. I have a small grindstone, at least," he continued, producing a cylindrically-shaped stone from an inside pocket. "That may suffice for my purposes. Now, I can't say when I shall be back, but I should be obliged if you would save me a little bread and cheese from your mid-day meal, as I may not have much opportunity to eat while I am out!"

With a little salute he was gone, and I was left to wonder what it was he intended to do. For a time I tried to distract my thoughts with the day's newspapers, but they contained little of interest and I soon found my thoughts returning once more to the strange business my companion was involved in.

It seemed likely to me that the brooch really did belong to our morning visitor, but as Holmes had remarked, it did not appear to be in need of repair. Why, then, had it been sent anywhere at all, and why, in particular, had it been sent to Holmes? Our visitor did not appear to have sent it herself, but how, then, did she know it had been sent to our address? Who had sent it and why? Did our visitor know who had sent it or not? Why was she so determined to withhold her own name?

One thing that seemed evident was that she did not want Holmes to learn anything of the facts surrounding the brooch, but Holmes, it was clear, was equally determined that he would uncover these facts. He had had a tiny message in the package he had received, pleading for his help, and he needed no further persuasion than that. As I was beginning to learn, it was only rarely that he refused his help when it was sincerely requested. This generosity of spirit put enormous demands upon his constitution, demands that would have quite exhausted another man, but which seemed only to spur my friend on to greater industry.

I should not wish my readers to think that I was excessively self-absorbed, but as I reflected on my fellow-lodger's intense and energetic activity, I was led inevitably to a consideration of my own contrasting circumstances. Little more than a year had passed since I had been invalided home from the war in Afghanistan, and I had stepped onto the jetty at Portsmouth with my health seemingly ruined forever. That had, in truth, not proved to be the case: I was definitely in somewhat better health now than I had been twelve months previously; but the slightest over-exertion was still likely to reduce me to the state of a limp rag. In these circumstances, I had come to look to Sherlock Holmes and his work to provide the zest and interest in my life which I could not provide for myself. I had begun to keep notes of his cases and had on a few occasions been able to accompany him on his investigations, although that was not always possible. Now, as I pondered the mystery of the jet brooch, I found myself glancing frequently at the clock on the mantelpiece, wondering when my friend would return, and if he would have managed to learn anything of the matter.

It was the middle of the afternoon before I heard Holmes's characteristically rapid footsteps ascending the stair. I could see at once, from the expression on his face, as he burst into the room like a whirlwind, that he had had some success.

"The bread and cheese is on the table, under the cloth," I said.

"Good man!" said he. "I am famished! I shall just remove this beard, which has begun to irritate me, and be with you in a moment. Do you know if we have any beer in the house at present?"

"Yes," I said. "There are some bottles of pale ale in the cupboard. I'll open one for you."

A few minutes later, he returned from his bedroom. The beard had gone, along with the grimy jacket and cap, and he had donned his old dressing-gown once more.

"Now," said he, as he laid into his simple meal with gusto, "I dare say you are wondering what I have discovered."

"I have been able to think of little else."

Holmes laughed. "Yes, it is an intriguing little problem, is it not! You will be interested to know, then, that I have learned a great deal – although there are still one or two small points that are not clear to me.

"I made my way to Cumberland Gardens, in Kensington. It is a short, handsome street, with plane trees along the sides. The houses are very smart, all in white stucco, and clearly the homes of the wealthy. I began my investigation by simply loafing about there and striking up a conversation with anyone who seemed likely to respond. I make a grand loafer, Watson, even if I say so myself. It seems to come naturally to me. Gradually, through conversation with some of the ostlers in the nearby mews, a man delivering vegetables from his cart, and numerous other people, I was able to accumulate information about the occupants of Number Eight. Needless to say, I also gathered information about the occupants of Numbers Two, Four, Six and Ten, which I endeavoured to forget as soon as I had heard it.

"Head of the household at Number Eight is Sir George Datchett, who was one of the founders of the Sea Eagle Marine Insurance Company, and who was knighted just two months ago for his services to commerce. His wife is Lady Hilary Datchett, and from the description I was given of her, I am fairly certain it was she who called upon us this morning. The family is completed by a son, Michael, aged about twenty, who is up at Oxford but returned home for the Christmas vacation two weeks ago, and a daughter, Olivia, who is seventeen and in her final year at the Cheltenham Ladies' College. She returned home last week. The domestic staff at the Datchett household consists of a butler, who organizes the household, a cook, a kitchen-maid, and a chambermaid.

"Having amassed this information, I abandoned my loafing about and called at the tradesman's entrance of Number Eight, where I offered my services as a knife-grinder. This was rejected, much as I had expected, but I did not give up.

"'My dear lady,' I said to the cook, who had answered the door to me. I was about to extol the benefits of having sharpened knives, but she interrupted me.

"'Don't you be so bold,' said she. '"Dear lady" indeed!' But she laughed nonetheless, and I could see that by amusing her I had gained a small foothold. I thereupon offered to sharpen a pair of scissors for her free of charge, 'to demonstrate the worth of my technique', as I put it. This she assented to, in grudging fashion, and I had thereby gained a few more minutes of standing in the kitchen doorway, which was of course my aim.

"As I did my best to sharpen the scissors a little, I chatted with her and watched as she and the kitchen-maid – who appeared to be called Lily – bustled about their work. When I'd finished, I declared that it was 'thirsty work' and asked if I might have a cup of water, which she brought me. Up to that point, to speak frankly, I hadn't really learned anything very useful, but all at once things changed. Another girl came into the kitchen in a maid's uniform. She was there for only a few moments, picked something up and left again, but in that few moments I thought I might have found my way to the heart of the mystery. I was already fairly confident, if you recall, that the brooch and the request for help had been sent to me by someone who was young, female, and a domestic servant. Neither the cook nor the kitchen-maid looked likely to be so imaginative or enterprising, and the butler could surely be ruled out. But in the few moments the other housemaid had been in the kitchen, she had glanced across to where I stood, in the doorway. For half a second, our eyes had met, and in that half-second I had seen an unusual depth and intelligence in her eye. Surely, I thought, this was my mysterious correspondent! I might also add that she was quite exceptionally pretty and attractive."

"I thought you always said," I interrupted, "that the appearance of your clients was a matter of complete indifference to you."

"Yes, of course, that is true when their appearance is irrelevant to the case, as it generally is; but there are odd occasions when a woman's appearance is not simply an irrelevant, peripheral matter, but a central feature of the case, and I found myself wondering if this might not be one such instance. Sometimes, a pretty face in a household or other group of people can have an effect akin to the tossing of a small pebble into a placid mill-pond: ripples are created which, although sometimes scarcely discernible, can reach a long way.

"'That girl who was in here just now,' I said to the cook as I sipped my cup of water, 'I believe I may know her. Is it not Susan, who used to be in the household of Lady Darlington?'

"'No, it ain't,' said the cook. 'It's Jane, who didn't use to be in anybody's household.'

"'Of course,' I said, 'but I do know her from somewhere. Is it Jane Robinson?'

"'No it ain't. It's Jane Page – and how would a shabby-looking fellow like you know someone as sweet as Jane?'

"I was saved from having to answer that question by the reappearance of the girl herself.

"'Here, Jane,' said the cook. 'This dirty-looking scoundrel reckons he knows you from somewhere. Do you know him?'

"The girl looked across the kitchen at me, a very dubious expression on her face. 'I don't think so,' she said.

"I glanced at the cook. She had turned away to put something in the sink, and I took the opportunity to take a card from my pocket and held it out so that the girl could see it.

"She took a step closer. 'You don't look like I thought you would,' she said in a doubtful tone.

"I leaned in at the kitchen door. The cook and the kitchen-maid were still occupied at the other side of the room. I dropped the rough accent I had assumed in my guise as a knife-grinder and, lowering my voice, I said, 'I'm in disguise. I've come in answer to your request for help. Quickly! Tell me what has happened!'

"She came to the kitchen-door and stuck her head out so that she would not be heard by the others. 'That brooch,' she began.

"'Yes? Is it Lady Hilary's?'

"'Yes. Someone put it in my box.'

"'Where was that? At the foot of your bed?'

"'Yes. And then Lady Hilary found it was missing from her jewellery-case, and asked me if I had seen it anywhere. I said I hadn't, but it was in my pocket. I was walking round all day with it in there, trying to think what to do with it. I couldn't tell her where I'd found it – she'd just think I'd stolen it. But I couldn't just put it back in her room, either, as she told me she'd looked all round there – on the dressing-table and on the floor underneath it. Then I thought of you. Mr. Boardman – '

"'Is that the butler?'

"'Yes. He'd read us out a report in the newspaper one evening of how Sherlock Holmes of Baker Street had solved some mysterious burglary when nobody else could, and I thought perhaps you could help me.'

"'I'll try. Who do you think might have put the brooch in your box? Are any of the other servants jealous of you?'

"'Oh, no,' she returned in surprise. 'We all get on famously. Hardly ever a cross word.'

"'Your master and mistress?' I asked. 'Do they treat you well? Are you happy here?'

"'Oh, yes,' she replied quickly. 'It's like Heaven. Sir George is the kindest man I've ever known.'

"'And Lady Hilary?' I asked as she paused.

"'She can be a bit sharp sometimes,' Jane replied, lowering her voice a little more, 'but I think she's quite nice underneath.'

"'The children?'

"'I never see much of Miss Olivia. She's been away at school all the autumn and only came home at the end of last week. She seems nice enough.'

"'And the son?' I asked as the girl hesitated.

"'He's very good looking, and they tell me he's quite clever.'

"'But?'

"'He's a bit bold sometimes. One night last week, I think he'd had a little too much to drink and got a bit over-familiar with me, if you know what I mean. I told him it was wrong, but he wouldn't take "no" for an answer, and I had to push him away. I was worried after that that I'd get into trouble.'

"'When did you find the brooch in your box?'

"'Just yesterday morning. Then, about tea-time, Sir George gave me some letters to post for him. I put them on the hall table and went downstairs to get my hat and coat. While I was downstairs, I had the idea of sending the brooch to you, so I put it in an old soap-box, filled it up with flour to stop it rattling about, and wrapped it up.'

"'Could anyone have learned where you sent it? Did anyone see you writing the address?'

"'No, I'm sure they didn't.'

"'Did you perhaps leave it somewhere unattended for a few moments?'

"'No – wait! – I did! When I got back up to the hall, I realized I'd not got my gloves, so I put the little packet on top of Sir George's letters and ran back downstairs to get them. It was only for a few seconds, though, and there was nobody about in the hall.'

"'But someone might have passed through the hall, and seen the packet lying there?'

"'I suppose so. But I didn't see anyone.'

"At that moment, the butler, Boardman, entered the kitchen and put an end to our discussion by asking what I wanted. I told him I was a knife-grinder, he said they didn't need any knives grinding and that was that. I thanked them for the water, gave the cup back to Jane, and wandered off.

"I then loitered near the end of the street for some time, sitting on a low wall, smoking my old clay pipe. I was just deciding what to do next when my mind was made up for me. The front door of the Datchett's house opened, and out stepped a smart and fashionably-dressed young man who proceeded along the pavement, tapping his cane as he went. I followed him until I judged we were far enough from the house that our encounter would not be visible from there.

"'Excuse me,' I said.

"'No, I haven't got any small change that I can spare,' he responded, scarcely glancing in my direction, and evidently taking me for some sort of beggar.

"'I don't want any,' said I.

"'Then you should be very happy that I'm not going to give you any,' said he, without breaking stride.

"I could see that the only way I could halt his progress long enough to speak to him would be to surprise him, so I again dropped my rough accent and in my ordinary voice simply said, 'Michael Datchett?'

"He stopped abruptly and turned to me. 'Who the devil are you, and how do you know my name?' he demanded.

"'It is my business to know things,' I said, and gave him my card.

"'Well, Mr. Sherlock Holmes,' said he as he handed back my card, 'what is it you want?'

"'I am looking into a matter concerning Jane Page.'

"'What, Jane the housemaid?' he cried in surprise. 'What has she done?'

"'She hasn't done anything. On the contrary, things have been done to her.'

"'Such as?'

"'You have recently forced your unwanted attentions upon her.'

"'Oh, I see,' said Datchett. 'That is what she told you, is it? Well, Mr. Sanctimonious Holmes, you don't want to believe everything you are told.'

"'Do you deny it?'

"'No. Why should I? What I dispute is the term "unwanted". The whole matter is, in any case, an utter trifle.'

"'And now someone has stolen something from the house and placed it among Miss Page's possessions, with the evident intention of getting her accused of theft and thus dismissed, or even charged with the matter in a court of law.'

"'Surely it is more likely, if anything is stolen, that she has stolen it herself.'

"'If so, she would hardly have told me about it.'

"'You might think that, but you can never tell what people might do. Look, if she's taken a silver tea-spoon from a cutlery drawer in the kitchen, or whatever it is, just tell her to put it back where she found it and no-one will be any the wiser. I certainly won't mention it to anyone. Now I really must be off.'

"He turned away, but I persisted. 'It would be natural to wonder if the attempt to incriminate her was a form of revenge, perhaps perpetrated by someone whose advances had been rebuffed.'

"'"Revenge"?' he repeated in an incredulous tone, then burst out laughing. 'Why on earth should I want dear Jane dismissed? Christmas is coming. In two or three days, there will be bunches of mistletoe hanging up, and then she will be obliged to accept a kiss from me. You can't go against the venerable traditions of antiquity, you know! You'll see – or, at least, she will!' With that, he turned away once more, and I was left to ponder the matter further."

"With any result?" I asked.

My friend shook his head. "There are several possibilities," he replied, "with little in the way of evidence to indicate which is true."

"What will you do, then?"

"I really think I shall have to go round to the Datchetts' house this evening and try to force matters to a conclusion. If I don't, Lady Hilary will call here again tomorrow morning and I shall have to give her the brooch. She will then take it away with her and the mystery will remain unresolved. For all we know, Miss Page might then be dismissed from her position, and that is not something I can contemplate with equanimity."

Holmes fell silent then for several minutes, and it was apparent he was considering the matter from every different point of view. "Would you care to accompany me?" he asked abruptly.

I was somewhat taken aback by this sudden and surprising invitation. "I think I should like that," I replied, "if I would not be in your way."

"Not at all," said my friend. "I think it would be interesting for you to see what I hope will be the final act in this little drama. It will be best if we call when the family are all present, but before they sit down to dine, so be ready to leave just after six. Make yourself as neat as possible, Watson, and I will do the same. We must make a favourable initial impression or we may not be seen at all."

It was starting to snow as we took a cab from Baker Street, and as we rattled along through the dark, raw evening, the street lamps we passed served only to illuminate the whirling and tumbling snowflakes which filled the air. By the time we reached Kensington, just after half-past six, I could see that the snow was beginning to settle.

The front door of the Datchetts' house was opened to us by a large and imposing-looking butler who took Holmes's card into a room on the left while we waited in the hall. A moment later, the door opened and the butler re-emerged, followed by a pleasant-faced, grey-haired man of about fifty, who held Holmes's card in his hand.

"What is this about, gentlemen?" he enquired in a puzzled tone, as he closed the door behind him.

"Something odd has happened to a member of your household," replied Holmes, "and I have been trying to help. I am here to conclude the matter."

Datchett frowned. "Perhaps we should continue this discussion in the study," said he, indicating a door on the opposite side of the hall.

"Excuse me, Sir George, but are your family all in the drawing-room?"

"Yes, they are, as it happens. We were just chatting, and are about to dine shortly. Why do you ask?"

"I think it would be better if I said what I have to say in front of everyone. It will not take very long."

"Who is principally concerned in the matter?"

"Your maid, Jane Page."

"Has she done something she shouldn't have?"

"No."

"Very well," said Datchett after a moment's hesitation, "if you think it best. But be aware that I am only agreeing to this because I have heard something of you, and your reputation is that of a gentleman. I do not want any unpleasantness. My wife detests anything of that sort, and my daughter is still a schoolgirl. Do you understand?"

Holmes nodded his head but did not reply, and, after a moment, Datchett opened the drawing-room door and we followed him into the room.

"This is Mr. Sherlock Holmes and his colleague, Dr. Watson," said Datchett, as his wife, son, and daughter turned towards us, their features expressing surprise. "They have something to tell us. Go ahead, Mr. Holmes," he continued as he seated himself on a sofa.

"I will be as brief as possible," Holmes began. "Your maid, Jane, found a valuable piece of jewellery – a jet brooch – among her own possessions the other day, which she recognized as belonging to her mistress. She had no idea how it got there. Before she could do anything about it, Lady Hilary found that the brooch was missing. Frightened that she would be accused of stealing it, and unable to think what to do with it, Jane, on the spur of the moment, parcelled it up and sent it to me. This removed the immediate danger from her, by getting the brooch out of the house. No doubt she also thought that my involvement might lead to the truth being revealed.

"Unfortunately for her, Lady Hilary learned where she had sent the brooch. I assume, madam," he continued, addressing Lady Hilary, "that you saw the package lying on the hall table."

"That is correct. I happened to pass through the hall, and as I did so I glanced at some items on the table that were awaiting posting. Most of them, I could see, were letters my husband had written, but there was also a small package which appeared to have been addressed in a different hand. When I mentioned it to my husband later, he said he knew nothing about it."

"You then conjectured that it might have contained the brooch?"

"Yes, from the size and shape of the package."

"When you called at my chambers this morning and gave me some rigmarole about the brooch needing repair, you did not assume I was involved in the theft of the brooch, or consider calling the police?"

"No, of course not. Like others, I have heard of you as one who solves crimes, not commits them."

"And yet, you presumably felt sure by then that it was Jane who had sent the brooch to me."

"Yes. What of it?"

"Do you believe that Jane stole the brooch?"

"No."

"Why not?"

"Because I don't believe it is in her character to do such a thing."

"Well, if Jane did not place the brooch under her own pillow, then someone else did. She was led, understandably, to the conclusion that someone had deliberately tried to incriminate her, so she would be accused of theft and dismissed, a conclusion with which I entirely concur. If you did not believe that Jane had stolen it, you must surely have reached the same conclusion. There is no other possibility."

Lady Hilary hesitated a moment, and glanced at her husband as if for support, but the expression on his face was one of complete mystification, and it was evident she could receive no assistance from that quarter.

"I repeat," Holmes persisted, "if Jane did not remove the brooch from your jewellery-case, then someone else did, and I believe you know who that someone is, which is why you were so keen to hush the matter up, and had no intention of pressing charges against Jane."

"Oh, all right," said Lady Hilary abruptly in a sharp tone, rising to her feet. "I took the brooch myself. I was looking for a way of dismissing her. I felt my husband was becoming too fond of her, and that she was almost eclipsing his own children in his eyes."

"What nonsense!" cried her husband.

"But when I realized she had sent the brooch to you," Lady Hilary continued, ignoring the interruption, "I decided it had all got out of hand. I just wanted to get the brooch back, brush the whole business under the carpet, and forget about it."

"So, let us be clear about it," said Holmes. "You yourself took the brooch from your jewellery-case, and you yourself placed it under the pillow on Jane's bed?"

"Yes, I did. So now you know everything."

"Unfortunately, I do not."

“What do you mean?”

“Madam, you are not speaking the truth.”

“How dare you call me a liar in my own house!”

“The house is irrelevant. I know you are not speaking the truth, madam, because you say it was you that placed the brooch under Jane’s pillow, and I know you did not do so. I know you did not do so because no-one did so: Jane did not find the brooch under her pillow, but in the box at the foot of her bed.”

“It is no good, Mother,” said Olivia Datchett, speaking for the first time since we had entered the room. “He has tricked you.” She rose to her feet. “Mother is trying to protect me,” she said, addressing Holmes, her voice breaking with emotion. “It was I that took the brooch, and I that placed it in Jane’s box.”

“Olivia!” cried her father. “Surely you would not stoop to such a low, mean trick!”

At this, the girl burst into tears. “It’s true,” she said, between sobs. “It was mean of me, and stupid, and I am very, very sorry.”

I took a handkerchief from my pocket and passed it to her, as no-one else seemed to be doing so, and she dabbed her eyes.

“Can this really be true, Hilary?” asked Datchett.

“Yes,” replied his wife. “Olivia came to me and asked if I had seen the jet brooch recently, as she said she had been trying to find it and couldn’t see it anywhere. But there had been an odd expression on her face as she spoke to me, and all the time I was looking for the brooch, I suspected that she herself had had something to do with its disappearance. Eventually, in the evening, I confronted her with my suspicions and she admitted the truth. I then remembered the package I had seen on the hall table, and told her I was fairly certain I knew where the brooch had gone. I said I would try to get it back the next morning, so we could put the matter behind us and forget it had ever happened. Unfortunately, things did not work out so simply as that.”

The room fell silent for a moment then, until, with a bewildered shake of the head, Datchett addressed his daughter. “Whatever can have possessed you, Olivia, to do such a thing? What has Jane ever done to cause you displeasure?”

“Mother told me in a letter that you have arranged for a special tutor to come in to coach Jane in English and arithmetic.”

“And you were jealous of the attention? It is only one afternoon a week, Olivia – I am not sending her to the Cheltenham Ladies’ College! She is an intelligent girl, and works very hard. I thought it was the least I could do. She has great potential, and could make someone a good housekeeper one day – or a good wife.”

“Then, in Mother’s last letter, she said that Jane had been singing so beautifully that it had made you cry.”

“Oh, that!” Lady Hilary interrupted. “I only put that in the letter to amuse you, Olivia. You know what Father is like: he cries when he hears sad songs, he cries when he sees a sad play, and sometimes he even cries when he sees a happy play! It is just his way, and I am sure we would not want him any different!”

“He never cries when I sing,” said Olivia through her sobs.

“Ah! I see!” said her father in a tone of enlightenment. “Now I think I understand! Sit down, sit down, both of you – and you, too, gentlemen – and I will tell you something you do not know. Perhaps then you, too, will understand matters a little better.” He closed his eyes for a few moments, as if gathering his thoughts, before continuing.

“When Jane was just a tiny baby,” he began at length, “she was left at the foundling hospital. Neither she, nor anyone else, has any idea who her mother and father were. She was simply left one morning on the doorstep in a little wicker basket. A few months later, she was adopted by an elderly couple called Page from the East End, who gave her the name of Jane. The man worked as a cobbler, and apparently did all right for himself, but just a few years later, both Mr. and Mrs. Page fell ill and died within a few months of each other. Thus, the only family little Jane had ever known had been taken from her. She was only five years old at the time. Mrs. Page's sister took her in for a little while, but she herself was elderly and could not cope with the child, and less than a year later she gave her up and she was placed in an orphanage. After a time, she was moved from that orphanage to another, and, later, to a third. In all, she remained in such institutions for nearly ten years.

"Two years ago, when we needed a new chamber-maid, Jane was recommended to me. I agreed to take her almost as soon as we had met, for I could see at once that she showed great promise, and I have not been disappointed. Despite her unfortunate and unhappy childhood – which might have embittered or spoiled the character of some people – she has fitted in to our household very well, and gets along well with everyone.

"Now I come to what occurred two weeks ago. I was in my bedroom early one evening, changing for dinner. My bedroom, as you know, overlooks the back garden, and through the window I could see that it was a dark, cold evening. All at once, as I stood before the mirror, buttoning my shirt, I heard someone singing in the garden below. I looked out, and there, illuminated by a light from the kitchen window, was Jane. She was putting some rubbish in the dustbin – not the most pleasant of jobs at the best of times – and singing softly and sweetly to herself. And do you know what she was singing, this girl who has never had any family, nor anywhere she could ever call her home? She was singing *Home, Sweet Home* – 'Mid pleasures and palaces though we may roam; be it ever so humble, there's no place like home.'

"As I stood there listening, I knew that the home she referred to was our house, that we had, without particularly intending it, given Jane the first real home she had ever had in her life. At that realization, as much as at her voice, I admit I began to weep, but I am not ashamed of it. Your mother came into the room then, and asked me why I was crying. I told her I had been listening to Jane singing, but it was getting late, we had visitors coming, and there wasn't time for me to explain all the circumstances to her. There," said Datchett in conclusion. "That is the story of how Jane's singing brought me to tears, and I hope, Olivia, that you will understand the matter a little better now."

The room had fallen silent, save for the girl's quiet sobbing, and remained so for several minutes. Then Sherlock Holmes rose to his feet and took from his pocket the jet brooch, which he handed to Lady Hilary.

"That, I believe, concludes the matter, from my perspective at least," said he.

"Thank you for unravelling it all for us," said Sir George Datchett as he stood up and shook my companion by the hand.

We had turned to leave when there came a sharp pull at the front-door bell, and I heard the sound of singing from outside the house. A moment later, the butler entered the room to announce that the carol-singers from St Mary's had called, collecting for the parish charity.

"Oh!" cried Olivia. "I forgot it was tonight. I wanted to go with them! May I go? Please, Father? I can get a bite to eat later."

"Of course you may," said Datchett. "But you must wrap up warm, Olivia. It is a very cold night."

"And may I take Jane with me?" she asked. "I know from something she said to me this morning that she would dearly love to go carol-singing."

"Certainly, certainly," said Datchett, "but see that she, too, wraps up well. Now I must speak to the carol-singers."

With a cry of delight, the girl ran from the room, and I heard her footsteps clattering down the stair to the basement. We followed her father to the front door and stood for several minutes, listening to the carol-singers. Behind them in the cold night air the snow was now falling heavily. As they finished their carol, Datchett spoke to their leader, but I was distracted by the arrival behind me in the hall of two girls in overcoats, hats and mufflers. I turned to see them, but they slipped quickly past us and ran down the steps to join the carol-singers outside.

Presently, as the carol-singers made their way out of the gate and along the street, Sir George Datchett turned to us and thanked my friend again for his help. "Please send me your account for the trouble you have been put to," he said.

Holmes shook his head with a smile. "That won't be necessary," said he. "Sometimes the elucidation of the truth is itself more than adequate recompense."

As we made our way down the street, we came to where the carol-singers had stopped before another house, and paused a moment to listen. A girl at the back of the group glanced our way and I had an impression of a pair of bright, piercing eyes in a happy face, framed in tight dark curls. Holmes made a little gesture and she left the group and ran over to where we stood.

"I am confident everything will be all right now, Jane," said he, leaning over to speak closer to her.

"Yes," she returned in a breathless voice. "Miss Olivia has explained it all to me. It's all right now."

"But," he continued, "if at any time you find yourself in difficulty once more, do not hesitate to write to me again."

She nodded her head, then, raising herself on her tip-toes, she gave my companion a little peck on the cheek. "You look better without your beard," said she in a gay tone, and ran back to re-join the carol singers.

"I feel I should point out to you, Watson," said Holmes in a tone of embarrassment, as we resumed our progress down the street, "that that is not a regular occurrence at the conclusion of my cases."

I laughed. It amused me greatly to see my logical friend, usually so cold and unemotional, discomfited by a young girl, and I confess that I teased him about it for some time afterwards. Trivial incident though it may have been, I thought it worthy of mention here as being the only occasion in all of my records when my famous friend received payment from his client in the form of a kiss.

The Deadly Soldier

By Spencer Perkins

This story first appeared in the MX Book of Sherlock Holmes Stories Volume I.

Spencer Perkins first discovered his passion for the world of Sherlock Holmes while watching the BBC's miniseries adaptation nearly a decade ago. Since then, he has enjoyed delving into the original source material and writing his own works set in Arthur Conan Doyle's universe. In addition to writing historical fiction, he has recently gone back to school for a second degree—this time in web development. Upon graduation, he hopes to split his time between writing fiction and coding websites. He currently resides in Portland, Oregon. If you'd like to know more about Spencer's upcoming publications and his thoughts on the writing process, you can visit his blog at;
https://spencerperkinswrites.wordpress.com

Bobby Franano has been featured in international exhibitions and is in numerous private collections. In recent years, Bobby has become known for painting large, colorful canvases in a style he calls "Pop Surrealism." , was born in Kansas City,Mo. He displayed talent in the visual arts, as well as, music even in his early years. As a musician, Bobby has recorded on many albums. He also has been in 3 videos on MTV with "The Front" & "Bakers Pink" and designed 2 album covers.
Bobby has also made many contributions through his art to various charities, even designing the logo for one international organisation.

Bobby Franano on Facebook.

Artwork size: 25 x 25

Medium: Free hand oil on birch

Someone was trying to kill him. Of that, Professor James Moriarty was certain. For three nights now he'd seen the shadow of a man standing outside his Conduit Street residence. The man stood just out of the way of the gas lamps that lined the street, so only the long silhouette of him was discernable in the light.

When a carriage passed by, it disrupted the play of light on the cobblestones, throwing the shadow into long contrast against the walkway to Moriarty's home, as if the shadow itself was an insidious beast, lengthening and reaching out to take Moriarty within its grasp.

However, Moriarty was a scientist and believed in nothing of the terror to be found in beasts and shadows. He was rational above all else, and though his pursuer had been careful to keep his face well hidden, his unmoving, attentive posture was that of an army man.

Moriarty had no personal quarrels with Her Majesty's Army, nor had he recently done business with anyone who had a bone to pick with a man from the service, which made him conclude that this man had been hired by someone else altogether.

While in the practice of thinking, and especially when puzzling over some incredibly intricate piece of mathematics or trying to decide in just such a way how he would deliver a certain client's request, he had taken to pacing long, sure strides along the floor of his library. The movement of his legs helped energise his brain, and occasionally his fingers would twitch about the window coverings, pulling them back to view the city's comings and goings.

It was a pity that the gas lamps gave off too much light to accurately see the stars; the view of such a thing would have settled his mind much more than watching the scurrying to-and-fro of the citizens of London as they rode by in hansom cabs or walked arm in arm as lovers – all inconsequential to him, like so many ants upon a hill.

Yet, the stars were obscured from him, so he contented himself with stalking his rooms, thinking and watching. It was during just such an evening days ago that he'd first noticed that shadow of the man standing too still and purposefully ensconced in darkness.

The sight had amused Moriarty; for if the man had been sent to watch him, he'd have a long evening ahead of himself indeed, as the professor had no plans to leave his home that evening.

By the time he'd risen the next morning, the spot on the sidewalk where the man had stood was vacant, and while not putting the situation out of his mind, he filed it away carefully to be recalled if need be, though he had far more important things to think about than mysterious men standing on sidewalks.

Yet the long shadow of the man was back the very next night, and then again the next. Moriarty had noticed him again in one of his pacing turns about his library when he'd pulled aside the curtain to imperiously view his little spot of earth.

As he stood with black silk curtains still grasped in one hand and in full view of the window, he imagined the man must be stalking him, and perhaps compiling information upon his whereabouts to present to a third party. Then Moriarty noticed the silver glint of a gun as it was aimed and *oh*, wasn't that just the thing to spice up a dreary evening?

Moriarty was a tall man, nearing fifty, though slender as a matchstick with viper-fast reflexes. The very sight of the gun had sent off the impulse in him to duck before his conscious mind had caught up, and rightly so – his pursuer fired once, then twice, straight through the window.

The glass gave way with a powerful crack and shatter, raining down upon him in slivers like razor-sharp snowflakes. Moriarty, flat on his stomach, face pressed into the dull pattern of the Persian rug that carpeted his library, pulled himself away from the window, not risking raising his head to look out. He scuttled further into the room to reach his own weapon.

Despite being a man of books and cunning, it would be folly of him to not carry a piece for these such very reasons. In the decade since he'd got into his particular brand of criminal acts, he'd made a laundry list of enemies, and attempts on his life had run the gamut from poisoned tea to an attempted kidnapping. Though the latter had been botched from the start and ended rather abruptly when, having been tied to a chair and threatened with the red hot tip of a fire poker, he calmly inquired to the man holding if it he was going to attempt to burn the soul from him. He'd wondered aloud if such a thing were possible if he were lacking a soul to begin with.

Whether it was his perfectly calm demeanor at the question, as if they were discussing something of no more importance than the weather over tea, or the fact that the pupils of Moriarty's eyes were coal black and betrayed no fear, he found the poker being dropped and his kidnapper backing away, muttering something about "This ain't worth it – the crazy bastard," under his breath. At the time, he'd laughed.

He laughed again, crawling across his floor three hours after sunset with broken glass crunching under his knees and the elbows of his jacket. The laugh was a low, unholy rumble, mad and lacking in any real mirth. It was a laugh that cautioned *you'll be sorry.* He got to his knees when he reached his piano, deft fingers feeling across the wooden seat, finding the catch underneath. Once opened, he lifted up the false bottom to unearth an opening the length of the seat in which he kept a loaded rifle.

Outside he heard voices. There had been shrieks at the shot and the tramping of feet – probably someone running to call a constable. He lived in too respectable a neighbourhood not to warrant the concern of the police when something as alarming as gunshots occurred.

How disappointing. I'd have liked to deal with him himself, Moriarty mused from his crouched position; his long spindly fingers still wrapped around the handle of the gun aimed directly at his window. He only stood once he'd heard an authoritative voice call, "Is there anyone inside?" with the accompanying light from a shining torch.

He rose in a fluid, near-serpentine movement, lowering his gun slightly – though not all the way in case the soldier was only pretending to be police – and took stock of his own countenance. His jacket and trousers were rumpled from his abrupt movements and a fine layer of white dust coated the dark garments. This he immediately tried to brush from his clothing, disliking the way it marred the fabric.

His features, too, he schooled into the look of bewildered apprehension he assumed the situation called for, his brow furrowing, eyes widening slightly. His lips, already a rather thin slash in his face, going even thinner with faux fear. By the time the constable peered in at him through the window, Moriarty was playing his part quite well.

"Alright in there, sir?" the constable inquired, reaching in through the broken glass of the window with his torch to widen the gap in the curtains. As his ruddy looking face came further into view, Moriarty lowered his gun completely and abandoned it on the closed piano bench, giving a nod.

"Quite alright now," he assured the policeman. "Though those gunshots were indeed a shock. Would you like to come in?"

The officer nodded his agreement and Moriarty crossed the room to let him in the front door. He showed the man into the library where the assault had taken place.

After a cursory glance around the room, both men's eyes followed the trajectory of the bullets, both of which were lodged into the spines of books upon Moriarty's shelf opposite the window. One had even pierced the spine of his own work, *Dynamics of an Asteroid*, and *oh*, whoever this shooter was would pay dearly for that.

"Do you have any idea who might want you dead?" the constable inquired, head tilted up to look into Moriarty's eyes.

Moriarty pretended to pause momentarily, as if to consider the question before replying in the negative. "I'm afraid not. I don't have any enemies as far as I'm aware. I suppose this means you weren't able to apprehend the suspect?"

The constable shook his head. "The ruffian must've fled the scene before I arrived."

"Pity, that."

Again, the constable glanced around, taking in the opulence of the room. Though Moriarty's upper-class residence wasn't out of place in Westminster, he did own rather a large collection of both ancient and new texts, not to mention a nice looking piano and a telescope in the corner of the room.

"Could be a thwarted robbery," the constable mused. "That wouldn't be uncommon in a neighbourhood like this. Thieves prey upon the wealthy."

Moriarty suppressed an eye roll. A thief, this assailant was not, nor could he imagine there being much call for astronomy books and scientific apparatuses to fence on the black market.

His gaze once again drew to the bullet holes. Judging by their relative height, the first shot would've struck him square in the chest had he not ducked, and the second was likely the assailant's second attempt to get him before he hit the floor. The fact that the man had got off two quick shots in succession like that spoke of his experience, which further bolstered Moriarty's suspicion that the man responsible had a military background.

The constable pulled him out of his musings by speaking once more. "I could have some of my boys do a patrol of your street if you'd like, to make sure he doesn't come back."

"No, no," Moriarty waved the suggestion away. "I'm sure I'll be perfectly alright here." He did have use for a police officer, but he'd already had one in his employ who understood the sort of business he conducted. "If I have further need for the police, I'll speak with Inspector Turner at the CID."

The constable's brows rose nearly to his hairline at the mention of the name. "Oh sure, of course, sir. I didn't know you were friends with the higher ups."

Moriarty just gave him a tight nod, growing bored and impatient with the constable's dull, bumbling presence, and crossed the room, opening his front door swiftly for him in an effective dismissal.

That night Moriarty was unable to sleep. The boarded up window marred the perfection of his library, looking crude and out of place, like a scar marring otherwise perfect skin. He shut the curtains to block it from view, but even having retired to his bedroom, he still could not rest for knowing it was there, so back down to the library he went, resuming his pacing. Upon every turn of his heel he glared at the window, eyes narrowed and full of simmering fury that doubled with each passing hour.

At the first light of dawn, he decided he could wait no longer to leave the house. He'd go to Clapham and see Andrew Turner right away.

Turner had been a former client of his. At the time, the up and coming constable had been aiming for the job of detective and it had come down to he and another man in the end. The other man, a Mr. Charles Woodlite, had at least a decade in age on Turner, and had been working as a constable a handful of years longer. That was where Moriarty had come in. At Turner's behest, Moriarty had arranged for Woodlite to be struck by a runaway carriage, killing him and leaving Turner as the only available candidate for the job.

Moriarty had been pleased to take on work for a member of the police and had waved away payment, telling him instead that if the time arose when Moriarty needed his particular services, he would call upon him. That had been a good eight months back, and they'd thus far parted ways without any contact, though with the attempt on his life, Moriarty now saw need for him.

When he came to the row house in which Turner lived, he gave three solemn raps on the door, and then waited a few moments before repeating the action when he heard no movement from within.

He imagined Turner and his family were still asleep upstairs, though that was no concern of his. He needed a job done and he expected his wishes to be attended to posthaste.

Finally, the door opened, revealing a sleep-rumpled Turner, his short blond hair tousled and sticking up on end. He was still in pyjamas and a plain navy blue cotton dressing gown, the sash of which he was still tying as he opened the door.

Upon seeing Moriarty, his posture immediately changed, eyes widening first in recognition, then apprehension, back straightening as though he were a marionette whose strings had suddenly been jerked. "Professor . . . ." he trailed off, seemingly at a loss, before swallowing thickly. When he spoke again, his voice was hushed. "It's early, what can I do for you?"

Moriarty made no mention of the time, though he was pleased to see the immediate deference and subtle hint of fear Turner gave off at the sight of him. "You can invite me in, for a start."

Immediately, Turner stepped back, allowing Moriarty into his home. "Can I get you anything?" he asked. "Tea?" He hesitated and added, "My wife and child are still asleep upstairs," by way of explanation for his lowered voice.

Moriarty took no care to lower his own tone, speaking instead in the same cold commanding note as ever. "No tea. This isn't a social call. We have business to discuss."

"Right." Turner nodded, his Adam's Apple bobbing again as he swallowed apprehensively, taking Moriarty's coat and hat before leading him into a sparsely decorated parlour. He immediately set about starting a fire in the fireplace while he beckoned Moriarty to take a seat on the sofa. "What can I do for you?"

Moriarty perched on the edge of the sofa, noticing the stitching worn threadbare in places. His lip curled up in a sneer of distaste, the lack of sleep he'd suffered only serving to make him all the more impatient and demanding. He explained the events of the previous evening in few words before arriving at the point of his visit. "I believe my assailant will try again. I'll need you to tail me over the next few days and keep an eye out for anyone else who might be doing the same."

He spoke the words to Turner's back, watching him stoke the fire with a poker before the man finally stood, turning to face Moriarty again. "Have you filed a report on it? I could try my best to get assigned to your case."

Moriarty's head swiveled on his neck, turning from one side to the other slowly, as if to stretch his muscles, though his eyes never left Turner's. It gave the appearance of a snake sizing up a rodent it was about to devour. "I'm not interested in filing a report," he answered at length, his tone clipped. "When my pursuer is apprehended, I'll not be handing him over to the police. I'd far prefer to *deal* with him myself."

The threat within those words were unmistakable, and Turner, of anyone, should know just what sort of things Moriarty did when he'd decided to deal with someone on his own terms. Turner nodded again, though he still looked unsure, his hands toying once more with the sash of his dressing gown. "Westminster isn't in my division. I'm not allowed to patrol whichever part of London I choose. Perhaps there is something else I could – "

Moriarty had heard enough and cut him off before he was able to get another word out. "The man pursuing me is clearly dangerous. Is it not your job to make London a safer place for all citizens?" he inquired. "With a wife and child, I'd imagine you'd want our streets to be free of murderers."

Turner swallowed again. "I – "

"It's just that it would be a shame," Moriarty continued smoothly, as if the Inspector hadn't spoken, "if something were to happen to your child. An infant girl, am I correct? Rebecca." He hummed the name out, a slow smile spreading his severe, bloodless lips even thinner.

Colour bloomed high on Turner's cheeks; anger and fear making him gawp at Moriarty wordlessly for a moment, before he reached up to run a shaking hand through his unkempt hair. "I – I can start as soon as you need me to."

"Glad to hear you've come around to the idea. Get dressed, Inspector. You have a long day ahead of you."

Moriarty's pursuer was more intelligent than he'd originally given him credit, because after employing Turner to tail him, he saw neither hide nor hair of anyone following him or acting suspiciously.

He would have assumed the soldier had given it up as a bad job now that Moriarty had an Inspector watching out for him, if not for the fact that the last three men he'd had appointments with had turned up murdered.

The first, a Mr. Jonathon March, a banker who had a case of sticky fingers and decided he'd wanted to start pocketing some of the money from his bank's safe, had been found dead in his home. Nothing from his residence had been stolen, but a single bullet had pierced his chest, straight through his heart.

After March had neglected to show up for his appointment, Moriarty decided to pay him a visit, because people did *not* back out on their appointments with him without consequence. When he arrived, he saw a swarm of policemen at March's residence and turned back, not wanting to get himself involved in a police matter in which he didn't control all the players. In the evening paper, he read of the murder, and though such a thing could be discounted as a coincidence, after having just survived an attempt on his own life, it didn't seem likely.

His assailant was clearly still on his tail and watching him close enough to know with whom Moriarty did business. Yet, why kill one of his clients? Beyond the minor inconvenience of it, Moriarty cared little for their lives, and the loss of money from March's business was minimal.

He shrugged it off as a desperate attempt on the soldier's behalf to rile him, and continued on as usual, instructing Turner to keep following him in case the soldier decided to show himself again.

Then, his next client was murdered three days later, and another two days after that. The papers started calling it the work of a deranged killer, though they were unable to find any connection between the murders. Each man was killed with a single shot through the heart, without any other assault or robbery of his person and an absolute lack of evidence as to who had done it.

It was starting to become . . . inconvenient. One murdered client didn't bother Moriarty overmuch, but if the murders continued, it would be only a matter of time until a connection between the men led back to him, and word would get around that anyone who hired him wound up dead.

Not to mention that the police, even as incompetent as most of them were, would eventually find the connection, and while he had Turner in his pocket and didn't doubt his ability to find weaknesses in the others to bend them to his will, it would take an amount of effort in which he did not wish to partake.

As ambitious as he was in things that interested him, he didn't appreciate feeling as though someone else was forcing his hand, and as Turner was proving worse than useless as a tail, Moriarty decided to approach this from a different angle. It was about time he did something to draw the solider out.

First thing the next morning, he invited Turner in and gave him a rundown of their new goal, before walking him to his door to dismiss him. He waited until the Inspector was on his doorstep in plain view of the street before arranging his features into his a scowl; brows knitted together, dark eyes narrowed in cool dissatisfaction, mouth curled into a sneer, as he informed the Inspector in a clipped tone, "Since you've been unable to find the man who attacked me, I have no choice but to relieve you from your duty."

Turner gave a nervous jerk of his head, Adam's Apple once again bobbing as he swallowed reflexively in fear. The sheer terror on the man's face amused Moriarty. Though this playacting was part of his plan, the Inspector looked genuinely terrified at Moriarty's cold fury.

When Turner spoke, his voice was hesitant and wheedling. "I'm sorry, Mr. Moriarty. I've been following you day and night as requested. I just haven't seen anyone that I'd consider suspicious, I – "

"I'm not interested in your excuses," Moriarty interrupted. "I made myself quite clear when I told you what I expected."

Turner's pallour faded almost to Moriarty's own near paper white tones. "Yes, but – "

"No." Moriarty gave a jerk of his head, cutting off any more excuses before they could issue from the Turner's lips. "I believe I told you what the price would be for your failure."

Turner's eyes widened. "Please, sir, don't hurt my family . . . ."

Moriarty watched the man dispassionately, tilting his head to one side and then the other slowly, stretching his neck out. "Then catch my assailant, Inspector." He reached into his pocket, withdrawing a small leather-bound appointment book and handing it to the other man. "In here you'll find the addresses of my clients and the dates of our appointments. Catch this man before he can kill another one of them. You have twenty-four hours."

He watched Turner take the book and then continue standing there, gripping it so hard that his blunt nails left small indents in the leather.

"Well? Off you go," Moriarty prompted, jerking Turner into action again.

He gave a start and then nodded, pocketing the book. "I won't let you down again," he promised, fitting his hat on and all but fleeing from the house.

"See that you don't." Moriarty smirked, watching him hurry off, before stepping back and shutting the door after him with a decisive click. Everything was going to plan so far. He'd just hoped the soldier had been lurking out of sight to witness that performance.

Most people's motives, Moriarty found, were easy to suss out – greed, malice, simple stupidity – they all drove men to act in ways that were tiresomely predictable, and this soldier of his was no different, he assumed. Greedy, yes, as he'd likely been hired to do this job and was therefore motivated by money. Malicious? Perhaps. The pattern of the bullets made for a quick death, and the use of a rifle meant he preferred to work from a distance, though Moriarty assumed that to be from his military training more than from any preference to not get his hands dirty.

As for stupidity? There'd been a surprising lack of it, thus far. The man had been careful not to get himself caught by police, nor noticed by Turner, and he'd been patient enough not to fire off another shot at Moriarty too soon after his failed first time.

Truth be told, he was the sort of man who Moriarty wouldn't mind having in his employ himself. Though Moriarty relished in his own intimidation tactics, usually needing little more than a few discrete, well- placed threats and a narrowing of his eyes, even he could admit that sometimes more drastic measures had to be taken. Having a trained muscle that was proficient with a gun had its advantages.

It really would be a pity for his assailant to be shot as Moriarty's plan came to fruition, but sometimes these things couldn't always be planned for. He was perfectly willing to pull the trigger if he deemed the man unreasonable after having a proper chat, but first he had to lure him in. Getting rid of Turner had only been the first step. Now to put the rest of the plan in motion

The soldier hadn't shot a single person in public thus far, preferring to take them down in their homes. As his first long range attempt had failed, Moriarty could only assume this time it would be something a little more close and personal.

So, to give the man time, Moriarty left his home quickly as if he had business with which to attend, immediately setting off for Regent Street. In his purported haste he neglected to turn the lock on his front door. If this soldier were to break into his home to await his return, he'd much rather there be as little destruction upon his property as possible. He didn't fancy another boarded up window.

Once on Regent Street, he allowed himself to get lost in the flow of pedestrians clamouring in and out of shops. His upper lip curled in distaste at the mass of swirling humanity around him; the cacophony of voices, the clomping of horses' hooves as carriages passed by, and a squeaking out-of-tune piano-organ ground by a boy looking for change. The boy gained nothing but a withering look from Moriarty as the professor passed by him.

A glance to his pocket watch told him it was barely nine in the morning; if this soldier were any sort of criminal at all, he'd surely wait until nightfall to make his move. He had hours upon hours to waste before then.

While it had been his plan to lose himself in the press of bodies along Regent Street, making it impossible to murder him without someone seeing, he quickly found being among that many people intolerable.

Surely, risking a bullet to the chest would be preferable to being amongst that much constant braying humanity, and after barely an hour he'd returned to Conduit Street once more, heading for Saunders, Otley & Co., a circulating library not too far from his home.

In addition to frivolous dramas and works of poetry, the library also had a large collection of practical and scientific texts. The professor whiled away the rest of the morning and much of the afternoon reading up on the management and keeping of bees, while pondering just how many stings it would take to overload a man's body, forcing it to shut down. It would be a waste for the bee to die as well, however inefficient insects that they were. He made a mental note to research the keeping of wasps instead.

When it was approaching dusk, he ate at a local pub before checking his pocket watch once again and meeting Turner outside. At precisely their agreed meeting time, Turner made his way through the crowd, a subdued expression making his cornflower blue eyes appear dull.

"Hello, Mr. Moriarty," he inclined his head in greeting. Despite his many shortcomings, at least he was punctual. That was a trait Moriarty valued highly. Men who kept him waiting tended not to live long.

"Mr. Turner," Moriarty answered, voice cool. "I take it you've brought the cuffs I requested?"

Turner nodded, reaching into the pocket of his overcoat to pull out a set of silver handcuffs. He produced a small revolver as well, which he dutifully handed over to Moriarty.

After a cursory glance, Moriarty slipped both items into the pocket of his own coat and then shrugged the garment off, handing it over to Turner along with his top hat. Turner followed suit and soon Moriarty pulled on the other man's coat, looking down in brief distaste at the poor quality of the fabric compared to that which he was used to. He nodded for Turner to lead the way while he kept back at a discrete distance.

The plan was simple enough; Moriarty was banking on his assailant waiting for him in his home, and though Turner lacked Moriarty's tall, slim stature, in the poor light, Moriarty assumed the soldier would mistake Turner for him. Once the solider made a move, Turner would disarm and cuff him. He had explicit instructions not to fire upon the soldier unless absolutely necessary, but it would be foolhardy to not at least have brought a gun in preparation.

Moriarty watched Turner's back as they walked in silence toward his home; the professor taking care to keep well back and into the shadows. Turner walked up to his front door, opening it as if he were the owner of the place and stepped inside.

Moments later, Moriarty saw the light in his library shine through the curtains; Turner obviously had lit the gas lamp once he was inside. All was silent and he resolved to give the Inspector a few minutes before approaching the house himself to see how he was getting on. As soon as the thought had entered his mind, the unmistakable crack of a gunshot pierced the air.

Moriarty's head snapped up in attention. He hurried toward the house, hoping that Turner had been wise enough to follow his instructions. Had he killed the soldier before Moriarty himself could get his hands on him, there would be consequences.

As Moriarty's hand reached for the doorknob, he saw it turn before he could grasp it and the door was pulled open from the inside. The gestured revealed a man a bit shorter than himself but nearly twice as wide, compact with solid muscle. The man's sandy blond hair was cut in a short military style and smoothed down with wax, and he had a bushy moustache the same colour; it twitched as his lips pulled up into a smile. The gesture of amusement didn't reach the man's hard green eyes.

"Professor," he addressed Moriarty, stepping back so Moriarty could enter. "You've proven difficult to hunt down."

The smell of gunpowder was pungent in the air. Behind the soldier laid Turner, a spreading red stain across the front of his vest, soaking into his white cotton shirt. He drew in a shallow breath, moaning as he exhaled.

Moriarty's eyes slid from Turner's body on the floor back to the solider and he stepped inside. The man was still holding his military issue Webley revolver, though Moriarty just tilted his chin up in defiance, unafraid.

"And you've proven a nuisance," he answered dispassionately, stepping over Turner. "How disappointed you must be that you've still not taken me down. I'll bet your employer is most displeased."

The soldier laughed, raising his gun at Moriarty. "What makes you think I won't shoot you right now and be done with it?"

Moriarty watched the silver muzzle of the revolver point directly at his chest, though if he felt any sliver of fear it didn't show on his face. He just slowly tilted his head from one side to the other, stretching his neck out in his usual serpentine movement. "You could," he agreed, "But then you'd never hear my business proposition, and you'd be the poorer for it."

He watched the soldier cock his weapon, finger sliding to the trigger, though the man then hesitated a beat and Moriarty took advantage of the hesitation, adding, "I'm not sure what your employer has told you about me, but just by this brief meeting, I can gather a few things about you. Judging by your posture and the type of weapon you carry, you are a military man. Your skin is far too tan for someone who has spent much time recently in London, which means you've been abroad. Perhaps in Kabul, the Battle of Sherpur? Yet your decision to dabble in crime is a curious one. Maybe you've been recently discharged and found yourself unsuitable for a life which doesn't include wielding a gun."

As Moriarty spoke, the cruel, self-satisfied smile slid from the soldier's face, to be replaced with a look that was first weary, then begrudgingly bordering on awe. "You've deciphered all that from just looking at me?"

Moriarty inclined his head in agreement. "I have. Yet I find one thing about your methods very curious."

Despite the look of awe on the soldier's face, his revolver didn't waver from Moriarty's chest. "And what's that?"

"If you've been hired to kill me, what purpose did the murder of my clients serve?"

The soldier's smile returned, and he let out a hearty laugh as though Moriarty had just told a particularly funny joke. "That, Professor, was just for my own amusement. You've proven more difficult to get to than I'd planned, and instead of trifling with the Inspector tailing you, it was far more entertaining to follow home the men you had meetings with and dispatch of them. I knew you'd eventually grow tired of the damage it was doing to your business and try to lure me out."

He let out another small chuckle, shaking his head, "It was quite a nice touch with the Inspector wearing your overcoat as well. Perhaps a lesser man might've fallen for the gag, but I recognised his gait the moment he walked up to your house."

As if on cue, another moan of pain issued from Turner on the floor. Without taking his eyes off Moriarty, the soldier turned his revolver on the Inspector, delivering a fatal shot.

The heartlessness of the action impressed Moriarty, as did the soldier's cleverness. Though he clearly wasn't as good at reading people as the professor himself, he was a great deal smarter than most men Moriarty employed. Moriarty could use someone skilled with a gun, since Turner was now no longer drawing breath.

"I have to commend you on your work," Moriarty told him. "You're far from the first man hired to take my life, but out of them all, you've got the closest."

"*Closest?*" The solider echoed with a raise of his brows. "My good sir, between the two of us I'm the only one with a weapon in hand and I've just ended another man's life. Whatever makes you think that I won't be successful in ending yours?"

It was a fair point and a lesser man might've conceded defeat and started to beg for his life, but Moriarty was not a lesser man. He only watched the solider intently, reaching up to remove the top hat he'd not had the chance to divest himself of earlier, what with the commotion he'd met upon entering his home. His overcoat was shed next and he took his time, drawing out the silence between them. He enjoyed the way the soldier's attention never left him as he waited for Moriarty's reply.

Whether the man realised it or not, he was already in Moriarty's thrall, and when Moriarty felt the tension in the room increase to such a level that the solider was about to speak again, Moriarty opened his mouth to reply. "I suppose you *would* be successful in your objective, if that's what you so choose, but you've just killed someone of use to me, and as such, a job opening has become available.

Whatever the solider had been expecting him to say, that clearly was far from the mark. He gaped at Moriarty, brows rising again this time nearly to his hairline. Slowly, he lowered his gun to his side. "Are you telling me you're looking to hire me?"

"I am," Moriarty confirmed.

"What makes you think I'd betray my boss to work for you?" he scoffed, though he didn't raise the gun again.

This time, Moriarty didn't even pretend to draw out the silence before answering. He already knew he'd won. The solider having lowered his gun was as good as a yes already. "It's steady work, and whatever you're currently being paid, I'll double it."

The solider stood motionless for a breath, thinking it over before slipping his gun back into its holster.

Moriarty added, "You can start by disposing of the Inspector's body. Then pay a little visit to your boss and bring him to me. Do we have a deal?"

He put out his hand to shake on it, like the start of all gentlemanly agreements. The soldier's brows knitted as he looked down at that hand, as though shaking it would be akin to making a pact with the devil.

"I'll even triple your pay, if you manage to impress me," Moriarty added, and the man's hand met his in a firm grip.

After they shook, Moriarty spoke once more. "Another thing. If you're going to work for me, I'll need to know your name."

The man nodded, reaching up to stroke his moustache before standing up straighter, heels clicking together. It was the move of someone used to standing at attention in front of a superior officer. "Of course. It's Colonel Sebastian Moran, sir. At your service."

The Case of the Petty Curses

By Steven Philip Jones

This story first appeared in the MX Book of New Sherlock Holmes Stories Volume VII.

Steven Philip Jones has written fiction novels for adults and young adults, comic books, graphic novels, radio scripts, non-fiction, and advertising pieces. Steven has also taught courses in comic book writing and enjoys mentoring other writers as well as editing. A graduate of the University of Iowa, he majored in Journalism and Religion and was accepted into Iowa's prestigious Writers' Workshop MFA Program in 1990. Steven can be contacted through his website at www.stevenphilipjones.com

Robert St. Croix is a sculptor and entrepreneur, and began his career in Northern California. While attempting to publish a book and several plays, Robert was introduced to his new neighbor, who called himself a "metal sculptor". His name was Bob Kitchen. Bob told Robert that if he wanted to earn some money, that Bob would teach him how to cut shapes of flowers and birds out of brass and bronze sheet, then braze the shapes together to make them look like wall sculptures. Bob Kitchen further explained that once they had enough wall sculptures they would take them to Embarkadero Plaza in San Francisco and sell them. And that's exactly what the two young artists did. Six months later Bob Kitchen had moved to Hawaii. While Robert St. Croix kept designing and creating new wall sculptures and soon added water fountains made from copper and driftwood to his artistic inventory. Robert around this same time opened an art gallery in Bodega Bay with his earnings from selling his sculptures and fountains. Robert St. Croix's sculptures are currently shown at his wife's gallery, Gallery Biba on Worth Avenue, in Palm Beach. Robert owns and runs the Robert St. Croix Sculpture Studio & Foundry, in West Palm Beach, which is open to all artists and to the public.

http://robertstcroix.com/.

Artwork size: 7.6 x 6.7

Medium: Digital collage

Few of Sherlock Holmes's cases have started so bizarrely, or ended so tragically, as the affair of the Angus-Burtons of Notting Hill, which began for me with a letter from my friend that arrived at my Paddington practice with the four-o'clock post on a blistering afternoon in August of 1889.

It read: *"Watson, if you happen to be free this evening, could you come round to Baker Street at seven? A young woman has presented me with a problem ripe with those unusual and outré features so dear to us both. Also, since the fair sex is your department, your opinions of this new client might prove beneficial to my investigation. Holmes."*

My wife, Mary, was in Whitby for a few days as a favor to my predecessor, old Mr. Farquhar. It turned out to be an excellent opportunity for her to escape the extreme summer heat, but I had no choice but to remain behind to attend to my new medical practice. I was feeling quite forsaken, and therefore was delighted by Holmes's request.

A storm was beginning to brew when I arrived at Baker Street. The wind had picked up, the air was thick and humid, and the sky was beginning to churn with purple clouds piled high over gray clouds. Holmes was standing at the curb waiting for me, careful to keep a tight hold of his hat, and gratefully climbed in my cab while giving the driver our destination, 17 Kensington Place. After settling in, he commented, "I see that your wife is away, Waston, and left you to fend for yourself."

"And how exactly do you deduce that?"

"A few little things told me," he chuckled, "but primarily your tie. It is not perfectly straight, as when Mrs. Watson brings it into regulation for you. Though circumstances have prevented us from seeing more than little of each other since your recent marriage, I am nevertheless confident that your tie has not looked quite this off-balanced since you resided at Baker Street."

"I see. Well, I won't bother asking about the other little things. You're right, as usual." I imagine it was the heat that put me in as petulant a mood to add, "Of course, your deductions always seem simple after you explain them."

A nettled expression came over Holmes. "Yes, the obvious always seems simple when it is explained."

Realizing I had been rude, I apologized and asked him to tell me about the facts of this new case.

Holmes unexpectedly looked less than sure of himself. "I shall, but first, Watson, may I ask you a theoretical question?"

"Of course."

"What would you do if your wife insisted that you had placed a curse upon her?"

For several moments I was speechless, the question being so nonsensical. All I could muster was to mumble, "Pardon me?"

"What would you do if the person you vowed to love, honor, and cherish so long as you live convinced herself that you have cursed her?"

"I suppose I would seek professional help. An alienist. It's ridiculous, though."

"In the abstract I would agree, but this is not a theoretical problem for the young lady that I wrote to you about, Mrs. Halima Angus-Burton. She is seeking professional help, but, rather than an alienist, she has sought my aid."

I was no nearer a resolution as to what to say than before, and could only think to resort to logic. "Holmes, if you're serious, then a situation like this definitely requires skills outside your talents."

"That may turn out to be so," he conceded with professional humility, "but consider that her husband, Malcolm Angus-Burton, is the sole heir of a respected family, holds a high position with the Foreign Office, and is one of the Queen's most trusted advisers in matters regarding China. Under the circumstances, wouldn't you eliminate all alternative explanations before you irrevocably stained the character of the person you most loved?"

"Under those circumstances – yes – but how could anyone even entertain such a thing? It's irrational!"

"I'm afraid the explanation I've been given will not sound any more rational." Holmes looked at the gathering clouds as if to collect his thoughts. As incredible as the situation sounded, or perhaps because of it, I listened to my friend with more than normal interest when he continued. "To begin with, Mr. and Mrs. Angus-Burton share the distinction of being raised in foreign lands. He was born in China to British parents, but Mrs. Angus-Burton is a pureblooded Egyptian who was adopted by a British father who married her widowed mother."

"'Halima'. I thought the name sounded foreign, but I couldn't recollect its origin."

"It means 'gentle', and if I am any judge of character, Mrs. Angus-Burton is precisely that. She is also loyal, levelheaded, and I would be remiss not to mention that she is a bonnie thing."

"Appreciating a woman's beauty? That isn't like you."

"On the contrary, Watson. My living is made by observing, and all I've done is state an obvious assessment. Tell me if you disagree when you meet the lady."

"Fair enough. I suspect this observation plays a part in whatever theories you may have buzzing in your head about this case."

As I should have expected, Holmes was appalled at my suggestion. "You know my methods. I never hypothesize before I have all the facts."

"Yes. I stand corrected."

"Angus-Burton's father was a representative of the British East India Trading Company in Canton, where his family lived until Angus-Burton entered university in 1878. Angus-Burton's father retired to London at that same time, but both he and Angus-Burton's mother have passed away within the last three years." Holmes paused to consider his thoughts again. "Make careful note of this, Watson. The reason shall be made clear when we meet Mrs. Angus-Burton. Ten years before Angus-Burton was born, his parents took charge of a Chinese boy named Tseng. Apparently Tseng's family was massacred by Muslim Chinese in Chinese Turkestan, and the boy wandered east where he managed to survive in the port cities of Kowloon, Hong Kong, and Macao until his plight came to the Angus-Burtons' attention. They raised Tseng, who has been the head of the family's household staff since he turned twenty-one."

"So noted, Holmes. Now what about Mrs. Angus-Burton?"

"Her adopted father worked in banking, and was part of the Goschen-Joubert Mission that established the *Caisse de la Dette Publique* in Egypt in 1875. This is when he met his wife, whose family reputedly once practiced black magic, beginning with their service to the Eleventh Dynasty of Egyptian Kings against the Theban priesthood."

I shook my head. "That sounds like something concocted by Haggard for one of his wild adventures."

"Nevertheless, the rumor is an element in this case, as is this: Our client met Angus-Burton while he was touring Cairo during the summer holiday prior to his final year at Cambridge, and when their plans to be wed were announced, only Mrs. Angus-Burton's father approved."

"On what grounds did the other three parents object?"

"Angus-Burton's parents wanted to see their only child marry a lady of pure British stock, while Mrs. Angus-Burton's mother was adamant that her daughter remain in Egypt, rather than move away to England. Eventually Angus-Burton's parents accepted their daughter-in-law, but the relationship between Mrs. Angus-Burton and her mother remained strained. Then, last June, Mrs. Angus-Burton's parents were killed in a railway accident near El Mahalla el Kubra. Any possibility of reconciliation between mother and daughter died with them, in this world at least. Mr. Angus-Burton insists this accident motivated his wife to curse him."

Abruptly something about Holmes's tale followed some train of logic. "I presume he believes her capable of such a feat because of her alleged hereditary strain of black magic?"

"Once more, I caution against the practice of presuming, Watson, but you are correct in this instance. I warned you that this would not sound rational."

"Does it really matter, so long as Angus-Burton sincerely believes it is true?"

Holmes started to concur when the cab came to a halt. We had stopped on the Notting Hill end of Kensington Place. Holmes instructed to driver to wait, then asked me for the time. Looking at my watch, I informed him, "Seven-twenty-eight. What is this place?"

"The home of Mr. and Mrs. Angus-Burton."

During our journey, the wind had grown stronger as the storm clouds grew thicker and the evening darker, but I could still make out that the Angus-Burton home was grand in scale and architecture, common attributes of the houses in this district. As we approached the front door, Holmes said, "Mrs. Angus-Burton informed me that her husband routinely leaves for his Pall Mall club at seven-fifteen each Monday evening. She assured me that he intended to keep to his routine tonight, giving us the opportunity to inspect the home without alarming him. I am particularly anxious to examine his study."

"Why the study?"

"Because Angus-Burton believes his wife has incorporated the study into her curse. Attend to the knocker, would you, Watson?"

When the door opened, we were invited within and Holmes introduced me to his client. Mrs. Angus-Burton warmly greeted me. However, I had been struck speechless upon my first good look at the woman. Not before nor since have I beheld so handsome a creature. Her sunset complexion, regal cheekbones, and large russet eyes were at the very least enthralling. If Medusa's loveliness in any way was comparable to Mrs. Angus-Burton's beauty, I can understand why the insecure Athena cursed that vain mortal woman. At Holmes's gentle prodding, I regained my composure. "I beg your pardon. My mind went elsewhere for a moment. I'm afraid I think too much at times."

"Yes, I'm forever admonishing Watson about thinking too much." Holmes then asked the mistress if she had given her staff the evening off.

"I did just as you instructed."

"Excellent. May I look about the house while you and the Doctor become acquainted?"

Mrs. Angus-Burton had barely given her leave before Holmes dashed away, asking over his shoulder, "Has there been any word from your butler, Tseng?"

"No. The police have still found no trace of him."

Recollecting Holmes's comments about the man, I asked, "Your butler is missing?"

"Yes, Doctor."

"For how long?"

"At least a month. Possibly two. As I told Mr. Holmes this afternoon, my husband and I departed for China in March and did not return until two weeks ago. It was our third trip there in as many years, but the Foreign Office insisted my husband investigate the possibility of Britain leasing the New Territories in the near future. While we were away, Tseng vanished."

"When was he last seen?"

"In July, so far as we know. When my husband and I are away for any extended time, our staff, with the exception of Tseng, is sent to work at an estate near Withyham that belongs to a friend of my late father-in-law. Tseng remains here by himself, except for a few days at the beginning of each month when the staff returns to help him clean the house. The rest of the time he spends tending to upkeep and repairs. He is a superb handyman." I asked if it would be simpler to shut up the house during their absences, but Mrs. Angus-Burton explained her husband preferred that Tseng remain to guard the home. "Our staff saw Tseng in July, but when they returned at the beginning of this month, he was gone. Nothing had been stolen. There was no sign of violence. It was almost as if Tseng left without giving notice, except that his clothes and everything he owned is still here."

"Did he have any provocation to leave? Perhaps a disagreement prior to your leaving in March?"

"No. Tseng never disagrees with anyone, and my husband adores him like an uncle."

A rude pounding erupted, interrupting our conversation, accompanied by Holmes calling out for Mrs. Angus-Burton to unlock the door to the study.

Excusing herself while I joined Holmes, the lady fetched a key ring from one of the servant's quarters. "Malcolm keeps this room locked these days. He apparently forgets that Tseng has a spare key." As she set to work finding the correct key, Holmes inquired, "You told me before that everything your butler owns is still in his room. I just looked at it. It's quite barren. Nothing really in the way of personal belongings except his clothes and some Chinese books."

"Yes, Tseng lived very simply." Unlocking the study, her expression, restrained to this point, became anxious. "I pray you will find some sort of clue to explain why my husband doubts me."

"Dr. Watson and I shall make every endeavor to do so. Now if you will excuse us." With that, Holmes ushered me into the study and followed, shutting the door behind us. I began to reprimand Holmes for being impolite before being mesmerized for the second time since entering the grand house. "My word," I said, at last. "This is like a private museum."

"As you can see, Mr. Angus-Burton owns an outstanding collection of ancient Chinese furniture, curios, and art."

"Now it makes sense why he wanted his butler to guard the house whenever he and his wife were away. You knew this was in here?"

"I did. According to Mrs. Angus-Burton, her father-in-law collected these treasures during his tenure in China, and they are her husband's prize possessions."

Without forethought, I found myself bemoaning the injustice of one man being blessed with such beautiful objects and an equally beautiful wife.

This delighted Holmes. "Ah! So you agree with my observation of the lady?"

There was no point denying it. "You know I do. As does she, I'm embarrassed to say."

Thus appeased, Holmes took some pity on me. "Think nothing of it, Watson. You were the model of *politesse*. Now, as I mentioned, Angus-Burton believes his wife has incorporated his study into her curse. Before he left in March, Angus-Burton would work in this sanctorum for hours, but since returning, he finds that spending more than a few moments in here arouses an uneasiness whose persistence drives him out of the room."

"If the curse were true, I suppose that would make a bizarre sense. The wife lost her mother, so in vengeance she bars her husband from the objects he cherishes most. But surely there must be a logical explanation. Perhaps Angus-Burton's anxiety about Tseng manifests itself in a subconscious way through the uneasiness he feels when in this room."

"You may be on to something, Watson," Holmes permitted. "My search of the rest of the house found nothing untoward, so – " Without another word, Holmes set about poking, prodding, and crawling throughout the study. I had seen him perform this bloodhound style of investigation a number of times, and, as on those occasions, he rummaged mostly in quiet, permitting himself only an occasional grunt or hum. As time passed, Holmes grew frustrated and may have been about to forsake this tactic when his attention fixated on a small cabinet.

He craned his neck to stare at the study's only window, which had its curtains drawn shut, then looked back at the cabinet. He rubbed the side of the cabinet, rubbed his fingers together, leaned his hawk-billed nose close to the cabinet, sniffed, then smiled. Then Holmes dropped flat on the floor to examine the carpet underneath the cabinet before standing to reexamine many of the surrounding pieces. He seemed to be seeing the collection from a totally fresh perspective, though I had no idea what that might be. Finally, Holmes paced the room to make what I assumed were a series of mental measurements in relation to the study's treasures, the room's dimensions, and the window. When he was finished he looked at nothing in particular and said more to himself than me, "Remarkable."

"Remarkable?"

"Yes. Elegantly remarkable, and yet there is the suggestion of bitterness. Resentment, I think."

"You're not making sense."

"Patience, Watson." Opening the door, Holmes called Mrs. Angus-Burton into the study to ask if anything in the room had been disturbed since their return two weeks earlier. After looking about, she said, "No. Everything is in its normal place."

"Can you recall when your husband last changed the location of anything in this room?"

"Never. As far as I know, this study is arranged as it was on the day Malcolm's father moved into it."

"I see. That window? Are those curtains ever drawn back to permit sunlight into the study?"

"Quite frequently."

Holmes appeared more than satisfied and thanked the lady, adding, "If you would give the Doctor and I another minute alone, we will be on our way."

Concern broke through Mrs. Angus-Burton's resolve once more. "I don't understand. You've found nothing?"

"Quite the contrary, but it is merely a thread. A thin, frail thread we will follow as best we can to see where it leads."

"So there is an explanation?"

"I did not say that."

"But there is hope?"

"There is always hope, madam. Never lose faith in hope."

Once alone again, I asked, "What thread did you find, Holmes?"

My friend ushered me to the cabinet he had been examining. "Come look at this. Specifically this faded elm wood along the side. Does it look natural to you?"

It did at first, but then something struck my eye as being amiss.

"You see it, don't you, Watson? Go ahead and touch it."

I did. It wasn't faded wood but paint. "Someone's painted the wood to appear faded."

"Faded from the sunlight shining through that window, as any wood in that location would be after years of exposure. I discovered similar camouflaging on that vase and this marble statue."

"These three pieces are frauds?"

"Expert copies of the genuine pieces that were here before the Angus-Burtons left for the New Territories." Holmes's eyes kindled with the thrill of this discovery. "The other cabinets in this room are either lacquered or are covered with decorative paint, so we were fortunate that the elm wood on the sides of this one cabinet were left to patina."

"Then there's been a robbery! Why didn't you tell Mrs. Angus-Burton?"

"Because this is not an answer. It is a clue. There is still much to discover. These forgeries and the disappearance of the butler make up the thread we must follow. If we can trace it back to its skein, then I believe we can confirm what happened to Tseng and the explanation for Angus-Burton's uneasiness whenever in this study."

"Surely you have some idea."

The spark in Holmes's eyes dampened, replaced by what appeared to be apprehension, but for who or what I had no idea. "What I have is an errand that I must attend to while you return to Paddington."

"Why should I return home? Don't you need my help?"

"As always when the hour of action arrives," Holmes assured me. "However, unless I'm mistaken, we will have to make a dark descent into a perilous place this night, and so we best prepare ourselves. We'll meet at Baker Street at ten o'clock, and be sure to bring along your revolver."

Doing as Holmes instructed, I returned to our old rooms in Baker Street as the familiar clock above the mantel struck ten. Through a miasma of blue smoke, I spotted Holmes sitting on the floor wearing his dressing-gown, legs crossed, a pouch of tobacco and a telegram in his lap as he puffed on his briar pipe. Taking my familiar seat by the fireplace, I felt most at home. Perhaps too much so, as I said, "Something is weighing on your mind."

"And how exactly do you deduce that?" he asked in a subdued voice.

"A few little things. For instance, you always smoke your black clay pipe unless your mood is blue, then you smoke your old briar pipe. You have also kept the windows closed despite the heat, most likely for the sense of confinement, which you insist aids your concentration."

"Excellent, Watson." His voice suddenly turned grim. "Of course, it all seems so simple after you explain it."

My friend's tone prodded me to acquiesce. "*Touché*, Holmes. Does that telegram have anything to do with where we are going tonight?"

"It does. It is from the Wapping headquarters of the Thames River Police, to inform us that safe passage has been arranged for you and I tonight to enter a certain shop in the Dockland."

"Why go there? And why should we need any sort of safe passage?"

Holmes inhaled deeply upon his pipe. "I fear I am asking you to risk a great deal by accompanying me tonight. That is what weighs on my mind. We must go to this shop because it is only there that the confirmations I spoke of earlier can be established." He pointed to the telegraph. "The necessity of the safe passage is because this shop is under the protection of the city's most notorious Oriental society, the Triad, who guard it as vigilantly as the Crown Jewels are guarded in the Tower of London. Without this safe passage, it would take the assistance of a regiment for us to reach this shop, and if for any reason the Triad decides to rescind it during our visit, the chances of us escaping are perilously slim."

I don't know if I had ever heard Holmes sound so worried, but there was never any question that he could depend upon me and I told him so.

"Good old Watson. Our safe passage begins at midnight, so until then I'm afraid all we can do is smoke a quiet pipe and wait." He said not another word until it was time for to depart.

From Baker Street we traveled to the East End and descended into that other London. Whitechapel. Aldgate. Spitalfields. Mile End. Ratcliffe Highway. Even at that hour, those mazes of alleys and wharves were brimming with the bawdy music from pubs, the luring aromas of food from around the world drifting from restaurants, the crude voices from various sailor boarding houses, and everywhere the children, those "*street arabs*" who were "*pale and always ailing*". The temperature had precipitately cooled when Holmes stopped to fix his bearings and then look at the sky again. "By the look of that lightning, Watson, it appears this storm is finally going to break. Thank goodness we've about reached our destination."

"Which is where? You haven't even told me the name of the place."

Instead of answering, Holmes pressed on. "Down this direction."

"This way is even bleaker," I said, convinced after a few steps we must be lost. "Where's everyone gone? All I see are courtyards, backyard slaughter houses – "

"And our destination. That rather exotic shop."

Through a brick archway that I failed to notice before, I dimly perceived the bland green painted façade of a waterfront shop. From this angle, the shop appeared to be tucked away by itself, with the exception of a large warehouse it abutted. Above the door was a sign, "'*The Way to Heaven*'. Scarcely an apt name, I would wager."

"Let's pray it is not a prophetic one for us." At that second, the skies opened. "Here's the rain! Inside, Watson, before we're drenched!"

Upon entering the shop, I realized that Holmes had been right to call it exotic. Walking through its rooms was, I imagine, like walking through the Great Yarmark, the famous summer fair at Nijni-Novogrod. Among the collectibles I saw were Javanese pottery, cow-tail coats, jeweled idols, and bizarre arms and armors. In the back rooms was a zoo stocked with animals from the four corners of the globe, including a black swan, a Sumatra civet cat, a black panther, even a pair of petulant crocodiles. We spotted no other human beings until we reached the rear of the shop, where an ancient-looking Chinese man waited for us beside a large ornate drapery.

"Mister Holmes. Doctor Watson. Welcome to The Way to Heaven. I am Hip Yee. This is my shop."

"Good evening," said Holmes. "I believe we're expected."

"Yes, sirs. Tseng is waiting. Through this passage, please. The way is dark, but not too dark. I will take you." The proprietor drew back the drapery to reveal a red-brick groined tunnel. We followed Hip Yee in, and, as we descended, I asked Holmes, "Tseng is here? How did you find him?"

"We have the Thames River Police to thank for that. I deduced that Tseng is involved with the Triad, so it seemed likely that they would be hiding him somewhere in the Dockland, where the Triad is strongest in London. I presented what details I had to the River Police, who used that information and their expertise of the Dockland to locate Tseng and contact him. We are here because the Triad agreed to give us safe passage after Tseng consented to speak with us."

"And here you are, gentlemen." Hip Yee stopped before a great oxidized iron door, which he opened with far less effort than I would have supposed. "Inside, please, gentlemen. Please wait here for Tseng." We passed through, the door closed behind us, and we found ourselves in a large chamber. What I saw was beyond belief.

"Holmes. This room. It's – it's – "

"Remarkable?"

"It's Angus-Burton's collection! Every piece of it! But this . . . this is incredible. No, it's impossible! Tseng could never have stolen it all and replaced it by himself."

"You are correct. He couldn't. And he didn't."

Before Holmes could explicate, the great door opened and we were joined by a Chinese man of proud bearing wearing a long loose white garment. Like many middle-aged men of Asiatic heritage, it was difficult to decipher his exact age. The newcomer could just as easily been in his early forties as his early sixties. His hair was black, his green eyes were bright and perceptive, and I appraised that he had likely been quite handsome in his youth. Speaking with a voice tinged by an accent, the man said, "I am Tseng. Welcome to my home."

Forgetting our circumstances, I retorted, "*Your* home? Everything in this room, sir, has been taken from the study of Malcolm Angus-Burton!"

"What you say is true, Doctor."

"Then you admit you're a thief!"

"I admit I have committed a crime, but I have no qualms about how other men shall judge me. I am content in my heart." Having dismissed me, Tseng turned towards my companion. "I am curious, Mr. Holmes. How did you know to have the River Police search for me here? Pains were taken to leave no trail."

With the respectful voice of a patient schoolteacher, Holmes told Tseng, "A man leaves trails throughout his life that can be followed by someone who knows how. In your case, when you were an orphan you lived for a time in Macao."

"I fail to see anything revealing in that."

"No, but I am a student of crime. Not only in England but across the world. So I know that for the past several years a Triad branch has operated in Macao, and that they often attempt to recruit orphans into their society."

Tseng pondered this, perhaps recollecting moments from his past, then nodded. "Lost souls can make dedicated if mindless soldiers. However, I never joined the Triad as a child. Instead, I fled to Canton."

"I must confess I was uncertain if you joined them then, although it seemed logical that you did not. If you had, there would have been no need for you to be taken in by the Angus-Burtons."

"Living with them was indeed a better option than joining the Triad. The Angus-Burtons cared for me well and saw to my education. No one could have been more grateful to his benefactors than I."

"Mrs. Angus-Burton sings your praises as a handyman. I see from the calluses on your palms and fingers that you are more than that. You are a sculptor as well as a carpenter."

"And he would have to be to make all the forgeries in Angus-Burton's study," I said.

"But he didn't make them all," Holmes told me, then returned to Tseng. "That is how I knew you had joined the Triad. The number of forgeries involved with this grand substitution was too great for one person to create, even if he had a lifetime to complete them, much less three years."

This piqued Tseng. "Why do you say three years?"

"That is how long both of Malcolm Angus-Burton's parents have been dead. That is when your former master inherited the family's estate and all its possessions, including these treasures taken from your homeland."

"So you think that was my motive for wanting to possess this collection? Because these treasures were taken from China?" Tseng appeared to be almost disappointed with Holmes.

"No. You lived in the Angus-Burton household ten years longer than their only son, but you received nothing in their will. Your motive was that you were not remembered."

This stunned Tseng, who remained silent for several moments. When he found his voice, he stammered, "How could you know that?"

"Mrs. Angus-Burton told me you left all your belongings behind when you disappeared, which is a most telling act in and of itself. To stay on point, however, when I searched the Angus-Burton home earlier this evening, I found nothing in your room that could be construed as an heirloom."

"It is a plain and mostly empty room. Tell me, why was leaving my belongings behind so telling?"

"To borrow a gambling phrase, you overplayed your hand. If you had taken your belongings and left a letter of resignation, then your disappearance would have been dismissed as unexpected but not unusual. Logically, that would have been the preferable effect if your substitution of the collection were successful. This would mean, though, that your former master would not suffer as you suffered when his parents forgot about you. Mrs. Angus-Burton told us her husband loves you like an uncle, so if you vanished inexplicably, then Angus-Burton would always wonder and worry what happened to you."

What Holmes was describing struck me as reprehensible. "If that's true, it's more malicious then the robbery!"

Instead of refuting, Tseng queried Holmes, "What evidence do you have to suggest that I could be so vindictive?"

"Evidence? How about the pieces in Angus-Burton's study that are not forgeries?"

This made even less sense to me. "Tseng didn't steal the entire collection?"

"Oh, I did, Dr. Watson. You have my word that every piece of the collection accumulated by Angus-Burton *père* is here."

Holmes explained, "Whenever possible I put myself in the shoes of the criminal, as it were, to try to think as he thinks. When I recognized that the small cabinet was a forgery I searched the collection for more. To my surprise most – but not all – of the treasures had been substituted. This puzzled me. Why only steal the vast majority of the treasure instead of all of it? Then I noticed that the authentic pieces were among the most intricate and detailed of the collection. That was when it became obvious that all of the collection had indeed been stolen. These authentic pieces would have been virtually impossible to accurately duplicate, so they were replaced with genuine identicals."

"I'm trying," I said, "but I can't see any reason for doing that. The trouble and expense of replacing a few items with genuine twins could not have been worth the effort."

"My friend is correct, Tseng. Such an action suggested bitterness and resentment. You could not permit Angus-Burton to keep one single item from his father's collection if it was in any way possible to leave him with none of it."

Tseng paced a bit, his faced turned from us all the while. "I repeat, I have no qualms about how other men shall judge my actions. Still, you have not told me how you knew I had joined the Triad."

"To accomplish this robbery, you needed the aid of artisans familiar with Chinese furniture and art. These would have to be men that you could trust not to talk about your plan. You also needed access to a good deal of capital, not just for these artisans, but to pay for materials. What other resource was available to you that had access to all of this than the Triad? Especially when in return you could offer them access to everything you had learned from your years of service to one of the Queen's own advisors."

"Ah. I see." Tseng halted and let everything he had just heard go round his head again before speaking further. "It is a rather obvious trail once it is explained, but one that requires extraordinary perception and skill to follow." He smiled at Holmes. "I congratulate you on your abilities."

"You are aware of the unexpected affect your robbery has had on your former master?"

"Which is?" Tseng asked half-heartedly.

"He senses that things are not as they appear to be in his study, but he cannot see what is out of place. This, coupled with your mysterious disappearance and, I suspect, the fatigue of three journeys to China in three years, have deluded him to believe his wife has cursed him."

Tseng started to raise his arms in alarm before catching himself. "He thinks the mistress could – that is absurd!"

I assured Tseng it was true, and his anger blazed. In a quiet voice, he cursed, "That fool." Then his calm demeanor returned. "Well, it does not matter. Your deductions are correct, Mr. Holmes. Go and tell him everything. When you do, he will see that there is no curse. The mistress is most innocent."

I suggested, "Perhaps it would be better if you returned what belonged to him?"

"No, Doctor. I couldn't do that even if I wanted. The Triad owns this collection and they own me. That is the price I paid for their help. Their wish is that I return these treasures to China and I must obey. As must Malcolm Angus-Burton. He has more in his life than this collection. He has influence. He has wealth. And he is married to the most beautiful and gracious woman in England. I ask you, how much fortune does one man deserve in a lifetime?"

Holmes interjected, "Such decisions are for providence, not men, to decide."

"I have decided. I only agreed to your request because my masters in the Triad believe it was the simplest way to bring this matter to a conclusion. Now it is time for you to go."

"Wait!" I said. "What did you mean that Angus-Burton must obey the Triad?"

A solemn but determined glint hardened Tseng's eyes. "The Triad defends what is theirs, Doctor. If Malcolm Angus-Burton does not wish to lose the abundance of all he still possesses, then he must be satisfied with matters as they stand and move on with his life, as I now must move on with mine."

The following day, with Mrs. Angus-Burton's permission, Holmes presented Tseng's warning to her husband. That should have been the end of the matter, but Angus-Burton was outraged to learn of the betrayal.

The next night, Scotland Yard stormed The Way to Heaven and – after a fierce struggle – recovered the stolen collection. They also found Tseng, murdered in the gruesome ritualistic way of the Triad to prevent the organization from losing possession of him to the police. As for the Angus-Burtons, a few nights later their Notting Hill home was broken into, and upon the morning they were discovered by their servants in the same condition as their former servant.

The tragedy shook the grand old city, inspiring magistrates to begin the clean-up of the slums that grew in earnest during the Nineties. I like to think that because of this, the Angus-Burtons did not die in vain, something that I mentioned to Holmes while we looked back upon this sad case a short time later.

"It's a fine thought, Watson, but for myself I am convinced that there was indeed a curse at work in this case. Two of them, actually. The petty curses of *hubris* and *desire*. Angus-Burton's hubris not to accept what was lost and be thankful for what he still possessed, and Tseng's desire to take what he could when he couldn't have what he coveted, all to hurt a man who had never done anything but love him. It cost them both dearly, but not as dearly as it cost a dear young woman whose only sin was to be caught between the folly of two men's pointless inhumanity to one another."

The Adventure of the Sleeping Cardinal

or The Doctor's Case

By Jeremy Holstein

This story first appeared in the MX Book of New Sherlock Holmes Stories Volume II.

Jeremy Holstein has loved Sherlock Holmes since childhood but is especially fond of listening to his adventures on radio. He currently serves as the Artist in Residence for the Boston based audo drama troupe the Post-Meridian Radio Players (www.pmrp.org) where he has produced new full cast Sherlock Holmes audio dramas every summer for the past eight years. He lives in the Boston area with his wife and daughter, who are very patient with him.

Eddie Mendieta is originally from Union City, NJ, Eduardo has been living in Florida for the last 25 years. His passion for the arts started at a young age, painting grati on abandoned buildings and walls. Locally known as EMO, this passion developed into a blend of raw urban art and graphic design that is now known as his signature style. In recent years, Eduardo has gained recognition creating many large-scale murals and curating projects in West Palm Beach and throughout South Florida. Some of the mural programs Eduardo has been a featured artist in are 46 for XLVI Superbowl Indianapolis Mural Project; Downtown West Palm Beach Stairwell Mural Project; Northwood Village Mural Project, West Palm Beach; Downtown Hollywood Mural Project; Broward 100 Mural Project; the Walls Project, Baton Rouge; Canvas West Palm Beach and Biscayne Green, Miami. Eduardo has also painted large-scale public mural for the Cities of West Palm Beach, Lake Worth, Hallandale Beach, Ocala, Delray Beach and Knoxville, Tennessee.

www.eduardomendieta.com

Artwork size: 30 x 20

Medium: Acrylic on canvas

My name is Watson, Doctor Watson, and it was my privilege to share the adventures of Sherlock Holmes. Throughout the many years I lived with Holmes in Baker Street, I came to know both his many gifts and his many faults. Chief among those faults was an intolerance of dull routine, an impatience that was often tested in the interim between clients when no new problems were available to challenge his active mind. It was during one such lull, in the summer of 1899, that my story begins.

It was early morning, and I was supping upon one of Mrs. Hudson's excellent breakfasts. Holmes, however, had declined the meal, and was instead pacing back and forth before the mantelpiece in our sitting room. Finally he threw up his hands and bellowed his frustration at the top of his lungs.

"Bah!" he cried. "This is interminable, Watson! Interminable!"

"What's that, Holmes?" I said, even though I knew the answer.

"This inactivity!" said Holmes. "Has the entire criminal population of London gone on holiday? Give me a case to solve, a problem to unravel! Anything but this endless boredom!"

"Calm down, Holmes," I said. "Something will turn up soon. Why don't you have some of Mrs. Hudson's breakfast?"

"I don't need food, Watson," said Holmes. "I need clients! I am a thinking machine, and my mind must be fed problems, lest it wither from languor."

"Perhaps there's something in the paper for your mind to chew on." I picked up the morning paper and leafed through the pages. "Ah," I said. "Here's an interesting item. They've found Henry Tuttle alive and in hiding! He'd faked his death to avoid his creditors."

"A cowardly act," said Holmes, "but far from interesting."

"I seem to recall you did much the same a few years back," I said.

"For entirely different reasons, Watson," said Holmes. "You know that."

I did my best to hide my smile. "If you say so." I turned another page, and a new article caught my eye "Ah, here's something. Apparently the *Sleeping Cardinal* has been put up for auction."

"The *Sleeping Cardinal*?" said Holmes. "Now that is interesting. I believe you were involved in the painting's recovery a few years back?"

"I played my part, yes," I said.

"Yet you've never told me the full story," said Holmes.

"It's never come up before."

"Well then, Doctor," said Holmes, "if the criminals of the present cannot challenge my mind, then perhaps the criminals of the past can. Tell me your tale."

"Are you, Sherlock Holmes, really asking me to tell you one of my stories? You usually dislike my writing in the *Strand Magazine*."

Holmes fixed me with the gravest of stares. "It's either your stories or the needle, Watson," he said. "I leave the decision to you."

"Very well," I said, and pushed my breakfast aside. "Where to begin?"

"You are the storyteller, Watson," said Holmes. "I place myself in your capable hands."

"I suppose," I began, "that the best place would be the summer of 1892. It had been over a year since your disappearance, Holmes, and some months before your reappearance in London. During the intervening time, I had left the world of criminal investigation behind, choosing instead to focus upon my medical practice and the health of my beloved wife Mary, God rest her soul."

"Indeed," said Holmes. "Pray continue."

I gathered my thoughts, and began.

It was a beastly hot summer, as I recall, and my list of clients had swelled as a result. I had just finished treating a patient for heat exhaustion over near Covent Garden when I, quite literally, ran into an old friend. I was walking home and so consumed with thoughts of my wife and her health that I didn't even see the gentleman until I had barreled into him.

"I beg your pardon, sir," I said.

The gentleman, however, did not want to give pardon and began to yell back at me. "Why don't you watch where you're . . . ." he began, but then stopped, his eyes widening in surprise and his mouth spreading into a grin. "Well, if that doesn't beat all," he said. "Is that you, Doctor Watson?"

My heart burst with joy at the sight of the man. "Why, it's Inspector Lestrade!" I said. "My dear fellow. It's good to see you."

"What brings you down to Covent Garden?" said Lestrade.

"Oh, I've just finished up with a patient," I said. "And you?"

"Business, I'm afraid."

"Ah!" I said. "A case?" I could not help but feel a tingle of the old excitement at the prospect.

"Still investigating crimes, Doctor?" said Lestrade.

"No, of course not. Not since Holmes's death at Reichenbach."

"Of course."

"I still follow crime in the paper, though," I said. "Try to puzzle them out as Holmes would have done."

Lestrade regarded me with a curious expression. "Actually," he said, "it's funny running into you like this. This robbery I'm looking into. It's exactly the sort of case your Mr. Holmes would have enjoyed."

"Really?" I said.

Lestrade considered me for a moment, and then said, "See here, Doctor, this is a bit irregular, but are you busy? I could use a fresh set of eyes on this one."

I smiled. "For old time's sake?" I said. "Why, Inspector, I'd be honored."

"Capital," said Lestrade. "Then follow me, and I'll outline the details of the case en-route."

"Lead the way," I said. "I'm your man."

We set off together down St. Martin's Lane, Lestrade talking as we walked.

"It's like this, Doctor," he said. "Last night, one Lady Margaret checks into the Hotel Metropole, carrying with her a very expensive painting, called . . ." Lestrade pulled a notebook from his pocket, and consulted his notes. ". . . *The Sleeping Cardinal*," he finished.

"I'm not familiar with it," I said.

"Neither was I before now," said Lestrade, "but they say it's a masterpiece and worth a king's ransom. Lady Margaret had brought the framed painting into town for an exhibition. Not wanting to leave it in her room, she asks the manager . . ." Lestrade checked his notebook again. ". . . one Patrick Pardman, if he'd store it in the hotel safe for the night. Mr. Pardman agrees, and locks the painting up in his office before heading home. You follow me so far?"

"Perfectly," I said.

"Well, Doctor," said Lestrade. "Imagine Pardman's surprise when he arrives the next morning, goes to open the safe, and finds the painting gone!"

"Stolen!" I said.

"One would think so, but there's no evidence of a break-in at all! The safe is stored in Pardman's office, a small room with no windows and only one entrance in or out, a door just behind the main desk of the hotel."

"And the desk was manned all night?" I asked.

Lestrade nodded. "They assure me it was. By one . . ." He checked his notebook again. ". . . James Ryder, I believe."

"James Ryder," I said. "I know that name from somewhere."

"Do you now?" said Lestrade. "Well, this Ryder claims no one else entered the office between the time Pardman left for the night and when he returned the next morning. So how did the painting disappear?"

"Was the office locked at night?" I asked. "Could someone have slipped in while Ryder wasn't looking? Or perhaps it could have even been Ryder himself?"

Lestrade shook his head. "Mr. Pardman assures me he locks the door when he leaves at night, and only unlocks it first thing in the morning."

"No sign of tampering, I suppose."

"None."

I thought about the problem as we walked. "This is a bit of a stretch," I said after a time, "but could Pardman himself have taken the painting?"

"Pardman was seen last night leaving the hotel by both Ryder and the porter," said Lestrade. "He wasn't even carrying a bag, let alone a framed painting."

"You're right, Lestrade," I said. "This is exactly the sort of case Holmes would have enjoyed."

"I thought as much," said Lestrade, "As you can imagine, Lady Margaret is quite distraught and demanding the hotel cover the value of her painting in currency. If we can't find the culprit and recover the *Sleeping Cardinal*, the hotel will find itself in quite a financial bind! Ah, here we are," he said, stopping on the street before the Hotel Metropole. "This way, Doctor," he said.

We entered into an opulent hotel lobby, empty save for a constable guarding three people by the main desk. The woman, who I took to be Lady Margaret, for she was well dressed and ample, stood beside the two gentlemen who could not have looked more different from one another. One, who I soon learned was Patrick Pardman, was a tall, handsome fellow. The other, James Ryder, was short and rat-faced.

Lady Margaret wasted no time in pouncing upon Lestrade. "At last!" she said. "What took you so long?"

Lestrade was ever the professional. "My apologies, Lady Margaret," he said, impassively. "Yard business."

Lady Margaret huffed at this. "I don't understand what could possibly be more important than my compensation."

Lestrade ignored her indignation, and instead introduced me. "This is my colleague, Doctor Watson," he said. "He'll be assisting me with the investigation. Doctor, this is Lady Margaret, Patrick Pardman and James Ryder."

We all mumbled, "How do you do?" to each other.

"Excuse me," said Pardman, "but are you the same Doctor Watson who works with Sherlock Holmes?"

I considered correcting his grammatical tenses, but decided to let it pass. "I am," I said.

Pardman seized me by my hand and began to shake vigorously. "Bless me!" he said. "It's an honor sir. An honor."

"You've read my stories?" I asked.

Pardman let my hand go, somewhat sheepishly. "Well, not as such, no," he said. "But you're quite popular among the hotel guests. They're always chattering on about your friend's exploits. Is he here with you now? It would be a privilege to meet him."

"I'm afraid not, Mr. Pardman," I said. "Holmes is . . ." I paused, searching for the right word. ". . . away," I finished.

"If we can get back to the business at hand, please," said Lestrade, never one to let a sentimental moment remain uninterrupted. He pulled out his notebook yet again, and flipped open to an empty page. "Now, let's review the details for Doctor Watson's benefit. Lady Margaret. You checked in to the hotel last night around seven. Is that correct?

"Correct," said Lady Margaret.

Lestrade recorded this in his notebook. "And while checking in, you turned the painting over to Mr. Pardman for safe-keeping?"

"Well, of course!" said Lady Margaret. "I couldn't have such a priceless masterpiece of art lying around my room, now could I? You never know who works at these sorts of places."

"Madame," began Pardman, with the greatest indignity. "The Metropole is among the top hotels in London . . . ."

Lady Margaret interrupted him. "The top hotels in thievery, you mean."

"If I can continue?" said Lestrade, waving his notebook about for emphasis. "Now then. Lady Margaret, can you describe the painting in question?"

"Certainly," said Lady Margaret. "It is a particularly lovely piece of impressionistic artistry by the painter Flemming. With sublime brush strokes, Flemming depicting a priest at rest upon an altar . . . ."

Lestrade cut her off. "Just the size of the painting will do."

Lady Margaret looked as if she might explode, but she answered with even precision. "Two by three feet, Inspector, mounted in a mahogany frame."

Lestrade wrote this down in his notebook. "Thank you. Now, Mr. Pardman. You put the painting immediately into your safe, is that correct?"

"Immediately, sir," said Pardman. "Security is a top priority."

"And you locked the safe thereafter?" asked Lestrade.

"Of course," said Pardman. "I even double-checked the lock." His lip trembled at this, as some of his professional composure broke. "Oh, Inspector, how could this have happened?" he said. "I'll be out of a job!"

"Have some faith in the force, Mr. Pardman," said Lestrade. "We'll recover the painting, never fear. Now what time did you leave the hotel?"

"Just after eight that night," said Pardman. "Ryder had come on to work the desk shortly before Lady Margaret checked in, and I retired to my office to finish some paperwork. When I was done, I locked the office and bid Ryder good night."

"Ryder," said Lestrade, "can you confirm the time?"

Ryder, who had been very quiet up until now, nodded his head. "Indeed, sir," he said. "Eight o'clock."

"And you're absolutely certain," said Lestrade, "that no one entered the office between eight that evening and when Mr. Pardman arrived for work the next morning?"

"On my honor, sir," said Ryder. "It was a quiet evening, and I never left my post at the desk."

"Excuse me, Mr. Ryder," I asked, "but you look very familiar. Have we met before?"

"I don't believe so, sir," said Ryder, but he never met my eyes. I could tell he was lying.

Lestrade noticed none of this. "What time did Mr. Pardman return?" he asked.

"Around six this morning, I think," said Ryder.

"Six on the dot, sir," said Pardman. "Punctuality is my motto."

"And it was then you discovered the painting missing?" said Lestrade.

"Well," said Pardman, "not immediately. It wasn't until Lady Margaret came down and asked to check on her painting that I opened the safe. But when I did, the painting was gone!"

"No sign of a break-in?" said Lestrade.

Pardman shook his head. "None that I could see, sir."

"And Lady Margaret," said Lestrade. "What time did you come down?"

"Just past six-thirty," said Lady Margaret. "I'd had a bad dream, and woke up convinced something had happened to my painting!"

Lestrade rubbed his chin. "A dream, eh?" he said. "That's quite a coincidence."

"Mr. Pardman," I said, "could we have a look at this safe?"

"Of course," said Pardman. "Anything I can do to help. This way, gentlemen."

We left Lady Margaret and Ryder behind in the lobby as Pardman ushered us into a spartan office, devoid of any charm or character. No pictures adorned its windowless walls, and the only furniture was a single desk, two chairs and the large safe pushed into the far corner. The only luxury the room offered was its fireplace; a prize, I was sure, during the cold London winters.

"As you can see, gentlemen," said Pardman, "the door is the only way in or out."

Lestrade studied the safe. "I see no signs of tampering. What about you, Doctor?"

I studied the safe, looking for the scratches and dents that might indicate foul play. "None that I can see," I said at last. "Who knows the combination to the safe?"

"Only myself," said Pardman, "although I do keep it recorded on my desk ledger."

"Isn't that a security risk?" said Lestrade.

"Maybe," said Pardman, "but I've got a terrible memory, so it's better to have it written down than not. Besides, the office is locked at all times when I'm not here."

Lestrade turned away, whispering aside to me so that Pardman could not hear, "Little doubt how the thief got into the safe, is there Doctor?"

"Indeed, Inspector," I whispered back. "But there still remains the question of how he got into the office in the first place."

Lestrade turned back to Pardman. "Who all has the key to your office?" he asked.

"There's only one key, Inspector," said Pardman. "I keep it with me at all times." From his pocket he withdrew a keyring, singling one out.

"That's a rather unusual looking key, Mr. Pardman," I said.

"A Roman design, Doctor," said Pardman. "A trick for my memory to know which key fits my office lock."

"Now then, this Ryder," said Lestrade. "How long has he been with the hotel?"

"Less than a year," said Pardman, "but he came with references from the Hotel Cosmopolitan. I know the manager over there personally."

"And how long have you been with the Metropole, Mr. Pardman?" I asked.

"It'll be twenty years this January," said Pardman. "I'm second only to the hotel's owner, Mr. Saul."

I knew the name of Zacharias Saul very well. He was reputed to be one of the richest men in London.

I looked around the room, trying to think beyond the obvious, searching for any clues for how the thief might have entered the office. "This fireplace," I said. "Is it possible someone could have entered the office by the chimney?"

Lestrade shook his head. "I thought of that, Doctor," he said, "but if they had entered by the fireplace, they would have left traces in the ashes, and as you can see the ashes are undisturbed."

"Besides, the chimney's only a foot wide," said Pardman. He began to chuckle. "We joke about it around here. Say that it makes it very difficult for Father Christmas."

"What did you say?" I whispered.

"Father Christmas," said Pardman. "He's supposed to come down the chimney . . . ."

Memories rushed into my head. "Ryder!" I said. "James Ryder! Of course!"

I rushed out into the lobby, pointing my finger in accusation.

"Constable," I cried. "Seize that man!"

The constable seemed surprised, but did as he was told, seizing Ryder by him arm. Ryder struggled, but soon realized the constable was too much for him and his resistance evaporated into pitiful wails.

"Please, Doctor Watson!" he cried. "I haven't done anything this time! Have mercy!"

"Holmes gave you mercy once, Ryder," I said, "but he's not here to do it again."

Lestrade barged back into the Lobby, followed by Pardman. "Explain yourself, Doctor!" said Lestrade.

"Certainly," I said. "It was several Christmases past that Holmes and I investigated the theft of the Blue Carbuncle from the Hotel Cosmopolitan. Holmes's investigation determined the thief to be this man! James Ryder!"

Lestrade blinked in disbelief. "Ryder stole the Carbuncle?" he said. "And Holmes just let him go?"

"A thief!" cried Pardman with indignation. "A thief working the desk of my hotel!"

"Why'd you do it, Ryder?" I said. "You promised Holmes you'd flee the country and never steal again!"

Ryder stifled back a sob. "I tried to leave, Doctor Watson," he said, "but London's the only home I've ever known! I even tried to stick it out at the Cosmopolitan, but the manager came to suspect me, so I had to leave. I was trying to make a fresh start here at the Metropole. I didn't steal the painting! Honest I didn't!"

"We'll see about that," said Lestrade. "Constable, hold him tight while I search his pockets." Lestrade turned Ryder's pockets out, and searched through their meager contents. Unsatisfied, he looked about the lobby for more. "Where's his coat?"

"I believe I saw it behind the lobby desk, Inspector," said Pardman.

Lestrade strode around to the back of the lobby desk, seized the coat and raised it aloft like a prize. He thrust his hands deep into the pockets and fished about until he seized upon an object which he pulled out with a flourish of triumph. "Ah-hah!" he said. "What's this, then? Do you recognize this little beauty, Mr. Pardman?"

In Lestrade's hand was a metal key with the same distinctive Roman design we had seen only moments before.

"Of course I do," said Pardman. "That is a duplicate of the key to my office."

"I thought as much," said Lestrade. "James Ryder, you are under arrest for the theft of the *Sleeping Cardinal*!"

"But that key isn't mine!" said Ryder. "I've never seen it before in my life!"

"That's what they all say," said Lestrade, but then he began to laugh.

"What's so funny, Inspector?" I asked.

"It looks like your Mr. Holmes was finally wrong about something!" said Lestrade. "Letting a criminal go free like that. Mercy, indeed! Just goes to show you; once a thief, always a thief."

Despite Ryder's protests Lestrade led him away, assuring both Pardman and Lady Margaret that he would procure the painting's location during interrogation at the Yard. I watched Lestrade escort Ryder away down the Strand with the nagging suspicion that I had missed something, some detail that would turn this case around, but I couldn't then put my finger on it.

Holmes interrupted me, taking me away from my tale. "Leave the dramatics for your readers at the *Strand*, Watson," he said. "Please limit yourself to the facts."

"If you'd rather I stopped . . . ." I began.

"Oh, not at all, Doctor!" said Holmes. "While your prose may be overly colorful the problem is to my liking. Pray continue."

The following evening I spent in the manner which had become my custom: working on my memoirs in the company of my beloved wife. Mary was seated by my side reading the evening paper, and cried aloud as she came across something that sparked her interest.

"Did you see that you're in the paper tonight, John?"

"Hm?" I said, putting my pen aside. "No, I didn't. What does it say?"

Mary cleared her throat and began to read. "'Inspector Lestrade of Scotland Yard arrested James Ryder for the theft of the painting, the *Sleeping Cardinal*, from the Hotel Metropole. Assisting in the investigation was the long-time associate of Sherlock Holmes, Doctor John Watson!' My famous husband." She smiled at me, but that smile crumbled as a fit of coughing overwhelmed her.

I poured Mary some water, which she gratefully accepted. "Mary," I said as she drank, "you should get to bed. You know you aren't well."

"I'll be all right, John," she said, putting the water glass aside. "I'm just so happy for you. There's a sparkle in your eye when you're involved in a mystery. It's just like you used to say about Sherlock Holmes; you're happiest when there's a problem to unravel."

"Perhaps so," I said. "I just can't get this *Cardinal* business out of my mind. Something doesn't feel right about it."

"But you have the right man, surely!" said Mary. "Ryder's a thief twice over."

"He certainly had ample opportunity," I said. "Although the idea that he thought he'd be able to get away with it strikes me as incredible."

"If Scotland Yard is happy," said Mary, "then you should be too."

"I suppose you're right," I said. "But I'd be even happier if we can get you well again, Mary."

Mary put her arms around me. "I'd like nothing better, John."

I kissed her then, relieved that her coughing had, for the moment, subsided.

In the days following Lestrade was kind enough to keep me informed of his progress, or lack thereof, with the investigation. James Ryder continued to insist he was innocent, but Lestrade assured me it would only be a matter of time before he'd crack and give up the location of the painting. And that would likely have been the end of my involvement in the matter if not for a message that arrived at our doorstep a week later.

I was writing again in my study when I felt Mary's slender hand upon my shoulder. "John?" she said. "A telegram's arrived for you."

I lay down my pen. "Oh? Who's it from?"

"It doesn't say," answered Mary. "Just an initial at the bottom. The letter 'M'."

"M?" I said, excitement building within me, spurred by the possibilities of that initial. "Let me see that."

Mary handed me the telegram and I read it aloud.

WHERE IS THE PAINTING? CONSULT SHERLOCK'S CONTACTS. CONSIDER THE ASHES.

– M

I confess to being puzzled. "Consider the ashes . . . ?" I mused.

"What does it mean, John?" asked Mary. "Who are Sherlock's contacts?"

"Holmes kept numerous sources among London's criminal class," I said. "They helped him in his investigations."

"And you know these gentlemen?" I could hear the disapproval in her tone.

"A few of them." I saw no reason to scare my wife with the number of miscreants who I had come into acquaintance with during my time in Baker Street.

Mary was not fooled for a moment. "John," she said. "It might be dangerous."

"It might be at that."

Mary sighed. "But there's no stopping you, is there? I know that look in your eye. All right, John. Just be careful."

"I will, Mary," I said. "For your sake."

The telegram had reawakened the case in my mind. What had happened to the *Sleeping Cardinal*? There seemed two possibilities; either it had been hidden within the hotel prior to Ryder's arrest, or it had been secreted away from the hotel to be sold on the black market. Seeing as the police had conducted a thorough search of the hotel, I decided to pursue the second possibility. To that end, I sought out a man I only knew as 'Jones,' a shady sort I had seen frequently in our rooms at 221B Baker Street. His information had been instrumental in solving the Darlington substitution case several years ago.

I found him drinking in a disreputable pub in the lower-east end of London. I sidled up beside him at the bar.

"Is that you, Jones?" I said.

Jones looked askance at me. "Who wants to know?"

"My name is Doctor Watson. You might remember from the times you visited Sher – "

Jones clamped his hand over my mouth, silencing me mid-name. "Shhh! Shhh!" he said. "Not so loud! You want everyone in the pub to know who you is? Yeah, I remembers you, Doctor." He dropped his tone to a whisper. "Did Mr. H. send you? Haven't seen him around lately."

"No," I said. "Mr. H. is not in London at this time."

"Pity," said Jones, turning his attentions back to his drink. "He owes me money, he does."

"I'm looking for information," I said. "I was wondering if you can help me."

"Well, guv," said Jones, "help ain't cheap. It'll cost you."

"And just how much will it cost me?" I said.

"Depends on just how helpful you want me to be," said Jones.

"I'm looking for a painting."

Jones chuckled. "Oh! And not just any paintin'! You be lookin' for the *Sleepin' Cardinal* that got lifted out of the Metropole last week."

"Why, yes," I said, surprised. "How did you know that?"

"'Cause you ain't the only one," said Jones. "Scotland Yard's been down here lookin' for it too."

I felt a tinge of excitement. "You have it, then?"

"Good lord, no, guv!" said Jones. "You think I'm going to touch somethin' that hot?"

My excitement withered. "Then this has been a wasted journey," I moaned.

"Aw, cheer up, Doctor," said Jones. "I might not be able to help you find the paintin', but I might be able to give you a hint as to who took it." He looked around to make sure no one was listening, and then spoke to me in low tones. "There's this fellow, see?" he said. "Works at the Hotel Metropole, and he's in for some serious money with the local bookies. They say he likes the ponies and isn't the luckiest man in the world."

"Can you describe this fellow?" I said.

Jones smiled. "Course I can," he said. "But not until I see some coin."

"How much?"

Jones rubbed his chin, considering his options. "For information that valuable?" he said. "Well, now. Let me see. Five pounds might loosen my lips."

"Five pounds?" I cried. "That's outrageous!"

Jones shrugged. "Well, you think it over, Doctor," he said. "I'm not going anywhere. Not with it being so blasted hot outside."

I couldn't help but agree. "It certainly is that," I said. "It hasn't been this warm since . . . ." I broke off mid-sentence as something fell into place within my mind. "Good lord!" I said. "I have it!"

"What's that, then?" said Jones, sensing his fish had fallen off its hook.

"The ashes!" I cried. "Consider the ashes! I know who took the *Cardinal*!"

"Calm down there, Doctor," said Jones. "You're not makin' any sense."

"I have to go to Scotland Yard at once!" I said. I seized Jones by his hand, shaking it vigorously. "Thank you very much, Jones. You've been most helpful." I fished a coin from my pocket. "Here's a crown for your trouble."

Jones snatched the coin from my hand before I could even blink. "Why, thank you, Doctor." I turned to leave, and heard Jones call after me. "You're welcome!" he cried, followed by a mumbled, "I think . . . ?"

As I left the disreputable pub behind, my mind buzzed with excitement. I could see it all now; exactly who had taken the painting and how.

"Absolutely scintillating, Watson," said Holmes, who was pacing back and forth again within our sitting room. "You had of course noticed that the ashes . . . ."

I interrupted my friend before he could ruin my tale. "Holmes, please. Let me tell my own story."

"Of course," said Holmes. "Do forgive me, Doctor. Pray continue."

I rushed to Scotland Yard and sought out Lestrade. Together, we then made out way back to Covent Garden and were soon standing before a small set of rooms near the Hotel Metropole. We knocked at the door, and a tall, handsome man answered.

"Yes?" said Patrick Pardman. "Ah, Inspector. And Doctor Watson! What a surprise."

"May we come in?" asked Lestrade.

"Of course, of course," said Pardman.

He stepped aside, and ushered us within.

Pardman's quarters were spartan, devoid of the luxury the Hotel Metropole provided. It was a single room, with a small bed, a dresser and side table. A decanter, some bottles and glasses were perched on top of dresser, and Pardman poured himself a drink.

"May I offer you gentlemen some brandy?" asked Pardman.

Lestrade shook his head. "I'm afraid we're here on business."

"Oh?" said Pardman. "You have news of the *Sleeping Cardinal*?"

"We do," said Lestrade.

"Well, that is welcome news," said Pardman. "Mrs. Margaret is demanding her compensation by no later than noon tomorrow. Mr. Saul is most unhappy with the situation."

"I can imagine," I said.

"Then don't keep me in suspense, gentlemen," said Pardman. "Have you located the painting?"

"We have information that points us in a direction," said Lestrade.

"Well, that is encouraging!" said Pardman. "And where is the *Cardinal* presently?"

"That is what we've come to ask you, Mr. Pardman," I said.

Pardman blinked in surprise. "Me?" he said. "But it was Ryder who took the *Sleeping Cardinal*!"

"No," I said, "but that's what you wanted us to think."

"You knew of Ryder's suspected involvement in the disappearance of the Blue Carbuncle from your discussions with the manager of the Hotel Cosmopolitan," said Lestrade, "and knew he'd make a perfect scapegoat should a robbery ever occur at the Hotel Metropole."

"All you had to do was somehow mention Ryder's involvement with the Blue Carbuncle theft to the proper authorities," I said, "and Ryder's arrest for the new robbery would be almost assured. My appearance at the scene must have seemed an early Christmas to you. Why raise the affair of the Blue Carbuncle to the authorities when a known associate of Sherlock Holmes could do it for you?"

"The spare key was a nice touch in the frame-up," said Lestrade. "Only you made a small slip up there."

"Really," said Pardman.

"You said you never let the key of your sight," I said. "How then could Ryder have made a copy? I suspect if we were to check with locksmiths in the area of the hotel, they'd remember making a copy for you, Mr. Pardman, and not for Mr. Ryder."

"That proves nothing," said Pardman. "I have keys made for the hotel all the time."

"But the rest of the hotel uses standard keys," I said, "while the key to your office is Roman. Something with that unique a design is bound to stick out in a locksmith's mind."

"You slipped the duplicate into Ryder's coat so I could find it," said Lestrade, "which completed your frame-up. A very clever touch, but not clever enough for an officer of the Yard."

Pardman drained his glass, and regarded us calmly. "An entertaining tale, gentlemen," he said, "but you still haven't told me where the painting is."

"The painting's disappearance is really only a mystery if we assume it was ever in the safe to begin with," I said, "and we only have your word for that. If, however, the opposite were true and the painting were never in the safe, then the solution becomes obvious."

"You walked out of the Hotel Metropole that evening with the painting in hand," said Lestrade, "determined to sell it on the black market."

"That's ridiculous!" said Pardman. "How could I walk out with a painting that size and not be seen? The idea's ludicrous!"

"It is ludicrous," I said, "until you remember the ashes in your fireplace."

Pardman blinked at me in surprise. "I beg your pardon?" he said.

"Lestrade noted the ashes in your office as evidence that no one had snuck down the chimney," I said, "but what we should have been asking is why you were burning a fire at all during the hottest summer in recent memory? The answer is that you were burning the frame upon which the *Cardinal* was mounted!"

"With the frame removed, the painting was much easier to conceal beneath your coat," said Lestrade. "You wrapped the canvas around your body and walked out of the hotel, right in front of both Ryder and the porter, with neither the wiser."

"But this is madness!" cried Pardman. "Why should I do such a thing? I've been loyal to that hotel for twenty years! Ryder's your man! He's a thief, I tell you, a thief!"

"Yes," I said, "I wondered about that too. Why would you steal from your own hotel? But then I did some checking with Holmes's criminal contacts and discovered a very interesting fact."

"We know about the bookies," said Lestrade. "We know about the gambling, and we know how much you owe them. The game's up Pardman. Why don't you give us the canvas and be done with it?"

Pardman stared back at us in defeat. "Fine," he said at last. "You can have the blasted thing. No one's buying it anyway. They say it's too hot! But you have to protect me, Inspector! If I don't have the money by tomorrow, they'll kill me!"

"Then it's a good thing you're going to the safest place I know," said Lestrade. "A jail cell at the Yard."

Pardman retrieved the *Sleeping Cardinal* from its hiding place, and Lestrade took him away to an awaiting cell. That evening, with the painting in hand, Lestrade and I visited Lady Margaret to return her property. She seemed oddly cold to the *Cardinal's* recovery. In fact she hardly even bothered to thank us! But justice had been served, and I felt satisfied.

"And that, Holmes," I said, "is the story of how we recovered the *Sleeping Cardinal*."

Holmes, who had been smoking as he listened, opened his eyes and laid his calabash pipe on the mantle. "An entertaining tale, Doctor," he said. "I'm sure the readers of the *Strand Magazine* will enjoy it."

"Oh, I'll never write it up," I said. "It's your adventures they want, not mine."

Holmes smiled. "Ah, but perhaps I had more to do with the case than you realize."

"How do you figure, Holmes?"

"Did you never wonder who sent you the mysterious telegram?"

"Well," I said, "I had always assumed the message came from your brother, Mycroft."

"You are only partly correct," said Holmes. "The telegram was indeed from Mycroft. The message, on the other hand, was from me."

"You?" I said, astonished.

"I had requested that my brother keep tabs on you during my absence," said Holmes, "along with sending me full reports of your progress. When he sent me Lestrade's police report on your involvement with the robbery of the *Sleeping Cardinal*, I could not help but smile."

I sighed. "At how poorly I performed the investigation?"

"My dear fellow," said Holmes, "you underestimate yourself. You had the tenacity to question the obvious while Lestrade rushed toward the easiest conclusion. I knew if we provided you a small push in the right direction you would find the truth. No, I smiled as, despite my absence, you were still in the game."

"Ah," I said. "Well, thank you, Holmes."

"You did, however, miss one avenue of investigation."

"Oh? And what's that?"

"I find it difficult to believe," said Holmes, "that a woman who has just had her priceless painting stolen would immediately demand compensation rather than the canvas' recovery. I find it very probable that she planned the theft together with Mr. Pardman."

"Now, Holmes, that really is too much!"

"Consider the facts," said Holmes. "Consider that Pardman knew immediately how to smuggle the painting out of the hotel, almost as if he'd had advance warning. Consider that Lady Margaret chose not to store her painting in the gallery where it was to be exhibited, but instead to store it in a hotel safe. Consider also that she chose not to stay in a hotel near the exhibition, but instead a hotel owned by the richest man in London?"

"Good Lord," I said. "I have been blind all these years."

"Ah, but we shall never know for certain," said Holmes. "It was her estate sale you saw in the paper. Lady Margaret died last week. But cheer up, Watson. You did find the thief and recover the *Sleeping Cardinal*. As good an outcome as could be hoped for."

"Well," I said, "after your telegram provided a thread to follow, the solution was . . . er . . . ." I hesitated, wondering if I should dare.

"Go ahead and say it, Watson," said Holmes. "You've earned it."

"Why, it was elementary, my dear Holmes," I said. "Elementary."

The Adventure of The Parisian Butcher

By Nick Cardillo

Nick Cardillo has been a devotee of Sherlock Holmes since the age of six. He is the author of *The Feats of Sherlock Holmes* and his short stories have also appeared in anthologies from MX Publishing and Belanger Books. Nick is a fan of The Golden Age of Detective Fiction, Hammer Horror, and *Doctor Who*. He writes film reviews and analyses at www.Sacred-Celluloid.blogspot.com. He is a student at Susquehanna University in Selinsgrove, PA.

Bruce Helander is an artist, writer and critic. He received a BFA in Illustration and an MFA in painting from the Rhode Island School of Design, where he later served as the Provost and Vice President for Academic Affairs. He studied at Yale University for journalism and storytelling, as well as at Harvard, and is a former White House Fellow of the National Endowment for the Arts. He recently received the First Annual Professional Achievement in the Arts Award from Palm Beach Modern + Contemporary and is a member of the Florida Artists Hall of Fame. Helander is a past recipient of the South Florida Cultural Consortium's award for Professional Achievement in the Arts and has won four separate grants from the New York Foundation for the Arts. His work in represented in over fifty permanent public collections, including the Solomon R. Guggenheim Museum, Whitney Museum of American Art and The Metropolitan Museum of Art, as well as the San Francisco Museum of Modern Art and the Los Angeles County Museum of Art. As a critic, he regularly writes for numerous publications such as *The Huffington Post*, *Sculpture* magazine, *Art Hive* magazine and One Art Nation, among others. His illustrations have appeared in numerous publications, including The New Yorker magazine. His most recent books include "Chihuly: An Artist Collects" (Harry Abrams, Inc.) and "Bunnies" (Glitterati Press). He is a seasoned juror and curator of museum exhibitions and serves on the board of the Center for Creative Education.

There are two anomalies in the artwork. Can you find them?

www.brucehelander.com

Artwork Size: 15 x 14

Medium: Original paper collage on museum board with embellishments

agenta. PARIS.
Landry
Compiègne
SCHAAL
CACAO
PARIS
MONTMARTRE
PYRENEES-ORIENT
CATHEDRALE D'AMIENS
PYRENEES-ORI
PAR AVION
PARIS-R
NOV
DEP
CARD
ADDRESS
"Pelikan"-Farben
GÜNTHER WAGNER
LONDON

It has always been my intention to give the public as accurate and complete account of my association with Mr. Sherlock Holmes as possible. However, there have been innumerable times in our career together that I found myself having to alter facts such as names, dates, and places in order to relate matters of a sometimes scandalous or sensitive nature. On other occasions, I've found it necessary to hold back an account in its entirety; deciding as I laid my pen aside that it would be for the best that the particulars of some of Holmes's cases never be exposed at all. Such is the manuscript which follows: One of the few times when I determined it best that the document be consigned to some obscure corner of the Cox and Co. Bank vault, never to see the light of day.

Sherlock Holmes was the very last of men to ever give credence to any sort of sixth sense, so it came as something of a surprise to me one humid, rain-bedewed morning in the late summer of 1886 when Holmes sat back in his chair and said: "I have the strongest intimation that something is wrong."

I set the paper down on my knee. "Whatever do you mean?" I asked.

Holmes passed me an open envelope. "That letter came to me last evening while we were away," he said. "It is, as you will doubtlessly notice, postmarked London. However, the writer of that letter is Monsieur Andre Dupont, a wealthy French businessman. Does the name strike your ear as familiar, Watson?"

"I cannot say with any certainty," I replied. "What does this Monsieur Dupont write to you about?"

"He does not say," Holmes replied, reaching for his cigarette case. "He was most irritatingly vague. However, he says that he will present himself at our rooms at eleven o'clock on the morrow – meaning, of course, today."

"Well, I don't see what makes you so particularly inclined to think that something is wrong."

Sherlock Holmes lit his cigarette and laid the burnt-out match into the ashtray at his side. "If you would do more than to observe the latest cricket scores in that very paper which you have currently splayed out across your lap, my dear fellow, you would find an article which announces that M. Andre Dupont will be arriving by the one o'clock boat from Paris, as he is conducting some business with a few prominent English industrialists."

"Which means that Dupont has been in London for a day already."

"At the least," Holmes replied. "Either M. Dupont had some business of a more illicit nature to attend to in the city, or he is very much in fear for his life. The fact that his arrival in the city has now been documented leads me to believe that he will have to go to some extremes to conceal his earlier arrival. By my estimation, a lookalike shall be disembarking from the one o'clock boat in M. Dupont's stead."

Holmes clicked open his fob watch. "It's nearly eleven now," he said. "If you would be so kind as to stay, Doctor, you could be of invaluable assistance."

I told Holmes that there was nothing that I would rather do than aid him in any way I could. No sooner had Holmes exclaimed, "Capitol!" and clapped his hands zealously together then did we hear the bell below chime. I could hear the sound of someone at the door conversing with Mrs. Hudson in the foyer and, a moment later, when our landlady drew into the sitting room, Holmes beamed at her.

"You may show M. Dupont up at once, Mrs. Hudson. His visit is not an unexpected one."

"I beg your pardon, Mr. Holmes, but it is not M. Dupont who is at the door."

Holmes knit his brow in confusion. "Who is it then?"

Mrs. Hudson produced our visitor's card and handed it to the detective. He read it, his face clouding further. Then, without a word, he gestured for her to bring the client in.

"Well," I said, once Mrs. Hudson had gone, "who is it?"

"The card is most certainly that of M. Andre Dupont," Holmes said passing it to me. "But, as you will perceive, written upon it are the words: *Alexandre – Valet.*"

"Why should Andre Dupont send his valet to you instead of coming himself?" I asked.

Holmes shrugged his shoulders. "I hope that the man shall endeavor to answer that very question."

Our landlady returned with a tall, lanky man in his early fifties. He was well-dressed, though I figured that the dark coat and bowler hat which he carried could not have been in the slightest comfortable, especially as the late summer weather had turned the atmosphere thick and cloying.

"I would not be incorrect in assuming that you have come on behalf of your master?" Holmes asked the servant.

"That is correct, sir," the man replied. He remained stiff as a board, totally unmoving as he spoke. "M. Dupont had all intentions of calling on you himself this morning, per his letter, but he decided otherwise at the very last moment. He would, however, be most grateful if you would accompany me to my master's home. He is still most anxious to speak with you."

"This business must be one of the utmost severity," Holmes said, more to himself than anyone else in the room. "Very well. I shall come with you, provided that Dr. Watson is allowed to accompany me. He acts as my associate in all my cases."

The valet nodded his head slightly. His total lack of movement made the man appear to be some kind of statue. "That shall be quite alright, Mr. Holmes."

"Excellent! Then the Doctor and I shall join you in the foyer in precisely three minutes."

Holmes quickly set out gathering up his things and, once we had made our way downstairs, we climbed into a waiting four-wheeler and soon found ourselves hurtling through the teeming streets of the metropolis.

"Tell me, Alexandre," Holmes began, "how long have you been in M. Dupont's employ?"

"This autumn will be my fifteenth year."

"Would you describe your relationship with M. Dupont to be a close one?"

"I should think that no man knows my master better than I," the valet replied.

"And you have no idea in the slightest what could be troubling him so?"

For a moment, a look of fear came into the valet's dull, grey eyes, before he said quite emphatically: "No, sir. I cannot think of anything."

I noticed the look and flashed Holmes quick glance. He locked eyes with me and I knew that he too had perceived the valet's clumsy attempt at deception.

Our cab drew up outside of a very well-appointed house, tucked back behind a mighty oak tree which grew out of the well-manicured front lawn. The valet produced from his coat a ring of keys and, once inside, he divested us of our hats and led us into a large, open sitting room. The room was lined with expensive-looking oil paintings on three of its walls, with the fourth taken up by a stylish set of French windows which looked out onto a neat stone veranda. At the furthermost end of the room was a large fireplace, before which stood the man I took to be Andre Dupont. He was tall and lean, and not a day over forty – though he looked considerably younger – sporting an elegantly waxed mustache. He was well-dressed in an expensive black suit. He looked as if he was destined to be in that room, as though he were one of the subjects of the portraits on the wall that had come to life, just to add flair to the space.

"Ah, Mr. Sherlock Holmes," he said, with the slightest trace of a French accent permeating his words. "Thank goodness you have come."

"M. Dupont," said Holmes as he moved further into the room to shake hands with the man, "you need not be a detective to figure that you are quite distressed about something."

"I should imagine that my urgent letter and my subsequent behavior was enough to convey that to you."

"Indeed," Holmes said, "I have seldom encountered so curious a starting point to an investigation in my days as a consulting detective. Dr. Watson, my friend and colleague, can testify to that point."

I shook hands with Dupont and verified Holmes's words, which seemed to put the aristocrat to some ease.

"I am in fear for my life, Mr. Holmes," Dupont replied. "Please, gentlemen, sit. I shall tell you the story through."

Dupont took a seat in a wing back chair while Holmes and I took seats on opposite ends of a plush-looking settee. After he had offered us cigarettes, Dupont leaned back in his chair.

"I am a wealthy man," he began. "As such, I have garnered a few *enemies* in my time. Business rivals have publicly threatened me, and I have more than once in my life avoided being brained by thrown rocks. I have developed a thick skin. However, petty threats and stones pale in comparison to the threatening letters which I have received in the past few weeks."

From his inner beast pocket, Dupont withdrew two envelopes. "The first," he continued, "was delivered to my home in Paris a week ago. At first I thought that it was yet another threat from a business rival. The message itself was short and quite vague: '*Your time on earth is running short.*' It was not until I examined the note more deeply did I truly begin to fear for my life. You see, Mr. Holmes, this message was written in blood."

I sat upright in my seat suddenly. Dupont passed the letter to my friend. He took it and observed it first with the naked eye before peering at it through his convex lens.

"It is genuinely blood," my friend said length. "You will doubtlessly recall, Watson, that when first we met I was in the midst of developing a test to determine whether a substance perceived to be blood is actually blood. The congealed quality of the substance is enough to tell me that it is not ink."

"Naturally, I was scared out of my wits," Dupont continued. "I made sure that all the doors and windows of my home were locked. I began to carry a gun on my person and slept with it under my pillow. My wife, Michelle, started to question me about my curious behavior, but I did not wish to disturb her.

"However, my genuine terror only increased when, shortly after the arrival of that first letter, my pet dog disappeared from outside my own home in Paris. I feared that he had run away, but after searching for little more than an hour, my staff and I discovered that it had been slain. My wife knew something was amiss and confronted me that very night. I showed her the letter which I had received and together we believed that it was for the best that we leave Paris. I did not wish to make public my intent to travel to London, but it somehow it ended up in the majority of both Parisian and British papers. It was for that reason that I plotted to arrive here in London a full two days before my public arrival this morning. We traveled with some of my most trusted staff so we should want for nothing here in London. I even managed to hire a man with a similar resemblance to me to publicly be seen leaving the ship. I was taking no chances, whatsoever.

"I thought, Mr. Holmes, that I was safe. And then, yesterday morning, I received yet another letter. It is postmarked London."

He handed the second envelope to Holmes. The threatening message was, once again, terse and to the point: "*Death is Coming For You.*"

"It, too," Dupont said grimly, "is written in blood."

He drew in a deep breath, attempting to calm himself. "Whoever has sent me these letters knew of my flight to London," Dupont continued. "*He* knew that I would leave early and has dogged my heels across the Channel. Mr. Holmes, I beg of you. Please protect me."

"I am not a common bodyguard," Holmes retorted, more coldly than I believed was warranted. He handed the letter back to our client, and eased back in his chair, crossing one long leg over the other in a deceptively languid manner. "I shall, however, do my utmost to help you in unmasking your stalker. However, I must insist upon one thing M. Dupont: You must reveal to me all you know."

"I have told you everything."

"I do not think so," Holmes icily replied. "You identified your stalker as '*He*' a moment ago, almost as though you know precisely who is responsible for these acts against you. If you gave me some indication of who this man might be, I can go a long way towards clapping irons about his wrists."

Andre Dupont sucked in another deep breath. "I know of only one man who would have cause to wish such misfortunate on me," he murmured. "But that man is dead. I am sure of it."

"Nevertheless, tell me about him M. Dupont."

Dupont leaned back in his chair and, for an instant, the ghost of a smile crossed his mouth. "You will notice," he began, "that I am a collector. These paintings on the walls are all originals. Are you an art enthusiast yourself, Mr. Holmes?"

"I can appreciate a Bond Street art gallery as well as the next," Holmes replied. I cast my friend a quizzical glance, silently asking him what this could possibly have to do with the matter at hand. Holmes met my eyes and seemed to silently address me, saying that all would become clear in time.

"I have amassed something of a collection," Dupont continued, rising from his chair and moving to a small, elegant-looking bureau in the corner of the room. From his waistcoat pocket, he withdrew a key, and inserted it into the lock. He opened a cabinet door and removed a small case about six inches across, wrapped in a light cloth.

"I have always had a fascination with art," Dupont continued, "and from time to time, I have been captivated by the *oeuvre*. I confess, that I have always been riveted by Bosch's depiction of Hell in *The Garden of Earthly Delights*. I suppose that is what led me on the path to having an eye for the fantastic and the *unique*."

Dupont accented the last word as he removed the cloth from the case. What lay beneath was a neat, glass container. It was the contents of that container which turned my blood to ice.

Within the case sat a neatly severed human hand.

Though I have a strong stomach and am immune to much, the sight made me feel dizzy for a moment. Perhaps it was the showman-like air which Dupont had adopted in revealing to us his unique piece of art. I looked to Holmes, but his face was cold and unreadable.

"Whose hand is this?" Holmes asked at length.

"The man's name was Jacques Bonnaire," Dupont replied. "He was a close friend of mine for many years until, after my wife and I married, he attempted to make love to her. I caught him in the act and shot him on the spot. He was severely wounded and, as he lay bleeding, I told Michelle to call for the police at once. When she had gone, I must have lost my head, Mr. Holmes, for I took up a knife and cut off his hand. I just wanted to make a point to the blackguard not to cross paths with me anymore. The police arrived and dealt with the matter. Luckily in France, crimes of passion are leniently treated under the law, and Bonnaire was hauled away a hospital. I have not heard of him since, but I cannot imagine that he survived his wounds."

Sherlock Holmes remained silent. For once, I could read Holmes's cold, inscrutable eyes like a book and it came as little surprise to me when he opened his mouth a moment later and said, "Frankly you disgust me, M. Dupont and I shall have nothing to do with you."

"But what about the threats to my life?"

"You seem like the type of man who is quite capable at defending himself," Holmes retorted. "And, should you be too much of a coward to face your threats, then do what cowards do best: *Run*. You have shown yourself quite adept at that as well. Run away. Perhaps, back to Paris. Surely, Jacques Bonnaire will have quite a time crossing the Channel once again minus a hand and a bullet in his chest. That is my advice and I shall do nothing else but offer that alone. Good day, sir."

So saying, Holmes spun around on his heel and started out of the room.

When I managed to catch my friend, he was already standing outside hailing a hansom back to Baker Street. Once we were ensconced in the belly of the cab, I could see Holmes silently gnashing his teeth.

"It is said that you can judge a man's character by the company he keeps," he said "and I should surely never wish to keep company with M. Andre Dupont and his penchant for hacking off the hands of his rivals."

"I do not blame you, Holmes," I said comfortingly.

Holmes drew in a deep breath and sighed. "But I cannot help but think," he murmured, "that I may have been hasty in my judgment and I have sent a man to his death. I fear that if my imitations prove to be correct once again, then M. Andre Dupont's death may very well weigh on my conscience."

Holmes refused to speak on the matter for the next few days and, it was only as I sorted through the first post of the day three days later, that the business of M. Andre Dupont re-entered our lives.

"Postmarked Paris," I said as I held a letter aloft. I read the return address. "Inspector Durand. I say, Holmes, isn't that –"

"Yes," Holmes interjected. "Inspector Durand was the most competent of investigators who we ran across during that bad business at the Paris Opera House five years back. Please, Watson, do me the service of reading the letter out."

I settled into my chair and opened the letter. It was written in an authoritative hand:

Mr. Holmes,

You will no doubt remember my name well. Though we seldom worked side-by-side so many years ago, I considered it a pleasure to have seen you in action. You have developed something of a following here on the Continent as your name has begun to appear in the press with frequent rapidity.

I wish then that it could be under better circumstances that I write to you, and I severely hope that when you receive this letter that you are able to drop whatever it is that currently occupies you and join me in Paris. To put it briefly, it is murder – the murder of Andre Dupont, the wealthy businessman. If it were only a routine investigation, I should not think on troubling you as I do. However, the savagery with which this murder was committed is unlike anything I have seen in many years of working as a police inspector. Both M. Dupont and his wife, Michelle, fell victim to the murderer. They were stabbed to death and discovered with one of their hands neatly cut off.

"Good Lord, Holmes!"

The inspector's words seemed to cut into me like a knife as well, and I felt a shiver run up and down my back. I hardly had time to register Holmes bolting from his chair and perusing the train directory.

"The boat-train to Paris leaves in two hours, Watson," he said. "If we make haste, we can still catch it."

"Don't you want to hear the rest of the letter?"

"On the train," Holmes said, as he rushed off to his room with a frenzied wave of his hand. "We must act while the game is still very much afoot."

The next hour disappeared in a flurry of packing of bags. Holmes rushed off a telegram replying to Durand, and we soon found ourselves charging across the station platform and ducking into a first-class carriage. I was only catching breath as the train became wreathed in smoke and pulled out the station. Once we found ourselves hurtling across the English countryside, I cast a glance across to my friend. He stared out of the window at the passing fields, his face betraying no discernible emotion. I wondered if the deaths of Dupont and his wife were, indeed, weighing on my friend's mind. Knowing him, he would blame himself for their violent ends. I was almost inclined to say something in an attempt to break him free from his reverie, but I decided against it.

We passed the voyage in relative silence, broken only by Holmes pressing me for more information from Durand's letter. After I had read a part through, he would sit in silence and contemplate the scant words for what masqueraded as hours before urging me to continue.

Inspector Durand had explained that the room in which M. Dupont and his wife were discovered was the locked sitting room of their well-appointed abode, located on a well-to-do road in the middle of Paris. The bodies had been discovered by the valet, Alexandre, who had contacted the police at once. Aside from a servant girl, there were no other persons in the house.

A silent passage by boat was followed by another sojourn by train. It seemed as though the foul weather which had descended on London had followed us to the Continent. Rain lashed the train compartment windows and, when we finally arrived in Paris, we found ourselves rushing to hail a cab and avoid the deluge. Holmes had done us the service of booking a last-minute set of rooms at a hotel and, after we checked in, he sent off another telegram to Inspector Durand announcing our arrival. It had been a long, exhausting day, and at the end of it I found myself famished. I ate a small repast, and was not surprised – and not pleased – that Holmes refused to take any nourishment. I had just gathered up my plates and silverware when we were arrested by a knock on our door.

Holmes answered the call and found the familiar figure of Inspector Durand in the doorway. The half-decade since last we had met had been good to the inspector. He was a tall, lean man, broad-shouldered, and rather statuesque in appearance. He had a long face with deep-set eyes, and a shock of fair hair atop his head. He furled his umbrella while my friend relieved him of his coat, gesturing for the representative of the Parisian police to draw up before the fire.

"You look as though you could use a drink, Inspector," I said as I poured him a brandy from the sideboard. He accepted the libation all too readily.

"*Merci*, Doctor," he said, draining his glass. "It has been quite a day."

Holmes took a seat opposite the inspector and lit a cigarette. "Dr. Watson did me the service of reading the details of the case," he began. "Are there any particularities which you were unable to convey to me?"

"None, M. Holmes," Durand replied. "All of the facts which are in my possession were highlighted. And, alas, very little has been gained from the investigation."

"I assume that you have conducted an examination of M. Dupont's papers and personal possessions?" Holmes asked.

"Why, of course," Durand said, appearing slightly injured by Holmes's question. Perhaps the inspector did not know Holmes well enough to understand my friend's low opinion of the official police.

"Did you happen to find any mention of a man called *Jacques Bonnaire*?"

Durand considered for a moment. "No," he said. "Why? Who is this Jacques Bonnaire?"

"At present," Holmes replied, blowing a ring of smoke about his gaunt head, "he is a suspect of particular interest. However, as it is a capitol mistake to theorize before one is in possession of all the facts, I shall do my utmost not to let the lamented M. Bonnaire enter into the investigation at this time."

"But if he could have an impact on this case," Durand said, "it would be a grave miscarriage of justice not to pursue this particular thread. Who is Jacques Bonnaire?"

"Holmes and I were contacted by M. Dupont in London three days ago," I began. "Dupont had been receiving a number of threatening letters – first, here in Paris, and again in London. He believed that they were sent by a man named Jacques Bonnaire, his one-time friend who tried to seduce Dupont's wife. In retaliation, Dupont shot Bonnaire and cut off the man's hand. Dupont lost all traces of Bonnaire after the incident, but seeing how these murders have a strong link to the incident involving Bonnaire, it is understandable how he should become a suspect."

"I should think so!" the inspector exclaimed. "I shall make it a priority to look into this Jacques Bonnaire character."

"No, Inspector," Holmes retorted rather coldly. "You should make it a priority to allow Dr. Watson and me to examine the bodies. I assume they have been taken to the mortuary? Excellent. Though the hour is rather late, I can think of no time like the present to visit the morgue."

In short order, the three of us had donned our hats and coats and had stepped into the street. The deluge had lessened and a mist was falling upon us. Inspector Durand hailed us a cab and, as we climbed inside, a palpable silence descended over us. I watched as Holmes peered out at the passing rain-soaked city. The City of Light took on a haunting yellow glow as the undulating flames of gas lamps mingled with the wall of fog and mist into which our carriage trundled.

We alighted before a small, stone building tucked on a side-street. Inspector Durand eased open the door and we stepped inside. The smell of death was overwhelming and I clapped a hand to my nose. Though I have in my time been in the presence of death and decay – as both a soldier and a doctor – I would never be able to become immune to the thick, cloying stench of loss. Holmes, however, did not seem to take notice and proceeded into the room. We approached two tables standing side-by-side, the familiar shapes of cadavers atop them, covered in shrouds.

Durand drew back the white sheets which covered the bodies, and I stared at the pale corpses. Holmes circled the table and, from his inner pocket, withdrew his convex lens. Leaning over the body of Andre Dupont, he held the lens close to the wound which had been the cause of his death. Moving swiftly to the body of Madame Dupont, he did the same. In life, Michelle Dupont would have been a lovely woman. She was tall and lean, with a head of charcoal-black hair which would have cascaded down her shoulders. Despite what I knew of Dupont's dubious past, I could not reconcile the claiming of the life of someone who I was sure was guilty of nothing.

Holmes stood and pressed the magnifying glass into my hand. "I would appreciate a doctor's opinion," he said. "The wounds – they were inflicted with the same weapon?"

Approaching the bodies, I held the lens close to my eye and examined the wounds in much the same manner as Holmes had just done.

"These wounds were undoubtedly inflicted by the same hand with the same weapon," I said. "And, from the looks of it, I should think that the knife which did this was a large kitchen knife. The wounds are deep and quite wide."

"And the hands," Holmes continued. "Would you say that the same knife was used to sever the hands?"

I examined the bodies once more. "From what I could see, a different knife was used in this operation."

"A *different knife*?" Inspector Durand echoed.

"I should imagine that the weapon was not as sharp as the one which dealt death to M. Durand and his wife. The cut is far more jagged and less clean."

I returned the lens to Holmes who pocketed it wordlessly. He tapped his long index finger against his lips for a moment.

"Why should the murderer carry two knives on his person? What kind of butcher could have done this thing" Durand asked.

"I would be most surprised if the murderer chose to carry two weapons when one would be more than sufficient," Holmes replied. "A kitchen knife of the type which Watson described is a formidable weapon indeed."

"What exactly are you insinuating, M. Holmes?" Durand asked.

Holmes smiled. "At the moment, nothing. I shouldn't wish to color your investigation more than I already have. The hour, I'm afraid, grows late, and it has been an incredibly trying day for both the Doctor and myself. First thing on the morrow, however, I must make an examination of the murder scene. That can be arranged, Inspector?"

"*Oui*, M. Holmes."

"Excellent," Sherlock Holmes replied, turning sharply on his heel. "Then, Dr. Watson and I shall bid you farewell. Or, perhaps, *au revoir*."

We parted ways with the inspector in the street. Our carriage conveyed us back to our hotel where we silently made our way to our rooms. Once inside, Holmes divested himself of his coat and took up his briar pipe as he settled in before the fire.

"You are not retiring for the night?" I asked.

"No," my friend replied. "The cogs of my brain have been set into motion and I would be doing myself a disservice should I try to halt their natural processes this night. But I am sure that you are exhausted, my dear fellow, so you needn't wait up for me."

I began to undo my tie as I moved towards my room. I looked forward to a good night's sleep more than anything but, as I neared the open door, I stopped and turned around to address Holmes.

"You have begun to develop some theory, haven't you?"

Holmes blew out a ring of smoke which encircled his head. "I have," he replied. "If it is correct, I fear that this case may only grow ever darker."

I roused myself early the following morning, only to find that Holmes was already awake. To my satisfaction, I saw that he was breaking his fast and, for a moment, I considered cajoling Mrs. Hudson into preparing French pastries at Baker Street if it meant that Holmes would take some sustenance more often. I joined him at the breakfast table and we exchanged pleasantries. I informed him that I had slept well, even after the grisly circumstances of the day, and was much relieved to hear that he too had made it to bed – albeit in the early hours of the morning. Holmes also informed me that he had sent an early morning telegram to rendezvous with Inspector Durand, who would convey us to the home of the late Andre Dupont.

After we had finished, we gathered our things and made our way into the hotel lobby, where we found the inspector standing at the ready for us. We exchanged a few words before we moved outside and into the awaiting cab. Though the rain had let up, the day was cloudy and foreboding. It did little to diminish the beauty of the city which, under the cover of darkness the night before, I had failed to truly appreciate. I have only been to Paris a handful of times in my life, but each time I have come away impressed by the splendor of such a lovely place.

Our carriage came to a stop on a picturesque road in the Sixth Arrondissement of the city. As we climbed out, I cast a glance up the street and saw the great tower of the Abbey of Saint-Germain-des-Prés peering over the rooftops of the nearby buildings. Inspector Durand led us through a small garden, the vegetation of which did go some way towards tucking the house away from the street. He withdrew a key from his inner pocket and inserted it into the lock of the front door. He eased it open and we stepped through.

"I have done the utmost to keep the space just as it was when the bodies were discovered, M. Holmes."

"Your consideration is much appreciated, Inspector," Holmes replied. "Your willingness to do so has already placed you above many of the inspectors at Scotland Yard. Now, can you show us to where the bodies were discovered?"

Durand led us through the foyer and into a well-appointed siting room. The room was small, surely not as grand as the room in which Dupont had entertained us in London, but a comfortable space nonetheless which clearly spoke to Dupont's obvious wealth. A set of French windows opened onto a small stone veranda, though I perceived that the glass had been shattered and the drapes undulated in the light breeze which circulated through the room.

"M. Dupont was found there," Durand indicated, pointing to a spot on the floor before the window. "His wife was found there by the settee. I have come to believe that the murderer forced his way in through the French windows and attacked M. Dupont. Madame Dupont was powerless to stop the murderer, as she was trapped in the room."

Holmes stepped further into the room and I watched as he swiveled his head around like a great bird of prey peering through the underbrush. His piercing grey eyes scanned each opulent surface. He turned quickly and, kneeling before the window, inspected the broken pane of glass. Holmes murmured inaudibly beneath his breath as he stood and then moved to the settee on the other side of the room. I watched him consider the space – the cogs in his brain almost visible through his eyes.

"You said that the valet, Alexandre, had discovered the bodies?"

"*Oui*. They were discovered late in the evening. M. Dupont, according to the valet, was in the habit of taking a nightcap and, calling on his master, he found the door to the sitting room locked. When M. Dupont did not respond to his knock, the valet forced the door open."

"And you said that there was no one else in the house at the time of the murder?"

"There was a maid, Jeanette."

"Did she have anything to add to Alexandre's story?"

"None whatsoever, M. Holmes," Durand replied. "She said that she was in the kitchen at the time of the murder and heard nothing."

Holmes tapped his lips once more in contemplation. "I'd like to see the kitchen if you don't mind, Inspector." He started out of the room before the officer had a chance to refuse. Durand exchanged looks with me and I shrugged my shoulders. Holmes had seemed to have lost interest entirely in the room in which the murder had taken place.

Durand drew our attention to a door at the head of a narrow staircase. Then he led us down the set of steps and into the kitchen which was furnished by an extensive series of counters.

"M. Dupont had apparently given his staff leave when he departed for London," Durand explained. "His unanticipated return meant that the number of the household staff was greatly diminished. As I understand it, the valet and the maid were the only ones in attendance, having accompanied their master to London and back again."

Holmes took a turn around the kitchen and, after he had performed what I could only imagine was the most cursory of examinations, turned to us and declared, "I should very much like to examine the veranda behind the house."

"There is a second set of stairs on the opposite end of the kitchen," Durand said, indicating the spiral staircase which sat tucked in the corner.

"Excellent," Holmes cried. "Oh, I have forgotten my hat and stick upstairs. You gentlemen need not follow me back up. I shall return presently."

Holmes climbed the steps and I heard him move about upstairs. He rejoined us a moment later and, insisting that we use the servant's stairs, we made our way to the ground floor of the house and, from there, out of the house and onto the small veranda.

Holmes took a turn around the veranda and stopped before the French windows. He examined a few shards of glass and then, standing, smiled as he clapped his arms behind his back and rocked ever so slightly from his heel to his toes.

"You seem quite pleased with yourself, M. Holmes," the inspector said.

"That is because I think that things are fitting together rather nicely," the detective replied. "However, I think the time has finally come for us to devote attention to Monsieur Jacques Bonnaire. I would very much appreciate it, Inspector, if you did a little digging. Find out all you can about the man."

"I shall start at once."

"Excellent," Holmes beamed. "As for myself, I shall take a walk. Paris is a city with which I am not too intimate and I think that a perambulation will do me some good."

"Would you like me to accompany you, Holmes?" I asked.

"You needn't bother, Watson," Holmes replied. "You will find me silent company for the next few hours. Treat yourself, my dear fellow, to some of this city's more sumptuous delicacies. I know that *le petit dejeuner* we had this morning will hardly be enough to satisfy your needs. Let us meet again in three hours' time at police headquarters. Shall be that sufficient for you, Inspector?"

Durand assured Holmes that it would be and we set off in separate directions. I figured that if Holmes was willing to lose himself in the city, then I should try to do the same. I walked aimlessly for some time until I came across a pleasant café. I stopped and enjoyed a cup of *café au lait* and a baguette which was quite to my liking. Wandering a bit farther afield, I soon decided that it was time for me to return to more familiar environs and, flagging down a cab, was conveyed back to our hotel.

As I sat alone in the carriage, I cast my mind back to the scene of the murder. Obviously Holmes had seen far more than either the inspector or myself, but I could in no way put my finger on what it was. What, I wondered, had he seen that helped him divine some more specific connection with the mysterious Jacques Bonnaire, whose name hung over this case like the grisly shadow of death? As usual, Holmes would not explain, and I wished that he would have shared with me his theory. He clearly saw some dark circumstances surrounding this already morose affair.

Deposited at the hotel, I spent the remainder of the afternoon in quiet contemplation and, I do confess, that I dozed off. I managed to rouse myself with time to spare and caught another carriage to the *Place Louis Lèpine*, home of the Paris Police Prefecture. The impressive grey stone building stared down at me as I made my way inside and, after asking for Inspector Durand, was told that I could find his office on the second floor. I ascended the staircase and walked down a corridor until I came to the inspector's small office and found him seated behind a cluttered desk; Sherlock Holmes seated across from him in the process of lighting a cigarette.

"Good of you to join us, Watson," Holmes said as I took a seat next to him. "Inspector Durand was just about to tell us what he has unearthed on Jacques Bonnaire."

I took a seat next to Holmes as the inspector opened a file which sat on his desk. "To begin," Durand said, "Bonnaire was the same age as Dupont. While Dupont was a self-made man, Bonnaire was born into his wealth. They would seem, then, to be at odds from the beginning, but from all accounts, the two were close friends.

"Bonnaire married a woman one year after Dupont married his wife. Bonnaire had two children – two girls – before the death of his wife, after only a few years of marriage. Bonnaire's children were only six and eight years old respectively at the time of his *contretemps* with Andre Dupont, nearly a decade ago.

"It appears as though the details of the incident as imparted to you, M. Holmes, by Dupont were accurate. Michelle Dupont did indeed contact the police at her husband's behest. The officer who answered the call, a man called August, has since left the force, but his report was easy enough to dig up. He says that when he arrived, Jacques Bonnaire lay on the floor of the master bedroom in a pool of blood. He clutched at his chest where he had sustained a bullet wound, his other arm at his side, minus a hand. Bonnaire was conducted immediately to a hospital. He was released after nearly two weeks and, since then, he has disappeared off of the face of the earth.”

“No contact of any kind you say? None made with his solicitors or bankers?”

“*Non*, M. Holmes.”

“What of his children?”

The inspector turned a page in his file. “The elder daughter severed all ties with the family and has gone to ground. I could find nothing on her whatsoever. The younger daughter – as we understand it – works at a cabaret, a well-known spot in the city called *Le Chat Noir*.”

Holmes leaned forward and crushed his cigarette into the ashtray perched on the edge of the inspector’s desk. “She would make a most interesting study, Inspector.”

“You wish to speak to Bonnaire’s daughter?”

“Of course,” Holmes replied rising. “The sooner the better.”

“We shall go tonight then, if it is your wish.”

Holmes beamed. “Capitol, Inspector!” My friend clicked open his watch. “Ah, how the time has flown. I confess I find myself rather taken with your Parisian cuisine – and judging from the crumbs which Dr. Watson has yet to remove from his lapels, I should imagine that he is too. I think you should dine with us, Inspector. We shall think no more of M. Bonnaire for the time being. I like to think that I am well-up on Continental crime, but I cannot pass up an opportunity to discuss it with someone first-hand. I leave the choice of restaurant to you.”

True to his words, Holmes refused to speak about the case for some time. Instead, we soon found ourselves seated before a sumptuous multi-course feast at an expensive Parisian restaurant. Holmes and the inspector discussed aspects of various cases which, I do confess, left me completely lost. I wondered if Holmes was purposefully distracting himself from the matter at hand. Perhaps, I reasoned as I drained a glass of fine wine, he knew all too well the trials which lay ahead of us in the unraveling of this case. This matter had already taken a toll on my friend. In his mind, he had failed his responsibility and now he was doing all in his power to bring the criminal to book, no matter how arduous the task might prove to be. I wondered just how close to the truth he actually was.

Night had descended when we quit the restaurant. The rain had continued to hold off and, still deep in conversation, Holmes insisted that we walk the rest of the way. Our perambulation was not a long way and we drew up outside of a very inauspicious-looking building. Stepping inside, I was at once struck by the loudness of the music and the cheers from the crowd. The room was wide and open, a stage situated at the furthermost end. Men and woman of all shapes, sizes, and apparent statuses were distributed at tables throughout the room, from which they looked at the stage, currently occupied by a group of women performing a dance which, I would imagine in London, would have raised a decent number of eyebrows. Holmes, of course, took no notice and pressed on further into the room.

We took an empty table which was tucked away in the back of the barroom. The inspector and I followed Holmes’s example as he sat, and in short order we were approached by a waiter. The detective ordered us a bottle of wine in perfect French.

“Well, Holmes,” I said trying to be heard in the loud room, “what exactly do you intend to do?”

Holmes smiled mischievously and put a long finger to his lips as the waiter returned to our table.

“*Parlez-vous anglais?*” Holmes asked the waiter.

Our man nodded politely. “*Oui, monsieur*,” he replied.

“Excellent,” Holmes said. He stood and drew up a chair from a nearby unoccupied table. “Then I invite you to join us for a glass of this most excellent wine.”

A confused look crossed the waiter's face and I am sure he was about to protest. However, Holmes all but forced the young man into the chair and had poured him a glass. Once the waiter had tentatively lifted the glass to his lips, the detective sat back in his chair.

"What is your name?"

"Henri, monsieur," the waiter replied. "Is there something I can do for you gentlemen?"

"I rather think that there is," Holmes replied. "My friends and I would like to speak with someone – one of the dancers, I believe. She would be about sixteen, I should imagine. Her surname is *Bonnaire*. Does she sound familiar?"

Before the waiter had an opportunity to answer, a big man, dressed in a garish waistcoat, sauntered up to the table. He was middle-aged, with a head of orange hair peeping out from under the brim of a battered billycock hat. He held in between his large fingers a chewed-upon cigar. He addressed the waiter sternly in French before turning to us, cocking an eyebrow.

"I am the manager of this club, *messieurs*. Henri tells me that you want some kind of information?"

"We're looking for a young woman named Bonnaire," Holmes replied. "If you could help us find her, it would be much appreciated."

Holmes coyly removed a coin from his inner pocket and slid it along the table. The glint caught the man's eye immediately and he picked it up, stowing it away as though he feared immediate robbery.

"I know precisely of whom you speak," the manager replied.

"We would like to speak with her at once," Holmes said. "It is imperative that we do so this evening."

"I shall take you to her," the manager replied, standing.

Holmes cast the inspector and I a beaming grin as the manager led us through the labyrinth of tables and chairs. Moving past the patrons of the club, we made our way to a small door which communicated with the backstage. The dimly-lit, private portions of the theater was alive with energy as dancers rushed hither and thither, and stagehands worked to lift and lower curtains and drops. I caught sight of Holmes casting a glance over the theatrical mechanisms before we were urged along by our guide.

"The *mademoiselle* you seek has not used the name Bonnaire in some time," the manager said, "but there are few girls working here who are quite so young."

I felt a sudden feeling of reprehension for the man. Having seen the *risqué* nature of some of the routines performed in this place, I couldn't imagine a mere adolescent being involved.

We came to a door which, I concluded, led into the ladies' dressing room. The manager addressed one of the dancers about to enter and, after she disappeared, he informed us that she would fetch the young lady we sought. The dancer was true to her word and emerged from the dressing room a moment later with a petite girl in tow. She was young – Holmes's estimation of about sixteen or seventeen seemed most accurate – but she had quite a pretty countenance which, enhanced with the elaborate makeup utilized in the cabaret, did give the girl something of a salacious appearance. She looked at the three of us and arched an eyebrow. Holmes asked if the girl spoke English, to which she nodded.

"*Mademoiselle*," Holmes began, "my name is Sherlock Holmes. This is friend and associate Dr. John Watson, and this is Inspector Erique Durand of the Paris Police Prefecture. You are the daughter of Jacques Bonnaire, are you not?"

The girl drew in a deep breath. "That is not a name I have heard in almost a decade, sir."

"Mademoiselle," Holmes continued, "we have reason to believe that your father is very much alive and responsible for the murder of Andre Dupont and his wife. It is most important that we speak to you at once."

Her eyes darted around the crowded backstage area. "Allow me a few moments, gentlemen," she said softly. She darted back into the dressing room and emerged again a moment later, a cloak draped about her shoulders. She then led us out of the building and into a narrow alleyway behind the theater.

"I apologize for the quality of the space," she said, "but we can speak privately here. I come here to think and, I do confess, my father is often in my thoughts."

"Naturally," I said, laying a reassuring hand on the girl's shoulder. "What is your name?"

"Emma," the girl replied. "Though, most of the girls around here just call me Em. No one has called me Mademoiselle Bonnaire in quite some time. You say that my father is implicated in the murder of M. Dupont?"

"That is correct, Mademoiselle," Durand said. "You have not heard from your father recently, have you?"

"*Non*," Emma Bonnaire replied. "I do not think that I would want to after what happened."

"Perhaps," Holmes said, "you ought to explain."

"My father and my sister were the only things in my world after my mother died," Emma said. "We were a close-knit family. My father was kind, decent man. However, he – like so many – took to drink as a way to cope with the death of his wife. He soon could only take solace in the bottom of a bottle and, in his fits, he was quite uncontrollable. He was a big man, gentleman. And strong. Once, I found him seated alone in our sitting room, clutching an empty bottle. He saw me and flew into a rage and grabbed me by the arm. He very nearly pulled my arm from its socket.

"I was too young to notice it, but I suppose my father was rather keen on Madame Dupont. She was a handsome lady, I will admit and, in one of his drunken rages, I can only imagine what went through his mind, but I cannot defend what M. Dupont did, gentlemen. It was wrong and . . . *savage*. I never thought that a man could stoop so low. It was not simply enough to shoot my father, but he went and cut off his hand too."

Emma Bonnaire held back a choked sob. I proffered my handkerchief, which she accepted as she dabbed at her eyes. "*Merci, monsieur le Docteur.*

"I can recall visiting my father in the hospital with my sister," she continued after a moment. "He was barely conscious and in a great deal of pain. I could read the look of disgust on my sister's face. She felt not pity for the prostrate figure laid out before her, but anger – an anger that he would attempt to seduce another man's wife and get caught in circumstances such as these.

"I suppose it came as little surprise to me then that she ran away shortly thereafter. It was one of the hardest things I have ever had to experience in my short life. It was made all the worse when, after I learned that my father had been released from the hospital, he did nothing to reclaim me. I was subsequently entrusted into the care of an orphanage, where I remained for some considerable time. I would often lie awake at night, simply contemplating my loneliness, gentlemen. That was until I decided to strike out on my own and join this cabaret. It has served as a home for me. Hardly an ideal one, but a shelter – and a family – nonetheless."

My heart simply broke for young Emma Bonnaire, and I laid another reassuring hand on her shoulder. She cast a glance up at me and her eyes looked like shattered mirrors. She pressed the handkerchief back into my hand and drew in another deep breath.

"Mademoiselle Bonnaire," Holmes said at length, "while you may not have heard from your sister or your father, can you think of anything unusual happening to you within the past few weeks?"

"I can think of nothing," she replied, "aside from, perhaps, the man who loiters outside the theater. But I cannot imagine how that could have any connection to this."

"Humor me if you please, mademoiselle," Holmes continued. "Who is this man?"

"I have never seen him clearly," Emma Bonnaire replied, "but he has become something of a legend amongst the girls. One of my friends, another dancer named Suzette, said that one night after a show she was exiting the theater through this very door and was making her up the alleyway when she heard someone moving about behind her. She turned and saw the outline of a man standing just over there."

Emma Bonnaire pointed to a spot beyond Holmes and the inspector at the foot of a small set of steps, leading down into the alleyway.

"Suzette said that she could not quite make out his face, but he appeared to be an old man. He was hunched over and seemed to have some difficulty in breathing. It was quiet night, Suzette said, and she heard his raspy breath as he leaned on the staircase railing. Suzette was about to go and ask him if he needed help, but she said that fear overtook her. You gentlemen have certainly heard tales of defenseless women in alleyways in the early hours of the morning. With that nightmare scenario running through her head, Suzette turned sharply and ran out of the alleyway.

"The next day, she told us about him and cautioned us to be on our guard. We heard and saw nothing of the mysterious man in the days which followed. However, one Friday evening a few weeks ago, a few of the girls and I decided to celebrate the end of the week. We all left together and were making our way of the theater when we caught sight of him, standing at the head of the alleyway. He was a tall, gangly-looking man dressed in a shabby, oversized coat. His hair was long and tumbled about his shoulders. And his beard was lengthy and dirty-looking as well. So shocked were we by his sudden materialization at the end of the alley that we all turned and raced back inside the theater.

"Since that day, gentlemen, we have heard nothing from the man. We have taken him to simply be one of the less fortunate who is forced to seek refuge on the streets. I very much fear that our minds ran away with ourselves and made a demon out of him."

The faintest ghost of a smile seemed to play upon Holmes's usually cruel, thin lips. "Mademoiselle Bonnaire," he said, "I cannot thank you enough for your invaluable assistance."

From his pocket, the detective withdrew a few francs and pressed them into the girl's hand. "If these can be of any help to you, mademoiselle, please take them."

Then turning to us, he added, "Come gentlemen, I very much suspect that – despite the lateness of the hour – the night is still young for us."

We bade Emma Bonnaire farewell and walked to the end of the alleyway and into the street.

"Well, M. Holmes," Inspector Durand said, "what do you intend to do next?"

"Part ways for the time being. I should very much like it if you could supply me with a city map, Inspector. If you could annotate it, as well, showing any spots in the city where you know there to be a large population without home or shelter, I would find it of great assistance. Let us all meet then once more at our hotel in an hours' time?"

Extending his arm, Holmes hailed a cab and I clambered inside after him, leaving Inspector Durand on the street with a look of stupefaction etched on his face.

Once we were within the cab, Holmes turned to me, and solemnly asked: "You did remember to bring your service revolver?"

"Of that you can certain," I replied.

"Excellent. I very much suspect that we shall be in need of it tonight."

True to his word, Inspector Durand met with us again at our hotel. He produced a valise, in which he carried a map of Paris. He spread out on the dining table.

"In an attempt to answer your question, M. Holmes," Durand said, "I consulted with a few of my fellow officers. They all agreed that here is the place where most of the city's poor some to congregate."

He pointed to a spot on the map along the River Seine. "The place is something of a colony," Durand replied. "They live along the river and under bridges."

"Excellent," Holmes said. "Then that is where we are headed now."

Holmes moved to the door and pulled on his hat and coat. "It has begun to rain, so take proper precautions. Now, come along."

Silently we made our way outside and into a tumultuous deluge. It was quite a feat in tracking down a cab, and I fear that I was soaked to the skin by the time that we three sat ensconced in the relative warmth and comfort of a carriage.

Chilled from the wet, as well as the anticipation and suspense in which I was being kept, I very nearly exploded once we found ourselves rattling through the deluge.

"What are we doing, Holmes? I am used to your characteristically dramatic behavior, but this is beginning to be a bit much."

Holmes replied in his usual, cool tone. "We are going to confront Jacques Bonnaire."

A shiver ran up and down my spine – a chill which I cannot fully attribute to the rain which had seeped into my clothing.

In short order, our carriage eased to a halt. Holmes gestured for Inspector Durand to lead the way and, alighting, we rushed out of the carriage, seeking shelter beneath the inspector's umbrella. We stood on a bridge overlooking both the River Seine, as well as a stone walkway below which ran parallel to the river. Durand informed us that the most likely place for us to find the homeless community was directly under the bridge. Locating a set of stone steps, Holmes pressed on undeterred.

In the darkness and rain which lashed at me, I lost sight of Holmes. I followed close at the inspector's heels, but it felt as if we were headed into some black void. The waters of the Seine looking indistinguishable from the inky darkness which surrounded us. Standing, disoriented and shivering in the pouring rain, it was something of a godsend when I felt myself bump into my friend. He pressed a finger to his lips and, from the folds of his coat, withdrew a bulls-eye lantern. I sheltered my friend's hands from the rain as he struck a match, letting the single point of yellow light pierce through the night.

"Now, follow me, gentlemen," Holmes whispered, "and, pray, keep silent. If he thinks that we are searching for him, then I'm afraid that the bird shall fly the coop."

We turned together as a small herd under the bridge and into the darkness, the pinpoint of light acting as our guide. I perceived, even in the dark, what appeared to be outlines of people shuffling in the night. Just as we had suspected, we were soon surrounded by an assortment of the city's beggars and vagabonds. I have witnessed much strife in my lifetime, but I felt additional pity to see such a concentration of sorrowful beings.

As we moved on, passing knots of people sprawled out on the cold stone, sleeping huddled under makeshift blankets or wrapped in their tattered coats, Holmes stopped suddenly and shone the lamplight on a tall, rail-thin specimen who lay before us. Even in the dark, I could make out something familiar about the man. Though I had never clapped eyes on him, I knew at once that this must be the mysterious apparition who seemed to haunt *Le Chat Noir*.

The creature was some kind of nightmarish vision. He was a tall, gangly-looking man, almost to the point of emaciation. His gaunt face was shrouded, however, by an unruly, unkempt beard, and a mangy, tousled head of long hair cascaded about his face. He was clad in a shapeless brown overcoat, done over in patches and stitched back together as though someone had tried to save it from the precipice of death itself.

Holmes whispered two, haunting words: "Jacques Bonnaire."

Movement came to the man's limbs and he opened one, bloodshot eye, wincing in the light.

"*Qui tu es?*" I heard the man rasp against the wind and rain. Despite my limited knowledge of the French language, I knew that the man was asking us who we were.

"My name will mean nothing to you," Holmes replied, "but this is Inspector Durand of the Paris Police Prefecture, and we have come to arrest you for the murder of M. Andre Dupont and his wife."

It is beyond my skills as a writer to attempt to describe the look of savagery which crossed the man's face at these words. In an instant, the pity for the poor soul who lay before us melted away as he transformed into some uncontrollable beast. I watched, helpless with horror, as he dug into his inner pocket and withdrew a long knife. I caught a glimpse of his shirtsleeve dangling about where his one hand once resided. With what I can only imagine was all of the man's limited strength, he hauled himself up from the ground and attempted an escape. So startled were we by the sudden convulsion which had overcome Bonnaire that Holmes, the inspector, and I completely failed to stop him. Time seemed to slow to a crawl before Holmes cried out, "Quickly! Cut him off on the other side!"

I took to my heels and returned the way we had come, soon finding myself sprinting along the stone causeway which ran along the river. The rain had made the stones into something as slippery as ice, and I almost lost my footing on several occasions. I could barely make out the scene which transpired beneath the bridge, but with little else place to go, I stood my ground and pulled the hammer back on my revolver. I aimed, not hesitating to shoot at whatever leapt out at from the darkness.

I heard the sound of Holmes's voice calling through the night, and I momentarily lowered my gun for fear that I might strike my friend on accident. No sooner had I done so then the figure of Jacques Bonnaire flew out at me from the void. His face contorted into some satanic visage, he screamed like a banshee as the knife flashed in the air, and I let out a gasp as its point caught my coat sleeve. I felt the cold steel against my flesh, followed by a moment of intense, searing pain, as though I'd been struck by a red hot poker. I dropped my gun and pressed a hand to my wound. The man seemed to have lost interest in me entirely, however, for he turned and started to run along the way I just come. I saw him raise the knife high over his head once again, in search of either Holmes or Durand.

In one swift movement, I had gathered up the gun from the ground and squeezed the trigger. The explosion sounded tremendous in the relative quiet of the early morning. The bullet met its mark in the back of Jacques Bonnaire, and I watched as he tumbled to the ground, his weapon falling from his hand.

A second later, I felt a hand on my shoulder and, looking up, I found myself staring at Holmes.

"Tell me that you are not hurt, Watson!" he cried.

He shined the light over me. I caught sight of a gash running along my forearm, but I was numb to the pain. The terror which had surged through my body had let to go of me.

"Jacques Bonnaire," I said breathlessly, "is dead."

That was the last I recall before total darkness overwhelmed me.

When I came to, I was seated upright in my bed in the hotel. Sherlock Holmes and Inspector Durand sat on two chairs at the foot, keeping vigil. I smiled as I came to and made to reach for my watch, only to find that my arm had been wrapped in a sling.

"It's barely five in the morning, Watson," Sherlock Holmes said.

"I haven't felt this bad since the war," I joked. My jest drew a smile from both men.

"Your wound was a superficial one," Durand said. "M. Holmes insisted that we get it dressed, and our physician at the prefecture concurred that we have it attended to . . . as you can see."

"A bloodletting was worth it, I should think," I said, "if we were able to stop Jacques Bonnaire and bring an end to this business."

"I rather think not," Holmes replied darkly.

At these words, the inspector and I both turned to face Holmes, our mouths agape.

"M. Holmes, what are you talking about? Jacques Bonnaire attacked both you and Dr. Watson in his attempt to flee from the police. He was carrying a knife which, I am told, matched the type which was used to sever the hands of M. Dupont and his wife. Are you insinuating that he was innocent all along?”

“Nothing of the kind, Inspector,” Holmes replied, crossing one leg over the other. “In fact, it was Jacques Bonnaire who did sever the hands of the deceased. But it was *not* Bonnaire who killed M. Dupont and his wife.”

“Well then, who is guilty?” I sputtered.

“Bonnaire’s elder daughter,” Holmes replied. “You, Inspector, will know her better as Jeanette the maid.”

“*Mon Dieu*,” Durand said. “M. Holmes, I think you ought to explain yourself.”

“Gladly,” the detective said, as he lit a cigarette. “From the outset of this business, I thought that there was more to the case. M. Dupont showed me two letters which were making threats against his life. The second of these was postmarked London, which meant that whoever sent it had to have been in the city and returned just as quickly when Dupont and his wife decided to flee. Now, ask yourself one question, Inspector: Would Jacques Bonnaire – a man who is minus one hand and who has been inflicted with a near fatal bullet wound – be capable of crossing the channel as quickly as he did in his condition? What’s more, you and I both saw how destitute he was. The man was living on the streets, and would surely have been unable to pay the fare for two consecutive trips, let alone one.

“Knowing that there was a conspirator involved in this affair was only made all the more plausible when I was struck by the presence of two different knife wounds upon the bodies. You yourself asked the question, Inspector: *Why should the murderer carry two different knives when one would be more than efficient?* The simplest answer is that there was more than one murderer involved. And, this became even more likely after an examination of the scene. You will doubtlessly recall that I took a moment to analyze a few shards of glass which I found on the veranda. You assumed that that glass was left after the murderer gained forceful entry into the house. If that had been the case, Inspector, the glass would have been found on the *inside* of the room and not *outside*. That window was broken *after* the murders were committed.

“And, lastly, you told me, Inspector, that the maid, Jeanette, was in the kitchen and heard nothing on the night of the murder. Perhaps you would be so good as to cast your minds back to the afternoon we examined the scene. I returned to the room to fetch my hat and stick –”

“And I clearly heard you moving about upstairs,” I interjected.

“As I figured that you would,” Holmes replied. “Jeanette would have to have been lying when she said that she could not hear anything transpiring upstairs. The design of the house and the kitchen would have placed her almost directly underneath of the room in which her employers were killed. The weapon itself is also connected with the kitchen. It would not be too difficult a task to search the kitchen for the knife, Inspector. And, if you find one, feel free to send it my way. I have developed something of a test which will differentiate blood from a whole host of other substances. Its presence on a blade should not be too difficult a thing to ascertain, given a few hours of concentration.

“As I see it, Jeannette – if her name truly is Jeannette – felt not repulsion for her father when she saw him lying, dying in a hospital bed all those years ago, but a yearning for revenge against the man who had done this. Her disappearance gave her ample opportunity to begin seeking employment in some of the wealthiest houses in France, bringing her into the social circle of M. Andre Dupont. After some years, I rather think that Dupont would fail to recognize the little girl who had once been the daughter of his friend, and he hired Jeannette, completely unaware of the conspiracy against him. Jeannette was working with her father to avenge him and began the persecution, creating fear in the Dupont household. Even when he attempted to flee, she would follow. Dupont told us that he brought only his most trusted staff to England, and you confirmed, Inspector, that Jeannette was in London.

“On the night of the murder, Jeannette aided her father’s entry into the house. She stabbed to death both M. Dupont and his wife before her father began his bloody task. Once she had managed his escape, Jeannette broke the window to convincingly approximate a break-in – inadvertently casting suspicion solely on her father – and then returned to the kitchen. I am glad only that the police investigation has run this long, Inspector. Should Jeannette have tried to flee before now, surely she would have been easily traced. However, I suggest that you apprehend her as soon as possible. News of the action by the river shall spread fast and, with nothing else to lose, I fear that she might do anything in so desperate a situation.”

Durand rose from his chair. “I shall put my best men to it immediately.”

“Excellent,” Holmes replied. The two shook hands. “It has been an absolute pleasure working alongside you on two separate occasions and, should the needs arise, please feel free to contact me again.”

“I shall do so only too happily,” Durand replied. “I shall see myself off. *Au revoir*, gentlemen.”

I found myself feeling in much better sorts during the remainder of the day, and the following morning, Holmes and I found ourselves once more trundling across the French countryside by train. Holmes had remained silent about the case but, as he sat, casting a glance out of the yet again rain-streaked windows, I noticed a certain melancholia descend upon him.

“You have vindicated yourself,” I said trying to coax him from his brown study. “You have seen justice served once again.”

“You are right, Watson,” Holmes replied, “but one cannot go unaffected by what we have witnessed here these past few days. This adventure of the Parisian Butcher has only reinforced to me what a bleak world we inhabit.”

“Well,” I said, “it should then reinforce what a role you must play in it, then. If the world is as bleak and dark as you make it out to be, then surely the world needs a Sherlock Holmes to maintain the light.”

The Adventure of The Long-Lost Enemy

By Marcia Wilson

This story first appeared in the MX Book of New Sherlock Holmes Stories Volume V.

Marcia Wilson is a research writer and freelance illustrator whose style has been described as 'spookily like Gorey'. She currently lives in the Pacific North Wet and has been writing for MX since You Buy Bones was published in 2015. The Anthology challenges keep her on her toes between pursuing her degree and holding down two jobs.

Her blog is https://graspthenettlehard.wordpress.com/ and artwork and photography are on www.deviantart.com/gravelgirty/gallery/. Consider her always game for a challenge in the Canonical Sherlock Holmes world.

Lupe Lawrence is a self-taught fine arts painter who is best known for her landscape and cityscapes paintings. Born in Havana Cuba, she migrated to United States at the age of five and lives in South Florida. Lupe loves to travel and takes inspiration from the cities that she visits. Lupe is a member of Artist Showcase of Palm Beach County, No More Starving Artist, Creative Center of Education, and the Norton Museum. Her artwork has been exhibited in numerous shows throughout Florida and South Carolina.   She enjoys her work and finds great joy and excitement in every project she works on.

www.Arttimesbylupe.com

Artwork size: 18 x 24

Medium: Oil on canvas

F rom *Cox & Kings* (formerly *Cox & Co.*), August 18th, in the Year of Our Lord, MCMXXX:

It is rare to discover a case that demonstrates the editing between Dr. Watson's natural verbose style and the final, polished result from Sir Arthur. The following may be the only one of its kind, being complete in the Doctor's original voice and in possession of no "failed" feats of deduction, nor the other alleged "failures" that led to so many adventures' consignment to the limbo of Cox. From the perspective of History, the worthy Detective will doubtless argue that this case is a paltry show of his abilities. We respectfully posit this manuscript is an insight into the unique methods that he used in solving crimes.

It was late on December the 18th, the Thursday before Christmas. It was my custom to pay my patients a last call before the holidays, and my rounds were circuitous. Frost sprinkled over the black ice-piles in the gutters like anthracite, and it was all any light could do to cast some feeble glow into the black lumps for my safe passage. My old wounds stung as a sour wind blew from the North, bringing flakes the size and texture of Brittany's bitter grey salt to gently rest a carpet over the cobbles. A haze grew around the nimbus of light hissing about the street-lamps as distant carolers practiced their arts, their songs and bells echoing softly back and forth over the valleys and mountains of brick and stone. Here and there winked the few brave lights of Christmas, and wafts of fresh greenery cleansed the nose of soot. More vocal proofs of midwinter rested on the countless playbills: tonight was the night to pay respects for Sebastian among the Eastern Orthodox. A newspaper pasted to the door of a Confectionary's advertised the feast of Winibald, brother of Walpurgis; a crude painting of the saint with his bricklayer's trowel in hand stood by a pretty little ikon of his sister cradling her corn dolly – doubtless a petition for her gentling hand against the storms that had plagued our city from the sea.

The closed-down Indian spice shops were liberally painted with festival. Thanks to my military days, I could read the praises for a peaceful Al-Hijra that had passed on the fourth, and in gold paint were notices of the Day of Ashura, so reminiscent to the Occidental eye of the Jewish Hanukkah. A child from somewhere in the high tenants' housing was singing a high, sweet ululation in praise of the Prophet. Typical of the tolerance of the sub-Continent, across the street the devout were winding down their day-long fast of Durgashtam. Lord Shiva's day had been on the Wednesday, and I could see his serene form behind beaded curtains. A plump Ganesh smiled in a tiny sill, the tip of his broken tusk winking by the light of a single butter-lamp.

In the Chut quarters, the prayers and fastings had ended with rich aromas that would have set an aesthetic's stomach growling. Earlier that day, I had passed this spot and paused to listen to two lively children excitedly relating to their younger siblings the moment when Adam created fire with two stones in blessing to God for the way of the world turning to darkness, then light. Now these children were in bed, their door-way empty but for a curled-up beggar, sleeping with a new loaf of bread inside his arms and two dozing moggies curled for warmth inside the folds of his oversized coat. A Rabbi prayed in a sing-song voice in an attic glowing from tiny seven-tier candelabras.

I passed from one country's street to another: The Irish feted their Saint Flannán with happy toasts. Strains of *O Adoni* wafted through the air where an Armenian chapel practiced late Vespers. I was surprised to find a Zoroastrian colony on my way, and stopped for a moment to regard the humble scenes in the barred glass, thinking of my wanderings between India and the East. These quiet folk were preparing for *Shab-e-Yaldā*, for they see Christmas as the first day of winter. Red being felicitous, they had arranged a brilliant display of tiny Christmas apples and the holly wreaths that could scarce be seen for the amount of scarlet berries and red marzipan pears and pomegranates. They must have been long residents of England, for they knew the trick of forcing the pale pink cherry blossoms to bloom in water. In accordance to their custom, this was the season for beaus to declare their sincerity to their fair maids, and I watched as three laughing sisters hurried out with baskets of fruits and nuts in response to the courtesy of their swains.

I was in a splendid mood despite the weather. London can demonstrate great beauty, and it is possible to discover such treasures if one is willing to see it. I never failed to feel that this season was the one time of year in which all hostilities are suspended; one can feel, in the slimmest hours between the old year and the next, that the entire world is resting content. It is indeed a time where one ought to believe in Peace on Earth.

I opened the door of our sitting room to discover Holmes organising his impressive collection of books.

My friend was well-read. When needs must, he attacked the unknown with gusto, questioned the experts without thought to his incommodities, and absorbed the smallest detail to be used at some unknown moment in the future. The urge to know drove him in the same way that food's finest sauce was the hunger of its diner. The thickest and most obscure tome could be devoured by his hungry eyes in mere days. The dullest sums were easily immortalized in the notes which were never thrown away, for he preferred to move ever-forward in his cases, and ordered his papers to keep memory for him as he cleaned his brain-attic for the next case to come. In concession to this voracity, Mrs. Hudson had granted him an unused room, and he was wasting no time in this advantage. A ziggurat of dictionaries teetered on the bearskin; natural history smothered most of the carpet. In the odd corners and inconvenient nooks, I could see the titles that had caught his fancy: foreign language, climate, bones of long-dead beasts, arguments of colour-vision, mental studies, and many other examples, some too fantastic to mention here. It was a tactile exhibit of his learning, which he preferred to call an omnivorous diet to feed the mind.

"Ah, I thought I heard you," Holmes said. As I navigated the rough seas to my sofa, he emerged laden with more books. These joined the pile on the bearskin and a cloud of dust curled up to rest upon the ceiling.

"I should think that will be enough for the night." He declared, and stepped back to better admire his achievement. With that, he rang for supper and changed the subject for a discussion of the weather and how it was affecting travel. London was always ripe for dull crime, he felt, but the wintry avenues harvested broad challenges for the cleverer brain, and it was to these that he wished to test his mettle.

Our usual after-supper custom was to enjoy one last conversation before the fire. Tonight, this required a bit of meandering around books, and I had to clear out my chair.

Holmes was mellow. He plucked up a small calabash that he prized but never used. He often smiled when he examined it, its secrets known only to him. "There is something about the element of fire which brings out my personal philosopher."

"I suppose that is part of being man, Holmes. We have ever gathered around fire for thought."

"Perhaps the season makes me more contemplative, but I find that strangely comforting." Holmes polished the pipe as he spoke. "I shall be sorting the last shelves this week-end; after that I may require some assistance in moving the boxes, should you feel Marcini's a proper payment."

"I would be pleased to help after I finish my two days for Dr. O'Neill. He is an interesting fellow, if a bit absent-minded, and he has a way of attracting patients with *outré* cases."

The following morning, I found myself standing on the steps of my patron's office with white sheets in the windows and a QUARANTINE card on the door. Through the mail-slot, the housekeeper assured me that the practice was indisposed for the week and I would be free to call upon the gentleman of the house by the following Monday – Wednesday the latest.

As I wryly observed this twist in my funds, a voice called from the London throng. I turned to see Inspector Lestrade, straining his small body in the crowd to get my attention. My second surprise in as many minutes left me speechless and worse the wear for descriptive powers, for he reminded me of nothing so much as a stubborn salmon flailing against the dominant current. In seconds, he was panting on the same lower step as I.

"Heavens! Is this why we couldn't reach Dr. O'Neill?"

I assured him he would eventually return.

"Well, that's a relief!" he exclaimed. "But here, do you know someone who could help the Yard in a pinch?"

"What is the problem?"

"We need a death confirmed to legally cart the remains to our Coroner. We're so overworked, we have been relying on outside contracts, and we pay a day's wage for each trip out."

I assured him that I would be pleased to be useful, if he felt it within my capacity.

The little detective looked up in surprise from batting a cloud of dust off his bowler.

"Bless you, but we'd be pleased to have you any day. I assure you we don't have a lot of cases that deserve your attention, that's true; our medical folk see humdrum work most the time."

I was still absorbing the fact that I had the reputation of being the surgeon's version of Sherlock Holmes in the eyes of the police when Lestrade put his hands to his mouth and whistled for his police cab. Without further ado, I followed him inside and we set off to an inconsequential slum tucked away on the opposite side of Clerkenwell.

The poorer slums of central London have an inexplicable lack of concern compared to the sensationalism of our city's "East of Aldgate". Since Elizabeth's time, the area has quietly upheld admirable creativity with lawlessness. This early an hour, the stacks were fresh and blankets of soot bathed the clouds, turning the day into a dark and sinister forest of buildings. Here and there, windows wanted glass and roofs dearly lacked for new slate, giving the impression of winking, ragged-cropped giants.

"They usually send Gregson over here," Lestrade complained as he kept up a futile dusting of his coat. "But he's out with the same sick, sulphur onions piled up to his chin! I am sorry this won't be a very interesting bit, but most of our days are thus."

"I shan't complain for the chance to work, and you feel it is within my abilities."

"It is unpleasant if simple. We have a matter of a long death."

"A long death?"

"A man died and his brother didn't take him from their rooms out of fear the body would be put to infernal use – oh, you needn't look so! I didn't mean cults. That's really quite rare. Tends to be the spoilt-up lads that conduct that sort of nonsense, and they hardly ever kill anyone on purpose."

I felt Lestrade's profession was not as boring as he believed. "What did he fear?"

"Oh, the usual. Those ghoulish students, or collectors wanting a fresh corpse to study. What with the recent stories of cremation, there's *that* worry amongst the poor." Lestrade stared out the window with a lordly air. "The newspapers think they can't afford to properly put the dead to rest, you know. But I know that's not the case. They'll starve if it sets a loved one to rights. And here of all places? No, they have been hard-used by others, and will do their best to keep one final indignity from the grave. This poor fellow was a common faith-healer of sorts, and he had some regard in the back-alleys for his way with thrush. It would be most unlikely someone would steal his remains – they're more likely to nick a piece of his clothing or a clip of his hair."

I wondered at his angry expression, which with his suddenly jutted-out jaw and crimped brow, gave the impression of a short-tempered bulldog. "His brother hid him from burial?"

"Who is now dead himself. Oh, not inside the room! Dear me, I've gotten ahead of myself, just like Holmes says." He shook his head sadly. "Tommy Shenk was a coal-swinger. Brother Jonas stayed home and earned a few bits with his faith-healing. It was an odd arrangement but it worked for them, but last night Tommy was killed at the docks. Too many new sailors fresh to the port and too much green beer and raw rum. Four dead in all, and six more abed! We thought we were taking poor Jonas news of his brother's death when we found out the hard way he was already talking to him from his side of Creation." In agitation, the little detective slapped his gloves upon his knee. "What a mess! We're worn thin enough as it is. Shenks' body was being kept in an old earthen cellar, and that whole map is bad for outbreaks. Typhoid, cholera, measles, every pox . . . what would happen if the waters were tainted again?" We both shuddered. "And it is Grim House, to make things worse."

I confess I felt a thrill, for everyone in London knows that place. A hundred years ago, the Grim name was revered in our architecture, but that respect ended with the last of the line's two sons. The eldest, Basil, was considered "The Good Brother" for his tireless kindness, but younger brother Garland was made of sterner stuff and dabbled, it was whispered, in the lucrative trade of child-selling. Many swore he was the true inspiration for Dickens' Scrooge, and the treatment of his four sons had been the stuff of legends.

Basil eventually grew sick enough of his family that he set his fortunes in Australia. Before leaving forever, he bound his brother by his last will to properly house his nephews. Garland had salved his fury by carving their house into four meagre-thin tenements. The sons reacted to this largess by following their uncle's example and dispersing. Grim spent the rest of his days as Scrooge would have done without Marley: alone, unloved, and unmourned. His solicitors tried to gain some financial solace from his work, and the curious came for miles to look upon this lump of stone, a fitting mausoleum to the absence of charity. I myself had glimpsed the nefarious James Tracks, his surviving partner in their vile trade. Tracks used his rat-catching trade to discover – and then steal – promising children from families too poor to protest. His breeding of yellow rats as pets for the wealthy gave him the chance to look over a house from the inside, and return later to rob it clean. Such was the terror behind his name that none dared help the Yard or even Holmes in hunting him.

We soon set our feet upon a crumbling street too narrow for the cab. Our way was overcast with a double row of glowering brick buildings and plain-scrubbed panes, and the air reeked of carbolic and boiled vinegar.

I prided myself in knowing London, but this was the first time I saw rats in broad daylight, if daylight this could be called, pinched to starving skeletons. Hoardes flowed over the kerb and street and paused in the narrow alleys to stare us with cold red eyes. In the thick fogs and stifling atmosphere, these streets were more congenial for the spirits and melancholy than the living. Rarely have I seen any slum without a congestion of humanity, but the people ran before us into the fog, and dogs barked incessantly.

"They know me," Lestrade muttered. The little detective scowled at dark nooks as though they meant something to him. "This is the worst of it. The sewer was closed on a cholera outbreak and they started rinsing the rats out, but the cold weather damaged the pipefittings . . . people are staying inside now until the vermin's cleared out, but right now I have more faith in rat-catchers like old Tracks supplying the pits." He sunk deeper into the scarf about his throat, angry that a man of the law would be forced to support an illegal cruelty. "If these buildings were wood, I fear someone would have cleansed it with fire long ago."

"Do they fear you more than the rats?"

"Not likely. Mind you, they are proud and often straight as a tack! They work hard to help themselves. You'd be amazed at the cleverness they possess, for they'll run right at a problem to solve it. But it is cold, most of the able-bodied are away on any jobs they can find, and . . . well. Times are hard." He shook his head in pity. "Christmas is the one time they can hope to make the year's money, and the rent will rise on Boxing Day."

The dirty mist parted to show four impossibly narrow, rib-thin houses. There was barely enough room for the stairs and a stingy bottle-window on each floor.

Lestrade rightfully understood my expression.

"They say good and evil both lives on after the man dies, but I've never heard a single good thing about Garland Grim." The detective shuddered. "He built this over a freshet that fed the Stamford, so no-one owns the building further than its earthen floor! In other words, small as his sons' rooms would be, they couldn't lengthen it by digging further down – and there's no means by which they could add further rooms on top. The neighbors still refer to him as "Grudging Garland.""

It was unlike Lestrade to deviate from business into personal gossip, but I could tell he was at the end of his wits over the affair. "We'll be going to the one on the far end there." He pointed with his chin, where two Constables guarded the doorway.

Up close, Grim House was dull with filth piled upon the paths between the listless street-sweepers and crawlers. The stench was marked and Lestrade warned me to keep my handkerchief across my face. He scurried over the slimy cobblestones to halloa. Lestrade's Constables straightened as we drew closer and tapped their brims.

"There you are, Balan. What news?"

"Some of the neighbors were nosin' about agin, but Ardalean and I put 'em back, sir."

"They should have nosed about weeks ago! This is a hazard!"

As they spoke, I caught the stench from inside the building and held my breath. "How could anyone have not reported this?" I cried. "Is there no Inspector of Nuisances?"

"They cannot come in without permission," Lestrade said through the muffling of his face. "The other tenants' wishes are not good enough when everything is all legally hide-bound. I appealed to the Magistrate as soon as I could, but until this is settled, these poor folk are living all doubled up like bees in a hive in the untainted three quarters of the house."

As this was being relayed, a bony driver squeaked up with a narrow van marked for the city's mortuary. It must have been designed for these alleys, for it was mostly canvas and too lean for more than the horse, the driver, and a coffin.

"Finally!" The little detective clapped his gloved hands in relief and rocked on the balls of his feet. "I'm taking Dr. Watson down. Tell them to be ready, for there shall be no time to waste!"

The constables looked at me in admiration. I was certain it was undeserved.

I followed Lestrade down a yard-thin flight of stairs. He had to inch slowly with Ardalean's bull's-eye, for it was dark and the wood creaked and moaned under our lightest steps. In the darker corners, I gleamed an astounding number of cobwebs. A dusty rope caught me in the face.

"They spin as soon as we walk through 'em too," Lestrade grumbled. "The poorest folk still use cobwebs for bandages." He lifted his walking-stick to knock down a large netting. "Especially for stab wounds. One sees a lot of blood around here. Here we are."

The cellar was small and rude and empty, save for a heavy red carpet upon which perched the coffin on a crude sawbucks bier. A single candlestick rested at the wall, prepared to light for a Christmas that would never come.

"I couldn't tell you if he died by fair means or foul, but I'm hoping you can verify that he has died. From there we can take the remains to our morgue." With that he set his jaw and lifted the lid of the coffin, holding his breath and hastily backing away.

I held my handkerchief over my nose and made a quick work of it. "He is clearly dead, Mr. Lestrade."

"Thank you!" Lestrade rolled his eyes in comical relief. "Thank you, and thank you. I am not asking you to make the determination of death – that shall be Dr. Pennywraith's duty, if the court deems it necessary. They might freeze him first to keep the air down."

"I would not know where to begin in determining cause of death." One last glance at the unsightly contents of the box and Lestrade returned the lid. "Most signs would be erased."

"I never know what the court will want from the Yard," was the weary sigh. "Lord help us! I simply do not understand." He shook his head from side to side. "The things people do. And those neighbors – pah!"

"Curiosity is normal, is it not?"

"I'd agree, but they were probably nosing about because of the rumours old Ghastly left a fortune in his house. They couldn't find it in their quarters, so they have decided it must be here, and as I said, they know their rent is upping."

"Lestrade, you appear to be very suspicious of human nature."

"Thank you." The little detective grunted as was forced to step closer to the coffin in order to put the lid back. He stopped across the clasp, and a strange look came over his pale face.

"What is the matter?"

"My foot just went down in something. Well, there's nothing for it."

I bent to see that his left foot was inside a depression in the carpet directly under the centre of the coffin. "For what, Lestrade?"

"I'm going to see what that is as soon as the lads take the coffin out of here."

The stairs were narrow and the coffin, awkward. At long last the wagon was off and the Constables were back on duty outside the front step.

I held the lantern as Lestrade moved the sawbucks and slowly rolled the carpet a bit at a time across the hard-packed floor. He suddenly gave a cry of satisfaction: below the spot where the corpse rested, a deep-set brick had been removed and replaced with hasty hands, allowing a half-inch gap between.

"Look at that, Doctor!" He pointed to the brick.

I did not understand his triumph. The brick had been written on with a sharp implement, such as a nail-tip. Hours of labour had gone into the careful engraving of a complex rune that, once I adjusted the lantern, could read:

> *Thou horseman and footman, you are coming under your hats; you are scattered! With the blood of Jesus Christ, with his five holy wounds, thy barrel, thy gun and thy pistol are bound; sabre, sword, and knife are enchanted and bound, in the name of God the Father, the Son, and the Holy Ghost Amen*

"What does it mean?"

"The missing fortune, I'll be bound. This is an old rune against thieves." The little professional sought with his gloved fingers, then yanked upwards, bringing the brick out of the little pit. At the bottom was a grimy oilskin. "Dear me, I wasn't expecting this." Lestrade tugged open the throat of a musty purse and shook out a handful of tarnished coin. "Real guineas! And eight of them! More than enough to slit a throat."

"A low enough sum against a life."

"Oh, I agree, but this won't be the end of it." Lestrade sighed and dropped the purse to his lap. "If one fortune is found in the cellar, there'll be rumours that two more are hiding in the walls, and who's to say? Desperation makes a person clever. But this is likely the Shenks' fortune, and not Grimey's."

"How can you be so certain?"

"He hated banks. There would be much more than this. Also, this swag-hole has been freshly used." Lestrade rapped on the brick. He sadly replaced the money in the purse and tied the throat up tight. "I suppose that explains why no one ever saw both brothers outside – one was staying home to guard the money."

"But he died."

"Tommy used his body to guard the money." Lestrade nervously fidgeted with his walking-stick. "Sanctity of death is one of the few things people respect here. They wouldn't have disturbed him . . . I might have known when I saw this carpet in a basement . . . too nice for a dirt floor."

"This carpet is not too fine for a brother's funeral parlour."

"It drew my attention when we came down here – I should have listened to my eyes." Lestrade was very glum at his self-chastisement, and it was all I could do not to tell him that I had seen this expression many times by Holmes.

"What happens to the money?"

"Escheats to the Crown, if it isn't disqualified as being disproven as their property."

"But it is under their floor!"

"And the property line ends at the earth. *Bona vacantia* is a nightmare, but it will see to their proper burial!" He tucked the purse inside a large pocket sewn inside the lining of his coat and looked in the crevice one last time. "Now what is this?"

I peered down. A whiff of something indefinably musty, and mildewed like a long-abandoned grave, blew into our faces. Cobweb wobbled before our eyes and Lestrade brushed it aside, angling the lantern without much hope. At last we succeeded when I pulled out the hand-mirror used for my examinations and we reflected the lamp-light into the hole, which I could see, was not a hole at all but a black wooden pipe.

"This is one of the original pipes of London!"

"An alderwood?" I marveled, for I had heard of but never seen the log pipes built to ferry water throughout the older parts of the city. "It is in poor enough condition that I can believe it was set over a hundred years ago."

"Alderwood's still being used in the cow-country where I was born. It stays good if wet and never splinters. It only falls apart when it dries out."

"It must have dried when a stream was diverted."

"Yes." Lestrade was scowling, and even though I could not see his face, I could hear his unhappiness. "This is very queer, Doctor. There appears to be something clogging it up . . . ." He poked and prodded with a persistence I found puzzling, and I said so.

"You wouldn't believe some of the swags we've found." With a grunt, he pulled out a well-preserved walking-stick of ebony, a matching peg-leg, and finally a wad of many-waxed and oiled skins well wrapped around a small book bound of cracked and crazed black leather, the pages uneven and thin.

Pow-Wows
Or
The Long-Lost Friend

"Someone wasn't taking chances, eh, Doctor? Saw a lot of these during the American War."

"But what is it?"

"Oh, just a spellbook." Lestrade coughed. "Let's get out of this! I'll beg to the Inspector of Nuisances to get on down here with his zymotic steam-oven . . . ."

Outside, the light was better. "Some of this appears to be a low form of German."

"It might be that, Doctor. It might also be a cipher. Those books are private, you know. They don't like the wrong eyes reading personal words." Lestrade shrugged. "A lot of countries have them banned outright. Or they'll just burn them. They – " He suddenly jumped back and swore as a blotched rat with a short tail staggered out of a narrow hole in the foyer wall and ran out the door in terror.

I chuckled and expected Lestrade to make a comment about rats, but he was staring where it had vanished with a strange expression.

"Lestrade?"

He laughed self-consciously and rubbed at his eyes. "Up too many hours, that's what. Eyes playing tricks."

"I can assure you that really was a rat."

"So it was!" He laughed again and it was a forced, false gaiety before his entire face changed to dread. "Doctor, do you think Mr. Holmes might be available for a bit of work? There's something about this that I don't like. He could make sense of it all, I'm sure."

I bade my farewells, accepting Lestrade's offer of a cab as part of my fee for the day and a promise to return, with or without Holmes, as an answer. The weather had lightened somewhat, but a light dance of ice had touched that larger streets. At a snail's crawl we half-slid, half-hobbled to Baker Street, where Holmes was finishing up a linseed-oil application to his now empty bookshelves.

"I do apologise for the smell, Watson."

My composure shattered. After a few minutes, I was calm enough to explain myself.

"You earned your pay after all, and with a story."

"A story and perhaps a diversion from your books?"

"It is a case with some interesting points about it."

"I wish I knew why. Lestrade was badly affected, but it was only a rat!"

"There is no knowledge without effort." Holmes rose. "You are chilled to the bone, and have time for a sandwich and coffee as I review a few notes." With that he plucked up a small brown journal perching on the books and paged through it. I followed his advice and had barely finished when Holmes leaped to his feet with a laugh of satisfaction.

"Watson, would you mind accompanying me to this puzzle? We need only to make a brief stop and send a wire to an old friend whom I feel will be most helpful!"

There was a peculiar smile to his face that I found untranslatable. When I asked he only shrugged.

"The best Christmas gifts can be years in the making, Watson."

Lestrade was waiting outside when we returned, and his countenance had taken a turn for the worse since our brief parting.

"I am all right." He tried to wave me off, but the open concern from his Constables compelled me to examine him. He was grey-green from some sort of shock, and the sweat on his brow was ice-cold. It was almost unthinkable to imagine him so moved after his stoicism in the cellar. "It's . . . we just found another body."

"Not much of one, if I may say," Balan spoke up. "All sticks inside a bag of skin."

"Too true." Lestrade suddenly sank to the bottom step and put his head in his hands. It was quite unlike the little professional to demonstrate any weakness before his Constables, but they were looking ill themselves.

"I assure you Watson and I will not place ourselves in any risk. If you could describe to me what you saw?"

"There wasn't much to see," Lestrade protested weakly.

"Nevertheless, I would trust your eyes."

Lestrade took a restorative breath of smelling salts and braced himself. "After Dr. Watson left, I was worried about that alderwood pipe. It isn't strictly the building's property, but we have a very ticklish Inspector of Nuisances, and if I couldn't convince him this wasn't a case of just another poor wretch and a long death, he'd be slower to bring down the disinfectors. There are at least twenty children living in the rest of the rooms, plus the elderly ones who can't get out, so I was hoping to find more proof in case it all came down completely to the Magistrate."

"You were trying to prevent an epidemic," I assured him. "Disease sweeps through these places like fire."

"Yes, well, that was what I was thinking, and there was at least one rat running in and out. So I took the lamp and your mirror and poked around that pipe again. I didn't see a thing, but I ran my walking-stick into it, and found something giving way. It looked like old leather. It took almost a quarter-hour, but I finally fished up a corner close enough that I could grab it and pull it up to the hole. What I thought was a leather bag wasn't a bag. It was a loose flap of skin. This poor soul, whoever it was, had been stuffed down that pipe years ago."

"You were quicker than I expected, Lestrade. But I must congratulate you for being quick and resourceful. I shouldn't worry about finding the missing leg – Basil Grim had it buried with a proper funeral at St. Mary's graveyard forty years ago after that unfortunate accident with the horse. The peg-leg you found was undoubtedly his."

Lestrade went from green to white. The police turned looks of dumbfounded awe upon my friend.

"Mr. Holmes," Lestrade said very slowly and clearly once his breath returned, "Had you been born sooner, they would have hanged you with the Yorkshire Witch."

"How did you know that was Basil Grim, sir?" Balan gasped. "And the missing leg?"

"Come, come, you know my methods." Holmes rose to his feet. "Now I believe I see our old friend Shinwell Johnson puffing up. He was the last man to see Basil Grim alive, and I am certain he is quite capable of identifying the remains."

"Porky Johnson?" Lestrade jumped up as the old criminal staggered to us, a swarm of dirty little urchins chattering and clustering about his battered working-slops.

"Is it true?" Johnson gasped. His tiny blue eyes blinked frantically under a fringe of hair that had he had been in the process of combing when Holmes's news came. Dried shaving-lather spotted his neck, and a flannel night-shirt peeped at the neck of his hastily-bound coat. "Did you find him?"

"I shall not take credit for another man's work, Porky. We have Lestrade for the credit."

The little detective could not have been more astonished when the old criminal grabbed up his hand and pumped it in gratitude.

"Bless you, bless you!" he cried.

"For what?" Lestrade shouted. "Holmes, what?"

"It means I was right and poor Mr. Basil was murdered all those years ago!" The stocky old criminal mopped at his face.

"His disappearance was suspect." Holmes added. "Johnson was one of the 'sons' and heirs to Grim House. Rather, one of the children kidnapped and made to serve Garland and his loathsome partner, Tracks the Rat-Catcher."

"Is this true?" Lestrade demanded hotly. "Man, why did you never say anything to us?"

"I am not from nice society, as you well know," the man answered with dignity.

"I know old Carpet-Tracks," Lestrade scowled. "I assure you we are always looking to catch him in the act!"

"He must have known you were too close to his old crime," Johnson grumbled. "No-one's seen a whit of him in weeks. Gone to ground, I'll be bound!"

"If his infernal rats are around, he can't be far. We'll find him, Porky." Lestrade pulled at his hat in agitation. "But you are positive you can identify the remains as Basil Garland's?"

"Just look close upon the head, sir. He had a left green glass eye."

"It would be common knowledge if he had one."

"It was Thuringian-made, with the stamp in the back. Two loops over a squat crossed T. 'Twas my job as a boy to wash it for him every night."

Lestrade's expression became positively stone-like, and even Holmes was surprised when he reached into his pocket and pulled out a shattered green glass eye.

"You have convinced me," he said quietly. "Mr. Holmes, if I may beg your pardon, I shall be asking questions of my witness."

Holmes was wordless until we returned home. After a quiet meal, he again plucked up his calabash for polishing. I joined him before the fire.

"Thirty years is a long time to solve a case, Watson." Holmes finally spoke. "The rat-catcher is still free, but I have my nets out as well as the police and he cannot be far. Betrayed by the special rats he breeds with pale fur and short, furry tails for fine ladies – we will find that beast before the year is finished, I'll be sure of that."

"Lestrade was as eager to snare him as you.'

"The child-sellers are beyond redemption. Fagin was an angel compared to the Tracks of the world, and I had no choice but to watch and wait. Were I endowed with powers of authority to match my intellect, there would be no criminal free from my hand.'

"How did you know of this?"

"I first met Porky as a torn man, wanting to reform, but also resigned that he could not find the proof that his kindly old master, Basil Grim, had been murdered. Who believes such an unworthy child? He was stolen with no memory of his past outside of his name, which comes from the Jewish quarters. His memory was much eroded from time, and what I suspect was the trauma of witnessing Brother Garland striking his own flesh and blood dead – dead, he recalls, because Basil wrote the will to provide for Porky and the other children.

"After the murder, Garland enlisted his partner James Tracks the Rat-Catcher to hide the body, and Porky was forced to help. Suspecting his own end, he ran away with his mind fogged in terror. It was years before he could recall a few details, other than Basil was stowed inside a large wooden pipe with his ebony walking-stick. The best I could do was keep a written record of what he could remember, and slowly piece together the smallest clues in hopes of drawing a larger picture."

"I begin to see. The Shenks must have dug into the cellar to hide their small wealth and re-discovered the pipe. They used it as a cache, not thinking that anything else was inside the pipe."

"To be discovered in turn by Lestrade."

"But you were the only one capable of seeing this for what it was."

Holmes held up the little brown book. "I am proud of my library, Watson, but I confess my vanity for what I have written. This is a compendium of all the Porky Johnsons in my life, all the murders, thefts, and imaginable crimes witnessed by the un-witnessable. Crime being what it is, the wicked often repeat themselves, and many are the cases where I have solved a crime because I have taken the word of a little street-urchin seriously, or listened to the babble of a woman in a madhouse. A parallel incident here – a suspiciously familiar circumstance there – and I have a new crime solved with an old crime. If not solved, at least brought to some sort of justice. There are many hard-earned victories, Watson, in which I can tell my applicant that justice of a sort has been served, if not the justice they had hoped to see.

"For I am the judge, Watson. And it is my right to declare if a person's testimony is worth hearing." He was smiling as he rested the little brown book upon a world atlas. "My belief in him aided Porky immensely in his departure from crime. Now he may rest this Christmas, vindicated that he was not imagining murder. To-night is the night of *O Radix Jesse*, and I am struck by the poetry of the closing lines, '*come and deliver us, and delay no longer*'."

"It would seem that you have granted yourself a Christmas gift, Holmes – I have rarely seen you so content."

"Ah, my gift will be the pinch of Tracks! But Lestrade has given me a nice consolation." Holmes produced the cracked book of *The Long-lost Friend*. "I asked him if I might keep this, and he was all too eager to oblige. It was below the legal property-line, and a policeman who brings in a book of witchcraft will not be taken seriously by his peers! The rats would soon eat up the paper and glue. I have always wanted one of these books, but they are guarded jealously . . . aha! Here is a fine one, Watson! A charm to immobilise thieves! Shall we try it out? But is that the bell? At this hour?"

We turned to our open doorway, for we could already hear Mrs. Hudson's exclamations and Lestrade's uneven stride hammering up the steps.

"Holmes!" Lestrade clutched the door-frame for support. "You said you wanted word as soon as we found Tracks! Well, we found him when the disinfectors followed the alderwood to the next building over! Dead as can be, picked clean by his own rats! Pennywraith said he must have died in his sleep, and the disinfectors have threatened to quit because the rats found we'd unblocked the pipe when we removed Basil's remains and they're running all over the place now and – I say! Do you think this is funny, Holmes?"

Addendum

Dr. Watson attached notes to the back of this manuscript explaining that a strange sort of justice had prevailed on behalf of the poor tenants of Grim House. Trask's unique rats were swiftly captured and, with the notoriety of the case, became more valuable than ever, leaving the people with the financial means to keep up with the higher rent upon Boxing Day. He understood that they made meek enough pets, but were absolute terrors in the rat-fighting rings. Eventually Shinwell Johnson was deemed the heir and lowered the rent even further, wishing no profit from a terrible past.

Sherlock Holmes
And The Other Eye

By Richard Dean Starr and E R Bower

This story first appeared in Sherlock Holmes – The Crossovers Casebook.

Richard Dean Starr has written or edited more than 200 articles, columns, stories, books, comics, screenplays, and graphic novels since the age of seventeen. His original fiction and non-fiction has appeared in magazines and newspapers as varied as Cemetery Dance, Science Fiction Chronicle, The Southeast Georgian, The Camden County Tribune, Suspense Magazine, and Starlog, among others. His licensed media tie-in stories have appeared in anthologies including Hellboy: Odder Jobs, Kolchak: The Night Stalker Casebook, Tales of Zorro, and The Lone Ranger Chronicles, just to name a few. In addition, Starr co-authored Unnaturally Normal, the first Kolchak: The Night Stalker / Dan Shamble: Zombie P.I. team up comic book with New York Times bestselling author Kevin J. Anderson and co-edited the Captain Action comics line with Matthew Baugh. As an industry-leading feature script consultant, Starr has contributed to produced films with multi-million-dollar budgets starring such acclaimed actors as Malcolm McDowell, Tom Sizemore, Amber Tamblyn, Haley Joel Osment, Costas Mandylor, Robert Culp, Richmond Arquette, and Zach Galifianakis, among others.

E.R. Bower began her publishing career as an editorial intern with prominent indie publisher Les Figues Press and went on to become a professionally-published author, editor, and consultant for fiction, non-fiction, motion picture, and poetry projects. Her first professional poetry sale, "James Brown in Springtime," appeared in Say It Loud: Poems About James Brown, released by Whirlwind Press in 2011. Following that, she co-authored several media tie-in stories and novellas, including "Sherlock Holmes and the Other Eye", published in Sherlock Holmes: The Crossovers Casebook, edited by the late retro-pulp editor Howard Hopkins, and "The Masque" in The Lone Ranger Chronicles. The latter volume was the first anthology of original Lone Ranger stories in the seventy-nine-year history of the beloved character and included contributions from multiple New York Times and USA Today bestselling authors. In addition to her poetry and fiction work, Bower is also co-editor, with Richard Dean Starr, of The Further Crossovers of Sherlock Holmes, an anthology featuring all-new stories by top writers from the worlds of film, television, and literature.

JR Linton is an unique artist who's talent spans many mediums. He works in pencils, paint, clay, cameras, digital computer art and even skin. His work embodies the Lowbrow art movement with focus on nerd culture, hot rods and pin-ups. He is an award winning tattoo artist and owns Ink and Pistons tattoo shop and co-owns and curates SlushBox Art Gallery in West Palm Beach.

www.SlushBox.com

Artwork size: 11x14

Medium: Acrylic on Board

Linton

"We never sleep," I said, wearily, staring down at the newspaper spread across my lap. The date below the masthead read Tuesday, May the third. Had I been asked what day it was before receiving that morning's edition of the *Times*, which I had yet to read, I might have sworn that it was actually Monday the second.

"Try not to be melodramatic, Watson," said Sherlock Holmes, gazing out through the front window of our sitting room on the second floor of 221B, Baker Street. "While it is true I require less rest than you do, on the whole I would say you sleep quite well, and often."

"It certainly doesn't feel that way," I said. "We have closed not less than three cases over the past two weeks, the last one just this morning, and during that time I have managed to obtain, on average, less than four hours of sleep each night. I think you can agree that is not very much at all, Holmes!"

"And prior to the two weeks in question? How many hours a night did you manage then?"

"About seven. But that is neither here nor there, I must get my rest!"

"Seven hours or four," said Holmes, idly, tamping some tobacco into the bowl of his pipe. "I see no great advantage in one over the other. I would suggest that you consider taking a cold bath, Watson."

"A cold bath? You must be joking!"

"In my experience," said he, lighting the briar-root, "the benefits of submersing oneself in well-chilled water can be substantial."

He drew in a deep breath, held it for a time, and then exhaled. For a moment his head was encircled by a small cloud of ash-gray smoke and the room quickly filled with the scent of bergamot and sandalwood.

"I daresay a cold bath might also help to nullify your persistent desire for marriage," he added, tipping his head to study the various pedestrians making their way along Baker Street.

I frowned. "I can't possibly see how a cold bath would have anything at all to do with my relationship with Mary. Nor do I fathom the connection between chilled water and rest."

My friend looked up for a moment, and I thought a fleeting smile appeared ever so briefly on his long, angular face. Then I wondered if it was anything other than my fatigued, over-active imagination at work.

"It is hardly a unique insight, Watson," Holmes said. "It is a well-known fact that prodigious amounts of cold water *do* have a tendency to 'wake' one up, in every sense of the word."

His tone, which could often be sardonic, was suspiciously lacking in obvious irony. I grimaced. Before I could formulate an appropriate reply, he had already returned his attention to the street below.

"Fascinating," he said, suddenly. I saw him take an uncommonly quick draw on his briar-root and then exhale it equally quickly. "Most interesting."

He turned back to me and frowned. "It appears that sleep, let alone reading the paper, will have to elude you for some time to come, Watson. I suspect we are about to have yet another client."

"This seems a bit soon, Holmes," I said, earnestly. "Would you not consider it prudent to allow some time to recuperate from our recent endeavors?"

"I think not," he replied, seemingly unaffected by my momentary distress. "Even if I did wish to grant you the sleep you desire, this person is of...particular interest to me."

I was momentarily taken aback by this declaration. There are very few men or women for whom Sherlock Holmes would express a unique fascination. Among them were the alluring and dangerous Irene Adler, and the nefarious Professor James Moriarity. For various reasons, I knew that the individual in question could not be either one of them.

"How do you know that this person will become a client, Holmes?"

"Elementary," he said, removing the pipe from his lips and staring thoughtfully into the bowl. "The visitor that Mrs. Hudson is presently receiving is none other than the notorious occultist, Aleister Crowley."

Holmes pointed to the newspaper in my lap. I looked down and saw that morning's headline, which in my fatigued state, I had as yet failed to read:

Sir Fallowgrove Dead; Famed Occultist Sought!

Below it was a drawing of the infamous Mr. Crowley, which in its dark and scowling representation, made him appear more than a bit sinister. To the right of the sketch was a second column topped by an equally sensationalistic headline:

Famed 'Other Eye' Blue Diamond Missing!

"I find it unlikely," said Holmes, "that such a man—especially one in what appears to be his present predicament—would seek us out simply for afternoon tea, Watson."

* * *

"'Death,'" said Aleister Crowley, regally, "is the wish of some, the relief of many, and the end of all.' And that, Mr. Holmes, is the essence of why I find myself on your doorstep today, for I fear that death may soon be the end of me!"

Sherlock Holmes sat back in his chair, taking long draughts from his briar-root and studying the man who sat on the settee across from him. I was seated to one side, listening intently and watching both men with equal fascination.

Crowley, whom I had read much about in the press, was more impressive than one might have expected from a man of his dubious reputation, and not particularly sinister at all. I noted with some surprise that he was dressed as well as any Mayfair gentleman, in a conservative and well-tailored suit. His dark brown hair was parted high and severely on the left, which served only to emphasize the pale and generally unhealthy pallor of his skin. Most notably, I could not help but observe that his pudgy, round and vaguely aristocratic face bore an expression of unshakeable confidence and conviction. Even when seated, he exuded a strange magnetism not unlike that of Sherlock Holmes himself.

"And was it not Lucius Seneca who also wrote, 'It is the power of the mind to be unconquerable'?" said Holmes, evenly. "It occurs to me that a man with powers such as those you claim to possess would be immune not only to death, but to the mundane efforts of such entities as Scotland Yard."

I searched my friend's expression for any signs of mockery, but his hawk-like features remained as implacable as ever. Crowley's face darkened for the briefest of moments, and in his keen eyes I saw a quick flash of immense rage. Then it passed so quickly that it might not have been there at all.

"Well, Mr. Holmes," said he, with a sudden smile that was disconcertingly affable, "you appear to be everything I've heard—and undoubtedly more. I hope, then, that you will consider my case. Have you by chance examined this morning's edition of the *Times*?"

"I have."

I was not aware that Holmes had already read the paper, which was now draped face-down over my knee. When I had come through the door that morning it had still been resting on the foyer rug, apparently untouched.

My confusion must have been evident upon my face, for Holmes noticed this and said, "That is why too much sleep leaves a man always a step behind, Watson, and why I counsel so much against it."

"But why," I asked, peevishly, "would you put the newspaper back down as if unread?"

"I have observed," replied Holmes, "that discovering a fresh newspaper each morning is an important part of your daily ritual. In fact, you seem to find it quite energizing. Given your excessive dependency upon sleep, I believe such a small and harmless delusion to be beneficial to your daily vitality."

I opened my mouth to protest, but upon reflection, found that I could not disagree with him. Reading the newspaper after it had already been paged through by other hands was not nearly as satisfying to me as being the first one to open it. I was loath to admit this fact out loud to my friend, however. I was also abruptly aware that it was uncommon for us to have such an exchange in the presence of a client, so therefore I elected to remain silent.

"As you may have read," interjected Crowley, impatiently, "the police have convinced the editors at the *Times* to help turn the public against me by suggesting that, as the so-called 'Wickedest Man Alive', I was somehow involved in the theft of the blue diamond as well as the death of Sir Francis Fallowgrove."

"More precisely," said Holmes, "the paper suggests that you performed certain spells which caused the stone to vanish and subsequently led to Fallowgrove's demise." He stared intently at our visitor. "Would you consider this to be a true statement of fact, Mr. Crowley?"

Our visitor blinked once. Then he laughed, sardonically. "Oh, most certainly! In fact, you may not be aware of this, Mr. Holmes, but I actually *am* in the routine habit of casting spells which kill everything from annoying children to the occasional small pet—especially those that bark incessantly."

He grimaced and shook his head in apparent disgust.

"Come now, I'm astonished that a rational man such as yourself could even consider such an idea. Really!"

"I did not suggest that I believe such a thing to be probable, or even possible," replied Holmes. "In point of fact, I have no belief or trust in the supernatural whatsoever. However, whether or not *you* believe that you are capable of such an act, and that certain others might agree, is entirely relevant to the present situation, I think. After all, Mr. Crowley, a man's actions are most often predicated by his beliefs."

He stood up and studied his pipe again for a moment, then stared intensely at Crowley. Our infamous visitor attempted to meet his gaze with equal force. However, following the example of my friend, from whom I have learned much of the art of close observation, I immediately took notice of a faint tremble at the corner of Crowley's mouth. He was, I realized, a man barely in control of some deeper fear.

"Let me be frank, Mr. Crowley," continued Holmes. "Although the *Times* implied that you are being sought for questioning, I am certain that Inspector Lestrade of Scotland Yard has, in fact, ascertained your whereabouts and shall be arriving at my door any moment, fully intending to place you under arrest."

Crowley's already pale countenance whitened even more, an effect I would have previously thought impossible, and in the somewhat muted light of the sitting room, his skin seemed momentarily translucent, each vein as clear against his face as the lines on some ancient parchment.

"But Holmes," I asked, puzzled by his conviction, "how could you possibly be sure of such a thing? And in all of London, why would Inspector Lestrade come *here* looking for Mr. Crowley?"

"When Mr. Crowley made his appearance," said Holmes, "I could not help but notice that he had been followed by one of Inspector Lestrade's sergeants. That very man, wearing a rather plain suit and bowler hat, immediately began skulking about on one of the stoops across the street."

Crowley started to reply, but before he could utter a single word the pounding of several pairs of boots sounded on the stairs, followed by a powerful and sustained knocking on the door of our apartment.

"And there you have it," said Sherlock Holmes. "It seems that the good Inspector has indeed arrived."

* * *

The entrance of Inspector Lestrade was uncharacteristically dramatic, something I knew appealed to my friend, although I also knew that he was not likely to openly betray such an emotion.

When Holmes opened the door, the plainclothed Sergeant that he had noticed earlier entered first, followed by a uniformed officer and another, stouter man whom I did not recognize. Then Inspector G. Lestrade made his entry, his penetrating eyes peering out from a narrow face whose skin was nearly as waxy and plain as that of Aleister Crowley. He took in every detail of the room, his rodent-like gaze pausing only for a moment on Crowley before coming to rest on Sherlock Holmes.

"I must confess, Mr. Holmes," said he, loftily, "I am a bit surprised to find you in the company of such a man. Did you not see this morning's *Times*?"

"I did," said Holmes. "It was, in fact, the events described within it which led Mr. Crowley to this very doorstep."

Before Lestrade could reply, Crowley stood up, indignantly. "I resent your inference, Inspector," he announced, imperiously.

159

The stout man with Lestrade, whose somewhat pudgy face seemed nearly taken up by enormous dueling eyebrows and a thick, well-pronounced moustache, remained silent but studied Crowley with intense focus, as if he might somehow evaporate at any moment.

"Sit down, Mr. Crowley," said Holmes, firmly. "And unless you wish to make your circumstances direr than they already are, please keep silent until I instruct you otherwise."

Crowley examined my friend's steely expression, then returned to his place on the settee, crossed his arms impetuously, and made the prudent decision not to speak. Holmes, disregarding Lestrade's comment, indicated toward an empty wooden chair beside the window.

"Please have a seat, Inspector," said he, "and introduce us to your companions."

Lestrade scowled slightly then lowered his slight frame into the chair, which was bereft of any padding at all. He shifted about somewhat uncomfortably, and I suppressed an impulse to smile knowingly. On certain occasions Holmes would invite a visitor to sit in that very seat when he wished him to be unsettled by the experience. Having sat there myself, I knew that in short order it could become taxing to the spine, not to mention the rest of one's lower anatomy.

"Of course, of course," said Lestrade. He gestured toward the plainclothed man in the bowler hat. "Holmes, you undoubtedly recognize Sergeant Litster from the Yard, and my other man here is Constable Powers." He nodded at the stout mustached man. "And this gentleman is William Pinkerton, here from America at the behest of Sir Francis Fallowgrove."

"The *late* Sir Francis," corrected Pinkerton. "However, since his death, I am now in the employ of Lloyds, which held the policy on the diamond while it was on display."

He stepped forward and jutted out one large, beefy hand, which my friend seemed to study much the way he would a rare insect or a mysterious crystal which had formed among his experiments during the night. Then, realizing that Pinkerton meant for him to respond in kind, Holmes took hold of the American's hand, his narrow fingers instantly dwarfed by those of the bigger man.

"I've been looking forward to meeting you," continued Pinkerton, pumping Holmes' arm with great enthusiasm. "Lestrade here has told me a great deal about you, and his tales of how you've helped him close various cases have piqued my curiosity."

Holmes studied Lestrade with one quizzically raised eyebrow. The Inspector shifted in the chair and became suddenly fascinated by the cuticles of his slightly ragged, yellow fingernails. Of course, my friend was content to allow Lestrade to take full credit for Holmes' contributions to their occasional collaborations, preferring instead to remain quietly in the background where his deductive abilities could be best put to use. Nevertheless, I suspected my friend had to be surprised that Lestrade had made such claims so boldly in front of him. Upon reflection, I realized that this said a great deal about the inspector's regard for the American, William Pinkerton.

"Inspector Lestrade," said Holmes, gravely, "can be prone to a certain amount of exaggeration when the mood strikes him."

I nearly laughed out loud at his serious tone, but restrained myself. Lestrade coughed into his hand and stood up. "Since you have read the *Times*," said he, quickly, "then you must know why we are here."

"I can easily deduce it, given the disappearance of the blue diamond being followed so closely by the untimely death of Sir Francis," answered Holmes. "I can also see that you have come with more men than you would normally require for the detainment of one unarmed prisoner. One, I might add, who seems perfectly sedate, and for the most part, accommodating. However, the more fundamental thing which I cannot discern is the evidence you have that merits the arrest of Mr. Crowley at all.”

“I believe,” said William Pinkerton, stepping forward once again, “that I am the best man to answer that question, Mr. Holmes.”

He removed a small leather-bound notebook from his vest pocket, opened it, and began to flip through its pages.

“We have a witness that claims Mr. Crowley performed some type of heathen ceremony two nights ago. The witness further stated that the purpose of this observance, which involved, and I quote, ‘an aspect of the Hindu Sita’, was to rid the suspect of his enemies, whoever they might be.”

“When we learned of the death of Sir Fallowgrove,” interjected Lestrade, “and examined other facts, which in the interest of justice I am not yet free to reveal, we were able to conclude that Mr. Crowley was a most suitable suspect for both crimes.”

“Is that so,” murmured Holmes. “Well, then, Inspector, am I to assume then that you subscribe to the supernatural as a means to theft and murder?”

Lestrade’s dull face darkened. “Of course not!” he said, peevishly.

“And you, Mr. Pinkerton?” asked Holmes. “Do you believe that a man is capable of summoning the otherworldly in his quest for vengeance, or even greed?”

Pinkerton frowned. “I am sorry to say that I find your question to be...offensive, Mr. Holmes. I am a Christian man, and I give no credence to fairies, ghosts, and the like. It is pagan, and against my faith. More directly, I can honestly say that such things are defied by all that I have seen and heard thus far during my life.”

“And yet, here both of you stand,” said Holmes, “each prepared to arrest a man on the basis of claims which you both assert to be false.”

“As I said,” replied Lestrade, testily, “there are things about this case which I cannot speak of, Holmes. For now, we have enough evidence to take Mr. Crowley into custody, and that we are going to do.”

“Please, Holmes!” cried Crowley as Sergeant Litster and Constable Powers took him by the arms and lifted him from the settee. “I am innocent!”

“Fear not,” said Holmes. “Inspector Lestrade is a fair man and you will not be poorly treated in his custody. I shall take your case, Mr. Crowley, for I believe you are innocent.”

“I think you have chosen poorly this time, Holmes,” said Lestrade, even as the still protesting Aleister Crowley was led from the apartment and down the stairs. “And I must say that it will not please me to see you proven wrong.”

“On the contrary,” said Holmes, “should Aleister Crowley be found guilty of the crimes for which you have detained him, I shall be pleased to acknowledge my error, Inspector. It is my hope, too, that in the ‘interest of justice’ you will allow me to be of assistance in whatever form that may take.”

After the police and Pinkerton had gone and the door was once more firmly closed, I turned to Holmes with more questions than answers.

"How can you be so certain that Mr. Crowley is innocent?" I asked.

Holmes picked up the paper and opened it to the second page. There, the front page story continued, stating that the occultist was alleged to have called upon the Hindu goddess, Kali, during the course of his ceremony, with no other details given.

"I believe Mr. Crowley is innocent," said Holmes, "because of two things. First, when Mr. Pinkerton recounted the statements of his witness, he said that the ceremony in question involved an 'aspect of the Sita'. However, Mr. Crowley did not object to this characterization."

"And what is the significance of that, Holmes?"

"As it happens, Watson, in the interest of general knowledge, I have made a study of Hinduism and can say categorically that Kali, the dark goddess known as 'She Who Destroys', has nothing whatsoever to do with Sita, a goddess considered to be the daughter of Bhumi Devi, goddess of the Earth."

"I must confess," said I, puzzled, "I still do not see the connection."

"The *Times* story quotes an anonymous source that associates Mr. Crowley's activities that evening with Kali," said Holmes, patiently. "Because Mr. Crowley did not object to the Sita reference, we can thereby conclude that Mr. Crowley believes the goddess Kali to be an aspect of Sita. That belief, as you now know, is incorrect."

"And the second thing?"

"That is less a question of fact than of personal belief," replied Holmes. "I am in general agreement with Mr. Pinkerton, in the sense that I have yet to encounter anything which leads me to believe in the supernatural or the spiritual. Furthermore, Watson, I happen to think that if the supernatural *does* exist, then it most certainly could not be manipulated by a man such as Aleister Crowley!"

* * *

It was just past six o'clock the following morning when Sherlock Holmes and I found ourselves delivered by Hansom Cab to the intersection of Cornhill and Threadneedle Streets. At that early hour, the city of London was shrouded by a thick and damp fog, and a bitterly cold wind gusted along Cornhill, whipping our cloaks about our bodies. I pulled mine tighter around my shoulders and glanced at my friend who, as usual, appeared unaffected by either the unfavorable temperature or the miserable dampness.

To our right the enormity of the Royal Exchange building rose into the pervasive dreariness, the columned Romanesque façade partially obscured by tendrils of gray-white fog that curled hazily around the high-peaked roof. Barely visible along the lower frieze of the portico were engraved, in Latin, the letters: *Anno XIII. Elizabethæ R. Conditvm*; *Anno VIII. Victoria R. Restavratvm.*
Because it was still quite dark, the coachman removed one of the side-lamps from the cab and held it aloft so that we could better make our way across the open paved courtyard, past the regal statue of the Duke of Wellington, and ascend the portico steps. Once there, we discovered that the gates which protected the enormous entranceway had been opened and secured, but beyond it remained two towering wooden doors, both tightly closed. Each was banded with thick metal and punctuated by a

large, iron door knocker, and it was one of these that Sherlock Holmes grasped with his gloved hand and rapped hard against the backplate, causing a great booming sound to echo across the broad arcade. After a moment we heard a deep rumble as the right door began to grind inward across the stone floor. Then a thin ribbon of light fell through the widening rift, and we saw illuminated in it the sour face of a man who looked none too pleased to be greeting us while it was so dark.

"Who are you?" he said, without preamble, staring at us with squinted eyes that glittered with a black and foul combination of impatience and distrust.

"I am Sherlock Holmes," replied my friend, "and with me is John Watson. We are here to see Mr. Peter Curtis of Lloyds."

"So he's expecting you, then?" asked the man, scowling.

"Without question," said Holmes. "Please announce our arrival, if you would be so kind."

"No need," said a voice from behind the door. "Admit them, Pack, and then lock up again."

"Yes, sir," muttered the scowl-faced man, reluctantly.

He stepped back from the opening and held his lamp higher, highlighting the narrow foyer behind him. At the edge of the lamp's glow stood a tall and exceptionally thin gentleman, expensively dressed in a suit of fine gray wool. His narrow, fox-like face was expressionless, and his eyes, while not as poisoned by the darker emotions as those of the watchman, nevertheless studied us with a level of weighted calculation.

During the course of my years of association with Sherlock Holmes, it was a look I had come to know well, one most often possessed by the cynical such as bankers, stockbrokers or policemen— and all too often, criminals.

"Mr. Curtis, I presume?" queried Holmes, stepping into the foyer.

I followed closely behind him. As soon as we were inside, the watchman slid the door closed behind us with some effort, and the sound of the heavy wood scraping along the stone was greatly magnified within the narrow confines of the space. As we followed Curtis out into the inner courtyard of the Exchange, I could hear the man, Pack, muttering darkly beneath his breath, but could not make our specifically what he was saying.

"Indeed," said Curtis, coughing into a white handkerchief that had clearly been soiled by repeated episodes of the same. "Welcome to Lloyds, Mr. Holmes." He glanced at me with quite obvious uninterest, but nevertheless extended his hand with at least a modicum of courtesy. "And again, you sir are...?"

"Watson," I said, taking his hand and briefly shaking it. "John Watson, M.D."

"A physician, then?" replied Curtis, raising one eyebrow. "Impressive, sir, impressive, indeed. You must pardon my impertinence, however, but in regards to Sir Fallgrove, it strikes me that the time for a physician has passed. Wouldn't you agree?"

I felt my face flush with momentary anger. Before I could respond, Holmes said, "Dr. Watson is my friend, but also a valued associate, Mr. Curtis. I think that you will find his input significant as we examine the facts of this case."

Curtis seemed to consider my friend's words, then sighed. "Mr. Pinkerton speaks quite well of you, Holmes," he said. "I can only assume, then, that Dr. Watson is also comprised of much more than he appears. If you would, please follow me."

The gentlemen, whom I now began to see as slightly emaciated, led us across the courtyard and into the westerly hall of the Exchange, then up a flight of tiered stairs to a broad landing. On each side were numerous offices, some of which overlooked the courtyard below. After leading us through a series of corridors and rooms as bewildering to me as any ancient maze, we found ourselves in a large windowed meeting room. In one corner sat a modest chimney, and within it a fire burned, casting the room in a warm light. At the center of the chamber stood an enormous polished table, its elaborate surface embedded with a variety of rare and beautiful woods. Around this magnificent table sat the American, William Pinkerton, and another, younger bearded man with whom I was unfamiliar. As we entered the room, the two of them stood up to greet us.

"Good to see you again, Mr. Holmes," said Pinkerton.

"Indeed," added the second man. "It has been quite a while since we last encountered one another."

I glanced at my friend with some surprise. Given the extensive time we had spent together over the past years, I thought I had come to know nearly everyone of Holmes' acquaintances, but this man was a complete stranger to me.

"When we last met, Ian, I believe you were a laboratory assistant," said Holmes. "It was mentioned to me last year that you had been taken on as a surgeon with Scotland Yard. I would say that congratulations are in order."

The man inclined his head, which was largely bereft of hair, and smiled, faintly, from beneath his generous facial hair. "After a great deal of education and altogether too much poverty, I must say that my station in life has, indeed, greatly improved."

"I do not believe I have made your acquaintance," I said, impatiently. "Would you care to introduce us, Holmes?"

"Of course," said Holmes, blithely. "Forgive me. Dr. Watson, allow me to present Dr. Ian Gallagher, formerly of the Royal College of Physicians and the London Hospital, now of Scotland Yard."

"I gathered that much," I replied, a bit irritably. "A pleasure to meet you, sir."

"Likewise," said Gallagher, unsmilingly. "I must say, it would have been better to have met for the first time under more favorable circumstances, Dr. Watson."

"Unfortunately, in our profession it is too often that colleagues meet at similar, melancholy junctures," I replied. "You are involved in the Sir Fallowgrove case, then?"

"Alas, replied Dr. Gallagher, "it was my sad duty to undertake Sir Fallowgrove's post-mortem examination."

Each of us took a seat around the table, and after a moment a servant entered the room carrying a tray bearing a silver tea service and a small plate of biscuits. He placed them at the center of the table and then backed silently from the room, leaving us to discuss the events at hand.

"Tell me," said Holmes, helping himself to a cup of tea, "what did you discover during your examination?"

"Although all indications were of a heart attack, Inspector Lestrade instructed me to search for any signs of foul play," recited Dr. Gallagher, his tone altogether clinical. "This would have included any marks indicative of violence, such as shiv wounds and the like. However, I found nothing of the sort." He shrugged. "In addition, I examined Sir Francis for any manifestations of toxic poisoning, including needle injection marks and so on. However, there was nothing at all detectable, no punctures of any kind, nor any chemical traces apparent in the stomach or in the tissue samples I examined."

"Thank you, doctor," said Holmes, "for your thorough examination and for sharing your findings with me. I must admit, I do find your profession fascinating. However, as I am hardly an expert in your field, perhaps you would be willing to enlighten me as to the procedural limits of such an examination?"

Dr. Gallagher looked perplexed. "I'm not sure what you mean, Holmes."

"For example," said Holmes, "was there anything else which caught your attention? Anything at all, no matter how trivial?"

Gallagher seemed to consider Holmes' question, then frowned. "There were two somewhat unusual things, but I'm sure they were unrelated to his passing."

"Perhaps so," said Holmes. "But please continue, if you would."

"Very well. The first were a number of small rashes evident on the palm of Sir Francis's left hand, as well as the Antebrachial surface of his right arm. However, I attributed them to his hobby of gathering woodland plants for his garden. In this case, the rashes were most likely caused by exposure to *Toxicodendron radicans*."

"Excuse me," said Pinkerton, irritably, raising his great, bushy eyebrows. "If you wouldn't mind speaking English, sir, I'd be quite grateful. Unfortunately, you have exceeded my rather limited grasp of Latin."

"*Toxicondendron radicans*," explained Holmes, patiently, "is more commonly referred to as Poison Ivy, while *Antebrachial* is the anatomical term which refers to the lower portion of the human arm."

"The forearm, as it is commonly called," I added, helpfully.

"Rashes," said Holmes. "Very interesting. Tell me, Doctor Gallagher, was Sir Fallowgrove frequently exposed to toxic plants?"

"Nothing that could be directly confirmed by anyone in his household," replied Gallagher, "but it did seem logical to me, as Sir Francis was a collector of certain wild plants, especially those located in the depths of the forest. On occasion he would even collect specimens nocturnally, which obviously would heighten the chances for accidental exposure."

"I see," said Holmes. "And what was the second unusual characteristic that you noticed?"

"An internal one, actually," replied Gallagher. "During the surgical autopsy I discovered that Sir Fallowgrove's lungs displayed a number of fresh scars."

"And to what cause did you attribute them?"

"When I interviewed his staff, they related to me that Sir Fallowgrove had been visiting friends in the countryside a few weeks past. Apparently, at some time during the journey he found himself assisting a fire brigade in suppressing a burning coach house. As such, I determined that the scarring had most likely been caused by excessive heat or by smoke inhalation."

"Very good. Thank you." Holmes turned to Pinkerton. "Tell me, sir," said he, "what are your thoughts thus far?"

"When I originally arrived in London," said Pinkerton, "I was in pursuit of the master thief, Adam Worth, a rogue you may be familiar with, as his exploits have been reported extensively throughout the press on both sides of the Atlantic."

"I am familiar with the name," said Holmes. "I believe the press calls him America's own 'Napoleon of Crime'."

Pinkerton winced as if the characterization pained him. "Worth has been called that by some yellow journalists, yes. And I'm sorry to say that, to date, he has eluded my agents at every turn. Even now they continue to scour the countryside for any sign of him."

"And how, if I may ask, did your pursuit of Mr. Worth lead to your involvement with Sir Fallowgrove and the blue diamond known as the Other Eye?"

"I believe I am the best one to answer that question," said Curtis, self-importantly. "But first, I should acquaint you with a brief history of the Other Eye and what is perhaps more relevant to this discussion: the alleged 'curse' rumored to accompany it."

* * *

For a moment there was a long and awkward silence around the table, and then the American, Pinkerton, leaned back in his chair and waved his hand dismissively.

"Absolute poppycock," he said. "As Holmes and I agreed upon yesterday, there is most certainly a mystery here but I am entirely convinced it is not at all supernatural in nature!"

"And I will reiterate," said Holmes, "that I quite agree with Mr. Pinkerton. However, the accusations against Mr. Crowley are already gaining credence amongst members of the public, as well as the press. I think it is in the best interests of justice to examine every aspect of the case no matter what our personal convictions may be."

"Do as you will," said Pinkerton, with a grunt. "But it seems a waste of time to me."

"Pray continue, Mr. Curtis," said Holmes.

Curtis steepled his fingers beneath his chin, seeming to consider carefully what he was about to say.

"When Sir Fallowgrove first made the decision to display the blue diamond at his home," he said, "he approached Lloyds to act as the insuring agent. We were, in a word, skeptical, as the tale he told of how he acquired the jewel in question seemed too fantastic to be believed."

"Did he happen upon it while playing a game of Loo?" I asked, innocently. "I must confess I never excelled at it myself."

"This hardly seems the time for humor, Watson," admonished Holmes, staring at me disapprovingly.

"Actually," said Curtis, gazing balefully from eyes sunken into a face that now appeared to me to be quite emaciated, "that is not too far from being accurate. In point of fact, Sir Fallowgrove claimed to have won the stone in a legal settlement against the owner of a small West Indian shipping company. Not a card game, precisely, Dr. Watson, but I imagine one could assume such an arrangement would provide better odds than most of them."

"Quite so," said Holmes, absently.

I noticed then that he was paying particular attention to Curtis's right hand, which was still positioned beneath his chin. I saw immediately what my friend was looking at: a burn mark on the leading edge of Curtis's palm, small but easily visible if one happened to be looking for it.

"That appears to be a rather painful burn you have there, Mr. Curtis," I said, indicating toward his hand.

"The perils of tea, Dr. Watson," said Curtis, lightly, "or to be more precise, the preparation of the hot water used to steep the leaves. I carelessly placed my hand too near the fire some days ago, you see, and received this for my inattention."

"I'd be inattentive, too," said Pinkerton, dryly, "if I began every day well before the dawn, as you seem to."

"Please continue with your recollection, Mr. Curtis," said Holmes, with some impatience. "I am especially interested in the curse that you mentioned."

"Of course, of course," said Curtis. "According to Sir Fallowgrove, the blue diamond, which he coined the 'Other Eye', was originally discovered more than one-hundred years ago by a grave robber in a temple somewhere along India's Coleroon River, and only recently resurfaced in the possession of the shipping company owner from which he received it."

"That story is familiar to me," said Holmes, rubbing his chin thoughtfully. "Are you suggesting, Mr. Curtis, that the *Times* is correct, and that the diamond in Sir Fallowgrove's possession actually is the lost companion to the famous Tavernier Blue?"

"What's that again, Holmes?" I asked, puzzled. "I'm not familiar with that particular gemstone."

"I am not surprised," my friend replied. "You would know it better by its current and much more familiar name, the Hope Diamond."

"But that's impossible!" I said. "There is only one such stone and at present it is in the possession of Lord Francis Hope."

"Had you found the time to examine yesterday's paper, Watson," said Holmes, "you would have stumbled across a brief history of the Hope Diamond contained therein."
He took one of the biscuits from the silver tray and bit into it with surprising delicacy, then took a moment to flick the fallen crumbs from his waistcoat. I opened my mouth to protest, but before I could speak he continued on, ignoring me.

"And had you kept reading," he said, "you would have discovered that the Tavernier Blue, as it was then known, was originally a much rougher stone and theorized to be one of two 'eyes', both stolen from the inveterate remains of a pagan god. Or the statue of one, at least."

"Quite right! Very good, Mr. Holmes," said Curtis, admiringly. "Of course, this brings us to the curse I mentioned. You see, gentlemen, the Hope Diamond has long borne the reputation of delivering upon its recipients all manner of bad luck—and under certain circumstances, even death."

"Which, if one grants credibility to such stories, would begin with Jean Baptiste Tavernier," said Holmes, reaching for a second biscuit. "He is, of course, the gentleman who allegedly removed the stone from the temple. Apparently, sometime after selling it, Mr. Tavernier journeyed to Russia, and while there on holiday was promptly torn apart by a pack of wild dogs. A thoroughly charming story, yes?"

"Not especially," I muttered, gazing sadly at the plate with its few remaining biscuits. I had been considering sampling one of them, but now my appetite seemed to have abruptly forsaken me.

"Quite the entertaining story, Holmes," said Pinkerton, irritably. "But it can be just as easily explained by coincidence. As I told you yesterday, I'm a Christian man and have no use for such ideas. Besides, I fail to see how these fairy tales bring us any closer to solving the murder of Sir Fallowgrove, or to recovering the stolen diamond!"

"If you would," said Holmes, "I would like to beg your indulgence for just a while longer, Mr. Pinkerton. As a consulting detective yourself, I am certain you will acknowledge that the best way to determine the facts of a case is to observe everything that is available to be seen—or in this case, unseen."

Holmes turned his attention to Curtis. "You mentioned that Lloyds was initially reluctant to insure the Other Eye because of the account Sir Fallowgrove related about how he came to possess the stone. What about its provenance provoked your doubts?"

Curtis shrugged. "We simply felt that his story was too convenient, as it were. Sir Fallowgrove cited privacy reasons and would not say how many pounds were at stake in his settlement with the shipping company owner. This made it impossible for us to determine the plausibility of the diamond being used as a settlement for that debt, especially given its high value. Of course, while that omission alone was not proof of any nefarious dealings on the part of Sir Fallowgrove, it still piqued our curiosity."

"I see," said Holmes. "And yet you ultimately chose to insure the stone anyway?"

"Yes. After examining it thoroughly—a task which I personally undertook along with two expert gemologists—the board agreed that the stone was legitimate and that Lloyds would insure it for the stated value of sixty-thousand pounds. Simply put, Mr. Holmes, we could proffer no reasonable explanation as to why we would not be willing to do so, as the contract promised to be quite profitable for us."

"And that," said Pinkerton, gruffly, "is where I had the bad luck to come into all this. When Mr. Curtis learned I was in London, he approached me at my temporary office with a proposal to provide security for Sir Fallowgrove. With every lead in the Worth case gone cold, it seemed a simple matter to provide the necessary security."

"It must have also been apparent to you as well," said Holmes, casually, "that your involvement with Sir Fallowgrove and the Other Eye would result in a great deal of positive press coverage for the Pinkerton Agency."

The American's face reddened. Before he could speak, Curtis said, "What makes it particularly embarrassing, Mr. Holmes, is that the Pinkerton men were on guard the entire night. It strikes me that this illustrious 'agency' has been made a mockery of by Aleister Crowley, a man who is little more than a degenerate murderer and thief."

"And that is why," said Pinkerton, fiercely, "I am determined to resolve this case as expeditiously as possible, one way or the other. To that end I will accept all the help that I can muster, even if it happens to come from the man working on behalf of the villain in question."

"Actually, you are mistaken," said Holmes, evenly. "While it is true that I have agreed to take up the case of Aleister Crowley, I do so not out of any special concern for his well-being, but as I have said more than once, in the greater interest of justice."

Shrugging, Pinkerton sat back in his chair and stroked his moustache absently. "Whatever your reasons, I'm quite content to allow them to remain just that—yours. What concerns me now is the reputation of my firm in London, not to mention the rest of Europe."

"Your concerns, Mr. Pinkerton, are duly noted," said Holmes. "I must admit, however, that one aspect of this case is particularly puzzling to me. It is my understanding that when the Other Eye was discovered missing, the display was nonetheless still locked and sealed. Is that correct?"

"Indeed," said Pinkerton, glumly. "It was as if the stone simply evaporated into the air." He shook his head sadly. "As much as it pains me to do so, I find that I agree with Curtis here. The Pinkertons are not accustomed to appearing as fools, but this case has become a public relations catastrophe for us!"

"Perhaps," said Holmes, calmly, "dire would be a more apt word. I do not believe that a catastrophe—a word with much more…permanent connotations—is a certainty at this point in time. One thing that *is* certain, however, is that the death of Sir Fallowgrove and the disappearance of the Other Eye cannot be attributed to the supernatural."

"Perhaps not in the usual sense," said I, sensing an opportunity to contribute something of use.

"However, I am aware of numerous instances where those who profess a belief in the supernatural have displayed severe psychosomatic symptoms after being 'cursed' by another person."

"Impossible!" exclaimed Pinkerton.

"Not at all," I said. "In point of fact, on certain occasions the subject of a so-called curse has died, ostensibly from his own conviction that death was now a foregone conclusion."

"I have read of such cases myself, actually," said Dr. Gallagher. "It is quite true that the human mind is capable of remarkable—and sometimes horrifying—acts upon the very body which serves to protect it."

"Assuming that you are correct," said Pinkerton, "then there may be an explanation here that makes some degree of sense."

He removed a slender notebook from his coat pocket and flipped through the pages, finally stopping in the middle of the book.

"Ah, yes, here it is. Apparently, Crowley has quite the reputation as a skilled hypnotist; perhaps he was able to employ some kind of power of suggestion to kill Sir Francis. What do you think of that, Holmes?"

My friend seemed to consider the proposition for some moments. "I think not," he said, at last. "I, too, have some skill and experience in that arena and have studied the field for many years. I can tell you with absolute certainty that the human mind possesses great power over the body, but that it is, at the same time, ruled by a tremendous prohibition against self-harm. While it is true that some unstable individuals can on occasion cause themselves injury, it is my considered opinion that a man of good mental health could not be hypnotized to cause himself significant harm. Based upon what I have learned thus far, I have no reason to doubt that Sir Fallowgrove was of sound mind."

Pinkerton frowned. "I see your point, Holmes. So what do you suggest, then? This seems to lead us back to where we began."

"Not entirely," said Holmes. "I think that it is time for us to visit the scene of the crime. Most significantly, we must summon the witnesses to Aleister Crowley's pagan ceremony, as well as Inspector Lestrade and Mr. Crowley himself, so that we may put all of the facts of this case in their proper perspective."

He looked into my eyes and I saw his pupils shining with a familiar anticipation that I had come to know well over the many years of our friendship.

"Come, gentlemen," said he, addressing the entire room, his voice betraying none of the excitement that I knew now gripped his imagination. "The game, as they say, is afoot."

* * *

Within the hour, Peter Curtis and his man, Pack, had dispatched a messenger to Inspector Lestrade as well as arranged for several hansom cabs, operated by a gaggle of street Arabs who had risen early and were available for the commission, to convey the five of us to the home of the late Sir Francis Fallowgrove. We were barely settled into our respective conveyances, each with its capacity of two passengers, when the crack of multiple whips echoed in the fading darkness, nearly in unison, and we plunged off down Threadneedle Street, the six sets of wheels and the horse's hooves making a terrible clatter in the relative quiet of the early, fog-shrouded morn.

As we rattled along, I noted that Sherlock Holmes was gazing out into the drifting fog, seemingly far away from the moment and deep in some thought, the meaning of which I could not readily discern. Ordinarily I was loathe to disturb my friend during such moments of introspection, but today I found myself disturbed by thoughts of the resurgent supernatural aspects which seemed to plague the case at hand.

"Tell me, Holmes," said I. "Do you truly believe we'll discover some mysterious meaning to all of this at the home of Sir Fallowgrove?"

"Undoubtedly not," said my companion, gravely, turning his gaze upon me. "You know all too well my philosophy on matters such as these." He waved one gloved hand in the general direction of the dark and torturously narrow side streets and alleyways which comprise so much of the city of London. "Mankind strives to find deeper meaning in all things, Watson, but he does so in deliberate avoidance of the prosaic reality which so slowly and inexorably consumes him. To put it more simply, the human soul is a darker and far more convoluted labyrinth than any city, and one need not look to the supernatural to understand that."

"How can you be so certain, Holmes?" I asked. "As complex as the human soul undoubtedly is, the world is also a large and intricate place, and there is much we do not yet understand. Why, just last month I was reading in the *Strand Magazine* an article which stated that the explorer, Sir Randolph Ceasley, recently discovered no less than three varied species of frog in the jungles of South America, all previously unknown to science."

"Unknown," said Holmes, dryly, "but hardly supernatural, Watson. Please alert me the very first time that a frog performs a verifiably magical act, and I will be suitably impressed."

I grimaced, but could think of nothing immediate to say, so I looked instead to the now fading darkness, which remained filled with a multitude of passing buildings and passageways, all of which I was utterly unfamiliar with.

"Is it my imagination, Holmes," I asked, suddenly, "or do the structures here seem...tidier than most?"

"It is not your imagination," said Holmes. "We are entering the district of Belgravia. I am sure you are familiar with it?"

"Of course," I said. "It's among the most fashionable districts in London!"

"Indeed," said Holmes, absently, as our coach began to slow. "Would you expect a man of Sir Fallowgrove's apparent wealth to reside anywhere else, Watson?"

At last, our cab came to a stop before a long row of adjoining four-story homes, all constructed of white alabaster, each with its own columned portico topped by a small, wrought-iron balcony overlooking the street. At this early hour most of the windows remained dark; however, a single gas lamp mounted beneath one of the porticos was lit, and I deduced, without much effort, that this must be the residence of the late Sir Francis Fallowgrove.

As we stood on the pathway in front of the house, two carriages approached from the opposite end of the street and pulled to a stop. A number of individuals stepped from each one, and as they hurried across the road toward us, I immediately recognized the thin, pale form of Inspector Lestrade as well as the broad, yet slightly stooped figure of Aleister Crowley, among the group.

"How do you do, Holmes," said Lestrade, irritably.

My friend merely nodded toward the other people who accompanied the Inspector, the curiosity in their faces clear in the ashen twilight. "Can I assume that these are the witnesses to Mr. Crowley's ceremony, Inspector?"

"Indeed," said Lestrade, "and they're none too happy to have been dragged out here before the sun's come up. Same goes for me, as a matter of fact. I hope you have a bloody good reason for calling us out this early, Holmes."

"Have patience, Inspector," my friend replied. "I believe you will find that all will be made clear in the next hour or so."

"I, for one, would much rather be warm in my bed," said Crowley, his pale, moon-like countenance creased by a sour pout that made him, in the moment, appear more boy than man. "And at home, mind you, not in some hideous cell at Lewes prison!"

"Shut up, you," said Lestrade, blithely. "You'll be lucky not to be hanged from the neck before this year is done, Crowley, so you'd best be silent for now."

The officer beside Crowley placed one hand on his shoulder, and I immediately recognized Sergeant Litster of Scotland Yard, whom Holmes and I had first met in our apartment on Baker Street just the day before. He nodded toward me in the cordial yet guarded manner so common to the members of London's police force, and I nodded politely back to him.

"So what now, Mr. Holmes?" asked Peter Curtis. He pushed his hands deeper into the pockets of the heavy, dark gray overcoat he now wore over his lighter gray suit. "I believe I speak for everyone when I state that frankly, I'm fascinated to see what you've come up with."

"And so you shall," said Holmes as he turned to climb the three short steps to the front door of Sir Fallowgrove's former home and then knocked upon it. After a moment, the door was flung open by a plump, matronly housekeeper dressed in a plain but well-made skirt and jacket, her hair neatly covered by a pretty lace cap. Her face appeared sorrowful, as if she had spent some time collapsed in tears, and I found this indication of loyalty to the late Sir Francis Fallowgrove to be quite touching.

"Oh!" said she, clearly startled to see the group of people standing on her porch so early in the morning. "You've arrived much sooner than I expected."

"My apologies," said Lestrade, gruffly, "but Holmes here felt it was necessary that we visit the scene of the crime at once."

"Quite so," said Holmes. "It is always advisable to pursue the facts of a case as close to the actual commission of the offense as possible so as to ensure that the recollections of all involved are suitably fresh, as it were."

"Old or new memories," said Pinkerton, "it strikes me that people will remember whatever they will, as they desire to."

"Possibly," said Holmes, cryptically, as we followed him into the home. "Or possibly not. I have found that the recollections of witnesses have something critically important in common with the physical location of a crime: it is best to preserve both, in their original state. And that is why I requested that Mr. Pinkerton keep the two original guards on duty, even going so far as to have them sleep here, so that the integrity of the crime scene would remain intact and unbroken until our arrival."

The housekeeper, whose name was Mrs. Georgina Rusnak, had been in the service of Sir Fallowgrove for more than ten years. She led us with assuredness to the large parlor where the Other Eye had been displayed, and where the empty case still remained, flanked by the two Pinkerton men whom Holmes had just mentioned. As we entered the parlor, the witnesses crowded in behind us. The two Pinkerton agents on duty immediately saluted their American supervisor in a fashion which seemed decidedly military, and which I greatly approved of.

"Nothing has been disturbed over the past forty-eight hours?" asked Pinkerton, without preamble.

The two men replied that nothing had, and that the room and the empty case remained undisturbed.

"Very well, then," said Pinkerton, "good work, men. Holmes, it's now in your hands. Take it away, then, as they say."

My friend studied the room, and then the empty case, pausing to rub his chin in that most considered of ways of which I knew so well. As for myself, I could see nothing special about the solid pedestal and the small pillow upon which the stone had rested before its disappearance; likewise the four panes of thick glass which surrounded it. Only the locked, copper lid was particularly unique, shaped as it was to resemble a diminutive Hindu temple.

Holmes turned back to the guards. "Tell me what you saw the night that the Other Eye disappeared, and leave out no detail, no matter how trivial you may believe it to be."

The two men glanced at each other, and I saw not guilt in their expressions, but embarrassment. They seemed to fidget for a moment, and then the taller of the two stared defiantly at my friend. "Truth be told, we hain't seen nor heard a thing," he said, "not two days ago, and not last night, either."

"'Tis true what he says!" exclaimed the shorter guard, whom I could see was greatly vexed. "Mr. Pinkerton pays us well to do our duty, and do it we did. Hain't nothing moved nor made a sound here since we come on duty!"

Holmes nodded but did not immediately speak. Leaning closer to the case, he took a short, deep breath through his nose, but did not reach out to touch the glass or the copper lid.

"Tell me," he said at last, "you men have—if you will pardon the unavoidable pun—touched upon two of the five human senses: sight and sound. In this instance I do not believe that the third sense, taste, is pertinent to the facts of the case. However, the fourth sense, touch, could very well be a different matter. During the night the diamond disappeared, did either of you men touch anything in this room?"

Both men declared that they had not, upon the specific orders of Sir Francis Fallowgrove. "He told us 'taint no one to touch the case," said the taller guard. "On his command we weren't to allow anyone within three feet of it, and weren't no reason for us to put our hands on anything else in here."

"Very good," said Holmes. "Continue guarding the case and do not allow anyone but myself, Mr. Curtis, or Mr. Pinkerton to touch it."

"There is one other sense," said I, "which you did not mention."

"Ah, yes," said he, "the sense of smell. Very good, Watson, I was just about to address that."

"How," said I, "will an examination of the olfactory provide you with any insight into this case, Holmes?"

"Patience, Watson," he replied. "As it happens, the sense of smell may very well provide the final clue necessary to bring clarity to this case." He turned to the guards once again. "Tell me, did either one of you notice any odd scents in this room during the night?"

"Not me," said the taller guard. "We stood separate watches, so there was only one of us on duty at a time, but I can tell you I hain't smelled nothing strange."

The other guard grimaced. "There was something," said he, "two nights past. For an hour or two I smelled something powerful strange, but it seemed to come and go. I di'nt think no more of it once it was gone for good. Figured it was from the sewers or somethin' like that."

"Strange smells, no one in sight, and a diamond missing from a locked case," said I, annoyed. "Once again, I find myself no closer to unraveling all of this than I was a day ago. Tell me, Holmes, what do you make of it all?"

"As I said, patience, Watson," repeated he, a bit sharply. "I assure you that all will be made clear." He turned to the witnesses, all of whom stood together along the parlor's back wall. "I understand that each of you attended Mr. Crowley's ritual where he claimed to have summoned Kali, the Hindu goddess? Is that correct?"

One of the witnesses, a young man perhaps twenty years of age, stepped forward, his jaw thrust out in defiance. "We all saw the Master perform the consecrated ritual, and we beheld the goddess, Kali, as she was sent forth to exact her revenge for the theft of the sacred stone!" When he spoke, his voice quavered slightly, yet I could see in his eyes that he was clearly a true and passionate believer in the teachings of Aleister Crowley.

"It's true!" cried a plump, older woman standing just behind the younger man. "Sir Fallowgrove brought the vengeance of Kali upon himself! He was given the choice to return the stone to the place from which it was stolen, but he refused and has now paid the price for his arrogance!" Holmes raised one eyebrow and studied the woman thoughtfully. "Refused?" he said. "If you would be so kind, please explain what you mean."

"On the first night that the stone was displayed," replied she, much excited, "we accompanied the Master here, each to bear witness to his warning. The Master foretold that the stone must be returned to India, and to its rightful place in the lost Temple of Sita."

"I do recall them, Mr. Holmes," said the smaller guard, peevishly. "They came the first day the diamond was on display, but Sir Fallowgrove would have none of it. He ordered us to throw Crowley right out the door." He nodded at the woman and the other witnesses. "And meaning no disrespect, but we threw these ones out right along with him."

Holmes glanced at Aleister Crowley, who appeared to have become rather puffed up from witnessing the devotion so evident in his followers. "I would not be so pleased with yourself, Mr. Crowley," said he, sharply. "Such theatrics may play well before an ignorant crowd, desperate to believe in nonsense, but it will be of no help to you in a trial. In fact, your success may become the end of you, as you so capably predicted yesterday."

Crowley's face flushed with anger. Then, just as it had in our apartment on Baker Street, it resolved back to the contented and vaguely arrogant expression which I had come to believe was his de facto condition, as it were.

"I will risk my fate with any jury," declared Crowley, imperiously, "for I command powers much more potent than the law, and considerably greater than the judgment of any man!"

"Quite," said Holmes, dryly. "But while you may win the battle of credibility with your followers, Mr. Crowley, your statements may, at the same time, cost you the war for your very survival. My counsel is as it was a day ago, sir: remain quiet so that I may, if possible, move to save your life!"

* * *

"So what shall we do now?" I said. "This all seems rather a condemnation of Mr. Crowley, Holmes, as circumstantial as the case against him may be."

"That would appear to be true," said Holmes. "However, I believe that we must seek further information before allowing the Inspector here to send Mr. Crowley to the gallows, Watson."
Mr. Lestrade opened his mouth to respond, but Pinkerton waved him off. "If he was, indeed, responsible for the theft of the diamond," commented Pinkerton, "not to mention the murder of Sir Fallowgrove, it strikes me that it would serve him right, Mr. Holmes."

"Once again, you assume guilt on his part," replied Holmes, calmly. "As I stated to Inspector Lestrade, I do not believe Mr. Crowley to be guilty of the crimes for which he is charged."
Lestrade laughed, sarcastically. "How can you be so sure, Holmes?" he asked. "There is no information pertinent to clearing Mr. Crowley of suspicion which you do not already possess."

"That is not entirely true," said Holmes. "When you arrived at 221B, Baker Street to arrest Mr. Crowley, you stated that there were additional facts of the case which you were not free to disclose at that time. I would suggest that now is the time to reveal them, or you risk sending an innocent man to his death."

Lestrade glanced at Pinkerton, who shrugged indifferently.

"Very well," said Lestrade, "but I am convinced that this information would be of no assistance to you, Holmes. In point of fact, the information actually helps to condemn your client, rather than help him."

"Your indulgence, please," said Holmes, pleasantly. "If you would, tell me what you know, Inspector."

"On Monday, the day after the diamond disappeared," said Lestrade, "Sir Fallowgrove sought out Mr. Crowley and openly accused him of stealing it. The altercation took place in a public restaurant, with many witnesses, several of whom recounted that the two men nearly came to blows. Mr. Crowley was ordered to leave the premises, and as he did so, was heard to utter several threats against Sir Fallowgrove."

"Pretty damning, eh, Holmes?" asked Pinkerton, rhetorically. "When you take that confrontation into consideration, it seems that we have quite the case against Mr. Crowley here."

"I would not be so sure," said Holmes, cryptically.

He stared intently at Peter Curtis, who had remained silent since entering Fallowgrove's parlor.

"Mr. Curtis, please confirm for me," said Holmes, "that the case has not been opened since the Other Eye was first placed within it."

"We've recounted to you all of the facts, Mr. Holmes," said Curtis, angrily. "Once again, the case has not been opened, and the Pinkertons have attested to that."

"Indeed," said Pinkerton. "If you'd like, Holmes, we're more than happy to open it for you now."

He took two steps toward the case, reaching his arms out toward the elaborate Hindu lid, when Sherlock Holmes took two great steps across the room and placed his hand upon Pinkerton's arm, interrupting the act.

"I would advise against that, Mr. Pinkerton," said he, gravely. "However, one of us must, and therefore I think that perhaps Mr. Curtis is the best one to assist us with this task."

I glanced at Curtis, and to my great surprise, noted that his skin had paled to such a degree that it resembled the unhealthy shade of spoilt milk.

"I...I would be honored," said Curtis, haltingly.

He removed a pair of gloves from his overcoat pocket and slipped them on. Holmes studied them curiously, and sensing the question unasked, Curtis proceeded to explain.

"At Sir Fallowgrove's request, no one is to touch the case without gloves," said he. "More specifically the lid, which is quite ancient and valuable."

For a moment, I thought Holmes might smile, and then his eyes appeared to darken in that ineffable manner which had so characterized the many cases we had worked on together. I now knew that my friend was near to revealing all, and I found myself thrilling in anticipation of this last, final bit of the game.

"By all means, then," said Holmes, "wear your gloves. But please be brief, Mr. Curtis, as the day is now wearing upon us."

Curtis stepped up to the case. I saw him lick his lips, nervously, and then reach for the lid and lift it, with some effort, from its resting place atop the glass. Almost immediately a pungent odor flooded the room, and Curtis hurriedly turned his head away and moved back from the open case, setting the lid down upon the floor.

"What is that wretched odor?" said Pinkerton, grimacing. "I've never smelled anything quite like it."

To my great astonishment, I realized that I recognized the odor, which had quickly dissipated, almost immediately. I opened my mouth to speak, but Sherlock Holmes held up his hand in warning, and so I remained silent.

"Now that the case has been opened," said Holmes, "I would request that you remove your gloves, Mr. Curtis, and examine the inside; more specifically, the area around the pillow which held the diamond."

"Whatever for?" cried Curtis, his forehead shining with sudden perspiration. "This is a complete waste of time, gentleman! Look for yourselves; it is clear that the diamond is no longer there!"

"Ah, but it *is* still inside the case," said Holmes, "I can assure you of that. Please remove your gloves, Mr. Curtis, and do as I ask. Simply touching the cushion will reveal the diamond's location, I promise you."

Curtis pulled off his leather gloves, and all who were in the room could clearly see that his hands were trembling. He reached for the case, hesitated, and then burst into tears, shaking his head violently. After a moment he retreated to the nearest wall where he stood alone, shuddering and sobbing uncontrollably, as the occupants of the room looked on in shocked surprise.

"I don't understand any of this," said Pinkerton. "Why will he not reach into the case? The diamond is gone, so what harm could it do?"

"As I said," replied Holmes, "the Other Eye is still there to be seen, if one only knows how to look for it."

"I'm not following your explanation, Holmes," said Lestrade, with a frustrated grimace, "for even I can see that the case is empty."

"All of these events," said Holmes, "have at their source the most prosaic of explanations. During our ride here, I actually spoke with Dr. Watson about the manner in which most human beings are absorbed by what they believe to be profound or important ideas, which nonetheless mask the more mundane aspects of their lives. For some, greed is as complex an idea, and a purpose as important, as any others one might imagine. This particular case is a clear example of what can happen when the basest of desires becomes the central focus of one's existence."

"Which means what?" I asked.

"Nothing more than that this case is about greed," said Holmes, "and little more. I will endeavor to provide all of you with the order of events as clearly as I can. Watson, please do not hesitate to add anything which I may have overlooked, which you feel is relevant."

"Very well," said I.

"First," continued Holmes, "please tell us what the strange odor was that briefly filled the room, Watson, if you would be so kind."

"Of course. It is hydrofluoric acid, an unusual and quite deadly chemical commonly used by etchers. I became familiar with it while purchasing a gift for my dear Mary, which I wished to have engraved with her name."

"Most excellent, Watson," said Holmes. "When the case was opened, I saw upon your face the realization of what was happening, but the time was not yet right to reveal that information."

"It would explain why Curtis would not reach inside the case," I said. "To do so would without a doubt have meant certain death. Even the fumes are poisonous enough to kill a man."
Several of the occupants in the room shifted nervously, but Holmes set them immediately at ease.

"There is nothing to be concerned about," said he, confidently. "Most of the chemical in question has already evaporated, and the stench of what remains is relatively mild and will not be harmful to us. The cushion inside, however, is a different matter altogether."

"Very much so," I said, peering at the cushion through one of the glass panes. "This stuff is quite difficult to work with, and in fluid form, is rapidly absorbed by the skin—or a cushion. For so much of it to be detectable after several days, it is reasonable to conclude that liquid hydrofluoric acid was utilized in this instance."

"Precisely," said Holmes. "If you would, Mr. Pinkerton, please have your men remove Mr. Curtis's coat and suit jacket, and then roll up his sleeves so that we may examine his hands and arms."
The two guards moved toward Curtis, who offered little resistance, and they were able to quickly strip away his coats and pull up his shirtsleeves.

"There, you see," said Holmes, "there are burn marks visible on his arms, in addition to the one on his hand which we took note of at the Lloyd's offices. As Dr. Gallagher indicated, similar marks were discovered upon the body of Sir Fallowgrove, and in addition, there were recent signs of scarring to his lungs. One can deduce that both men came into contact not with poison plants, as Dr. Gallagher had surmised, but the liquid form of hydrofluoric acid."

"Which, as I already mentioned, when absorbed the skin can have deadly consequences," said I. "As it happens, when this type of acid interacts with blood calcium it is known to cause heart failure."

"And that," said Holmes, "is what I believe occurred here. Clearly, Sir Fallowgrove inhaled more of the fumes than did Mr. Curtis, which resulted in his rapid demise."

"But to what point, Holmes?" asked Lestrade. "Why would the two of them take such risks? I fail to see how this acid plays a significant role in the disappearance of the Other Eye."

"That is perhaps the most ingenious aspect of their plot," replied Holmes. "Please have your men turn over the lid of the case. Carefully, now, Inspector, and please ensure that their skin does not come into direct contact with the metal at any time."
Two of Lestrade's policemen moved over to the lid and bent down beside it. Both men were wearing gloves, but they still moved carefully as they turned it over, revealing the bottom.

"If you examine the inside of the lid," said Holmes, "you will see that there are the remnants of a small, glass capsule attached there."

"Well I'll be damned," said Pinkerton, "he's right!"

"Ah, but this time, Holmes," said Lestrade, smugly, "you've hurried out the facts of the case without considering all of the ramifications. Even this rare acid cannot dissolve a diamond. Everyone knows that."

"You are correct, Inspector," said Holmes, and Lestrade's eyes widened in surprise. "The strength of a diamond could not be compromised in any significant way by this acid, most especially one of this size."

"You see," said Lestrade, "even the finest of investigators can overlook a critical fact, Holmes. I would not feel too bad about it."

"Again, you are correct, Inspector," said Holmes. By this time Lestrade fairly beamed with anticipated victory over the great Sherlock Holmes, but alas, my friend had not yet finished with him. "There is one thing you did not consider, however, and that is that the diamond never existed at all." Lestrade's mouth fell open, but thankfully, he stayed silent this time.

"It is my belief," said Holmes, "that Sir Fallowgrove and Mr. Curtis conspired together to create a fake diamond. Based upon the faint stains which I detected upon my examination of the cushion inside the case, I believe it was mostly likely constructed from jeweler's paste." He pointed to the lid. "The glass fragments there are all that is left of a vial which contained a substantial amount of hydrofluoric acid, which, among its many properties, is capable of eating through glass. Once that occurred, the acid dropped slowly down upon the false diamond, eventually dissolving it and leaving nothing behind but a slight odor and the most minimal of stains. I detected both when I first examined the case, and as you can see, the evidence which has now been revealed confirms my theory."

"And how did Curtis play into this?" asked Crowley, suddenly, from across the room. "I'd like to know, as he very nearly cost me my life!"

"Elementary, Mr. Crowley," said Holmes. "Sir Fallowgrove required the cooperation of Mr. Curtis in order to authenticate his fake diamond, as well as to facilitate the insuring of it by Lloyds of London. Undoubtedly, Mr. Curtis bribed his 'experts' to confirm his findings about the Other Eye, and this final act set in motion the events which followed."

"Unfortunately, he's not directly responsible for the death of Sir Fallowgrove," declared Pinkerton, "or we'd hang him, sure as the day is young."

"I believe you would have no need to do so," said Holmes, dispassionately. "Curtis has been exposed to the acid as well, and while it may take him some time longer for his life to end, I have no doubt that a premature death will ultimately be his fate."

"And so it goes," said I, "for those who seek to unlawfully acquire the possessions of others."

"As Sir Walter Scott so aptly wrote in his memorable poem, *Marmion*," said Holmes, "'Oh! what a tangled web we weave, When first we practice to deceive!' Sir Fallowgrove and Mr. Curtis have no one to blame but themselves, Watson, and in the end they will have both paid dearly for their actions."

"I must say, Mr. Holmes," said Pinkerton, "that I am greatly impressed. Very much so!" He reached into his vest pocket and removed a flat metal object and thrust it toward my friend. "Please take this as a token of our appreciation and respect, sir, and by all means, feel free to call upon us should the need arise."

Holmes took the item, which I now recognized as a Pinkerton National Detective Agency badge, and slipped it into his coat pocket.

"Thank you, Mr. Pinkerton," said Holmes. "I shall bear that in mind."

"Please do," replied Pinkerton. "As it turns out, bringing you on board was the best decision I could have made." He turned toward Inspector Lestrade, who had suddenly become quite busy herding the witnesses from the parlor. "Had I left it up to the police, the Pinkertons might very well have been left with a highly visible *black* eye!"

"I am pleased to have been of service," said Holmes, "but now the sun is well up and I believe it is time we considered breakfast. Would you not agree, Watson?"

"At the risk of being rude, I would very much like to join you, Mr. Holmes," said Pinkerton. "Given your success with this case, I'm quite curious to hear your thoughts on our pursuit of Adam Worth."

"Perhaps another day, Holmes?" I asked, pleadingly. "I am ready for a nap, and a full breakfast will only compound my desire for rest."

"Remember, Doctor," said Pinkerton, with a thin smile, "there is no rest for the wicked. And because of that, a Pinkerton never sleeps!"

"You make an excellent point," said Holmes, thoughtfully. "I must confess, I find Mr. Worth's activities to be of substantial interest. Please, do join us for breakfast."

"A Pinkerton never sleeps," said I, wearily, "and so it appears, neither do we."

An Affair of the Heart

By Mark Mower

Mark Mower is a member of the Crime Writers' Association, the Sherlock Holmes Society of London and the Solar Pons Society of London. He writes true crime stories and fictional mysteries. His first two volumes of Holmes pastiches were entitled *A Farewell to Baker Street* and *Sherlock Holmes: The Baker Street Case-Files* (both with MX Publishing) and, to date, he has contributed chapters to seven parts of *The MX Book of New Sherlock Holmes Stories*. He has also had stories in two anthologies by Belanger Books: *Holmes Away From Home: Adventures from the Great Hiatus – Volume II – 1893-1894* (2016) and *Sherlock Holmes: Before Baker Street* (2017). More are bound to follow.

Amber Tutwiler (b. 1988) is an emerging artist from South Florida. Her work is a meditation on interface; specifically, it is concerned with the interface between our physical, corporeal world and the digital landscape arising from the world. Focusing on an interdisciplinary practice, she works across oil painting, sculpture and installation, audio, video, and performance. She attended Alexander W. Dreyfoos School of the Arts, Massachusetts College of Art and Design, and received her MFA in Visual Art from Florida Atlantic University (2017). From 2017-2018, she completed a residency at the Armory Art Center in West Palm Beach, Florida. She is an adjunct instructor at Florida Atlantic University and Palm Beach State College. She has won various awards, including the Women in Visual Arts Scholarship, the Thesis and Dissertation Scholarship, and the Williamsburg Painting Award. In 2018, she had her first solo exhibition, *Interface*, at the Fritz Gallery, and collaborated as Creative Designer with Lauren Carey of Ballet Florida in an immersive dance, *Welcome*. In this time, she has established West Palm Beach's only artist collective, H/OURS Collective.

www.ambertutwiler.com

Artwork size: 18" x 24"

Medium: Oil on Canvas

In my long association with Sherlock Holmes, I only ever knew him to be an honourable and loyal friend, who could be relied upon to act with the utmost tact and discretion on any matters of a personal nature. So it was that when I found myself embroiled in a distinctly delicate family matter in the autumn of 1886, it was to Holmes that I naturally deferred.

We were sitting in the congenial surroundings of Brown's Hotel in Albemarle Street having just met with the establishment's proprietor in his newly refurbished lounge bar. Holmes had been engaged to tackle a potentially damaging case of jewellery theft from one of the more expensive suites in the hotel, occupied at that time by a crown prince from Eastern Europe. I had high hopes that this would turn out to be a colourful and absorbing episode, which might showcase my friend's remarkable talents. In reality, what I had envisaged somewhat prematurely as *The Curious Case of the Ukrainian Emerald* was solved by Holmes in less than half an hour, leading to the very public arrest by Scotland Yard of both the crown prince and his criminally-complicit manservant. It was clearly not the outcome that the hotel owner had anticipated and, having paid Holmes very discreetly for his services, the red-faced manager left us to finish what remained of our strong Turkish coffee and Panamanian cigars.

Holmes turned towards me with a telling grin. "Not one for your journal then, Watson? I fear that a simple case of insurance fraud is unlikely to excite the interests of your expectant readers. Still, while we have a quiet moment, it might be a good time for you to share with me the concerns you have about your nephew Christopher's impending marriage to Mrs Virginia Aston-Cowper."

His offhand comment caught me completely by surprise. "Holmes, I had no idea that you had spoken recently to young Christopher. I do indeed have some reservations about the match, but cannot see how my nephew knows of these – it is a good six months since we last had any sort of conversation. In any case, it was only four days ago that I received the wedding invitation, which, I have to say, came very much out of the blue."

"My dear friend, I have had no such conversation with Christopher. In fact, if you remember, I have only met him but the once, on the infamous occasion that he called upon us at Baker Street, claiming to have lost his wallet and being without the train fare to enable him to get back to his student digs in Oxford."

"Yes, of course," I replied, remembering how embarrassing the incident had been. "Not the first time his excessive gambling has got him into trouble. But how, then, do you know about his recent news and my thoughts on the matter? Please tell me this isn't some elaborate parlour trick on your part."

Holmes laughed heartily. "From a lesser man, I might have taken that as an insult, Watson. There is no trickery I can assure you. As you said, the wedding invitation arrived four days ago. It was the only letter addressed to you from the pile that Mrs Hudson brought up to me that day. I cast a glance at the envelope and then placed it in your post rack."

"I trust you didn't return to the letter and open it without my knowledge?"

"Of course not – the envelope told me all that I needed to know. The letter was postmarked 'Oxford' and the address was written in that small, spidery hand which I have come to recognise as that of your nephew. While you may not see or speak to him often, I have observed that Christopher's letters have been arriving more frequently of late, no doubt linked to his gambling debts, but expressed to you in his polite requests for small amounts of money to support his continuing medical studies at the university. That this particular letter was not one of those regular communiqués was apparent from the oddly-sized envelope, which enclosed a card of some sort. Coupled with the clearly displayed 'RSVP' on the back, it was not hard to discern that this was a wedding invitation. And on reading through the announcements in *The Times* that same day, I couldn't fail to see the notice regarding the forthcoming marriage of 'Mr Christopher Henry Watson of Trinity College, Oxford, to Mrs Virginia Belvedere Aston-Cowper of Bexley Heath, Kent'."

"Very neat, Holmes, but how did you know that I had failed to greet the news with any great relish? It is true, that I have tried to support my nephew through all of the troubles he has encountered since the death of my alcoholic brother. I have a great affection for the boy, especially since he has chosen to devote himself to a course of study which mirrors my own. But this latest caper is indeed troubling. And yet, I cannot recollect saying anything to you about the matter."

"Precisely so, and the very fact which prompted me to take note. It is not every day that one receives an invitation to a family wedding and yet you chose not to mention it. Of late, you have been less garrulous than normal and given to periods of intense introspection. The invitation also required a prompt response - something you would attend to ordinarily by return of post. Thus far, you have seen fit to leave the invitation inside the envelope, which this morning still sat within the letter rack. Lethargy is not a characteristic you are prone to, Watson, so I can only conclude that you have chosen to delay your response, being troubled once again by the imprudence of your nephew."

His pinpoint accuracy in targeting such a raw nerve left me deflated. "I was unaware that my innermost thoughts were so easily exposed," said I. "What do you make of the situation?"

He lent across to the low coffee table in front of us and stubbed out what remained of his cigar. "As you know, I am not given to any moral panics or ethical dilemmas when it comes to affairs of the heart. I do not profess to know what drives a man to declare his undying love for another and be content to live out his existence in the shadow of *a better half*. In this case, I take it that your main concern is the fact that Mrs Aston-Cowper is both a widow and a woman some years older than Christopher?"

"Eighteen years older, to be precise!" My anger had surfaced finally and I could no longer hide my frustrations of late: "Christopher is a rash, happy-go-lucky, sort of fellow. But his heart has always been in the right place. A more devoted, loving individual it would be hard to find - exactly as my brother had been, before he descended into poverty and took to the bottle. What I fear, is that his mounting debts and overriding material desires are clouding his judgement. Mrs Aston-Cowper is a wealthy woman, who is no doubt flattered by the attentions of a younger man. As such, they both have something to gain from the union. And yet, I fear it will be a marriage of simple convenience that one or both parties will live to regret."

"Watson, you have the upper hand on me. I feel disinclined to venture any opinion on Christopher's romantic inclinations and cannot claim to know his wider motivations. But what of the lady herself – what more do you know of her?"

"Alas, very little. I made some discreet enquiries at one of my dining clubs. A steward there knows of her, and furnished me with a few particulars. She is the widow of Sir Ashley Aston-Cowper, the eminent anatomist, famed for carrying out some pioneering arterial surgery on one of the Queen's continental cousins. When he passed away in February of last year, he left his wife a fashionable and expensive home in Bexley and a tidy annual income to match. Inexplicably, she has, since that time, ceased to use the honorific title of 'Lady Aston-Cowper'."

"Yes, indeed. But there is something more. I cannot recollect all of the details, but seem to remember that she was embroiled in some sort of scandal involving the younger son of the Duke of Buckland."

"Well, that is news to me!" I spluttered. "And what was the nature of this impropriety?"

"Given the delicacy of the situation, Watson, I am loath to tell you anything that is not completely accurate. I suggest we retrace our steps back to Baker Street, where I can consult my files and tell you all of the pertinent facts surrounding the *Cheddington Park Scandal.*

****

The two-mile walk back to Baker Street lifted my mood considerably and I felt reassured that I had, at last, confided in Holmes. But at the back of my mind, I was now anxious that the matters he had referred to might exacerbate my woes about the marriage.

On entering 221B, we were greeted immediately by an agitated Mrs Hudson. "I'm so sorry, Mr Holmes, but the lady insisted on waiting for your return. I have just taken her a cup of tea, but she seems very emotional and has already sat upstairs for the best part of an hour."

"Understood, Mrs Hudson, then we will delay her no longer," Holmes replied, removing his overcoat and hat and nodding for me to do the same. "But do please tell us – who is our resolute, yet excitable guest?"

Mrs Hudson's reply came as a surprise to us both. "Her calling card says 'Aston-Cowper'… 'Mrs Virginia Belvedere Aston-Cowper'."

We climbed the seventeen steps to the upstairs room and entered the study. Mrs Aston-Cowper stood promptly to greet us, dropping her small handbag on to the chair she had been sitting in. It was clear that she had been crying and she still held within her delicate, gloved left hand a small handkerchief which I gathered she had been using to dry her tears.

The lady appeared to be considerably younger than I had expected. While I knew her to be just over forty years of age, I could not in all honesty say that she looked a day over thirty. She was slender in build and around five feet, ten inches tall. Beneath her heavy black shawl, she wore a long, exquisitely tailored dress of green silk, which accentuated her slim figure. Her bright, delicate face was framed with a mass of dark curls, on which sat a velvet bonnet festooned with a colourful assembly of flowers. As I approached her, I was transfixed by her intense blue eyes.

Holmes greeted her warmly. "Mrs Aston-Cowper! I am so sorry to have kept you waiting." She raised her right hand towards him and he shook it gently. "I am Sherlock Holmes, as you may have

184

guessed, and this is my colleague, Dr John Watson, the man you have really come to see. Please, be seated.”

Her face took on a look of gentle surprise and she smiled pleasantly as I too shook the hand that was extended towards me. She then sat back down and proceeded to remove her shawl, black gloves and the green velvet bonnet, revealing the full extent of her brunette locks. “I suppose I should have guessed that a celebrated consulting detective would have little trouble in discerning the primary reason for my visit,” she said, in a confident tone.

We both took seats facing her and I could not resist the opportunity to make an immediate observation: “Mrs Aston-Cowper, no doubt you wish to talk to me about your forthcoming marriage to my nephew Christopher? I imagine that he asked you to come here, knowing that if he had come himself, I would have expressed my displeasure at his hasty matrimonial plans. You may view me as overly-protective and unreasonably paternalistic towards him, but I think I should point out that Christopher is, in many respects, the closest thing I have to a son of my own. I have no reason to question your affections for him, but fear that he may be marrying you for his own selfish reasons.”

Her response was both earnest and considered. “Dr Watson, I thank you for your honesty and directness, as I much prefer a man who says what is on his mind. Christopher knows nothing of my visit today. He holds you in high regard and has told me much about your loyalty and steadfast support for him and his studies. I have taken on the task of arranging all of the preparations for the wedding in order that Christopher may concentrate on the final batch of his university examinations. Of all the invitations I had sent out, yours was the only one which had not prompted any sort of reply. I am told that you are a proactive man, with a military disposition to get things done, so could envisage only two reasons for this. Either, you had not received the letter, or, having taken delivery of it, you had decided that you did not wish to attend the ceremony. My visit today was designed, in part, to clarify if the latter was the case and I recognise now that it was. I know how hurt Christopher will be if you are absent on the day, so I implore you to reconsider, for both our sakes.”

I could not fail to be moved by her appeal and apologised for having not replied to the invitation. At that same time, I resisted the temptation to glance at Holmes, and wondered what he must be making of all this. I then found myself agreeing to attend the wedding, which elicited a most radiant smile from our guest.

“I am so happy to hear you say that, sir! And please, rest assured, I have the measure of Christopher and his wayward habits. Since we first met two months ago at a charitable event in Oxford, we have been the closest of kindred spirits and have both determined that there should be no secrets between us. I have been candid in telling him about my first marriage to Sir Ashley Aston-Cowper and some of the incidents in my life of which I am less than proud. He, likewise, has been open in sharing with me his addiction to gambling and his dishonesty in approaching many of his family and friends for funds to support his compulsion…”

Holmes shuffled in his chair and stifled a chortle with the pretence of a cough.

“…I am convinced now that he has put all of that behind him and is genuinely determined to complete his studies and take up a position he has been offered at Guy’s Hospital.”

I could but marvel at the turnaround in my nephew's fortunes if what I had heard was true. Having now met his intended and listened to her passionate defence of him, I hoped that this was indeed the case. I turned to the question of his career prospects - "And you say he has been approached by Guy's?"

"Yes, well, *approached* may not be an accurate interpretation. I will be honest in sharing with you that it was I that secured the offer. My late husband was very well regarded in his surgical role at Guy's and I have maintained close friendships with some of his former colleagues. It was not difficult to put in a good word for Christopher, knowing that he has both the skills and determination to succeed in his career."

This time it was Holmes who spoke. "It seems you have taken an extraordinary risk in placing your faith and love in a young man you have known for such a short time and who has yet to establish himself in society. You are a woman with both status and wealth. Are you not concerned that others may judge your betrothal to be reckless?"

"I have ceased to worry about what others may think. Call it an affectation of age, but I have reached a point in life where I choose to do those things which *feel* right, rather than those which are deemed by others to be the most rational or sensible course. Knowing something of your professional approach, Mr Holmes, I imagine that may be anathema to you."

My admiration for this woman was growing steadily and I could understand now why my nephew had become so infatuated with her. Undoubtedly, she had the measure of most of the men she encountered.

Holmes ignored her passing remark and changed tack, as only he could. "Mrs Aston-Cowper, it seems you have resolved the matter of Watson's attendance at your wedding. Perhaps now you will turn to the other pressing issue which has brought you here today. If I am not mistaken, you are seeking my help on the delicate matter of the *Cheddington Park Scandal*.

The lady was quite taken aback. She looked to me fleetingly, possibly seeking some sort of explanation or reassurance, but then turned her gaze back to Holmes, her penetrating blue eyes fixed on his. "That is most remarkable. How could you possibly know that?"

"Aligning a few facts and observations into a feasible hypothesis is the very essence of my craft – the science of deduction. Your earlier comments suggested that beyond the immediate matter of the wedding, you had a further, *secondary* reason for travelling across to Baker Street. This was clearly an issue of some importance, for you were prepared to wait over an hour for our return. And yet, you had not thought to send a telegram or to alert us in any other way to your impending visit. That this is also a very personal matter is evident from your emotional state. Putting both facts together suggests to me that something has happened very recently which has made this a more immediate concern, which you feel unable to deal with on your own. Perhaps there was also a degree of opportunism in coming here, knowing that your visit to Dr Watson might also provide you with access to his colleague, the detective. I am also aware that last year you were embroiled in some delicate matters at your Cheddington Park home, which may now have ramifications for the planned wedding. All in all, it seemed most likely that that would be the topic on which you would wish to consult me."

She continued to look at him in astonishment. "I declare that I am rarely shocked by much these days, Mr Holmes, but that has certainly caught me by surprise. I hope you will be able to assist me, but fear that I may be clutching at straws, as this is a most delicate and intractable problem. I would, of course, be pleased to reward you handsomely for any help you can provide..."

Holmes looked troubled by the reference to money and was quick to interject. "My dear lady, you need not concern yourself with the latter. I ask only that you acquaint me with the relevant facts of the case, so I may determine if there is any way that I can assist. Without the data, I can do nothing."

Mrs Aston-Cowper appeared to take this as a positive signal and offered up another of her beguiling smiles. "I will, then, begin at the very start and tell you all that I can. I am not sure how much will be relevant, but will let you decide the matters of substance. You will then understand why it is such a personal and immediate concern."

I took the opportunity to ask a quick question: "You have indicated that this is a very personal matter. Would you prefer it, if I were to leave at this point?"

"Certainly not, Doctor. I know that you work in close collaboration with Mr Holmes and can be trusted to be discreet. You have thus far been very open and honest with me. It is fitting that I should extend you the same courtesy."

I smiled and nodded. Holmes brought his fingertips together and raised them to his chin. He then planted his elbows on the arms of his chair and closed his eyes. Mrs Aston-Cowper then began her narrative.

****

"My story begins in the summer of 1863, when I was just nineteen years old. My parents, Henry and Vivienne Melrose, felt strongly that all four of their female progeny should experience as much of life as was possible before marrying well and settling down to a quiet life of domesticity. Central to this enlightened ethos was the belief that travel would broaden our horizons and enrich our conversation. I had no great desire to travel, but faced with the gentle encouragement of my mother and the generous financial backing of my father, found myself that year in the colourful city of Paris. All of the arrangements had been made for me to stay for a period of six weeks, to see all that the metropolis had to offer and to make good use of the conversational French I had been learning for about a year. Travelling with me was Mrs Rose Sutherland, a seventy-year-old chaperone chosen by my mother, who had earlier accompanied my three older siblings to their favoured destinations in other parts of Europe.

"From the outset, the carefully formulated plans of my sojourn began to unravel, when dear Mrs Sutherland contracted a debilitating stomach complaint on the sea crossing to France and then spent the first week of the trip confined to her bed within the Hôtel de Crillon. I was content to amuse myself in and around the hotel while she recuperated, each day gaining the confidence to walk a little further from my base, seeking out whatever cultural diversions I could find. Of course, I told Mrs Sutherland nothing of these little excursions.

"On my third day, I visited the impressive gothic cathedral of Notre-Dame, and while walking close to the River Seine chanced upon a group of English artists painting an exterior view of the building. The party had travelled across to France together - a mixed group of male and female painters of all ages who seemed to revel in the relaxed bohemian atmosphere that Paris afforded them. My eye was drawn, in particular, to a watercolour by one of the older men, Gerald Stanhope, who told me that he was a student of the Royal Academy. Imagining that the picture would make a perfect gift for my parents, I asked him politely if it was for sale. He smiled and said that while he could not possibly take any money from me, he would be prepared to let me have the painting if I agreed to sit for him the next day.

"You will no doubt think me naïve, gentlemen, when I say that the proposition - put to me as it was on that fine, sunny day, along a beautiful stretch of river and among a group of talented artists – did not at the time strike me as odd or offensive. I agreed to meet up with the very charming Stanhope the next day, in the Pigalle garret he had rented for the duration of his stay. The following afternoon, I found my way to the garret and climbed the stairs to what was a small, but luxurious attic complex with access to a rooftop terrace overlooking the city's fine skyline. Stanhope had been true to his word and already had the watercolour wrapped for me to take away. That left the small matter of the sitting.

"Looking around the garret, I could see that he had been extremely industrious in his work; the walls, floor, tables and sofas of the apartment were covered in sketches, watercolours and canvases of all sizes. I could also see various bits of equipment which Stanhope informed me he had acquired for his developing interest in amateur photography. But the two small canvasses which really caught my attention were those hanging in pride of place on the wall of the main room. Both were of young women no older than myself, and each had been captured reclining and naked. I felt myself flush in embarrassment as I realised that this was what the artist now had in mind for me. With the bargain struck, I was immature enough to believe that I had no alternative but to go through with the sitting.

"I should say at this stage, that Stanhope acted without any hint of impropriety, busying himself with the easel and canvas and selecting his oil paints, as I began to remove my clothes. I thought only of the classical tradition of creative muses and the many women before me who had bared themselves in the name of art. It all felt very wrong, but I convinced myself mentally that it would all soon be over and no lasting harm would result. The artist then directed me to recline on the chaise longue he had prepared and which I recognised from the two paintings on the wall.

"Little by way of conversation passed between us, as he seemed to prefer to work without interruption and with an intensity of concentration that I had rarely seen in a fellow human being. The one concession I did extract from him was that in naming the finished painting, he was not to make any specific reference to the identity of the artist's model. This he agreed to happily, pointing out that he had already done that with his two earlier models. In any case, throughout the short time that I had known him, I had only ever referred to myself as 'Virginia'.

"Time passed very slowly in that cramped garret and within a couple of hours I announced that I would have to get dressed and make my way back to the hotel, as my elderly chaperone would, without doubt, be wondering where I was. As ever, Stanhope was friendly and obliging, but indicated that he was far from finished and would have to carry on the following day, expecting clearly that I would make a return visit. Realising this to be the case, my emotions got the better of me and the tears welled up within my eyes. He could see my obvious distress and suggested an alternative, which in the awkwardness of the moment seemed to be preferable. He would set up his camera and take a single photograph of me, from which he could then work at his leisure without any further imposition on me.

"That then was that. When I arrived back at the hotel, I found that Mrs Sutherland had barely missed me. I vowed never to tell a soul about the incident and believed that no one could possibly know what I had done. I realised, of course, that in my haste to get away from that claustrophobic apartment, I had not even paused to look at how Stanhope had portrayed me. Had I done so, I may not have been so confident that this was the end of the matter.

"There is little more to say about the Parisian trip beyond that. Mrs Sutherland failed to return to full health after that first week and we concluded that our best course of action would be to return home early. Over time, I put the whole affair out of my mind and it would only re-enter my thoughts when I glanced occasionally at the Notre-Dame watercolour that graced the wall of my parents' conservatory.

"When I was twenty-five, I met and fell in love with Sir Ashley Aston-Cowper, a distinguished medical man, some years older than me. We were not to be blessed with children and despite his status as a surgeon he suffered with persistent heart problems, exacerbated by his extravagant lifestyle and love of fine wine and rich food. Ours was a happy marriage for the most part, although we had distinctly different circles of friends with whom we spent time, when not together. My preference was to visit my parents and sisters. Sir Ashley liked to mix with the more elite and wealthy members of his various clubs, societies and medical institutions. Occasionally, he would invite some of these to stay for the weekend in the exterior lodge close to the entrance of our Cheddington Park home. It was during this time that I first became acquainted with Roger Morton, the youngest son of the Duke of Buckland.

"From the outset, I disliked the man intensely. He was close to my own age, and younger than most of the group that my husband entertained on a regular basis. In short, he was brash, uncouth and self-obsessed. But what I particularly detested, were his barely concealed attempts to flirt with me in the presence of my husband. Sir Ashley seemed not to notice and clearly saw something in the man that eluded me. Morton lived off the not insignificant allowance that he received from his father, but maintained that he was an art dealer. And it was in this capacity, that he was to bring the past back to haunt me.

"Sir Ashley had invited a dozen guests over one weekend in February last year. Morton had arrived ahead of the others and seemed particularly pleased with himself, saying - out of earshot of my husband - that he had a surprise for me. He explained that the previous week he had purchased a job lot of paintings and ephemera from a major dealer in Brussels. This had included a number of works by British artists, including 'Gerald Stanhope'. He paused, allowing the name to hang in the air and watching for my reaction. I froze instantly, in the dawning realisation of what he had just said, and felt a cold chill descend through my body. 'So, it is you in the painting - I guessed as much!' he whispered with a smirk, before following one of our servants who was carrying Morton's bags and cases in through the door of the lodge.

"I recognised that Morton had the upper hand and the future of my marriage, if not my standing in society generally, would indeed be precarious if he were to reveal the painting to anyone. That Friday evening he seemed content to let the matter rest, casting me lascivious looks every time our eyes met. And it was only before lunchtime the following day that his intentions became clear. Catching me in the grounds of the house as I strolled through my favourite rose garden, Morton took me by the arm and announced that he wanted me as his mistress. He then added that if I were to refuse, he would reveal the painting to our guests that very evening. He left me to think it over.

"In that instant, I determined that I would not be held to ransom by the scoundrel and realised one immediate fact. Namely, that in threatening me, he had clearly brought the canvas with him. If I could find a way to get to the picture and destroy it, my future might yet be saved. As luck would have it, Sir Ashley had provided me with a perfect opportunity to put my plan into action. Over lunch, he announced that all of the guests were invited to take part in a bridge tournament in the main house, a proposal that all agreed to readily.

"That afternoon, feigning a headache, I left our guests to their card playing and headed for the kitchen, where I took from one of the cutlery drawers a small, sharpened fruit knife, which I hoped would be sufficient to cut the canvas from its frame. I then took a side door from the house, out of sight of the servants, and walked the short distance down the drive to the lodge. With all of the guests being entertained at the main house, I knew that the lodge would be deserted.

"When I entered Morton's room, I could see no obvious place in which he could have hidden the painting. All of the bags and cases he had brought with him were empty, their original contents having been placed in the drawers and wardrobe of the bedroom. That left only the small loft space above the bed. I retrieved a set of wooden steps from an adjoining room and climbed until I was able to push open the loft door and look inside. To my frustration, I could see nothing in the darkness and had to come back down the ladder to find a hurricane lantern in a store cupboard, which I lit to take back up with me. My second attempt met with success as I could now see, some five feet from my grasp, a wrapped package which I guessed to be the canvas. But as I went to climb further up the ladder and into the loft, I felt a rough tug on my left ankle and heard Morton shout loudly for me to come down. Startled, I lost control of the lantern and it fell heavily, the glass globe breaking and igniting the paraffin which spilled out from the lamp.

"Morton dragged me bodily from the ladder and pushed me aside before climbing on the steps and trying to ascend into the loft. I seized the opportunity and ran from the room as he was driven back by the flames now engulfing the tinder dry rafters of the roof space. When I managed to get back to the safety of the house, I raised the alarm and soon both servants and guests were running to and from the lodge with buckets of water in a futile attempt to extinguish the inferno.

"Sir Ashley knew that at the time of the fire only Morton and I had been at the lodge. Morton had dropped out of the card game early on, saying that he needed to retrieve something from the lodge. Having raced back to the house to raise the alarm, it was obvious that I had not been in my room suffering with a headache. That evening, with the lodge now completely devastated by the fire, my husband called both Morton and I to his study and asked for an explanation. My initial fear was that our guest would now take his revenge by telling Sir Ashley all about the painting, which had also been destroyed. However, he went one step further in his vengeance, claiming that we had been having a secret affair for months and I had talked about the prospect of marriage once Sir Ashley had succumbed to the inevitable heart disease with which he was afflicted.

"I need hardly tell you, Mr Holmes, that what Morton did that evening was far worse than revealing the existence of a scandalous painting. When Sir Ashley looked at me for some challenge or corroboration of the story, I fell mute – unable to defend myself or tell him what had really gone on. Morton was told in no uncertain terms to leave Cheddington Park immediately and to never show his face in front of Sir Ashley again. I was instructed that while we would give outsiders and household staff the impression that our marriage was solid we would, from that moment on, cease to be husband and wife. In the event, there was no need for any such pretence. The shock of the alleged affair was more than my husband's heart could take and during the night he suffered a fatal attack.

"Of course, with a house full of well-connected guests whose weekend had been cut short by the drama of what had gone on, it did not take long for the rumours to start circulating. A mysterious fire, the unexpected death of a Knight and talk that his Lady wife had been having an affair were bound to have a resonance. Some of Sir Ashley's friends and colleagues began to shun me, but on the whole most were supportive in my hour of need. Most significantly, Roger Morton seemed to have disappeared and I was told later by one of our circle that he had gone to New York to work for an auction house.

"The fact that the provisions of Sir Ashley's will remained unchanged and I was left both Cheddington Park and an annual income helped to persuade some doubters that there had been no obvious rift between the two of us. But I felt distinctly uncomfortable about the bequest and decided to cease using the title 'Lady Aston-Cowper'. It was a small gesture, but it was my way of showing that I did not want to dishonour the memory of my dear husband.

"After some months, my life began to return to some semblance of normality, helped by the unerring support of my family. And, most recently, I met Christopher, who has proved to be the most loyal and compassionate man I have ever known. As we became closer, I took the decision to share with him the full story of what the newspapers had called the *Cheddington Park Scandal*."

Our guest paused briefly, and Holmes – who had to that point given every impression of being fast asleep – opened his eyes quizzically, and prompted our guest: "Please, Mrs Aston-Cowper, I think you were about to bring us up to date and reveal the telegram you received this morning from Roger Morton threatening to make public the photograph taken of you by Gerald Stanhope."

The lady swallowed heavily. "Yes, indeed, Mr Holmes, but I am again in awe of your deductive capabilities. I made no mention of the telegram…"

"No. But you did not challenge me when I put it to you earlier that something had happened very recently. And when we entered the room it was clear that you had been re-reading something which had once again brought you to tears. For reasons of vanity, you were quick to dispense with the pince-nez which you slid swiftly into your chatelaine bag. The telegram did not fare so well – it still sits beside you, now looking rather crumpled, but clearly displaying today's date. As for the photograph, it struck me from your account that if Morton had managed to purchase Stanhope's original oil painting - and had been so sure that you were the model in it - it was also extremely likely that he had acquired the accompanying photograph. In my experience, blackmailers relish a solid back-up plan."

"Simply astonishing!" she uttered, a broad smile now covering her face. "So, vanity was my undoing, yet again. And you are quite correct about the content of the telegram. I had not heard one word from Roger Morton since the night of the fire and believed that he had no further hold on me with the destruction of the canvas. The telegram came as a complete shock."

"It would be helpful to see the precise wording of the message," said Holmes.

She rose from her chair and passed the telegram to my colleague. He looked it over for some minutes and then read aloud: '*More to come on Cheddington scandal…a photograph…will prevent marriage = M.*' Very interesting - it seems that Mr Morton is determined to scupper your wedding plans, Mrs Aston-Cowper, and is prepared to go to great lengths to do so. That recent announcement in *The Times* has clearly been picked up by our man in America who now plans to travel back to England to sow the seeds of your undoing."

I then interposed. "Why do you say that, Holmes?"

"Well, he has no way of knowing that Mrs Aston-Cowper has already told your nephew about the canvas and photograph so is labouring under the delusion that his disclosure of the latter would prevent the wedding. That said, if the photograph were to fall into the wrong hands, it could still be tremendously damaging to both their reputations. And yet, Morton clings to some hope that he can negotiate a deal. If that were not the case, he would already have exposed the photograph to the American press, who would no doubt relish a story about the fall from grace of a British Lady. The telegram was sent from New York yesterday evening by the Western Union Telegraph Company. It seems to me that Morton despatched it before boarding a passenger liner for the transatlantic passage to Liverpool."

With that, he leapt from his seat and began to rummage through a pile of loose folders in a corner of the room. Mrs Aston-Cowper looked on with some consternation. When he returned to his seat a minute or two later, Holmes was waving a bright-coloured pamphlet.

"Here it is - a brochure for the British and North American Royal Mail Steam-Packet Company. The passenger liner *Scotia* was due to set off yesterday for the eastbound crossing. This is the oceangoing steamer that won the *Blue Riband* for the westbound passage three years ago. The voyage is estimated to take between ten and fourteen days, which should mean that Roger Morton will be docking at Liverpool in early September."

Mrs Aston-Cowper continued to look confused. "And what happens then?"

"Why, it should be a simple matter of greeting him at the port and persuading him to hand over the photograph," Holmes retorted. "That is a task you can leave to the inestimable talents of Dr Watson here."

I was flattered by Holmes faith in me, but not a little disturbed at the thought that the social standing of both my nephew and his bride to be might depend on my success in completing the mission. Mrs Aston-Cowper seemed delighted by the plan, rising from her chair to come and shake me warmly by the hand, before offering some words of encouragement.

"Doctor, I will forever be in your debt if you can manage to resolve this issue. It is more than I could have hoped for in coming here today, when my principal objective was to persuade you to attend a wedding! And I will be eternally grateful for the professional assistance you have offered, Mr Holmes. You have a rare set of talents. I must now take my leave. And while I am loath to keep anything from Christopher - as I hinted at earlier - I do believe it would be better for all concerned, if nothing more was said about our meeting today."

"That would be best for us all," agreed Holmes, with a mischievous smile. "Without any disrespect to you, Mrs Aston-Cowper, I would not wish it to be known by my colleagues at Scotland Yard that I am now providing guidance on marital matters."

Our client left us in good humour and I looked forward to meeting her again at the wedding that October. For the next week or so, I sought regular updates from the steamship company on the likely progress of the *Scotia* and made plans to travel up to the Port of Liverpool to greet the arrival of the passenger liner. When it berthed at the Albert Dock on Monday, 3rd September, I was more than prepared for the encounter with Roger Morton.

He emerged from the dock office in the company of a porter who was pulling a hand trolley on which sat a large cabin trunk. Morton was well over six-feet tall and solidly built. He was dressed in a knee-length tweed frock coat, a white shirt and wide dark-red necktie. On his head sat a tall top hat. He looked every part the English aristocrat.

As I stepped forward, he pre-empted my challenge. "Dr Watson, I take it? I understand that you are here to collect this from me," said he, thrusting a large envelope into my hand. There was no warmth in his tone and his dark brown eyes fixed on mine with a degree of menace. Not to be intimidated, I continued to hold his stare and then turned my attention to the envelope. As I opened it, I could see that it contained the salacious image of the young Virginia Melrose.

"Our business is concluded then, Mr Morton," I said, turning briskly and walking away to be bemused looks of the porter.

It was clear that Morton felt he had to have the last word. "For what it's worth, you can tell her that she was never a great beauty!" His words echoed around the dock office. I carried on walking.

When I arrived back at Baker Street a couple of days later, Holmes was waiting for me with a stiff glass of brandy. "Warm yourself up with this, Watson, it is unseasonably cold today."

I could not resist chiding him for the unnecessary display. "Holmes, I have known you too long to be fooled by any of this. You knew full well that Morton could be persuaded to hand over the letter. When I met him at the docks he already knew who I was. So, how did you do it?"

Holmes smirked, knowing that I was more relieved than upset by his intervention. "My dear fellow, I could not send you into battle without providing you with reinforcements. A quick visit to my brother Mycroft was all that was required. Having heard the story, he travelled up to Liverpool ahead of you and arranged to be taken out by tug to the *Scotia* as the liner began its entry to the port. When he tracked Morton down on board the ship, he made it clear that if the rogue did not hand the photograph to you at the dockside, both he and his father, the Duke of Buckland, would be blackballed in every gentleman's club in London. Furthermore, the Duke's loans on the current refurbishment of his Highland estates would be called in, rendering the family bankrupt. I suspect that was sufficient to seal the matter."

I was warmed by the subterfuge. "Then that is an end to the matter, Holmes. A job well done - I have destroyed the photograph, Mrs Aston-Cowper can rest easy, and we can all enjoy the wedding. Let's drink to that!"

A Ghost from Christmas Past

By Thomas A. Turley

This story first appeared in The MX Book of New Sherlock Holmes Stories, Part VII.

Thomas A. Turley has been "hooked on Holmes" since finishing *The Hound of the Baskervilles* at about the age of twelve. His first Sherlockian pastiche, *Sherlock Holmes and the Adventure of the Tainted Canister*, appeared as an MX e-book in 2014. He has two stories (*A Scandal in Serbia* and *A Ghost from Christmas Past*) in The MX Anthology of New Sherlock Holmes Stories, Parts VI and VII. Tom recently finished *The Case of the Dying Emperor* which will appear, along with "Serbia" and two new stories, in the forthcoming collection *Sherlock Holmes and the Crowned Heads of Europe*. Although he has a Ph.D. in British history, Tom spent most of his career as an archivist with the State of Alabama. He and his wife Paula are proud family members of two grown children, a beautiful new granddaughter, and a bossy little yellow dog. For more about Tom and his stories, see his Amazon author's page www.amazon.com/Thomas-A.-Turley/e/B01FL645TO and his occasional blog on Goodreads www.goodreads.com/author/show/8135315.Thomas_A_Turley.

Nune' Asatryan has been a professional artist and designer for 35 years. Nune participated as a jury member for selection of nomination of the best artwork at the 7th Annual Student Exhibition, The Fine Arts Center, Englewood, NJ. Her paintings are in the museum of Modern Art of Armenia, in the collection of Government of Armenia, and in private collections in Armenia, Russia, USA, Germany, Belgium, Canada, Iran, Lithuania and Poland. Nune is also Art Educator at Armory art Center, West Palm Beach.

www.artnune.com

Artwork size: 18 x 24

Medium: Oil on canvas

No doubt it is a sinful thing to rue the Christmas season. I do not mean the day itself, which remains for me—and all mankind—a day of joy, and hope, and spiritual renewal. I am no Ebenezer Scrooge; indeed, the tale of his redemption is my favourite of the many memorable works left to us by Mr. Dickens.

Yet, for the Watson family, the season surrounding Christmas Day has always been a time of sorrow. My mother's early death, occurring on its very eve in 1858,[i] haunted my father and my brother until their own lives ended, decades later, in misery and squalor. As a three-time widower, I have not escaped the curse. It was but eight years ago, just after Christmas, that my beautiful Priscilla was diagnosed with the cancer that would kill her within weeks.[ii] On December 22, 1891, I lost my beloved Mary with appalling suddenness. That remains a story, even now, that I am not prepared to tell.[iii]

But it is of my first wife, and an even earlier Christmas, that I shall write today. Hitherto, I have said little of Constance in my memoirs of Sherlock Holmes, so little that some readers, understandably, have confused her with Mary in cases that predate *The Sign of Four*. My reticence has not been due to a lack of regard for my poor angel, although our marriage was not, by its untimely end, a happy one. Rather, it was the uncanny manner of her death that led me to keep silent. Unlike Sir Arthur Conan Doyle, my friend and literary agent, I am not a believer in the supernatural. I remain quite sure that I myself have never seen a ghost. Yet, on the night that Constance died, I was moved to consider, for the first and only time in my long life, the possibility that ghosts exist.

To tell this story properly, I must begin by writing of my brother. I have done so only once before, and then misleadingly. *The Sign of Four* contains a passage in which Sherlock Holmes, after deducing Henry's tragic history by examining his watch, defends himself against my anger by protesting that he never knew I had a brother. That account was fiction. In fact, my friend had been aware of Henry for some years, for Holmes' substantial loan had financed my attempt to save him. Early in 1884, I left Baker Street to take up residence in San Francisco, California. There my brother and I spent our last days together, and there I met and fell in love with Constance Adams.[iv]

In many ways, my relationship with my elder brother helped to prepare me for my relationship with Holmes. Henry, like the great detective, possessed a far more agile mind than I do; he, too, had scant patience with slower-moving intellects. In his youth, my brother had seemed destined for a brilliant future, and it was our father's final disappointment that he abandoned law to follow me into the army. For a brief time, we served together in Afghanistan. My role as regimental surgeon ended with a wound at Maiwand; Henry, after an unhappy love affair, drowned his promising intelligence career in alcohol.[v] He never recovered, for my brother far exceeded Sherlock Holmes in his capacity for self-destruction. I arrived in San Francisco to find him sick and destitute, having in three years squandered his entire inheritance.

Oscar Wilde, who visited the bayside city shortly before I did, posited that "anyone who disappears is said to be seen in San Francisco."[vi] He concluded that it must be a delightful place, but that part of his *bon mot* failed my brother utterly. I found him settled in the most squalid corner of the city, known as the Barbary Coast. As a den of iniquity, it outstripped both Whitechapel and the worst haunts of Paris, but Henry had taken to his foul surroundings like an alligator to a swamp. He invested our father's legacy in a waterfront saloon, was swindled by his partner, and quickly lost himself in debt and dissipation. To my further horror, he had also married a young girl from the streets. She, at least, proved to be a gentle-natured, pretty creature, who nursed Henry devotedly when he became too ill to work. Even then, there was little wrong with my brother that rest, a better diet, and abstinence from whiskey would not cure. His situation was by no means hopeless if his self-respect could be restored.

In order to support the three of us, I sought employment as a *locum tenens* at several local hospitals. The Sisters of Mercy, a group of Irish nuns resident in San Francisco since the 1850's, put me to work at their clinic in Stockton Street.[vii] Here I ministered daily to the dregs of Barbary Coast society: drunken sailors, syphilitic prostitutes, and opium-addicted Chinamen. Unpleasant as it was, my experience later aided me in treating my poor friend Asa Whitney, although sadly he was one victim of the poppy whom I failed to cure.

I learned from the Sisters that San Francisco ran an Almshouse for its indigents, located on an old Mexican ranch outside the city. When I visited (expecting some Dickensian horror), I found eighty acres of arable, well-watered land, sheltered behind two prominent hills known as the Twin Peaks. The Almshouse operated as a communal farm, its inmates providing labour in return for lodging, food, and medical care. So successful were they that the farm produced a surplus for sale in San Francisco's markets.[viii] In short, it seemed an ideal place for my brother to recover. I felt sure that a few months of fresh air, hard work, and—above all—clean living would make a man of him again. Henry was not easy to persuade, angrily declaring that manual labour was beneath his dignity as an ex-officer. Considering his recent degradation, I took this protest as a healthy sign. Fortunately, even a younger brother may assert his authority as a physician. By late summer, Henry and Alice had translated to Laguna Honda, where they settled into their new life very well.

With my brother in an improved financial and physical condition, I began to seek a more advantageous personal arrangement that would allow me to pay off Henry's debts, as well as my own considerable arrears to Sherlock Holmes. In the spring of 1885, I was able to obtain custody of a small practice in Post Street,[ix] whose incumbent had (in the parlance of the day) "gone to Texas" to escape his own pecuniary troubles. Debt seemed to be a common theme in San Francisco! My office was close to the city's financial district and only a short cable-car ride from its hospitals, where I was by now well known. After hanging out my shingle, I looked forward to a better class of *clientèle* than I had met so far.

"A young lady to see you, Doctor."

The speaker was my nurse Miss Bivins, a relic (in every sense) left by my predecessor. Tall, elderly, and dour, she nonetheless was fully competent, and admirable as a chaperone when examining young ladies. In this case, no chaperone was needed; for the patient she admitted was accompanied by another incarnation of Miss Bivins, dressed in the regalia of a Spanish *dueña*. The young lady introduced her companion as Teresa. Her name was Miss Constance Adams.

"I've come for my spring tonic."

Her voice was light and clear, with traces of the graceful drawl found only in the southern states. I judged her to be no more than one-and-twenty: short of stature, but with a pleasingly full figure and a rounded, dimpled face. The hair beneath her bonnet was dark auburn, and her prominent eyes a striking shade of blue. Although Miss Adams looked to be in perfect health, I noticed that she dressed severely, almost as though she was in mourning. Otherwise, her attire exhibited both wealth and taste.

"Are you in need of a tonic?" I enquired. "You don't appear to be."

"I have *catarrh*," she insisted, with a charming pout.

"Dr. Richards prescribes Peruna for Miss Adams every spring," Teresa interjected.[x]

"Dr. Richards has 'gone to Texas,' and Peruna is little more than alcohol."

My comments evoked a frown from the *dueña*, but a smile from my new patient. "What would *you* recommend, then, Dr. Watson?" she asked impishly.

"Fresh air and exercise, primarily. Do you walk?"

"I walk each morning in our garden, and in Golden Gate Park[xi] some afternoons. In fine weather, we often make excursions to San Francisco Bay."

"Sea air is normally healthy, but fogs from the bay can be uncomfortably cold, even in mid-summer. Not the best thing for catarrh. Have you ever visited Laguna Honda? The ground is higher there, and fog dissipates quickly in the morning sun. Most of the area is open farmland, with a spring-fed lagoon that's quite delightful. My brother is a patient there. Perhaps," I found myself proposing, "I could accompany you one day."

"That," proclaimed Teresa sternly, "would not be acceptable to Colonel Adams."

"I had not thought of inviting Colonel Adams. But he would be more than welcome, if Miss Adams feels she needs a chaperone."

"That role is mine, *Señor*." The *dueña* rose. "Come, Miss Constance. It appears that the only suggestions this new doctor has to offer are improper ones."

"Your pardon, ladies," I said quickly. "Let me assure you that I meant no impropriety. I shall be more than happy to prescribe a tonic for Miss Adams. Though not one," I added firmly, "containing alcohol." I wrote out a prescription for a harmless nostrum and handed it to her.

"Thank you, Dr. Watson." Placing the prescription in her reticule, Constance also rose. "I must not detain you further. I am volunteering at St. Mary's Hospital this afternoon."

"As it happens, I go there later for my evening rounds." My association with a Catholic institution earned a nod from the *dueña*. At the door, Constance suddenly turned back to me.

"You're from Scotland, Doctor, are you not?"

"Yes, I was born in Stranraer. However, I lived most of my life below the Tweed before coming here from London."

"My mother is English." She seemed to muse on that fact momentarily. "It's been many years since I have seen her."

"Come, Miss Constance." Teresa took her charge's arm and positively hustled her from my consulting room.

After they departed, I pondered my unseemly conduct with dismay. I realised that I had, of late, enjoyed little social contact with young ladies, passing my days with the "soiled doves" I treated at St. Mary's Hospital. Had I, like Henry, lost the manners of a gentleman by associating with such company? Resolving to behave correctly towards her in the future, I was nonetheless determined to see more of Constance Adams.

In pursuit of that objective, I revised the schedule of my daily rounds to coincide with my fair patient's hours as a volunteer. Her *dueña* did not join in these public duties, so it was easy to arrange "fortuitous" encounters on the cable car that took Constance to the hospital. Soon this became our regular routine. Over the weeks, we progressed to less defensible excursions: joint attendance at receptions for St. Mary's volunteers, post-luncheon strolls through the park in Stockton Street, even late-afternoon visits to the zoological gardens.[xii] Once—daring greatly—Constance persuaded an old schoolmate to invite us both to tea.

In the course of these adventures, I learned more about her. She had come from a region of Alabama known as the Black Belt—so called for the richness of the soil, not the hands that tilled it. Her father, a wealthy cotton planter, had married a young English lady while on a European tour. When the South seceded, he—like most of his class—joined the Rebel army, rising to the rank of colonel. Constance was conceived during her father's convalescence from a wound in 1863. From the moment of her birth (as she mournfully expressed it), "everything went downhill" for the family. Union raiders cut a swath of destruction through the Black Belt, freeing the slaves on whom its affluence depended. Constance's older brother died of fever. Following Lee's surrender, Colonel Adams returned to find a grieving wife, a ruined plantation, and a daughter he had never seen. His wife left for England two years later. In 1869, Constance and her father removed to San Francisco. She could scarcely remember any other home.

With each passing day, our liking for each other deepened, and by early summer I had begun to think of Constance Adams as a potential wife. However, when I proposed making the acquaintance of her father, she at once demurred.

"Oh, no, John. Papa's health would not permit it."

"Then could I not call upon him in my medical capacity?"

She shook her head decidedly. "Papa has his own physician: Dr. Victor. He wouldn't like it if I brought in another doctor—especially anyone who was interested in me!"

This seemed an odd criterion for rejecting a physician. I was intrigued by Constance's continued reticence about the Colonel, whom she seldom mentioned of her own accord. On my next visit to Laguna Honda, I decided to ask Henry (who, after all, had run a public house) if he knew anything about the man.

After a year residing in the Almshouse, my brother had improved considerably from the shattered wreck I met on my arrival. The doctors had managed to cure his opium addiction, and he had recently forsaken alcohol. By day, Henry laboured almost frantically in the ranch's fields and orchards, having long since abandoned his objection to hard work. His nights were quietly occupied with Alice in their rooms in the communal dormitory. I was pleased to see that he had resumed his study of law books. Not unnaturally, my query about Adams—bringing with it a reminder of his old life—seemed to disturb him, but he answered readily enough.

"Old Adams? Yes, I remember him. They say he came here nearly twenty years ago; took up the shipping business and made a modest fortune. Unhealthy-looking ogre. I've been told he fought with Bedford Forrest's cavalry, but if he was anything like his present weight in those days, I pity the horse that had to carry him! Used to rent our spare room at the Parrot: 'eighty-two or -three, it must have been. Sometimes I'd go in to take them whiskey. *God*, I wish I had some now!"

"Steady on, old man," I murmured, as Alice smiled consolingly from her seat beside the hearth. Brushing back the hair from his perspiring forehead, Henry laughed ruefully and continued his account.

"Anyhow, Adams would meet back there with a handful of other wicked-looking fellows: Southerners as well; I got to know the accent. Sailors from a vessel called the *Lone Star*. Pretty little bark; got a look at her once down at the harbour. They'd spend hours discussing some dark business, sitting around a pile of ledgers and a strongbox. One night they were arguing over timetables and plotting courses on a map. Got the idea they must be after someone; maybe there was money missing. Never asked them anything about it, naturally. That was one group of fellows, John, you didn't want to cross."

As a depiction of my future father-in-law, I found my brother's tale disturbing. Even so, I thought little about it in the coming days, for my attention was more closely focused on the Colonel's daughter. On an afternoon in late July, as we idled through the zoo in Woodward's Gardens, I asked Constance whether I might call upon her father formally to request her hand. She blushed furiously, but quickly nodded her assent. Raising her chin, I kissed away the tears that sprang into her eyes, feeling certain that they must be tears of joy.

We arranged for Constance to call at my office the next morning to convey the Colonel's answer. At the appointed hour, after cheerfully replying to Miss Bivins' knock, I rose to greet my *fiancée* but found instead her *dueña*. Teresa offered me a pitying smile.

"Do you think I am a fool, *Señor?* How do you suppose Miss Constance so often escaped her father's vigilance over these past months? Remember, I myself was young once, long ago. I have been on your side almost from the first."

"But why?" I asked in stupefaction.

Teresa sighed, accepting the chair I offered her. "I have spoken of you to the Sisters, Doctor. They acknowledge that you are a good man, for a Protestant. They even pray your soul may be consigned to Purgatory, after only a few aeons in Hell. I have done as much for you and my poor girl as I am able. But you must be careful now.”

“Where is Constance?” I demanded. “Why has she not come herself?”

“She was not permitted. Nor would she have wished to meet you, bearing the bruised cheek her father gave her.”

“The blackguard! I shall have it out with him at once!” I leapt to my feet and started for the door, then realised that I did not know precisely where the Adams lived. Teresa seized my wrist in order to detain me.

“That would only make more trouble for Miss Constance, so long as she remains within his power. Be patient, child; you shall be with her in due time. Even the Devil cannot preserve the life of that foul man much longer.

“And now I must go, Doctor,” she concluded, patting my face gently as she stood. “You will have another visitor this morning, and I should not care for him to find me here.”

The *dueña* was not lacking in clairvoyance, for scarcely an hour passed before a thunderous pounding sounded on my door. The intruder pushed roughly past Miss Bivins before she could announce him, but I had no doubt of his identity.

I was never privileged to meet Professor Moriarty, the arch-enemy of Sherlock Holmes, but I did encounter two other lurid villains: Dr. Grimesby Roylott and Colonel Sebastian Moran. Wicked as they were, neither gave me the impression of unmitigated evil that I saw in the eyes of Colonel Alexander Adams. Between their drooping lids and leaden pouches, they were as cruel and lifeless as a cobra’s eyes. Yet, his dropsically gross body, the bluish pallor of his fleshy cheeks, even the phlegm that choked his rasping breath—all unmistakably announced his coming death from heart failure. I knew at a glance that soon my Constance would be free of him.

Colonel Adams glared at me with evident dislike, panting raggedly behind his walrus mustache. “I hear from my daughter, Doctor, that you want to marry her,” he growled.

My bow of assent seemed only to enrage the Colonel further. “Well, now,” he snarled, removing his top hat to mop the moisture from his balding pate. “What makes you think I’d let my only child wed some penniless Scots sawbones, the brother of a drunken bankrupt? Hey?

“No, sir!” he continued, lifting a hand to forestall my response. “She’ll not give herself to any blasted Britisher while I’m alive! Where was your country, Doctor, when Yankee cavalry was burning Alabama cotton destined for your mills? When the scions of your oldest families lay dying on the field at Gettysburg or Shiloh? You shall *never* have my consent to marry Constance! I warn you: better men than ‘Dr. John H. Watson’ have learned the danger of defying me. Damn you, sir! Keep away from my daughter, or I’ll—horsewhip—”

Adams’ tirade ended in a choking gasp, followed by a prolonged bout of coughing. Offering the man no aid, I waited for him to recover before making my reply.

“As a physician, Colonel, I should advise against such violent exercise in your condition. However, I can promise you that if you ever again lay a hand upon Miss Constance, you will find yourself on the wrong end of that horsewhip!”

The Colonel’s rage was awful. He raised his stick to strike at me, but I held my ground and stared him down. With a scowl befitting a stage villain, Adams turned ponderously upon his heel, snorting and wheezing as he lurched from my consulting room. The next day, Teresa sent a note advising me that Constance’s father had suffered an apoplectic fit upon returning home. He had taken to his bed and, according to his doctor, might never rise from it again.

Thereafter, the difficulties of our position were substantially reduced, for Constance and I could see each other openly. During that autumn, we enjoyed the most carefree times together we would ever know. I took her to concerts, receptions, even a masked ball. We boated on the San Francisco Bay and climbed one of the Twin Peaks. From its summit, I showed Constance the rolling pastures of Laguna Honda. We later visited to help its inmates with the harvest, and I introduced my *fiancée* to my brother. To my delight, they warmed to each other instantly. Nor did Constance show constraint towards Henry's wife, for both possessed an innate goodness that overcame disparities of background. The four of us were soon fast friends, and it gladdened my heart to see the ones I loved escape their woes and move towards happiness.

Yet, all was not sunlight and roses, for planning our future together was another matter. Constance, torn by guilt, steadfastly refused to leave San Francisco while her father was alive. For his part, the Colonel stubbornly declined to die. He had grown mortally afraid (Teresa said) of the hellfire that awaited him, and was now utterly dependent on his daughter. Consequently, our engagement languished unresolved into the spring of 1886. By May, I had paid the last of Henry's debts, as well as mine to Sherlock Holmes, and even accumulated a small profit. I decided to return to London in advance of Constance, intending to purchase a new practice that could support a wife.

When I think back upon that time today, my mind lingers on our final meeting at the docks in Market Street.[xiii] There I took leave of my tearful bride-to-be and bade farewell to my brother. I still cherish my last sight of Henry: tanned and healthy, full of cheerful confidence in his plan to qualify as an attorney, loving toward his pregnant wife, and for once treating "little brother" as an equal. Indeed, he was touchingly grateful for my help and seemed as reluctant as Constance to see me depart for England.

"Why not leave that Holmes fellow to his London fogs," entreated Henry, "and come back to us in San Francisco permanently? We can always use another doctor at Laguna Honda. I feel free here, brother—as free as when we were boys back in Australia.[xiv] As for your future bride," he added, giving her a hug, "we'll take good care of her 'till you return. I know you'll not forget her!" An anguished smile from Constance told me that she felt less sure.

And why (I ask myself, with forty years of hindsight) did I never consider remaining in America before that final afternoon? After two years in San Francisco, I had everything a man should need to make him happy. My only remaining family member was at hand, our relationship restored. A beautiful and charming woman had agreed to be my wife. My medical career was as successful as it could ever be in London. Was not a brother's love more to be valued than the sincere but unemotional regard (so I thought then) of my one real friend in England? As for my beloved, why risk her health and happiness by transplanting her from a temperate California bay into the foul and chilly fogs of London?

Had I known then what was to come, or could I have viewed my life as a Victorian from my vantage point today, I might have made a different choice. But at the time, neither my *fiancée's* wishes nor my brother's were paramount in my decision. Constance was to be my wife; she would follow where I led. Henry, having come at last to a safe harbour, was well content to become an American. I could never be anything other than a subject of our Queen; and I felt it my calling to be the friend, colleague, and biographer of the world's first private consulting detective, Sherlock Holmes. So I returned to London, purchased a small Kensington practice, and waited for my bride to join me. Late in September, after Colonel Adams had finally given up his wretched life, she came. We were married on the first day of November, with Holmes as my best man.

In our early weeks as man and wife, Constance and I seemed to make a good beginning. Our part of Kensington, near the palace and Hyde Park, was not unlike the area in San Francisco where she had resided. Though it was a costly neighbourhood, I had been able to acquire the house and practice of a retiring colleague on favourable terms. My wife, with Teresa's guidance, had previously overseen her father's household; so I was able to leave domestic arrangements in her hands. While she turned the building's upper storeys into a pleasant refuge, I installed my office and consulting room on the ground floor.[xv] Whenever we were free from medical duties or domestic chores, I showed my bride the sights of London. We walked daily in Hyde Park and often ventured on more distant forays, as we had done in San Francisco.

Initially, Constance was of much assistance in my practice, acting as receptionist and book-keeper. Although I hired a nurse, my wife's skills in this arena were considerable. Until her own health failed, she remained a bright and cheerful consolation to my patients, possessing both a sympathetic nature and an appreciation of their suffering through years of caring for her father. Had she chosen this vocation, Constance would have been a credit to Miss Nightingale.

Yet, there were also problems in the marriage from its outset. For all her joy at our reunion, my wife seemed ill at ease in her new country. British middle-class reserve conflicted with her Southern upbringing. Our neighbours, in my view, appeared to welcome the "young couple" in their midst; she found them "stand-offish." Disconcerted by London's size and dismal weather, Constance soon grew homesick for California. She also missed Teresa greatly. That formidable lady (by now dear to both of us) had declined to accompany her charge across the water, rightly declaring that "a married woman does not need a *dueña*, child."

This last word was in truth the essence of the trouble. Having abducted my bride from the cloistered life in which I found her, I now realised that she *was* child-like in many ways. As Holmes remarked soon after meeting Constance: "She is extremely young, Watson, for a woman of nearly three-and-twenty." Annoying as I found this ruthless honesty, I could not dispute the justice of his verdict.

I have often pondered whether my wife's immaturity would have posed a long-term problem in our marriage. It undoubtedly postponed my hope of Constance bearing children of our own. Time, of course, cures many ills; but time was not a blessing to be granted us. All other questions were soon cast aside by the steady decline of my wife's health, almost from the day that she reached England. For those whose lungs are delicate, the mild and cleanly fogs of San Francisco are no preparation for a London winter's filthy smog and eternally foul weather. Henceforth, Constance's "catarrh" would no longer be a joke between us. In the first months of 1887, she was laid low by a series of bronchial infections—each worse than the last—that undermined her health and, even more, her happiness. Spring brought no improvement, only a mild case of pneumonia. While Constance carried on bravely between bouts, the vivacity and sweetness that had so attracted me gradually diminished. My poor young wife became morose and irritable, red-eyed from weeping, as much from sheer misery as from her respiratory symptoms. Before long, I could read the unspoken accusation in her eyes: *"You brought me here."*

As her physician, it became obvious to me that unless Constance removed at once to a more forgiving climate, her lungs would be damaged irreversibly. How that imperative could be reconciled with establishing my practice became a vexing question. Fortunately for my wife's health—if not necessarily for our marriage—a solution soon appeared.

Even during our days in San Francisco, Constance had talked eagerly of reuniting with her mother when she arrived in England. She had no idea of where to find the woman, who had departed Alabama when her daughter was but three years old. Colonel Adams would never speak of the wife who had deserted him. Although Constance did not even know her mother's name, she had a vague idea that her family had lived along the coast. "Mama used to tell me stories of the sea," she recollected.

I decided to enlist Sherlock Holmes to aid us in our search. In mid-December, before my wife's first serious illness but after we had settled in sufficiently to welcome guests, I dropped by Baker Street to invite my friend to Christmas dinner. As usual, it was an invitation he declined.

"Thank you, Watson—and please thank your charming bride—but it is quite impossible. I leave tomorrow for Odessa to investigate the Trepoff murder.[xvi] It promises to be a *most* intriguing case. Are you sure you do not wish to accompany me?"

"That is quite impossible as well," I laughed. "Have you no suggestion that might help my wife to find her mother?"

"You *have* tried Somerset House?"[xvii]

"Assuredly, Holmes. But Constance is not even certain of the year her parents married, and 'Alexander Adams' is an absurdly common name."

"Does her birth certificate not identify the mother?"

"It was lost after the war, when the courthouse in her county burned."[xviii]

"Humph!" he chortled, refilling his pipe from the Persian slipper as I stirred the fire. "Well, it is a pretty little problem. You know, Watson," Holmes pondered, puffing contentedly, "I have a certain friend with contacts in the Home Office. I'll ask him to have those lazy fellows dig up what they can."

The "friend" was, of course, his brother Mycroft, whom I would not meet for two more years. A response was slow in coming, but early in March I received a letter from the Home Office that supplied the information we desired. Constance's mother, Margaret Burke Adams, lived with her parents on the Sussex coast, just outside of Brighton. At the time, my wife was suffering from a heavy cold that would turn into pneumonia. Rather than arouse her hopes in vain, I wrote to Mrs. Adams and enquired whether she was willing to renew relations with her daughter. Her reply surprised me: she asked that I visit her before informing Constance that she had been found. Once my invalid improved, I concocted an excuse to undertake the journey, which involved a day trip from Victoria on the Brighton line.[xix] The route would become all too familiar to me over the succeeding months.

I arrived at the Burkes' large, ramshackle cottage prepared to dislike Margaret Adams thoroughly. The woman who met me in its vestibule bore but slight resemblance to my Constance. Once beautiful, perhaps, she was now gaunt and faded, looking older than the fifty years I knew to be her age. We endured an awkward dinner with her ancient parents, who found little to say in my presence and retired with evident relief. Mrs. Adams then escorted me into the parlour, took a decanter of whiskey from a hidden cabinet, and poured us both a brimming glass. Without further preamble, she began to tell the story of her marriage.

Margaret Burke had met her husband at the seaside, during his visit to Brighton in 1856. "Alex was a handsome devil then," she sighed, "with charming manners and every evidence of wealth." In view of her limited prospects ("Father being a Nonconformist cleric during a Catholic revival"[xx]), it seemed a better match than she was likely to achieve in England. "I've never fathomed why such a man as Alex desired to marry *me*. Satan must have sent him to make my life a living hell."

Once arrived at Glenburn, his Black Belt plantation—"acres upon acres of pine woods and cotton fields"—Margaret met the brute behind the mask of Southern gentleman. As a clergyman's daughter, she was horrified by the reality of human bondage. Her husband beat his slaves and bedded them, equally without compunction. "Can you imagine, John, that he left my bridal bed to spend nights in the quarters? I saw a dozen children on the place who were his progeny." Nevertheless, after a son was born to them in 1858, she abandoned any thought of going home to England.

"When the war came, and he joined a regiment, I prayed to God he would be killed. But, no, so ravenous a beast was bound to make a gallant soldier! He *was* wounded once, in Tennessee,[xxi] and came home long enough to beget little Constance. After that, my hero went back to defend his glorious 'Cause,' leaving me to preserve his wretched domain from the Yankees."

As I had already learned from Constance, the rest was a saga of disaster. Union cavalry wrecked Adams's plantation and removed his slaves ("save for his concubines, who stayed behind to sneer at me"). Their son ("dear little Charlie, the epitome of everything his father should have been") died of fever late in 1864. Embittered by defeat and destitution, the Colonel ignored his baby daughter and treated his wife more brutally than ever. When Reconstruction brought Federal occupation and Negro suffrage to the Black Belt, he, along with other ruined planters and ex-soldiers, took up what Margaret called "night riding."

"I can't say where they went or what they did on those excursions. After my first question was answered with a blow, I never dared to ask. But for the next two years, there were burnings and murders all across our region. Negro politicians lynched; freed slaves driven from their farms; Northern sympathisers vanished. Even women were not safe. An acquaintance of mine in Greensboro, a young teacher, had her hair shorn off for instructing Negro children.[xxii] I knew my husband and his cronies well enough to believe that no crime was beyond them.

"At last, I could bear my life no longer." Mrs. Adams, who was now inebriated, set down her glass unsteadily upon the table. "I told Alex that I was taking our baby and going back to Brighton. You cannot imagine the man's fury. He swore that he would hunt us down and kill us both unless Constance was allowed to stay with him in Alabama. It was pure hate and selfishness; he'd hardly looked at her before that night. But never in our marriage had my lord and master made an idle threat. So, God forgive me, John, I left my daughter there and fled alone."

In early April, after Constance had recovered fully, we journeyed back to Brighton; and Margaret Adams' daughter was restored to her. From that afternoon, a balance shifted in our lives, and my young wife began to drift away from me.

There is no doubt that her condition was improved by the salubrious climate and mineral waters of the Sussex coast, nor that she regressed immediately whenever she returned to London. Accordingly, Constance spent much time in Brighton as the months advanced, interspersed with forays in her mother's company to Bath, Cornwall, and other seaside resorts upon the Continent. I, meanwhile, stayed behind in Kensington, establishing the practice on which these costly trips depended. My wife had no resources of her own, for Colonel Adams left his fortune to found a Confederate soldiers' home in Alabama.[xxiii] In fairness, I should add that the Burkes provided every financial assistance in their power. It was no sacrifice to those of us who loved poor Constance, for the benefits to her health—however transient—were undeniable.

Yet, as often as I returned to the Burkes' cottage, I saw that the benefits were not all upon one side. In their grandchild's presence, life returned to the old couple, while the careworn Mrs. Adams bloomed anew. My own jealousy was perhaps at fault, but each time we met it seemed that they were more possessive of our angel. For her part, my wife had regained the object of her childhood love and loyalty. Constance believed she had come home, and that home lay in Brighton, not in Kensington. I, if not yet an intruder, was now no more than a welcomed guest. By late summer, my visits to Sussex had become infrequent, while hers to London had ceased altogether. After little more than half a year of marriage, my wife and I were leading separate lives.

Therefore, when not actively engaged in my medical practice, I had much time upon my hands. Our house in Kensington seemed sad and lonely without Constance, so occasionally I would visit Mrs. Hudson and spend a few days in my old quarters. Sherlock Holmes was often absent from Baker Street in the early months of 1887, involved in several cases of international importance that I have noted elsewhere.[xxiv] By mid-April, when over-exertion led to a breakdown of his health, I was called upon to retrieve him from Lyons. Thereafter, Holmes and I were able to resume our friendship and detective partnership, almost as they had been before my time in San Francisco. A series of new investigations followed, the most consequential being the affair of Irene Adler and the King of Serbia.[xxv]

In truth, my participation in these cases provided a welcome relief from the uncertainties of my domestic situation. Holmes obviously could not fail to notice my wife's lengthy absences, nor the element of guilt in my enjoyment of our renewed association. To the extent that we discussed such matters, my friend offered a more sympathetic ear than his emotional reticence would have led me to expect. Insofar as possible, however, I tried to keep my work with Holmes entirely separate from the issues of my marriage.

It was at the end of September that my two lives finally intersected, in a case I have recorded as "The Five Orange Pips." For the great detective, it was a brief and inconclusive tragedy, a rare professional failure soon overcome by his next triumph. Its effect upon my marriage was far more lasting and severe.

Having progressed thus far in the present tale, readers who recall "The Five Orange Pips" may wonder why my knowledge of the *Lone Star*, and night-riding ex-Confederates, was not enlisted in the aid of poor John Openshaw. It was quite true, as stated in the story, that the strange words "Ku Klux Klan" meant nothing to me, for Mrs. Adams had not linked her husband's band of ruffians to any such society. I did apprise Holmes of the probable connexion between Colonels Openshaw and Adams, based on the latter's association with the *Lone Star*. By then, unhappily, young Openshaw had met his doom; and my father-in-law was long past earthly retribution. The remaining culprits, though identified by Holmes, were lost at sea before they could be apprehended. When I later came to write "The Five Orange Pips," my wife Mary was still living. I decided, for her sake, to omit any reference to my first wife's past, as those facts ultimately had little impact on the solution of the case.

Would that I had employed such discretion with poor Constance! Unexpectedly, my wife returned to me early in October, soon after the *Lone Star* sailed from London. September's equinoctial gales had damaged the Burkes' cottage, leaving her room there uninhabitable. After a week in Kensington, Constance again developed chest congestion and a hacking cough. One evening as we sat together, desultorily reading and warming ourselves before the fire, my mind returned to the mysterious bark that was carrying John Openshaw's murderers away from British justice.

"Constance, did your father ever mention a sailing vessel called the *Lone Star?*"

"I don't believe so," my wife answered, with a puzzled frown. Since arriving in England, she seemed more averse than ever to discussions of the Colonel. "Papa never talked to me about his business, John. Why should you want to know?"

"Oh, just an odd coincidence. Calhoun, her captain, figures in a case that Holmes and I have been investigating. I remember Henry saying, back in San Francisco, that your father had had some connexion with the ship."

"*Oh*, you and Mr. *Holmes*," sniffed Constance peevishly. I had overheard more than one disparaging remark in Brighton about the time my "hobby" took from serious pursuits. Evidently, my wife had paid more attention to her mother than I realised.

"Well, I don't know anything about it," she insisted, "or—for that matter—why Papa's shipping connexions should be any of your brother's business. I'm sure one hears all kinds of rumours in a waterfront saloon!"

This remark was so unlike the woman I had married that I stared at her in consternation. Constance seemed caught between defiance and apology, a flush colouring her pallid face. As I saw the misery in those red-rimmed eyes, I felt a surge of anger and compassion that had become familiar over the preceding months. Now, for the first time, anger won.

"As it happens, my dear, *these* connexions of your Papa hounded our client and two other people to their deaths. They appear to be part of a society of murderers—something called the Ku Klux Klan—to which he himself belonged, from what your mother told me."

"That's ridiculous! How *dare* you?" Constance stifled a cough and rose unsteadily, her forgotten novel falling to the floor. "I'm going to bed now, John, and I hope that you'll continue to sleep here so I can rest. Please send a telegram to Mama after breakfast. I want to know how soon I can go home."

Sometime in the early-morning hours, I was awakened by a scream from my wife's room. I rushed in to find Constance cowering against her pillows as she sobbed hysterically. Lighting the bedside lamp, I took her in my arms and tried to comfort her, as one would a frightened child. It was a long while before she calmed enough to tell me of her dream.

"It was as though I was a little girl again, alone in my room at Glenburn, and it was darkest night. I woke up to the sound of hammering, and lights were flickering in the yard below my window. Oh, John, when I looked out, there were demons on the lawn! Robed and hooded demons, carrying torches that made shadows all around. The biggest one—dressed all in red—had stolen Shiloh, Papa's horse. He sat there bossing all the other demons, who were hammering big wooden crosses in the ground. Then two of the demons dragged out Cassie from the smokehouse. She was my nurse, John, after Mama left. Most nights, she slept in my room, but some nights she slept in Papa's. Cassie had been gone for days, so at first I was glad to see her. I wanted to call out to her, but she was screaming, and I was afraid. The demons brought out another darkie, too, a man I didn't know. They tied them to the crosses, John, *and then they burned them both alive!* I couldn't stand to watch it, so I hid in my bed. But I could still hear Cassie screaming, and smell that awful smoke!

"I hid from the demons for the longest time. The next morning, Papa came to find me. He held me in his arms and told me it was all a dream—only a bad dream—and when we looked out my window, there weren't really any crosses in the yard. Papa promised we would go away from Glenburn and live someplace else. It was after that night that we left for San Francisco. But when Papa was hugging me that morning, I could smell the wood smoke on his shirt! It must have been real, John. *It must have been real!*"

She burst into a fresh torrent of weeping, and there was little I could say to reassure her. Knowing what I did, it seemed certain that Constance had indeed witnessed the Klan's execution of her father's escaped concubine. The wonder was that her childish mind had managed to suppress such memories, until my angry accusation of the Colonel brought back the "demons" of that evil night.

To my dismay, however, my wife's fears were no longer buried in her childhood. She was irrationally convinced that the murderers of Cassie and the Openshaws would mark her as a quarry. ("Those men—the ones who killed your client—they'll come for me now. *They know what I've done!*") I could fathom neither this strange reference nor the reason for her fear. In vain, I assured Constance that the men aboard the *Lone Star* had sailed far away, that soon they would be brought to justice. My words gave her no comfort. From that October morning, the demons who had haunted Colonel Adams's little daughter would be with her always, even unto death.

The last months of our marriage are soon told. Despite her shock and illness, Constance insisted upon an immediate return to Brighton. We lodged at a nearby seaside inn until her room at the Burkes' cottage was repaired. Naturally, my wife's mother and grandparents were distressed by her mental state, and I received much blame for "upsetting" her. Had it been legally possible, I would have been banished by my in-laws.[xxvi] As matters stood, I visited twice more during the autumn, only to find that Constance had recovered neither her physical health nor her equilibrium. I urged her to see a specialist in Harley Street, or at least to spend the winter in San Remo with her mother. Although sweetly patient with my pleas (for she was always loving while in Brighton), my wife refused both courses. "I'm safe," she told me with a child-like faith, "as long as I stay here."

So there I was compelled to leave her, while I remained in London with my patients, my writing, and my detective work with Sherlock Holmes. Fortuitously, the last months of 1887 provided us with a succession of interesting cases. I also oversaw the publication of *A Study in Scarlet*, which Doyle and I had completed earlier that year. Thus, although I greatly missed my wife, I was usually kept busy during the hours my medical duties left me free.

On December twenty-second, I received a letter in which my mother-in-law discouraged me from joining the family for Christmas. Constance, she said, had lately been less well than usual; so they planned a quiet observance of the holiday. In compensation, I was invited to come to Brighton for the New Year. Having learned that the Burkes' wishes were likely to prevail in any contest, and knowing their local physician to be thoroughly competent, I sadly acquiesced.

Instead, I accepted a belated invitation from my old commander, Colonel Hayter, to keep Christmas at his house in Surrey. Returning to London on the morning of the twenty-seventh, I stopped in Kensington to retrieve a copy of my memoir, then called at my old lodgings to wish Sherlock Holmes the greetings of the season. My friend was less pleased to receive *A Study in Scarlet* than I might have wished.[xxvii] He did, however, inveigle me into his latest case, which involved a Christmas goose, a stolen carbuncle, and—in the end—an act of mercy proper to that season of forgiveness. It was late when the reprieved James Ryder fled our sitting-room, so I spent the remainder of the night in Baker Street. Only at mid-morning did I return to Kensington, to find the telegram left at my home the day before: *"Constance dangerously ill with diphtheria. Come at once."*

By late afternoon, I arrived at the Burkes' cottage, where a heavy snow had fallen.[xxviii] My wife was in a serious, but not yet critical, condition. According to the family physician, Dr. Hargrove, Constance had been sick for nearly a fortnight. Her complaints—sore throat, cough, and a low fever—were by now so chronic that at first they caused no real alarm. The classic symptoms of diphtheria had been slow to manifest themselves, but they were unmistakable by the time that I examined her. My wife was very breathless; her throat and neck were swollen; and a grey membrane of dead tissue had settled on her tonsils. The heart rate was more elevated than the level of her fever justified. Hargrove and I discussed tracheotomy should her breathing become more obstructed, but so dangerous a procedure was at best a last resort.[xxix]

This bald and clinical account is written from my perspective as a doctor. As a husband, it was a time of agony. My delayed arrival had been met with outrage by my in-laws, which I recriminated for their neglect to notify me sooner when Constance became ill. Naturally, we did not air these grievances before our invalid. Mrs. Adams, to her credit, maintained a brave face and an outwardly cheerful disposition, while I employed my best "bed-side manner" in an effort to keep Constance from despair. Poor child. She had been ill so long that she seemed to have accepted illness as her lot in life. There was no longer any censure from that quarter; instead, my wife responded to my care with all the sweetness that had been her hallmark when in health.

Constance's condition remained stable through the night. On the morning of the twenty-ninth, she seemed improved, and I cautiously allowed myself to hope. However, in the afternoon her fever rose and she became delirious, thrashing about restlessly and calling for her Papa. Mrs. Adams and I exchanged a startled glance, but the paroxysm soon ended. Our patient sank rapidly thereafter, for no compelling reason that Hargrove and I could discern.

By nightfall, Constance was very weak but quietly sleeping. My colleague departed, and the elder Burkes soon went to bed. Only her mother and I kept vigil in that dark-beamed, dreary bedroom. Near half past ten, Mrs. Adams slumped wearily upon the window seat, gazing out on the still-virgin snow. I sat staring at the dying fire, reflected in a standing mirror slanted towards the open door into the hall. When I turned back to my wife's bed, I saw that Constance was awake and watching me. I took her hand, and she smiled with gentle wistfulness.

"Oh, John," she whispered, "why did you leave San Francisco? We could have been so happy there." At last the censure I deserved had come, but more in sorrow than in anger. "Papa was so sick . . . he couldn't have stopped us. We wouldn't have . . . *needed* his consent to marry. We could have lived . . . just as we liked." Each clause emerged as a breathless gasp; I had to lean close to understand her.

"We can go back," I told Constance brokenly. "You must get well, my darling, and we *will* go back." It was a hopeless promise to make then, knowing I would never be required to keep it. Already my wife had travelled far from me, reliving the long months of our separation.

"But then you *left* me, and I was so lonely, John. The time went by . . . day after day. . . . He just *lay there* . . . and he *wouldn't die!* . . . John, I missed you so. I knew that you were never coming back to San Francisco. . . . Finally, I just *had* to, don't you see? He was never going to let me go, John . . . so I had to—"

"*Hush*, child!" Rushing to the bedside, her mother placed a trembling hand on my wife's lips. "Hush, now, and rest. You mustn't speak of this."

"No, Mama, I *must* confess my sins . . . or go to Hell. That's what Teresa says. . . . I'm dying, Mama, and I—"

Suddenly Constance sat bolt upright, her face stricken with terror as she pointed to the standing mirror. "*Oh, PAPA!*" she screamed hoarsely, and fell back against her pillows, silent. One look into those shocked blue eyes informed me that the light in them had fled.

There was no one in the hallway. In a kind of daze, I turned back to reassure my wife, when I felt my wrist clasped in a frenzied grip. Ashen-faced, Mrs. Adams stared into the mirror that had been her daughter's final sight on Earth.

"John," she uttered, in a quiet but deadly monotone, "*I saw him, too.*"

Was it a ghost, or only a final, shared delusion by two victims of a mortal demon? Even now—despite my long relationship with the most rational of men—I cannot answer that question in my mind with certainty. Yet, I never doubted that *believing* she had seen her father's ghost caused Constance's demise, not "heart failure due to diphtheria" as I wrote upon her death certificate. Whether by supernatural intervention or her own guilt-ridden conscience, Colonel Alexander Adams had reclaimed his daughter in the end.

I did not oppose the Burkes' request to have Constance buried in the family churchyard. She was interred there on the first day of 1888, a fortnight past her twenty-fourth birthday. After the funeral, I returned to Kensington and—with no desire to linger where fond hopes had turned to bitter memories—put my house and practice up for sale.

Holmes at once invited me to rejoin him in our old quarters, where he and Mrs. Hudson showed much devotion in their efforts to restore me. In truth, I found my grief, however sharp, less oppressive than my role in driving my poor darling to madness and despair. It had been with a degree of malice that I told Constance of the Ku Klux Klan, and reliving the horrors of her childhood had unbalanced her. A fresher source of guilt was my relief at settling back into my old routines. Inside our rooms in Baker Street, or with "the game afoot," it was possible to forget for hours that my wife had ever lived.

As for Sherlock Holmes, in those weeks he revealed the caring heart that lay behind his formidable intellect. Our friendship took on a new dimension, for long, personal discussions had never been our habit in the past. With his usual relentless logic, my friend sought to assure me that much of my guilt over Constance's death stemmed from the loneliness and frustration I had felt throughout the marriage. I could not concur with this conclusion, but his genuine concern was comforting in coping with my loss. Holmes also pooh-poohed my assertion (after repelling the advances of an importune young lady[xxx]) that I had no interest whatever in remarriage.

"No, my friend, it will not do." Lounging at our window on a foggy February morning, he had endured my long complaint in silence, save for a few muttered musings as he watched the passers-by. Now Holmes set down his coffee cup and reclined on the settee. "Not for you the bachelor's life," he proclaimed loudly. Recognising this remark to be preamble, I prepared to suffer a lecture in my turn.

"You appear to believe, Watson," he unexpectedly began, "that I myself am immune to feminine attractions. I can assure you, however, that such is not the case."

"Indeed," I replied to this astonishing digression, "I could not help noticing your obvious admiration for Miss Irene Adler, during our service to the King of Serbia last May. It struck me then as rather more than a purely intellectual attraction."

"Ah, Doctor, *that* woman eclipses the whole of her sex in my experience, limited though I admit that it has been. You see, after disappointing a most worthy young lady in my youth,[xxxi] I made a conscious decision to lay aside that troubling aspect of my life, in order to devote myself—utterly and without distraction—to what your *Study in Scarlet* called 'the science of deduction.' (Yes, Watson, I *did* read it!) Even for a man of my peculiar disposition, it has not been an easy vow to keep. Certainly, it is not one that *you* should ever make or even contemplate. I have seen the way your eyes light up when a pretty client glides across our threshold. That has not changed in recent days, despite your grief. Your regrettable encounter with Miss Withers—whom you were right to spurn—proves that you still possess attractions of your own. So, my dear fellow, mourn your lost Constance in her season. But when the time is right, you *will* remarry."

In an odd way, these were the most comforting words that Sherlock Holmes had ever said to me, perhaps because he had descended from Olympus to take note of the concerns of common men. Yet, it was hardly his only contribution to my recovery from my wife's death. The early months of 1888 saw us engaged in some of our most fascinating cases: the theft of the Eye of Heka; the Norbury affair; and of course the Birlstone murder, which I chronicled as *The Valley of Fear*. My friend even arranged for my participation in the first of his many diplomatic missions against Imperial Germany, which would occupy him intermittently until the war began.[xxxii]

Some weeks after our return from Charlottenburg, I received a letter from Laguna Honda. The hospital's director regretfully informed me that my brother Henry had taken his own life, a week after losing his wife and son to typhoid fever. Despite my shock and crushing sorrow, the letter's conclusion filled my heart with pride:

Your brother is much lamented at Laguna Honda. His brilliant mind and legal training were of great assistance to us here. Until this sudden tragedy unhinged him, Henry Watson was becoming one of the finest men I've ever known.

Late in the summer, I received a package that contained our father's watch, which Henry had left to me as a last remembrance. That part of *The Sign of Four* was true.

On the very day I showed the watch to Sherlock Holmes, there came a knock upon the door into our sitting room, and a card upon a salver announced the arrival of Miss Mary Morstan in my life. For three brief, blessed years, we were allowed to share the kind of happiness that Constance and I had been denied. My later, longer marriage to Priscilla was a happy one as well.

Yet, even now I still return upon occasion to that small churchyard in Brighton, where my young wife lies beside her mother. I offer a prayer for the first of my lost angels, in the hope we will be reunited in whatever lies beyond.

The Adventure of the
Paradol Chamber

by Paul W. Nash

This story first appeared in the MX Book of New Sherlock Holmes Stories Volume XIII.

Paul W. Nash grew up in the shadow of the Bodleian Library at Oxford, where he worked as a junior library assistant between 1981 and 1994 and as a senior library assistant from 2007. He makes his living as a bibliographer, cataloguer, editor, book-designer and printing historian, pursuing the mysteries of bibliography very much as Sherlock Holmes might have done, had he been a librarian. He is fascinated by the traditional processes of printing and has his own private press at which he prints small works of fiction, poetry and humour. Writing stories and musical composition have been hobbies throughout his adult life and he is now officially a doctor, albeit not in a useful sense (like Dr Watson), holding as he does a doctorate in Publishing History from Oxford Brookes University.

Pat Crowley was the Editorial Cartoonist and Creative Director for the Palm Beach Post (Florida) from 1978 to 2008. He was a founding staff member and first political cartoonist for The Hill newspaper in Washington D.C. (1994-99) and contributing artist to the New York Times. His political cartoons were distributed to hundreds of newspaper and periodicals throughout the United States by the San Diego based Copley News Service.

www.patcrowleyartist.com

Artwork size: 11 x 12.5

Medium: India ink and water color paint

The year 1887 was a busy one for Sherlock Holmes. He was engaged in a dozen cases of note, including the adventures of the Five Orange Pips and of the defeat of Baron Maupertuis, the Hoxton Devil, and the Amateur Mendicant Society, not to mention the very curious case of the Hollow Effigy, all of which are recorded in my notes (though some cannot be made public until the noble and gentle personalities involved have been forgotten). Perhaps the strangest case of the year, however, was that of "The Paradol Chamber". It represented a triumph for Holmes's powers of ratiocination, and marked for me the end of an old phase of life and the beginning of a new.

It began one balmy afternoon in July. Holmes was still in delicate health after his prolonged battle of wits (and fists) with the Baron, but he was in good spirits again after the black reaction to his herculean efforts of the spring, cheered by his successes and the recent Jubilee. We were both lounging in the rooms in Baker Street, Holmes toying with one of his musical compositions, humming short snatches to himself as he scratched with his pen, while I was absorbed in the latest outrageous tale in *Blackwood's*. Suddenly Holmes threw aside his manuscript and jumped to his feet.

"I had quite forgotten," he cried. "We are to receive a visitor this afternoon." He plucked a letter from the mantelpiece and threw it into my lap. I picked it up and read as follows:

Dear Mr. Holmes,

I am sure you will not mind if I call upon you this afternoon at four o'clock to discuss a little matter which has troubled me. My name will, I am sure, be known to you, but I do not seek any favour on account of my fame. Please treat me as you would any common client.

Yours most sincerely,

Beresford Lamb

"I received it this morning," said Holmes. "What do you make of it?"

Knowing my friend's methods, I addressed myself first to the physical characteristics of the letter. "Well," I replied, "it is written on very good-quality paper, with a broad-nibbed pen, in a round, confident hand. The writer has not commissioned a printed heading for his letter-paper, but has attached a copy of his calling card to the top of the sheet with a pin. The card gives an address in Endell Street and is somewhat pretentious in execution, with rather too many curlicues. I suppose Beresford Lamb must be well-to-do as well as being, as he remarks, quite famous."

"*Is* he famous?" asked Holmes. "I confess I had never heard of him before I read his name here."

"He is certainly known to me."

"Really? Is he, perhaps, a celebrated jockey or tipster upon the turf?"

"No indeed," I replied gravely, feeling that Holmes was chaffing me rather. "He is an author."

"An author? Of what cast?"

"He writes dramatic stories of crime."

"Not *reports* of crime? Surely, I should have heard of him had he been a recorder of criminal proceedings."

"No. His work is pure fiction. But I am surprised, nevertheless, that you have not heard his name. He has become well-known from these very pages." I raised the copy of *Blackwood's Edinburgh Magazine* that I had been reading.

"I see," said Holmes. "Have you read all his works?"

"Hungrily," I replied. Lamb was among the more successful of a group of writers who had taken to inventing bloody and unlikely tales of crime and detection in the past decade or so. I remembered with pleasure Mr. Collins's *Who Killed Zebedee* and Miss Green's *The Leavenworth Case*, and almost as fondly the serialisations of Dr. Casterman's cases in *The Cornhill* and those of "Lupus" in *Once a Week*. My black bag contained, at that moment, an unopened copy of *The Mystery of a Hansom Cab*, of which I had heard very good reports.

"Well," said Holmes. "We have a few minutes before our visitor is due. Perhaps you would tell me a little of Mr. Lamb's works."

"I have just finished reading the final part of his latest story," I replied, "and will be delighted to give you an account of it. It is a tale of love and attempted abduction called "The Adventure of the Paradol Chamber", and is the latest in a series of *The Chronicles of Lord Pinto*. This Pinto, the Viscount son of the Earl of Fullerton, is an amateur detective."

Holmes held up his hand. "A detective?" he said. "Like myself, rather than of the official variety?"

"Not quite. Pinto is a rich man who pursues detection as a hobby, while you are England's foremost professional consulting investigator."

I felt a little flattery would do no harm to my friend, or my narrative, at this moment. Holmes smiled with a mixture of pleasure and condescension. "Pray continue, Doctor," he said.

"Although Pinto is a noble amateur, I have noticed, once or twice when reading of his exploits, that there are echoes of your own work and methods. Accounts of your successes have been available in the public prints, and I am sure Lamb has taken a little inspiration from you." Holmes continued to smile.

"The story concerns a stage magician who calls himself 'Paradol'. He works with a young assistant on various astonishing illusions, and soon forms a powerful regard for the beautiful daughter of the owner of one of the theatres in which he performs. He pays court to this girl, but she spurns him and, in the way of such stories, her rejection turns his genius from light to dark, and he plots his revenge. The climax of his act is the appearance of The Paradol Chamber. This is a gaudily-painted vanishing-box, six feet tall and three feet wide, with a door on the front, which the assistant brings on to the stage. It is raised to a height of about a foot on four wheels, which allow it to move easily and the audience to see beneath it while the trick is performed.

"Paradol would invite a beautiful woman from the audience to join him on stage, and ask her to step into the Chamber. The door was then closed and the assistant would turn the Chamber round upon its wheels through three-hundred-sixty degrees to allow the audience to see the back and sides. All the while, Paradol would make exaggerated signs and passes as if conjuring powerful magic. He would then open the door of the Chamber to reveal that it was now quite empty. The audience would inevitably gasp. Then Paradol would bow and step into the Chamber himself and close the door. The assistant would repeat the revolution of the Chamber and this time when the door was opened the beautiful lady was standing again inside the box and Paradol had disappeared. This was the end of the act and, while the lady left the stage and the audience clapped loudly, the Chamber was wheeled into the wings.

"We are told how the trick was done. It was a very simple matter. The interior of the Paradol Chamber was covered with black velvet and was divided vertically into two compartments by a velvet-covered board which revolved on a central pivot. When the door was opened, only the front half of the Chamber was actually visible, but this was not obvious because of the blackness of the interior. The lady chosen from the audience was, of course, a confederate of Paradol, and once inside the Chamber knew how to revolve the central board and pass into the back compartment. When the door was opened, the audience could again see only the empty black interior of the front half of the box. Clearly, when Paradol himself entered the front compartment, the whole process was reversed and the two compartments changed places.

"So much for the trick as it was usually effected. But on one night Paradol practised a dramatic and potentially fatal variation." Holmes snorted. Perhaps I had grown a little caught up in the narrative and decided to continue it without embellishment. "He paid his usual lady accomplice to feign illness, and suggested to the theatre-owner that his daughter might take her place. To this he readily agreed, and the daughter was initiated into the secret of the trick. At the climax of the act she was picked out, seemingly at random, by Paradol and entered the Chamber. While the magician's assistant turned the box to show its faces to the audience, the young lady revolved the central board and entered the hidden compartment.

"But the ingenious Paradol had prepared the Chamber differently that day. He had drilled a number of holes in the floor of the hidden half of the Chamber, and beneath them fastened a shallow metal box stuffed with cotton-wool soaked with chloroform. The girl naturally fell into a deep sleep. Rather than enter the Chamber himself, Paradol then bowed to the audience, received their plaudits, and left the stage, while his assistant wheeled the Chamber after him. Usually the Chamber would be halted and opened as soon as it was in the wings, but now Paradol took charge of it and, with his assistant's help, wheeled it to the stage door, which he opened. Then he departed through it, quickly to return driving a small cart and pair. The Chamber was loaded into the cart and the magician drove off into the night with his sleeping prize."

"The next part of the story is a curious dream or vision which Paradol enjoys as he drives away, thinking of his new life with the young woman he has abducted. He fancies he will open the Chamber and take out her sleeping form and lay her on the bed in the cottage he has rented, to recover from the effects of the chloroform. When her head is clear, she will perceive her situation and give herself willingly to her abductor in marriage. Paradol will revert to his own name, which no one in the theatre world knows, and a priest will be called to conduct the service. Then he will choose a new stage-name and continue his career. But when he arrives at the cottage and opens the Chamber he finds it quite empty.

"In the third part of the story, Lord Pinto makes his appearance, called in by the theatre-owner to trace his missing daughter. The official police have, naturally, failed to solve the mystery and have suggested that the disappearance was merely a carefully planned elopement. Pinto begins his investigation and learns that the magician's young assistant has also disappeared. After much circumlocution, and not a few co-incidental discoveries, Pinto traces the assistant to a rented room where he is living with his new wife, the theatre-owner's daughter. It transpires that the assistant too had been in love with the girl and, perceiving at the last moment what Paradol was about, had rescued her from the Chamber while his master was fetching the cart and replaced her sleeping form with a couple of sandbags which were used in the theatre to secure scenery. Upon waking, she had recognized her rescuer, declared her love, and willingly run away with him, believing that her father would no more welcome as a son-in-law a young stage assistant than he would a mature stage magician.

"The story then turns to the pursuit of Paradol. Pinto gains from the assistant certain clues which allow him to locate the magician's cottage. He alerts the local police who meet him at the cottage, where they confront Paradol – and Pinto recounts, to the magician's astonishment, the full story of his abduction of the girl. When he has finished, however, Paradol asks the police inspector what crime he is going to be charged with, since there is no evidence of any of Pinto's claims and the girl was not, in fact, abducted by him but eloped with his assistant. The inspector scratches his head, but Pinto smiles and leads the party to an outbuilding where they find the Paradol Chamber, newly-painted in a different livery, but still the same machine. He produces a hand-bill for the magic act of one *Eggestein the German Wonder*, and opens the Chamber to reveal the unconscious body of another young woman. It is her abduction with which Paradol is charged.

"Upon finding that he had been cheated of the prize for his ingenuity, Paradol's heart had turned quite to wickedness, and he had determined to use his skills to take possession of the most beautiful young women of the region, repeating his trick in local halls and theatres under a series of different names. At the last, he is led away to prison, and the girl wakes to find herself in safe hands, with no knowledge of the fate which she has so narrowly escaped." I paused and looked at Holmes, trying to gauge his reaction to the story. His face was quite impassive however, like a severe carving of granite. "I enjoyed the story very much," I said. "Indeed, I found it . . . thrilling. But, I admit, it is a ridiculous tale, full of melodrama and implausible detail."

"I disagree," said Holmes sharply. "It is certainly romantic and melodramatic, even grotesque, but not wholly implausible. I can see only one possible flaw in the logic of the tale as you have related it, and that is the question of the chloroform held in a box beneath the floor of the Chamber. Would such an arrangement have been effective? And would not the odour have alerted the young woman that she was entering a trap? But then, why would she recognize the scent of chloroform?"

I had not expected Holmes to consider the story quite so seriously. "Perhaps," I said, "you should read 'The Adventure of the Paradol Chamber' for yourself."

"Perhaps I should," he replied. "But all that must wait, for here, if I am not mistaken, is the creator of that story." The small clock on the mantel chimed the hour and, in the same instant, there was a ring on the doorbell. After a few moments, we heard the regular footsteps of our visitor, and momently there was a firm rap upon the door.

Holmes paused a moment then called out, "Come in."

A tall gentlemen in a long brown coat entered. His brown bowler was held in the long, elegant fingers of his left hand, and in his right he held a gold-topped cane. He must have been well over fifty years of age, but his hair was coal-black, and swept back from his face in a sharp peak which he must have smoothed down just before entering our door. His face wore an expression of alert interest, and his blue eyes were especially piercing and earnest. At Holmes's invitation he handed over his hat and stick, removed his coat, which Holmes also took, and sat down beside the empty fireplace.

"So," said our guest when he was settled, "you are the famous Sherlock Holmes?"

"I am he," replied Holmes. "And this is my friend Dr. John Watson, who is has occasionally been good enough to assist me in my cases."

Lamb nodded to me, then turned back to Holmes. "You will know my name, of course," he said. "Have you read my stories?"

"I have some familiarity with them."

"Very good. I have followed your career too, as far as I have been able, through accounts in the daily papers. I must congratulate you on your triumph in the case of the Baron and the British antiquities. I gather you saved the French government something like a million, and the Greek nation a similar sum, and ended by knocking the Baron down the steps of the British Museum when he took exception to your interference . . . ."

"The accounts of the Baron's downfall in the papers were, I fear, a little purple. But I can count the case among my successes. Now, what can I do to assist you, Mr. Lamb?"

"I have received a letter," he said, "which has troubled me. It came last Friday, and I have been wondering ever since how to understand it. This morning I decided my best course would be to show it to you." Lamb took a sheet of folded paper from his pocket and handed it over. Holmes read it carefully, then took the sheet to the window and used his glass to examine the paper in the summer sunlight which shone in. Then he handed the sheet to me and, for the second time that afternoon, I found myself reading a letter addressed to another man. This time, however, the text was not a little shocking. It read in this way:

Mr. Lamb

You are a basterd and murderer! You are responsable for my Ellen's death, as sure as if you had strangled her with your own hands. She would never have left the comfort and safety of her own home and gone off with that man but for you and your wicked story of the Dashing Carman. Be sure, Mr. Lamb, that I will have my revenge, if it takes all my skill and cost my life. Yours is forfit, Sir, for the wickedness you have done.

Your most bitter and determind enemy

Tom Charlett

Having read the text, I studied the physical properties of the letter, attempting to follow the actions I had seen Holmes take. It was written with a sharp-nibbed pen with such force that at times the nib had quite broken through the paper, which was smooth and white, octavo in size. It had been folded twice, clearly for insertion into an envelope, since there was no sign of a seal, address, or stamp upon the back. I held it up to see the watermark and read "*JOYN*" and "*SUPER*". Holmes would surely have recognized this at once, as I did – as all that remained of "*Joynson Superfine*", the mark of one of the commonest writing papers in the Empire.

"Well," said Lamb at length. "Should I take it seriously? It seems a very bitter threat to me – and yet I cannot believe the writer is quite in earnest . . . ."

"Do you still have the envelope?" Holmes asked.

"Regrettably, I threw it away. I remember it was buff and was addressed to me, care of *Blackwood's* London office, using the same handwriting."

"What is this reference to your story of 'The Dashing Carman'?"

"Have you not read it, Mr. Holmes . . . ?"

"I regret not, but perhaps Dr. Watson?" He glanced in my direction.

"Yes, indeed," said I, "I remember 'The Adventure of the Dashing Carman' very well. It concerned the beautiful daughter of a cruel Banker, who was loved by an ugly Viscount, who was far above her station, and a handsome Carman, who was far below. Lord Pinto was consulted by the Viscount when the young woman disappeared. He discovered that she had secretly married the Carman and was living with him in a humble place. When the Viscount learned this, he attempted to murder the girl, which had been his intention all along, as revenge for her rejection of him, while her father hunted down the Carman with the same end in mind. Pinto saved them both, defeating the Banker – who was ultimately reformed – and the ugly Viscount, who ended by fleeing into the path of a locomotive at Paddington Station. I have noticed, Mr. Lamb, that your stories often involve a beautiful daughter, and an elopement."

"You are perfectly right," said Lamb. "My readers like nothing better, and I try to please them. The other factor in my stories is, of course, crime, most usually a murder or abduction, and here too I do my best to satisfy my public."

"How very admirable," said Holmes. If he was being sarcastic, Lamb did not detect it.

"You are most kind," he said. "And Dr. Watson – though he has omitted all the most interesting and original points in my story – has put it into a nutshell and touched upon the vital element – that this tale might be seen as an encouragement to a romantic young woman to defy the wishes of her father and elope with a good man of lowly station."

"What of the woman, this 'Ellen'?"

"I know only what can be inferred from the letter," said Lamb, "that she was among my readers, eloped, and was later murdered.”

“And Tom Charlett?”

“A relative, I presume. Most likely her father. I have never met the man, and yet he blames me for Ellen’s killing. It is perhaps one of the hazards of the occupation of writer, that some deluded person may read a great deal more into your words than was ever there. It is as if Macbeth were to be blamed for a case of regicide, or Mr. Dickens for a cruel gynaecide.”

“Not quite,” said Holmes. “I do not believe either Shakespeare or Dickens could be said to have encouraged murder. Both Macbeth and Sikes suffered for their crimes, while your story, if I understand it, might encourage not homicide, but elopement.”

“You are quite right, Mr. Holmes. But what should I do?”

Holmes took up the letter again and peered at it narrowly. “Since we cannot know, at present, whether this letter is real or its writer’s extremity of feeling continues, we must, I think, treat the threat as very serious indeed. For the time, Mr. Lamb, I would advise you to lock your doors securely and keep a pistol always to hand, to guard yourself most carefully and, if possible, never to venture from your house except in the company of some trusted male friend.”

“Thank you, Mr. Holmes.”

“There is one further course of action I should advise. You should take this letter, and your fears, to the official police. A very serious crime may be in contemplation, and the police would, I am sure, take these threats most seriously.”

“I hesitate to go to the police, for I know what fools they are.”

“I am surprised to hear you say so.”

“As you know, my experience, reflected in my stories, is that there is nothing more slow-witted and slow-moving than the average British policeman. They are inclined, I believe, to see crime everywhere except where it is actually taking place, and to judge by the merest appearances all cases that come before them.”

“There is some truth in what you say,” said Holmes. “But not all policemen are such imbeciles, and a few, a very few, come close to being able in their profession. In any case, the official force can assign a man or two to your protection and can put the entire metropolis on watch for this Tom Charlett.”

“Very well,” said Lamb. “I will do as you ask. But I do not trust the police to get at the truth.”

“I will do my best to find the truth,” said Holmes, “both about the letter, and about the murder. Once the killer is apprehended, Tom Charlett will have a more just focus for his bitterness.”

“Thank you.”

“You will not mind if I keep the letter for a while?” said Holmes.

“Will I not need to show it to the police?” Lamb asked.

“If you tell them of its content, and that I have the original for safe-keeping, the police will take your story seriously enough.”

Lamb rose and bowed to each of us in turn. Holmes put the letter away in his pocket-book then fetched Lamb’s coat, cane, and hat. Without another word, the famous author left our sitting room.

“Well,” said Holmes, “what do you make of our writer and his story?”

“It seems serious to me,” I replied. “If this Charlett blames Lamb, however unjustly, then his life must be in danger.”

“Indeed. That ‘if’ is a most important word. I cannot help but feel that we have had today, from start to finish, nothing but fiction. Yet parts of the story may be, indeed *must be* true. I did not mention the fact to our client, but I well recall the case of the murder of Ellen Charlett. It was reported early last week. As you know, I make it my business to keep up with the criminal news, and read especially the more sensational literature on the subject, though pure fiction concerning crime I have always considered beyond the pale. I docketed the crime and no doubt have a few notes upon it my index.

Perhaps you would reach over to the shelf to your left and draw out the volume for '*C*'? Thank you."

I passed the heavy, green-bound volume to Holmes who turned through the pages slowly, smiling and muttering to himself. "Camden Theatre Mystery. Castle Graham Imposture. Cats, Seven Black. Cervical Vertibrae . . . Ah, here she is, the Charlett Murder, lying neatly between the Chadlington Horror and my late lamented friend Charlie Peace – a long entry for him, but only a scrap for the unfortunate Ellen Charlett." He passed the book to me and I found a very brief newspaper clipping from *The Daily News* of the twenty-seventh of June, 1887, which ran in this way:

> *The murder, by strangulation, of Miss Ellen Charlett, daughter of Thomas Charlett, master-tanner, of Clerkenwell has been reported this morning. Inspector Lestrade of Scotland Yard told* The News *that it was a simple case and he expected to announce the arrest of the killer imminently.*

"Well," said Holmes, "that gives a little useful information. Our friend Lestrade is on the case, and we have Mr. Charlett's address and profession. In the morning I will summon Lestrade and we can begin our investigation. But for now we may perhaps best occupy ourselves with a little reading. I will assay the final episode of Lamb's "Paradol Chamber" in *Blackwood's.* You may perhaps have some similarly uplifting work to occupy your mind."

I remembered the copy of Hume's *Mystery of a Hansom Cab* in my bag and needed no further prompting to draw it out and begin the story.

The next morning, Holmes's telegram brought Lestrade to our rooms, where he told us what he knew of the Charlett case. It seemed the manager of Willis's Private Hotel in Highbury had reported the death of a young woman in one of his chambers. Lestrade had been called in to find it a clear case of murder. The girl had been strangled with a bootlace. The hotel register showed that the room had been taken by "Mr. and Mrs. E. Smith", but of Mr. Smith there was no sign. His clothes and possessions were gone from the room, while the girl's remained. The body was identified as that of Ellen Charlett, the daughter of Thomas Charlett, who had reported her missing a few days earlier. Charlett believed his daughter had run away with her lover, an unsuccessful actor named Elias Smith, whom he had forbidden his daughter to marry. Lestrade sought a description of Smith, but Charlett had only seen him once, and that from a distance, as he had been afraid to come to the house. The hotel clerk and porter gave similarly unhelpful accounts of his appearance, as he had worn a long coat and scarf, though the night was warm. All Lestrade could gather was that Smith was tallish and of middling build. The inspector enquired around the theatres of the city, but no one had heard of Elias Smith, so that he must either have given Ellen a false account of his profession, or a false name.

"We are still looking," concluded Lestrade, "but I wish you would give me a hint or two as to how, or where, to look."

"I believe I can help you best," said Holmes, "by suggesting that you may never find Elias Smith, at least not alive."

"What, you mean that he has done away with himself?"

"Not at all. I think it quite possible that he too has been murdered, by the same hand that did for Ellen. I am reminded of a story I heard recently of a Dashing Carman whose beloved was the focus of a rival's jealousy and a father's anger."

"Why, yes. A rival for the girl's affections . . . or perhaps her father – he had cause to hate Mr. Smith, well enough, and perhaps his own daughter too . . . ."

"It is a thousand pities that I was not able to visit that hotel room myself after the body had been found. The killer must have left some marks. I suppose the room has now been cleaned and re-let, and the girl is buried?"

"Yes, indeed."

"What of her possessions and clothes?"

"She had little enough, but what she had is still in store at Highbury Station. There is a little jewellery, a book, a couple of magazines, some money, and several sets of clothes. You can see it all, all except her shoes. We never found those."

"That is a curious circumstance, is it not?"

"I thought nothing of it at the time," said Lestrade, "assuming Smith had taken them with him by mistake, among his own things."

"Possibly . . . Yes, Lestrade, thank you, I should like to examine the young lady's clothes and possessions."

"You can come to the Highbury Station, any time you like, and see them."

"Perhaps you would be a very good fellow and have them packed up and sent to me here. Thank you. Now, before you leave, I wonder if I might ask one more question? You mentioned that the lady had been strangled with a bootlace. What sort of bootlace?"

"A common brown bootlace," said Lestrade laconically.

"A *leather* bootlace?"

He brightened. "Why yes, I see. Thank you, Mr. Holmes. I am sure I would have thought of it in time, but I am most grateful for the hint all the same."

Lestrade rose and bade us farewell. As soon as he was gone, Holmes said, "I, too, must leave for a short while."

"Really?" I replied. "I believed you had quite made up your mind to solve this case without leaving your chair, as you have done once or twice before."

"I would like to get to Mr. Charlett before Lestrade arrests him. Perhaps you would pass me the *London Directory*? Thank you."

I handed him the great red book and he opened it near the beginning and turned over a few pages. "As I suspected," he said. "There is only one *T. Charlett* listed as a tanner, at No. 5 Ray Street, Clerkenwell."

"Would you like me to accompany you?" I asked.

Holmes shook his head. "Thank you, no. You would help me most materially by remaining here, in case there should be any correspondence or visitors to receive."

I thought this rather unlikely, but perceived that Holmes would rather make this journey alone. I was not entirely unwilling to fall in with his plans, as in truth I felt indolent that morning, and relished the opportunity to idle in our rooms for a few hours. The prospect of another chapter or two of *The Mystery of a Hansom Cab* had more than a little appeal. So I said farewell to Holmes and settled myself in my favourite chair with Mr. Hume's excellent story.

I was to be disappointed, however, in my fancy for a spell of idleness, for Holmes turned out to be correct in his prediction of both correspondence and visitors to our rooms. I had not been reading for more than twenty minutes when a telegram arrived. It was from Beresford Lamb, who wrote as follows:

New Development. Coming Baker Street Soonest.

I tried to settle to my reading again, but my concentration had been broken and I had hardly turned another page of the mystery before I heard a cab in the street, and within a minute the great author was again in our sitting room.

"Thank you," he said when I had taken his hat and cane. "Dr. Watson, I have received another frightful letter. Is Holmes not here to help me?"

"He will be back presently," I said. "Will you wait?"

"I wish I could speak with him now," he replied. "I have an appointment with my publisher in a quarter-of-an-hour and had hoped to see Mr. Holmes at once. May I leave the letter with you, and return later to discuss the matter with Holmes?"

"Certainly."

Lamb handed over a small buff envelope which had been rather carelessly torn open. It bore a penny stamp and Lamb's name and address in Endell Street written in what looked like the same hand as the letter we had seen the previous day.

"I must depart if I am to make it to Bloomsbury in time, and so I bid you farewell, Doctor. Please do read the letter. I will return after lunch to discuss it with Holmes." I returned his hat, coat, and cane to him and, with a nod of farewell, the author quitted our rooms.

I felt, a little ruefully, that it was my lot in this case to read important correspondence intended for other men, but I drew the letter from the envelope:

Bastard, prepare to meet your maker! So end all murderers! I see before me every moment the sweet face of that innocent girl whose life you have ended with as much certainty as if you had killed her with your own hands. Indeed, you did just that, albeit your weapons were pen and ink instead of the power your grip. Damn you for the Dashing Carman! Damn you! Your life is forfeit, and I will take it, for Ellen's sake.

Your most bitter and determined enemy

Tom Charlett

I examined the thing closely. It seemed in every respect the brother of the previous letter. There was the same heavy pressure of the pen which had scored and torn the paper, as if the writer were squeezing out his fury through the nib, and there was the familiar watermark of Joynson. I put the letter aside, all thoughts of reading Mr. Hume's narrative now quite expelled from my head by the real mystery which lay before us. I turned the matter over in my mind, but as so often when I considered the tangle of evidence which Holmes seemed to cut through with such ease, I found only questions which I had no power to answer.

Holmes returned to Baker Street shortly before lunch. He threw off his coat and hat and wiped his face with his handkerchief. "I have endured two cab journeys," he said "and a painful interview with the bereaved tanner of Ray Street, on one of the hottest days I can remember. I have also smoked no fewer than seven cigarettes and my mind has turned upon our little problem."

"I have had a busy morning myself, having received Mr. Lamb. He has been sent another threatening letter, which he left with me, and promises to return to talk with you after lunch."

"Well, well," said Holmes rubbing his hands together. "How very interesting."

I handed over the buff envelope and Holmes examined it and its contents carefully for some minutes. Then he took out the earlier letter from Charlett and laid the two side by side upon the table, comparing first the paper, then the writing.

"Most singular," he said. "Now, before Mr. Lamb joins us, let me tell you of my little outing this morning. I found Charlett's tannery in Ray Street a very superior establishment. He is a tanner, leather-dresser, saddler, and felt-manufacturer. But he is a ruined man, quite broken by the loss of his daughter. He is certain that the stories she read of romance and elopement had a strong influence on her decision to defy his wishes with Mr. Smith, and blames these stories, their authors, publishers, and illustrators – he particularly derided the last for their depictions of pretty heroines in the arms of handsome soldiers and the like – for the loss of his daughter.

"But, although he knew well the story of the Dashing Carman from his daughter's effusions on the subject, I could not persuade him to name Mr. Lamb as the architect of his misfortune. I asked him plainly if he had written Lamb a letter, and he denied it. I contrived too to glance at some specimens of his handwriting, which was clearly different from that we see here." He indicated the two letters which still lay side by side upon the table. "Yet that may signify very little, for a man may write memoranda in a quite different temper and style from that he would use for a furious threat to a hated enemy. That he denied writing the letter is also far from conclusive. Our interview was interrupted, as I rather expected it would be, by the arrival of Lestrade and a constable who arrested Thomas Charlett on suspicion of the murder of his daughter and of Elias Smith. Charlett greeted this turn of events with horror, and I confess I felt considerable sympathy for him, for I had put the idea into Lestrade's head."

"I noticed your doing so," I said.

"I regret having added to his woes," Holmes replied. "But, since my return cab-ride and those seven cigarettes, I am all the more convinced that it was necessary."

"You believe him guilty then?"

Before he could answer there was a ring on the bell, followed by footsteps and a knock at the door. It was a fresh-faced police constable bearing a large cardboard box containing the clothes and other property of Ellen Charlett. Holmes wrote the lad a receipt and, when he had departed, slit open the box with his pocket-knife. The contents were very much as Lestrade had described them. The book he had mentioned was an edition of *Jane Eyre*, and the magazines were copies of *Blackwood's*, both including episodes written by Lamb. Holmes examined these objects and the girl's clothes with minute care.

"Look here, Watson," he said, pointing to the hem of a dark blue dress. I looked and saw, adhering to the fabric, a smear of white crystals.

"Salt?" I suggested.

"Possibly." He carefully scraped the crystals into an envelope with his knife, then re-packed the box, which he took through to his bedroom. "Now perhaps you would call on Mrs Hudson for a cold luncheon," he said.

After lunch, while we sat smoking, we heard again the doorbell and the now-familiar tread of Beresford Lamb in the passage. When the pleasantries were over, Holmes invited our guest to take a chair and asked him a somewhat surprising question.

"Why," he said, "did you think you could deceive Sherlock Holmes?"

"What do you mean, sir?"

"The letter you brought Watson this morning was a forgery, was it not?"

Lamb sighed. "I should have known better," he said. "But how did you know? I thought I had done it rather well."

"There are six points in the handwriting alone which mark the two out as different. The style of the second is more literary. But the most obvious suggestion that the two were not written by the same hand is that the writer has apparently learned to spell correctly in the few days between." Lamb looked crest-fallen. "Why did you do it, Mr. Lamb?"

"I confess I thought you were not taking the matter seriously enough. I detected some doubt, even levity, in your manner, and though I feigned as much indifference as I could, I have been very much afraid for my life, and felt that a second letter from Charlett would concentrate your mind and powers upon my problem. I am sorry, Mr. Holmes. I should not have done it."

"No doubt you should not have done it. But it is done. Did you do as I advised and tell the police of the letter?"

"I did, and they promised to protect me. A police constable has been stationed in Endell Street each night, and another will make a special patrol of the area during the day."

"That is good. But these precautions will now be withdrawn, for Thomas Charlett has been arrested for the suspected murder of Elias Smith and his own daughter.”

“Then the case is solved?” cried Lamb.

“Not quite. Watson and I must find Elias Smith, dead or alive, to bear witness to the killer’s guilt.”

“I wish you the very best of luck with your quest,” said Lamb. “But my own mind is quite at rest as a result of what you have told me. Thank you.”

“We still have a good deal of evidence to collect and analyse.”

“Indeed,” I said. “Barely an hour ago we received . . . .” My words were interrupted by a low groan from Holmes, and I looked round in time to see him crumple sideways upon the table then crash to the floor taking with him a vase of flowers which Mrs Hudson had placed there that morning. I rushed to his side. He was dreadfully pale and my first thought was that the day’s heat and excitement had been too much for him after the huge stresses of his recent cases. It took me only a few seconds, however, to realize what he was about.

“Is Mr. Holmes ill?” asked Lamb.

“I am afraid so,” I said. “His health is still poor after his encounter with Baron Maupertuis, and I fear he has overstretched himself. He needs rest now. Perhaps you would leave us and I will help him to his bed.”

The instant Lamb had departed, Holmes sprang up from the floor.

“I perceive you wished to stop me telling Lamb about the box of Ellen’s things,” I said, nodding towards the bedroom. “But why? Surely you cannot suspect Lamb? Is not forging this second letter just what an innocent, but terrified, man would do?”

“For the moment I will say only that I wish to keep Mr. Lamb innocent about the details of my investigation. My next task is to identify the crystals found on that dress, and I would ask you to leave me alone with my apparatus for a few minutes to achieve that end. Thank you.”

I sat beside the fireplace while Holmes repaired to the stained table at which he conducted his chemical experiments and lit his burner. He took out the little envelope of crystals and began to work on them, first tasting a few on his finger tip, then placing a few more upon the handle of a spoon and passing it through the flame, which briefly turned purple. Then he mused for a minute or so, and finally ground up the last of the crystals and mixed them with two other chemicals drawn from his numerous bottles and jars.

“Come, Watson, and observe the final proof,” he said. I stood beside him as he scraped the tiny mound of black powder he had made into the bowl of a spoon, and then touched a lighted match to it. There was a flash and a hiss, and a tiny genie of smoke rose from the spoon. It had an unmistakable odour. “*Et voilà tout*. Potassium nitrate.”

“Gunpowder,” said I.

“Quite. I knew it was a Potassium salt by the taste and purple flame. Presuming it was a common compound, it could not have been the chloride because that is hygroscopic and would not have remained as crystals, so it had to be the sulphate or nitrate. The easiest way to tell which was to make gunpowder with the sample – if it fulminated it was the nitrate and if it was inert then it was the sulphate. Saltpetre was, in fact, what I expected to find. But the test is proof positive. And now I must again leave you to amuse yourself for a little time, while I make a further enquiries. We may bring the business to a conclusion this evening, when I hope you will accompany me in the adventure. I will either return to collect you, or send for you, if you are you willing to assist me.”

“I most certainly am.”

“Until this evening, then.”

It was a long and weary wait. The heat of the afternoon was oppressive, and though I tried to bend my mind back to *The Mystery of a Hansom Cab*, I was constantly distracted by thoughts of Ellen Charlett and her sad fate. I ate a little supper. Soon night fell. It was past nine when I finally heard from Holmes. He sent a telegram which ran thus:

Meet 17 Buckler Street Woolwich. Ten. Bring Revolver.

I collected my pistol, drew on my coat, and went out into the street to find a cab. When I arrived at Buckler Street it was a little before ten. The sky was still not quite dark, but the streetlamps were lit and I could see Holmes on the street-corner, apparently lounging against a pillar-box while he smoked a cigarette.

"You see there," he said when I had joined him. "That warehouse?" He indicated a brick-built building. I nodded. "I hope you will not mind breaking an entry in a good cause?" Again I nodded. "I have been watching, and there is no one there now, but we can expect our bird to return to the nest before too long, now that night has fallen."

The door of No. 17 was heavy and locked both with a padlock and a mortice-lock. Holmes produced a set of burglar's tools, and quickly picked the padlock and opened it. The mortice-lock proved more difficult, however, and he had to unscrew the plate of the mechanism before he could release it.

"It is important," he whispered, "that our man does not suspect we are inside when he arrives, so we must leave no traces. I will slip in and open that window. Then I will close the door and while I lock it perhaps you would re-fasten the padlock, then climb in by the window?" Yet again I nodded, though I did not much fancy the window, which was narrow and nearly six feet from the ground. Nevertheless, once I had completed my task, I managed to scramble up and squeeze myself in, and close the window behind me. I found Holmes working by a narrow blade of light from a dark-lantern, relocking the door from within by reconstructing the lock.

We were in a small store-room which appeared to be empty, save for a few piles of rotting timber, perhaps once floorboards or ship's timbers. At the far end was a blanket, nailed up as a curtain, and Holmes nodded towards this. Beyond was a doorway into a gloomy space which smelt damp and acrid. Once through Holmes said, "I think we might risk a light here, as there are no windows." He lit a dark lantern and the place was flooded with light. Ahead of us lay a short brick-lined corridor with three chambers leading off each side. We walked slowly along and Holmes directed his lamp into each in turn. In one was a workshop, with a carpentry bench, tools strewn about and planks of timber leaning against the wall. In another was a bed, with a night-stand and dressing-table. In the third was a desk bearing books, papers, and a typewriter, with a bookcase and two chairs beside. In the fourth was a modest larder of tinned and preserved foods, a table and chair, and some plates and cutlery. In the fifth was a motley collection of objects – two bicycles, various trunks and boxes, several children's toys, and a great stuffed bear. The last room contained, however, a truly astonishing sight. When Holmes swung the beam of his lantern into the space I could scarcely believe it.

"Good Lord," I whispered. "It must be the Paradol Chamber!"

Before us stood a wooden cabinet, six feet tall and three feet wide, mounted upon wheels. It was painted deep red and decorated in blue and gold, just as the Chamber had been described in *Blackwood's Magazine*. When we opened the door, we found the interior covered with black velvet. Holmes reached in and pushed at one side of the central panel, which began to revolve.

"Surely," I said, "There cannot be someone in there?"

"I doubt it," he replied, and was proved correct. The hidden compartment of the box was empty, but, when Holmes directed his lamp at the floor, we could clearly see the holes drilled there and I could detect still a faint odour of chloroform coming from below.

"What does it mean?" I asked.

"Little in itself," he replied. "But I believe we will find something more conclusive." We returned to the room which was equipped as an office and Holmes began to search through the papers, then the contents of the desk drawers. From the bottom drawer he drew forth a pair of black patent leather ladies' shoes. They seemed ridiculously small, like a child's.

"This, I think, will be enough to convict our man," he said. "And now, we must wait for him. You have your revolver? Excellent."

We took our places on the two chairs beside the desk, and Holmes shuttered his lantern. I feared we might be in for a long wait, but I was happily in error, for only fifteen minutes had passed before we heard the crunching of a key in the great lock and footsteps entering the outer room. Then a gas jet was lit in the corridor and a tall figure stood in the doorway before us. Holmes uncovered his lantern, and I drew my revolver. Beresford Lamb uttered a foul oath.

"I am afraid we have you, Mr. Lamb," said Holmes. "My friend has a revolver and will not hesitate to use it, and I have these shoes, which I am sure Mr. Charlett will identify as having belonged to his late daughter."

"May I light the gas?" said Lamb urbanely.

"I will do it," said Holmes. He did so and then shuttered the lantern again.

"Now my good friend Watson will remain here, keeping you covered, while I fetch those forces of law and order which you so despise. Did you lock the outer door behind you?" Lamb thought for a moment, then nodded. "Then be so good as to throw me the key – Watson, watch him!" Holmes caught the key and slipped past our prisoner into the corridor. A moment later I heard the outer door open and the sharp note of a police whistle.

Lamb smiled, then moved very slightly towards me.

"Remain perfectly still," I said. "Or I will shoot you."

"I doubt that," he said. "You are a man of feeling, unlike Holmes, who is a mere reasoning machine. You would not harm a fellow creature, especially one who is innocent."

"You are quite right," I replied. "I would not harm an innocent. But I do not believe you are any such thing."

"Oh, I am," he said. "I am the victim of a most unfortunate error on Mr. Holmes's part. I beg you to believe me. Whatever evidence he has found he has misunderstood . . . . You will admit that it is possible."

I felt that it was, but was in no mood to argue the toss so said nothing more.

"Now let me show you something, something which will convince you of my good intentions." He began to reach towards the left inside pocket of his jacket.

"What is it?" I asked.

"It is a letter from Ellen Charlett. The truth is that I did know her, as a friend. She wrote to me after one of my stories touched her, and we struck up a correspondence. Her letters told of how she feared the anger of her father and wanted to run away with Smith to a safe place. I helped her with money. But her father found her all the same. This letter proves it."

"Move your hand no further," I said, "or you will find yourself quite unable to move it." He ceased the gentle creeping of his hand towards his pocket. "If you are innocent, how did you come by Ellen's shoes?"

"I confess I took them from her room, but after she had been killed. I went to the hotel to give her money, and found that Charlett had been there before me and strangled her. I took her shoes for a base reason, I am afraid – I intended to plant them in the possession of her father, so that the evidence against him would be all the stronger. I wanted him brought to justice. Only let me show you the letter, and you will see it all."

I thought this story convincing. He could see I was wavering in my resolve, and his hand moved slowly again towards his pocket, while he smiled. His face was a picture of honesty and candour. But at that moment I recalled the shoes, how small and pathetic they had seemed, and I squeezed the trigger and fired.

I am a good shot, and the bullet caught Lamb squarely in the right shoulder. With a terrible cry he was thrown back onto the floor in the corridor. A moment later Holmes rushed in followed by a constable.

"I should not have left you alone, Watson" he said. "Are you hurt?"

"Not at all," I said. "Lamb told me he had a letter that would prove his innocence in his left breast pocket . . . ." Holmes reached gingerly into the pocket and drew out a small, pearl-handled revolver.

Lamb groaned. "Your friend tried to kill me," he said.

"Nonsense," said Holmes. "Had he tried to kill you he would have succeeded. Now stand up and let me search you while Watson keeps you covered. I do not think you will twice doubt his determination in the matter." Lamb dragged himself to his feet, and Holmes went through his pockets, removing nothing else but a leather-bound notebook and gold-plated fountain-pen.

"Very well," said Lamb. "You have captured and wounded me, and I will tell you all. But not before the police inspector arrives. I want my story properly recorded, and known across the world."

"I doubt very much that there would be a word of truth in your story. Let me propose an alternative. When the inspector arrives, I will tell your story and you will kindly correct me if I go wrong in any particular. Now sit here – Yes, against the wall – and I will hold the pistol while the Doctor examines you. Do I hear the delicate footsteps of the excellent Lestrade approaching?"

Indeed, there was a thunder of footfalls in the outer room and Lestrade and two further constables burst into the corridor. Lamb sat down against the wall and I gave Holmes the revolver while I examined the wound that I had inflicted. The bullet had passed through the shoulder-blade, shattering it and the collar-bone, and out the other side. The wound was not life-threatening, but was no doubt very painful and would leave Lamb with a permanent weakness in his right arm. I did not have my bag with me, so that all I could do was apply a compress with a clean handkerchief. Holmes handed the revolver back to me.

"So you've shot him," said Lestrade, stating the obvious. "Why?"

"Let me enlighten you," said Holmes. "It is a grotesque story which your constable may care to record, for it contains a full confession. Beresford Lamb was not given that name at birth, but assumed it as one of a number of personalities in his life of crime. It became, perhaps, his dominant persona. Lamb, the successful writer, the great man of letters, famous, and now rich too because of the popularity of his stories. He has recently bought a new house in Endell Street on the profits of his writing. No doubt he has a considerable talent with his pen, but what makes Lamb remarkable is that he bases his stories, as far as possible, on realities, and the feelings of his protagonists, especially his villains, upon his own feelings. He is a sensualist, and has, I venture to suggest, so little of what a normal man would call conscience as to be practically devoid of any such virtue. He is probably the third cleverest criminal in London."

"Twaddle!" said Lamb.

"And possibly the most remorseless. He has also, until now, been able to continue his career, and to write about his crimes quite openly, without detection. That is the genius of the man. His mistake, his final mistake, was to take on Sherlock Holmes. For that was what you intended to do, was it not?"

Lamb made no answer, but gestured towards the desk where we had found the shoes. Holmes retrieved from it a sheaf of typewritten pages.

"It would have been my greatest triumph," said Lamb. "Or rather, Lord Pinto's."

"I see the story is called 'The Eclipse of the Great Detective'. A very lively title."

"It is all written," said Lamb, "all but the last few pages, in which the famous consulting detective fails, and Lord Pinto succeeds."

"The crime," said Holmes, looking through the papers, "is the murder of Ellen Charlett. I see you have given her another name, as you have to your failing detective, but the circumstances are identical. A young woman, seduced by an intelligent older man who pretends to be a failed actor, persuades her to elope with him against her father's wishes. When he has her at his mercy in a cheap hotel, he strangles her and flees into the night."

"You could never have solved such a crime," said Lamb.

"I suppose you think that because you see me as a rationalist? For Sherlock Holmes, there must be a rational motive for every crime, while this murder was committed for no rational motive. It was not for gain, or love, or hate, or revenge, or even for expediency. Why did you kill Ellen Charlett?" Lamb was silent. "In the story, I suspect the motive was one of pure sensuality. Your heartless older man merely wished to know what it was like to have a young woman at his mercy, and to take her life with his own hands. He wanted the experience. And that was something you believed I could not understand. Sensual pleasure was part of your motive too – for we must not forget that this murder has been done twice, once in fiction and once in fact. You wanted the experience. I daresay you enjoyed it. But you had two further motives. Firstly, you wanted to live out, to *try* out, the plot of your story, and secondly, you wished to confound Sherlock Holmes.

"In order for the last motive to succeed, however, I had to be brought into the case, and that was why you came to me with a forged letter in your hand. I could do nothing else but investigate the case, and fail to identify the killer – yourself – while every false move I made was noted and ascribed to your Great Detective, whose defeat was the heart of your story."

"Quite untrue!" said Lamb. "The heart of my story was Lord Pinto's success."

"I knew I was being led a dance, and so I danced, and tried to perform in every way as you wished me to, even leading Lestrade to believe I thought poor Tom Charlett the true killer. I am heartily sorry that I had to do that."

"I am confused," said Lestrade. "If this Pinto solved the case in the story, would that not reveal who killed Ellen Charlett?"

A look of irritation came over Holmes's face. "The story," he said, "reveals only the name and nature of a fictional character who killed a girl for pleasure, and the cleverness of Pinto in his deductions. It would be clear enough that the case was based on that of Ellen Charlett, but this would hardly be the first time a story had been inspired by a real crime. I believe Mr. Poe wrote something of the sort forty years ago."

He turned again to Lamb. "You almost succeeded. But I had three clues that guided me, and one scrap of evidence you overlooked. The first clue was in the letter which you forged from Thomas Charlett. I had no way to prove it a forgery, but I believed it was."

"Come now," said Lamb. "You must admit that the letter was a masterpiece, a brilliant piece of both writing and forgery."

"You betray one of your greatest flaws, Mr. Lamb. You are conceited. The letter was good, but it was just a little too florid, too much the work of a man of letters, to be genuine, while at the same time the poor spelling and coarse language was too strong for a man of Charlett's education and standing. My second clue came when Lestrade told me the name of Ellen's lover, Elias Smith. I was reminded at once of another Lamb, the poet Charles, who assumed a pseudonym for his essays. What were they called, Doctor?"

"'*The Essays of Elia*'," I replied.

"Quite so. Lamb had suggested to you Elia, and Elia had suggested Elias. Perhaps it was merely the unconscious signature of a self-regarding man of letters. The third clue came with the second letter which you forged. This was a very clever strategy. Your intention was to bring me a letter which was sufficiently unlike the previous one to be detectable as a forgery. When I uncovered the deception, as you knew I would, your stated reasons for undertaking it would do nothing but guide me further from the truth, and quite convinced Watson here of your innocence. However, I saw something else in the second letter, which you may not have considered when you wrote it. Although it was obviously different in a number of respects from the first letter, it was also obviously similar in a number of ways. The hand and language were so similar – as they had to be, if I were not to see immediately that this was a crude fake – that I asked myself how, without the earlier letter before you, you had done it. At that time, you will remember, the first letter was safe within my pocket-book. You either had a truly remarkable memory for handwriting and words, or you had written both letters yourself. Although I could not prove it, I inclined to the latter opinion.

"The final scrap of evidence was a few crystals which I scraped from the hem of Ellen Charlett's dress. You removed her shoes from the hotel room because your feared there were traces on the soles which might lead me to you, but you missed a very small trace on the hem of the dress which, I will wager, Ellen wore when she last visited you here. The crystals turned out to be of saltpetre. Where would one pick up such a chemical except in a manufactory of gunpowder? There is only one such in London, and it is hardly likely Ellen would have visited the Royal Arsenal. I recalled, however, that some years ago the Woolwich Dockyard had been part of the Arsenal, but had been closed down and many of the warehouses let to private companies. In such a building, where munitions had been made and stored for decades, was it not likely that saltpetre would be found upon the floors, and picked up by the boots and skirts of a visiting lady? I spent part of this afternoon with the agent for the former Dockyard buildings, and learned that only one of them, No. 17, had been rented in recent years – to a Mr. Charles W. Holmes. Guessing a little of Mr. Lamb's manner of choosing his *noms-de-plûme*, I suspect the compliment was due not to me, but to the American poet and essayist. So Watson and I came here and found your second home, your lair, in which your crimes were planned, your devices perfected, and your plots written."

"You have not bested me," said Lamb. "I am still the better man. That you found me out was sheer luck, Holmes!"

"I would expect you to believe nothing else."

"What of the Paradol Chamber?" I asked.

"That was an example of Mr. Lamb's practical approach to the writing of mysteries. He conceived his vain-glorious magician, Paradol – we may perhaps detect another self-portrait here – but had to know whether his device would work in practice. So he built the Chamber. It was an easy task for one who had once worked as a carpenter."

"How the devil could you know that?" said Lamb.

"When I first shook your hand, I remarked how much larger and stronger the right was than the left. You had clearly not developed such musculature wielding a pen, and I deduced some physical labour. Carpentry was suggested by the fragment of your story which I read, in which the construction of the Paradol Chamber was described in very precise terms. I would further venture to guess that you have worked in the theatre, both as an actor – witness your recent performances in my sitting-room – and in other roles, perhaps as a scenery-builder." Lamb regarded Holmes with malevolence, but said nothing. "Perhaps you tested the Chamber on Ellen Charlett."

"I did!" said Lamb. "That was back in February when I had first made her love me, and was initially drafting that great story. I had just told her my real name – well, I had revealed that I was Beresford Lamb, the very writer she admired with such a passion. I swore her to secrecy, and she was willing, eager even, to step into the Chamber and try my experiment. It worked wonderfully. Within a minute she was quite unconscious and I could enter and draw her sleeping body out. You cannot imagine my delight. Ellen came back here many times after that, to serve me. 'The Eclipse of the Great Detective' required that we elope – which I effected easily – and that she be strangled by her lover – which was also a simple matter. I brought her here that evening, so that I could tell her the story of the great victory of Lord Pinto over Sherlock Holmes."

"Did you tell her that you intended to take her life?"

"No, though perhaps she guessed. Had I asked her consent, I am sure she would have given it and offered her throat gladly. But it was important to me that she did *not* give her consent."

"You know," said Holmes, "in some ways, the letters you wrote in the person of Tom Charlett were your most truthful expressions. When you told yourself, '*You are a bastard and murderer!*' and '*You are responsible for my Ellen's death, as surely as if you had strangled her with your own hands*', you were, for once, writing the literal truth."

"I should kill you for that," said Lamb in a low voice. "I regret that I will probably not have the opportunity to do so."

"Probably not," said Holmes. "After you had taken her back to the hotel and done the deed, you thought to remove her shoes, just in case they bore traces which might lead the police, or an astute sleuthhound, to your door. But you missed the smear of saltpetre on her skirt, and that was your undoing. I wonder if you had another motive for taking the shoes? Did you wish for a memento of Ellen? Or of your sensual experience in bringing about her end?"

"I will not answer that," said Lamb. "I see that the constable has been taking notes, and there will no doubt be an official report on the case, and perhaps a confession which I shall be called upon to sign. I will do so, but on one condition. That my story, 'The Eclipse of the Great Detective', be published in *Blackwood's* as it stands, with my confession included as its termination." There was a moment's silence. "I had hoped to write more stories. I had a dozen plots in mind – all ingenious, all delightful – but I have done enough that the name Beresford Lamb will live for ever."

Lamb would say no more, and soon afterwards was taken away by the police surgeon. He stood trial for the murder of Ellen Charlett, and was convicted, but his sentence was commuted to one of life imprisonment as the judge believed him a lunatic. Holmes believed differently. He thought Lamb neither mad nor wicked, but a curious anomaly of nature, a man born without a conscience who regarded his mind, imagination, and senses, as the centre of all things. The case had been a triumph for Holmes's powers. He had defeated a great intellect in a game played by his opponent's rules. Thomas Charlett was naturally released by the police, and attended Lamb's trial, but betrayed no emotion when the sentence was passed. It is said that Lamb continued to write in the asylum, but his stories were always burned on the orders of the Governor. "The Eclipse of the Great Detective" was never published.

For my own part, I returned to our rooms after the adventure, and picked up again *The Mystery of a Hansom Cab*. I read it to the end, but found it dull and flat after the excitement of recent adventures with Holmes. This set an idea loose in my mind. These stories, these tales of murder and romance, had always an emptiness at their centre. Even those of Beresford Lamb had proved unsatisfying, because they were, in the end, untrue. What if I could write stories, based not on imagination but on *fact*, on the adventures of Sherlock Holmes, which had often been reported in the press with such scant regard for the truth? Some few years before, I had written a memoir of my time in India and Afghanistan and of my return to England, which had been lost in circumstances associated with the case I later called "The Adventure of Nightingale Hall". I had included short accounts of three of Holmes's cases in that lost book. Perhaps now was the time to recall those cases, and seek to publish those accounts, and others. I certainly had notes enough, and fancied I could write as fluidly as Beresford Lamb, and a good deal more honestly. I decided then to try to publish an adventure or two of my own. It did not occur to me until some days later, when I had completed the draft of the first such story, to wonder what on earth Holmes might make of the idea.

> *The year '87 furnished us with a long series of cases of greater or less interest, of which I retain the records. Among my headings under this one twelve months I find an account of the adventure of the Paradol Chamber . . . .*
>
> Dr. John H. Watson – "The Five Orange Pips"

The Adventure of
The Smith-Mortimer Succession

Daniel D. Victor

Daniel D Victor is a retired high school teacher who lives with his wife in his native Los Angeles. His doctoral dissertation, *The Muckraker and the Dandy: The Conflicting Personae of David Graham Phillips*, led to the creation of the Sherlock Holmes pastiche *The Seventh Bullet*. Originally published by St. Martin's Press, it was reprinted by Titan Books, UK and later translated into Russian. His fascination with Sherlock Holmes and American literature has led to his MX series entitled *"Sherlock Holmes and the American Literati"* in which Holmes and Watson encounter such writers as Raymond Chandler, Stephen Crane, Samuel Clemens, and Jack London. More recently, Victor has expanded his literary approach to Holmes' adventures by including writers from more varied backgrounds like Guy de Maupassant, Robert Louis Stevenson, and Fyodor Dostoyevsky.   Victor is currently working on a novel about Holmes and American journalist Richard Harding Davis.

Andy Pereira is a self-taught contemporary artist working primarily in acrylics, Andy was born in Guatemala City, Guatemala in 1960. Many of Andy's paintings are influenced by impressionism. Andy is a fulltime resident in the Northwood neighborhood of West Palm Beach, FL. His exhibitions include The Box Gallery (2016), Bohemia Gallery A. G. *"The End of the Year of the Monkey"* (2017), Common Hope Charity Fundraiser (2017), Palm Springs Elementary School, leading a four-hour student work shop about the importance of the arts in society (2018). Andy may be contacted via Facebook @ Andy E. Pereira.

www.andyepereira.com

Artwork size: 30" x 45"

Medium: Acrylic on canvas.

No detective, not even an amateur, wants to admit that he has been the victim of thieves. And yet that was precisely the situation in which I found myself after moving back to Baker Street in late April of 1894, some two weeks after the dramatic return from the dead of my friend and colleague, Mr. Sherlock Holmes.

By now the whole world knows the astounding story of how Holmes had appeared to plunge to his death at the Reichenbach Falls in Switzerland on 4 May, 1891, how he had spent the next three years traveling incognito, and how he had finally reappeared in London to solve the murder of one Ronald Adair. Today, of course, such facts are readily available. Yet it must be remembered that for reasons never made entirely clear to me, Holmes prohibited my publishing an account of the case for some ten years following the actual events.

Adhering to Holmes's request, I waited patiently until the autumn of 1903 before he allowed me to produce the sketch I entitled "The Empty House", the narrative that detailed Holmes's so-called "hiatus". Even though he had made it quite clear that my account would not be published for a decade or more, I stood firm about recording the facts as soon as Holmes reported them to me – that is, in April of '94.

Only by noting the details while they were still fresh would I be able to fulfil the role of faithful Boswell that Holmes had attributed to me. To that end, I maintained a notebook in which I set down the salient features of the Reichenbach Affair as provided by Holmes. I kept the thin volume in a drawer of the writing desk in our sitting room, and it was the purloining of the notebook in question that placed me in the predicament to which I referred at the start of this narrative.

I discovered the theft one balmy afternoon in late May. It happened this way. Upon returning from my surgery, I encountered the perfect opportunity to write. There was no Sherlock Holmes to be found, and an hour yet remained before Mrs. Hudson would bring up our tea. No sooner had I seated myself and opened the desk-drawer, however, than I discovered that my notebook had gone missing.

I immediately summoned Billy the page. "Has anyone entered our rooms recently when Mr. Holmes and I have been out?" I asked him.

"Why, um, yeah, Doctor," said the boy, tugging self-consciously at his burgundy tunic. "Funny you should ask."

"And why is that?"

Billy shifted uneasily from foot to foot. "Some bloke, a young man 'e was and very short, came in yesterday with a bucket and sponge – said 'e was 'ere to wash the windows."

"And you," I charged in disbelief, "let him in without so much as a 'by your leave'?"

Billy blushed, unable to conceal his miscalculation. "Mrs. H. was out, Doctor, so I couldn't ask no one about the fella's story. Both you and Mr. Holmes was gone, and, strange enough, the chap sounded like an educated fellow. I reckoned no 'arm could be done, so I opened your door for 'im. You know 'ow Mrs. H. allows the police inspectors free run of the place."

"Window cleaners are not Scotland Yard detectives, Billy," said I, shaking my head in annoyance. "You should be aware, young man, that this window cleaner took an important notebook that belonged to me."

Rather than apologizing for his blunder, Billy raised a forefinger and said, "Do you know, Doctor, I thought something seemed a bit dodgy about 'im – besides 'is posh speech."

"And why is that?" I said, my voice tinged with irritation.

"Because 'e 'aint been in 'ere but five minutes, and then out 'e rushed, bucket in hand, saying 'e'd forgot 'is soap, and just like that 'e run out the front door."

Now that Billy had mentioned it, the windows looked no different from how I remembered them, dark soot sullying the glass of each pane. The strange behaviour of the window cleaner certainly seemed to confirm the intruder's guilt.

Whilst I could not let Billy leave without admonishing him for his poor judgement, I also found myself thanking him for offering so straightforward an admission. Only after the lad had gone did I stop to consider the peculiarity of the theft. Nothing else seemed missing, and I had no clue concerning what vital interest there could there be in my simple notes of Holmes's return to London. They contained no secrets. If the details of Holmes's escape from Moriarty's clutches were not already public knowledge, Holmes's reappearance in the fight against London's criminal class most certainly was. How could it not be? Elsewhere I have noted the many cases he tackled in 1894, and his presence was obviously known to all the participants in each of those investigations.

Holmes himself returned in time for tea, and I related to him the mystery involving my notes.

"Curious, Watson," said he, cocking an eyebrow. "But 'tis no great matter. Disturbing as it is to be the victim of a minor crime, no great harm can come from missing the notes of my reappearance. I shall merely repeat the details for you, and you may take them down again. More to the point, during my long absence a number of criminal acts have occurred that demand our attention. Fear not. I have no doubt that with the passage of time, your little puzzle will be solved."

Although we did not know it as we sat sampling Mrs. Hudson's tea and biscuits that afternoon, the solution to that so-called "little puzzle" was destined to appear much sooner and with greater implications than we had expected.

It was a week to the day since I had discovered the invasion of our sitting room, and I had almost succeeded in pushing the matter out of mind. Having questioned Holmes once more and recorded for a second time the facts required to complete a satisfactory account of his actions in Switzerland, I no longer had the need to dwell upon what I had come to call "The Strange Case of the Missing Notebook". That morning, however, along with the breakfast dishes and the coffee, Billy presented a letter that had been left for Holmes.

"Brought in early this morning by a footman in livery, sir," said Billy on his way out the door.

Holmes examined the envelope with its thick-stock paper, overly large monogram, and red-wax seal.

"Someone important," said he with a wry chuckle, "or at least someone who thinks he is." Holmes broke the seal and quickly scanned the letter. "Note the shaky hand in contrast to the firmest of tones," he said as he pushed the paper in my direction. It was dated that morning at Windstone Hall, Gloucestershire.

> *Dear Mr. Holmes* [it read],
>
> *I shall meet with you this morning at ten a.m. in your rooms. It is of the utmost urgency, and I must insist that you cancel any other plans you might have.*

It was signed, *"Sir Lionel Smith-Mortimer, Bart"*.

"Watson," Holmes said over the rim of his coffee cup, "The *Who's Who?* if you please."

I gulped down a piece of toast and rose to fetch A.C. Black's familiar listing of influential people. It took but a moment to locate the book with its dark-blue boards and gold-lettered spine. I thumbed the pages, found the appropriate entry, and handed the open volume to Holmes.

Sipping his coffee, he read the entry quickly and summarised the salient features: "Lionel Smith-Mortimer, Baronet. Born 1822. One son named Leigh. Wife died in childbirth. In addition to an inherited title and fortune, he is the owner of Windstone Hall, a manor house in Oxfordshire. He – "

"Wait a moment, Holmes!" I cried. "I remember reading something about the man just yesterday in *The Times* – a rather tragic piece about a suicide, as I recall." I retrieved the newspaper from the small pile of spent dailies residing on a nearby table. It took me but a moment to locate the report. "Here!" said I, pointing to the story. It was indeed a melancholy announcement – "*Death of Baronet's Son*" – so sad an account that I had not gone on to read the details. Had I done so, I would certainly have called them to my friend's attention.

"Holmes," said I after quickly reviewing the piece, "it says that the young man died in the Falls of Reichenbach."

Sherlock Holmes put down his cup and stared at me with his steel-grey eyes.

"'*The coat of the deceased*,'" I read, "'*was discovered neatly folded on the path above the falls. His footprints along the path led to the edge of the precipice above the water – a drop of more than eight-hundred feet. His body has yet to be recovered.*'"

I laid down the paper and looked at my friend. If I did not know better, I could have sworn that the slightly upturned corners of Holmes's mouth displayed a hint of amusement.

"I returned from death but a month-and-a-half ago," said Holmes, "and already I seem to have created imitators." He looked at our mantel clock. "Come. It is almost ten, and unless I am very much mistaken, I hear the hooves of a pair of disciplined horses pulling a four-wheeler to the kerb. We should prepare to meet our distinguished guest."

Sherlock Holmes exchanged his mouse-coloured dressing gown for a dark jacket, and I proceeded to don my coat. It was a matter of minutes before Mrs. Hudson herself climbed the stairs to introduce our guest. No pageboys for the likes of a Baronet.

"Enter!" Sherlock Holmes commanded at her knock.

Mrs. Hudson stood at the portal and announced, "Sir Lionel Smith-Mortimer." Then, bowing her head and straightening her skirt, she backed out into the hallway and closed the door.

I must say that, whilst I knew this Baronet to be a septuagenarian, I nonetheless expected to behold someone of erect and noble bearing. Instead, I saw before us a scowling old man with a stoop to his back and a hand curled like a great claw over the round, silver head of his walking stick. With a nod to fashion, he wore an expertly tailored suit, its dark frock coat contrasting with his yellowing white hair. Patent leather boots and kid gloves complemented his attire.

"Sir Lionel," said my friend, "I am Sherlock Holmes." He introduced me as well and gestured towards the armchair reserved for his clients.

The Baronet gave a quick frown in my direction and then, with some effort, shuffled to the proffered seat and sat down. Holmes and I took chairs opposite him.

"Let me first say, sir," announced the elderly client with a thump of his stick, "that I don't fancy being here one bit." He rapped his stick on the floor a second time to punctuate his point. "Only because of Leigh's faith in you have I come at all."

Holmes stared at the man, offering no discernible response.

"Without doubt you have seen the reports of my son's accident."

We both nodded respectfully.

"Simply put, I don't believe them. I want to know what really happened. All I do know is that he was off in Switzerland wandering about with a friend."

"A friend?" Holmes asked.

"Yes. One Reginald Bentley. A barrister by profession. Known each other for about a year. Bentley and my son travel together when the opportunity presents itself. London not good enough for them. They want to see the world."

"And where was this Bentley at the time of your son's death?" Holmes asked.

"*Alleged* death, may I remind you. He remained at the hotel near the Reichenbach Falls, don't you know."

"At the *Englischer Hof?*" I asked. Noting the similarity to our own ill-fated trip three years before, I guessed the two men might have stayed in the same hotel Holmes and I had occupied.

As if he suspected that I possessed too much arcane information, Sir Lionel knit his brow. But all he said was, "By Jove, when I hear of a mysterious death and no corpse is produced, I have my doubts. You may think I sound like some suspicious figure in one of your adventures, Holmes, but that may be in part because of the interest that Leigh expressed in reading them himself."

"I appreciate the compliment, Sir Lionel," said Holmes, "but under the circumstances, one cannot escape an uncomfortable conclusion. The apparent death of your son mirrors – however imprecisely – my own rumoured demise. Given the fact that I have only just returned from that narrow escape, one has to marvel at the coincidence."

"Quite," muttered Sir Lionel.

It was all I could do not to call attention to the theft of my notes. The young man posing as a window cleaner whom Billy had observed, the one with an educated manner of speech – might he be none other than Leigh Smith-Mortimer, whose father now sat before us? Recreating the death of Sherlock Holmes, someone he admired, might have been his morbid motivation. Perhaps Leigh Smith-Mortimer had sought to end his life in dramatic fashion not unlike the storied suicide of young Romantic poet Thomas Chatterton.

"I must confess," said Holmes, "that my personal history in this situation adds impetus to my curiosity. I, too, would like to know what happened to your son, Sir Lionel. I shall take your case."

The Baronet withdrew a wallet of light-coloured leather from inside his jacket. "Name your fee, Holmes," said he.

"Later," my friend replied. "All my clients pay at the same rate, Sir Lionel. But concerning this case in particular, its proper resolution will furnish me with additional reward."

The Baronet gazed at his wallet. "I almost forgot," said he, extracting a photograph and a small card from the billfold. "My son and Bentley," he explained in reference to the photograph. "Inseparable friends. The card contains information about Bentley's chambers in Gray's Inn."

Holmes took the items, examined them briefly, and handed them to me. In the photograph, two serious-looking young men in straw boaters – the taller one with a moustache, the shorter, clean-shaven – stared back."

"Leigh is the one without the whiskers," said Sir Lionel as, using his stick as a brace, he struggled to rise. "As for Bentley, he works at Mapplethorpe and Ruggles, and I have already prepared him for a possible visit from you."

"We'll see him post-haste," said Holmes, ushering the old man to the door.

Sir Lionel stopped to address my friend. "This matter is of great importance to me, Holmes. In addition to the welfare of my son, I feel compelled to point out that he is my only issue. He arrived late in my life, and his mother died tragically during his birth. It was quite horrible really. The babe chose to appear when Lady Smith-Mortimer and I were vacationing in the mountains near Lake Windermere. It was all so sudden. We were alone in the woods, and I had to deliver the child myself as my wife lay dying."

"Horrible," I said.

Sir Lionel ignored my sympathetic response. "What's more," he added, standing up as straight as seemed possible for him, "neither can I neglect the deposition of my estate."

"It is entailed?" Holmes asked.

"Indeed. All I possess will be inherited by my closest male heir. If Leigh is truly no longer living, then Windstone Hall will be dealt off to some distant cousin in Canada. That is why it is imperative that I find out what happened to my son."

"Understood," said Holmes. "I will report to you as soon as I learn anything."

We listened as Sir Lionel made his way down the seventeen steps, his walking stick producing a distinctive thump on each one.

Holmes moved a window curtain aside so he could watch Sir Lionel enter the four-wheeler that awaited him by the kerb .

I heard the latch of the carriage door and then the rumble of the coach as it clattered down Baker Street.

"Come, Watson," said Holmes. "This investigation will begin with an interview of Leigh Smith-Mortimer's traveling companion, Mr. Reginald Bentley, Esquire, at the Inns of Court."

The chambers of Mapplethorpe and Ruggles had been established in Gray's Inn during the early years of the century. It was in the Gray's Inn Gardens that Reginald Bentley had agreed that we meet him. To that end, we flagged a hansom at our front door and were soon rattling along Oxford Street. Southampton Row brought us to High Holborn and the Inns of Court. We alighted at the wood-panelled frontage of the Cittie of Yorke public house that stands at the narrow alleyway leading to Gray's Inn. Entering the grounds through the main gate, we passed the South Square to our right and made our way under the archway leading to the green swards of the Walks, as the spacious gardens are commonly called.

Holmes had arranged our meeting for one o'clock, and under the mid-day sun we strolled along the gravel path enveloped by the iridescent colours and sweet aromas of the season. Spring seems so wrong a time to hold discussions of death – especially among the yellow daffodils and blue hyacinths and roses of pink and white and red attempting to distract us. After a few additional paces, however, we recognised the moustachioed chap from the photograph seated on a nearby bench.

Reginald Bentley was sitting in the shade of the London planes and elms that populated the Walks, and he rose upon our arrival. "Gentlemen," said he, "Thank you for agreeing to see me outside of chambers. This tragedy is no one's business but our own. Besides, I also appreciate the moments I can spend away from my desk." He pointed to a low-slung block of yellow-brick offices across the lawn. "Mapplethorpe and Ruggles suffer the confinement of the Raymond Buildings over there. As you must already know, Leigh and I always enjoyed our walks through the countryside."

"Which leads us to the Falls of Reichenbach," said Holmes. "As I understand it, your friend seemed intrigued by my personal history – so much so that he literally walked in my very footsteps. How does one account for this obsessive interest?"

"Let us sit," said Bentley, gesturing towards the bench. "Justice was paramount for Leigh," he explained once we were settled. "I should imagine his concern was based upon his own sense of victimhood."

"Victimhood?" I echoed, imagining the rich surroundings of Windstone Hall in which the boy had grown up. "In what way?"

"I know what you're thinking, Dr. Watson – the money that must have smothered Leigh when he was a child. But, you see, it was that very legacy that constantly weighed him down. His father had made it clear to Leigh that he had to marry and have sons to carry on the line – you know, gentlemen, the usual upper-class prattle."

"You don't approve of the British aristocracy?" I could not refrain from asking.

"Look," he said, "my own father is a banker, and fortunately for me was able to send me to university. I have benefitted greatly from my education. After all, here I sit, installed in the legal profession and quite able to pay my own bills."

"Rather proves my point, eh?" I said.

"Within reason, Doctor. I don't believe one should be forced to live the life one's father confers upon him, however much money that involves, if that is not the life one chooses for himself."

The young man may have had a valid point for the common fellow, but one cannot allow the upper classes to make such choices. Where would we be if the heirs to the throne could choose willy-nilly whether they wanted to be king? One could scarcely imagine a royal monarch giving up the crown to marry a commoner. Of course, such dilemmas did not concern a mere medical man like myself – not that sort of money in my family, I'm afraid.

Holmes brought the conversation back to practicalities. "Tell me about this trip the two of you took to Switzerland," he said.

Bentley patted down his moustache. "When Sir Lionel notified me that you'd be coming to talk about Leigh, I assumed you would ask about that final journey." He withdrew a map from an inner pocket and, unfolding it, proceeded to lay the sheet flat on the bench between Holmes and himself. "Leigh invited me to join him with the understanding that I would follow his instructions without questioning them. He told me he had a plan, and I agreed to go along."

Sherlock Holmes studied the chart, his eyes flashing as he noted the familiar route now coloured in red.

"I took the liberty to mark our course," said Bentley. "It was a singular excursion." As the young man spoke, he traced the progress of their trip with his forefinger. "We boarded the *Continental Express* here at Victoria. I had originally thought we would cross the Channel at Dover and sail the twenty-two miles to Calais, but Leigh had other plans. He insisted we change trains at Canterbury for the run to Newhaven, a decision that caused us to switch twice more at Ashford and Lewes. When I asked him why, he answered with your name, Mr. Holmes."

"Quite so," Holmes nodded. "Pray, continue."

"I'm sure you yourself can supply the details. At Newhaven, we sailed to Dieppe – " Here Bentley's finger on the map slid across the blue of the Channel. " – a crossing, I might add, three times the duration of the crossing at Dover. From Dieppe we travelled by train to Brussels, and then on to Strasbourg and Geneva. Following a week's walk through the Rhone Valley, we made our way to Leuk, climbed the Gemmi Pass in the Central Alps, and finally arrived just a short distance from the Reichenbach Falls in a town called Meiringen. We stayed in the *Englischer Hof*, run by – "

"Let me guess," I interrupted, "Peter Steiler the Elder."

"Correct, Dr. Watson. But from what I understand, you and Mr. Holmes stayed in the same hotel."

"Quite so," said Holmes again. Then he added vaguely, "It was all done for professional reasons."

Leigh Smith-Mortimer may have stolen my notes concerning the geographical route Holmes and I had taken to Meiringen, but obviously Holmes still wanted to conceal the details connected with the criminal activities of Professor Moriarty and his associate Colonel Moran.

"We had travelled so far a distance in so roundabout a fashion, gentlemen, that once we had reached our destination, I saw no reason to suddenly start doubting my friend's sanity. Thus, when early the next morning Leigh told me he wished to go alone to view the Reichenbach Falls, I acquiesced. It was the last time I ever saw him." Here Reginald Bentley hung his head. Had I been less sympathetic, I might have regarded it as an altogether too theatrical a pose.

"And then?" Holmes asked. "No doubt you alerted the police."

"When Leigh failed to return, I myself walked up to the Falls – ran, really."

I nodded with appreciation. Had I not made the same fateful run under the most similar of conditions?

"That," Bentley resumed, "was when I found Leigh's folded jacket and tweed cap lying at the end of the small path leading to the rushing waters. Once I saw those personal items, I suspected that something was truly wrong, and I summoned the police. We all returned to the scene, and they examined the footmarks leading to the edge and not returning. Alas, there was but one sad conclusion to draw – that Leigh had thrown himself from the precipice, his body disappearing in the churning waters below."

Holmes arched his eyebrows. "It would certainly seem so," said he. "Did you detect anything in Leigh Smith-Mortimer's nature that would lead you to imagine he could do such a thing?"

Sighing heavily, Bentley stared up into the cloudless blue sky. Perhaps he was hoping to find an answer somewhere in the heavens. "I can only tell you," he said, "that he hated the role in which his father had placed him. But I assure you, gentlemen, that I never suspected that Leigh was unhappy enough to do himself in. There's really not much else I have to say on the subject – except that I miss my friend greatly."

Holmes stood up. "Thank you, Mr. Bentley," said he. "You've been a great help to us."

The barrister collected his map and gently folded it along the creases. Replacing it in his coat pocket, he shook hands with the two of us and wished us well. We accompanied him as far as his chambers and then bade him good day.

"Do you realize, Watson," said Holmes once we reached High Holborn, "that thanks to Mr. Bentley – not to mention the dead Mr. Smith-Mortimer – we are going to have to return to the scene of some of our most unpleasant memories." When he raised his hand to flag a hansom, he bore the gravest of expressions.

Unlike our first trip to the Reichenbach Falls, we required no subterfuge on this occasion. We faced no adversary like Moriarty in his special train to fool into thinking we were going to Paris. The *Express* from Victoria took us directly to Dover. From there, a ship conveyed us to Calais. With no need to pose as carefree pedestrians touring the Valley of the Rhone or exploring the Alps of central Switzerland, we utilised the various railroads traversing the French and Swiss countrysides to deposit us at the chalet-like train station in Meiringen.

Holmes and I may not have looked like the tourists we had hoped to resemble three years before, but even on that earlier occasion we had no cause to conceal our true identities. When we reached the *Englischer Hof*, therefore, old Peter Steiler greeted Holmes in particular like an old friend.

"*Ach*, Herr Holmes," said Steiler, his English helped by an earlier stay in London, "it is as though you come from the dead. I heard of your return and am pleased to know that you did not die in the Reichenbach waters."

"And yet someone else just did, *nicht wahr*?" Holmes asked.

"*Ja*," answered Steiler. "A young Englishman. Like you, from here he went walking on his own."

"It is his death, Herr Steiler, that I am here to investigate. How was he dressed?"

The old man thought for a moment, then smiled broadly as he remembered the details. "Heavy trousers. Heavy coat. Good boots. Flat cap."

Holmes nodded. "Nothing else?"

"But of course," said Steiler. "*Schon vergessen*. A very large rucksack he carried on his back."

"Ha!" ejaculated Holmes, slapping his hand on the counter. "Precisely as I expected. Come, Watson. We shall soon get to the bottom of this mystery."

Snow-covered mountain peaks served as backdrop when, for the second time in our adventures, Holmes and I marched up the incline towards the series of falls. From the bottom of the road one cannot see the water itself, only the winding trail leading up and past the three mighty torrents that ultimately rain down as one. It took us some ten minutes to reach the lowest of the falls, an additional fifteen to reach the central, and another thirty to get to the uppermost.

Veiled in the shadows of the numerous fir trees, we plodded upward. Holmes kept his eyes on the ground searching for any tell-tale clues. For me, however, the path served only to conjure terrible memories. During that first ascent three years before, I had been called back to the hotel on a ruse, and I shall never forget the horrible fear I experienced when I rushed back up this same mountain trail hoping against hope that my friend still lived.

Now as then, the fearsome roar of the waterfall attracted us like a magnet. Skirting the ominous rock walls that towered above, I followed after Holmes in the direction of the thunderous din. To witness the waters cascade in waves of white foam down the glistening black walls of stone and plunge into the cavernous abyss is to see unmasked the overwhelming power and beauty of Nature.

Yet once we reached the narrow path leading to the edge of the final precipice, my morbid recollections eclipsed the grandeur. A wave of nausea overcame me as soon as I encountered the very boulder against which Holmes had leaned his Alpine stock and upon which he had left his farewell note. Enveloped by the clouds of mist and spray that hovered above the roiling waters, I forced myself to halt at a safe distance from the brink. The world around me was beginning to spin. With the mountain wall on one side and the straight drop a short distance before me, I placed my palm against the wet stone and took a series of deep breaths.

Holmes, who was stooping over a handful of black soil a few steps ahead, looked back over his shoulder and saw my condition. Whether my unsettled appearance affected his judgement, I shall never know, but with a quick shake of his head, he shouted at me over the water's roar, "No need to go any farther!" Then he gave the dirt in his hand a final peremptory look and tossed the stuff to the ground. "The path is of no use to us," said he loudly, slapping his hands together to rid them of any residual muck. "It's too moist, and too many footprints have already marred the trail. I should imagine that the authorities themselves have stomped across it and obliterated whatever clues we might have hoped to find."

"Are we done here, then?" I shouted back hopefully.

In answer, Holmes looked up at the sheer mountain wall by our side. "Do you see it, Watson?" he asked, pointing to a projection some twenty feet above our heads. "The ledge that shielded me when you brought the police here to examine the scene."

So long ago, and yet the memory of my exclusion from his plan still stung. I imagine that I will always harbour some resentment towards Holmes for letting me continue to think him dead. It was only the ultimate jubilation I experienced upon his return that alleviated the pain.

"We need another point of vantage," said he and, keeping his eye on the wall to our left, he proceeded to march back in the direction from which we had come. Though each step away from the edge helped restore my strength, I suddenly feared Holmes was searching for the invisible footholds he had employed in his earlier escape in order to scale the wall once again. At the point where the wall fell away, however, he stopped and, turning to his left once more, stared at a network of overgrown brambles and ferns.

"A-ha!" he said at last and roughly pushed aside the overgrowth.

In an instant I perceived a hidden pathway ascending round the back of the mountain, and together Holmes and I scrambled up the steep terrain. Only when we reached a small plateau did I realise that we must be at the same spot where Colonel Moran had watched the struggle between Moriarty and Holmes unfold. It would have been here that Moran, intent on completing the job that Moriarty had thankfully been unable to consummate, rained down upon Holmes a shower of large rocks and stones.

Today, of course, there were no such dangers. In spite of the tumble of tree branches that blocked part of the view, we could now readily discern some twenty yards beneath us the rectangular outcropping that had served as Holmes's hiding place. The ledge was several feet deep, and verdant moss, like a green wool rug, blanketed the small nooks and crannies of its stone floor.

From an inner pocket, Sherlock Holmes drew a pair of binoculars, which he trained on the area below. "Owing to the proximity of the Falls," he observed as he peered through the lenses, "the moss-bed remains continuously moist. I can assure you from experience that not only does it provide a comfortable nest, but it also retains footmarks exceedingly well.”

For a few moments more he proceeded to scan the ledge. “*Eureka!*” he suddenly shouted and, handing me the glasses, commanded, “Look for yourself.”

I adjusted the lenses and observed the patterns in the moss more closely. Where before I had seen only gentle folds, I now made out among the rear shadows a long indentation where someone had recently lain. I could also begin to distinguish a few scattered footprints. At one edge of the projection, I detected what appeared to be the broad marks of a man’s boots. At the other edge –

“Hold on,” I said to Holmes. “Are those not the footprints of a woman’s shoe?”

“Precisely what I expected,” said Holmes, clapping his hands together.

“But what can such footprints mean? For that matter, Holmes, what does any of it mean?”

“To London, Watson!” said he by way of answer. Motioning me to follow, he hurried along the downhill trail, his eyes focused on the path before him. Thanks to the information furnished by the binoculars, we now knew for what to look. And truth be told, clearly discernable along the way were the occasional woman’s footprints mingling with all the other marks that had churned up much of the earth.

“We have learned all that we could hope for here in Switzerland,” proclaimed Sherlock Holmes. “It is now time to reacquaint ourselves with Mr. Reginald Bentley.”

Amberwell House, a modest building of soot-darkened stone, can be found in Southampton Row between Russell Square and Theobalds Road. Thanks to its proximity to the Inns of Court, the establishment provides lodgings for many of the solicitors and barristers who work nearby. Two days after our return from the Continent, Reginald Bentley suggested the Amberwell in response to our request to speak with him.

“*Amberwell House at the end of my workday,*” he had wired back.

As he led us to a group of grey-leather-backed chairs in the corner of the small lobby, the moustached barrister seemed ill at ease. He continually looked round although, except for the clerk at the front desk and a man across the way hidden behind a newspaper, the lobby was deserted.

“We have just returned from the Reichenbach Falls,” Holmes began. “Let us get straight to the point, shall we?”

Avoiding Holmes’s gaze, Bentley fidgeted with the cuffs of his jacket. “I don’t know what you mean,” he mumbled.

“We believe that your friend, Mr. Leigh Smith-Mortimer, stole Dr. Watson’s notes that dealt with my near-death experience three years ago. Just a few days later, you accompanied him in the re-creation of our previous trip to Switzerland. You have alleged that he left you in your room at the *Englischer Hof* in order to go walking on his own. Further, you maintain that he never returned – that he fell, or hurled himself, to the bottom of the Falls.”

“As I have already said.”

“Then, sir,” came Holmes’s blunt reply, “not to put too fine a point on it, I do not believe you.”

Bentley’s eyes grew wide. He was about to sputter out some retort, but Holmes kept speaking.

“Oh, I do not doubt that Smith-Mortimer went off to the Falls on his own, but I must conclude that you knew of his plans from the start – that, in fact, the two of you conspired to make it appear that Leigh Smith-Mortimer had leaped to his death never to be heard from again.”

“Now, see here, Mr. Holmes,” Bentley countered, “I won’t have you disparage Leigh that way, not to mention myself. Do you not remember that it was I who notified the police?”

“And yet, Mr. Bentley, it was also you who failed to inform them that the presumed-dead Smith-Mortimer was in reality hiding on the ledge not twenty feet above them. You, must admit, sir, that – ” But Holmes never finished the sentence.

"Enough!" came the forceful, high-pitched voice of the man whom I supposed to have been reading the newspaper. He slammed the pages to the floor and stalked over to us. "Leave Reginald alone, Mr. Holmes. *I* am the one you seek. I am Leigh Smith-Mortimer."

Holmes and I both stared up at the man – though, in truth, not very far up. From his photograph, we knew him to be shorter than his friend. But in the flesh, his entire stature appeared much slighter in spite of the well-cut, dark suit that must have come from Saville Row. His face bore delicate features, and his dark hair was cut short.

Reginald Bentley offered him his own seat while Bentley himself collected the chair that Smith-Mortimer had just been occupying.

"Well, well," Holmes said with a quick smile. "The very man we speak of. He who has dogged my footsteps to death's door at the Reichenbach Falls appears very much alive. What do you have to say for yourself, *sir*?" This last word was heavily emphasised, and at the same time there appeared in my friend's eye the same inexplicable twinkle that I had seen when he had first heard the details of the young man's disappearance.

"Reginald has told me," Leigh Smith-Mortimer replied, "that you already know how much I detest my father and his domination – all in the name of his legacy. A plague on that legacy! I tell you, Mr. Holmes, that I could take it no longer. I wanted a means of escape. I've read of your investigations, and when I heard of your so-called death and resurrection, it gave me the idea to do the same.

"Your return being so recent, I assumed that Dr. Watson would have his notes concerning the affair lying about. As you have surmised, I entered your rooms in disguise and stole his notebook. Reginald and I then followed all of your steps to be certain we didn't miss any of the planning that led to your success."

"Stealing my notes," I muttered. "Not very sporting."

"I'm sorry, Doctor, but your notebook furnished me with the kind of details I needed – like the footholds leading to the ledge above the path. As did you, Mr. Holmes, I hid there from the police during their investigation, and when they had gone, I made my way back to London. Under a pseudonym, I took a room here at the Amberwell down the hall from Reginald. Now, I suppose, you will notify my father, and he will attempt to have me return to Windstone Hall."

"Your father is my client," said Holmes. "He has contracted me to find you. And yet, should I so choose, a rejection of his money would rid me of the responsibility."

The young man's eyes suddenly blazed with hope. "You'd do that, Mr. Holmes?"

"I assure you, Mr. Smith-Mortimer, that in the name of fair play, I have committed a number of unconventional actions. I am no official police force, you understand. But I must give your situation some thought. I don't overturn my clients' requests lightly. And whilst there is no law that will force you to go back to your father, the law of decency makes it imperative for me to let him know that you are alive and well. I suggest that we meet at Baker Street tomorrow afternoon. I shall send you a telegram once I have arranged the matter with Sir Lionel."

With that Holmes rose, and I followed. As we exited the Amberwell, I could not fail to notice that behind us an animated discussion was going on between the two young men.

"Well, Watson, what do you make of the situation?" Holmes asked once we had found ourselves in Southampton Row again and walking towards the Strand.

"I believe that you were quite right in reserving additional time to consider your responsibilities. Still, I must say that there seems no let-up in young Smith-Mortimer's grudge against his father. Unreasonable, I should think – in light of the rules that dictate the responsibilities of a titled son."

Sherlock Holmes stopped in his tracks. "Good old Watson – forever faithful to the traditions of our culture. And yet you miss the salient feature."

I could not see where Holmes was leading me. The antagonisms between father and son seemed quite clear.

"My dear fellow," said Holmes. "You have failed to recognise the fact that Mr. Leigh Smith-Mortimer – 'the titled son', as you call him – is in reality a woman."

Even I, the so-called man of words, was speechless. At last I spat out, "You – you can't be serious, Holmes."

"But I am, old fellow. Of course, you noted the delicate features, the short but luxuriant hair, the small frame, the lilting voice."

"Yes, all of which proves nothing."

"But when you couple those decidedly feminine characteristics with a masculine life dictated by the unforgiving laws of primogeniture, you discover a wretched soul forced to play a part counter to her nature."

"But, Holmes. Surely birth certificates, doctors' statements – all would discount your inflammatory charges."

"Remember the birth, Watson. The couple were alone wandering the woods. Who knows? Perhaps Sir Lionel had purposely arranged their isolated perambulations to coincide with the time the birth was expected. Fortunately, he managed to deliver the child, but unhappily could do nothing regarding the complications that killed Lady Smith-Mortimer. Clearly, there would be no more children. I imagine that in the confusion that followed, the doctors devoted their attention to saving the poor mother and simply taken Sir Reginald's word for the sex of the baby. Money paid out to wet-nurses and nannies would have purchased the silence of any others who knew the truth.

Such a wild plan certainly explained Holmes's fantastic accusation.

"I suspected some sort of ruse," said he, "as soon as Sir Lionel began complaining so bitterly about his son. I thought the old man protested too much. Upon observing the young person, I am now convinced."

"But the pretend suicide, Holmes, the climb up the mountain to the ledge. Surely, no *woman* could be expected to perform such feats!"

"Ah, Watson," Holmes smiled, "how did Hamlet put it to Horatio? '*There are more things in heaven and earth than are dreamt of in your philosophy.*' I find women quite as capable as men in accomplishing whatever they put their mind to." He turned silent, and I knew he must have been thinking of the machinations set up by Irene Adler a few years before that had succeeded in thwarting him.

"But what's the point, Holmes?" I asked breaking into his thoughts. "Even if Sir Reginald had succeeded in passing the girl off as a boy, there could be no children in her future, no male heir to claim the estate."

"A crazed old man trying to hold on to what is his for as long as possible," Holmes offered. He grew silent again. In fact, the only words he uttered after we had reached Aldwych, were, "Let us continue on and dine at Simpson's. Afterwards, I shall make arrangements with Sir Lionel for tomorrow's meeting."

With the late-afternoon sun to our backs, we negotiated the Aldwych Crescent, our long shadows stretching out before us. I remember thinking at the time how well those shadows epitomised the case. Whatever had been going on in the mind of Sir Lionel Smith-Mortimer for the past twenty years must have been very murky indeed.

Mrs. Hudson had prepared tea for five people as we had requested. The stooped form of Sir Lionel arrived first, his trek up our stairs punctuated by the beat of his cane. He looked at the tea service and chocolate biscuits set out on the dining table, shook his head, and selected an armchair to sit upon that was far removed from the table.

"Tell me your news, Holmes," he demanded.

"In due time, sir. We await the others."

"What others?"

As if in answer, a sharp knock rattled our door. Holmes opened it to Reginald Bentley. The barrister entered the room, but not by himself. He was accompanied by a magnificent young woman in a dress of yellow cotton, accented in white at the neck and cuffs. Adorned with a white feather, a small yellow hat perched coquettishly upon her short black curls. It nearly took my breath away to realise that only the day before I had been conversing with this very person under the impression that I was speaking to one Leigh Smith-Mortimer, the only son of a Baronet.

"Watson," said Holmes with a gesture towards the lady, "may I re-introduce you to Leigh Smith-Mortimer. That is, *Miss* Leigh Smith-Mortimer.

"Now see here!" interrupted Sir Lionel. "I won't stand for this *charade*."

Miss Smith-Mortimer had been about to take my hand when she wheeled upon her father. "*You* won't stand for this *charade*?" she charged, cheeks reddening, nostrils flaring. "I've been play-acting in your little game for as long as I can remember. Always the boy – to preserve the line! Even though you've always known that the line would end with me. You knew I could never marry as a man. And now I have found someone who has seen through this masquerade and wants to love me as a woman should be loved. I am through with your game, Father. May Windstone Hall crumble to the earth for all I care!"

"Leigh," Sir Lionel said, holding out both hands. "After your mother died and there was no possibility for a male heir – "

"Stop, Father!" she cried. "I have heard all this before. Let the succession fall to cousins twice-removed – or *three*-times removed. It doesn't matter anymore. You robbed me of my proper childhood, and I won't allow you to rob me of my marriage." She turned to Bentley. "That is," she said, her voice now lowered, "if you'll have me."

Reginald Bentley took her in his arms. "I love you, Leigh. Your beautiful nature has always shone through your disguise. We did our best to kill off the male version of yourself, and now, thanks to Mr. Holmes, you've been able to speak the truth."

The young woman stood as tall as she could. "I am leaving you now, Father," she said simply. "As you've just heard, Reginald and I will soon be married. Good man that he is, he has convinced me to invite you to the wedding. It is your choice whether you want to gain a daughter and, God willing, grandchildren or live on in isolation. The choice will be yours."

Before leaving, the couple turned to Holmes and me. "Thank you, gentlemen," said Bentley. "At first I feared you might bring ruination upon us, but now I see that shining a light on this bizarre story has brought us salvation instead." The two of them smiled and hand in hand slowly made their way down the stairs.

With a dissatisfied grunt, Sir Lionel leaned on his cane in order to stand. He took a deep breath and, without looking at either of us, placed a one-hundred-pound note on the table as he shuffled to the door. Not a word was spoken by anyone.

Once the door closed, I walked to the table set for tea and sampled one of Mrs. Hudson's chocolate biscuits.

Reginald Bentley had relatives who lived in the hamlet of Icomb in Gloucestershire. It was there in the tiny church of St. Mary the Virgin that he and Leigh Smith-Mortimer chose to marry a few short weeks after the events described. Although Holmes and I were invited to the ceremony, we decided not to attend. It was to be a small affair, and our presence would only serve to raise uncomfortable questions. Happily, there were no pressmen in attendance, and Miss Smith-Mortimer sent us an account in her own hand of all that had transpired.

True to her word, she did request her father's presence. And I am pleased to report that, difficult as it was for him both physically and emotionally, Sir Lionel travelled to Gloucestershire to give his daughter away. Villagers must have wondered about the splendid carriage and liveried footman at so simple a ceremony, but their wonder never reached the spiteful arena of London gossip – at least not then.

Three years later, however, Sir Lionel died, and the facts regarding his mistreatment of his daughter became the fodder of scandal throughout the land. Just as the Baronet had predicted, with no son to inherit the estate, the grand manor house along with the rest of the riches was passed on by virtue of entailment to a distant Canadian cousin called Randolph Carlton Smith.

It had been my desire to maintain the privacy of the newly-married couple. To that end, I included the Smith-Mortimer affair in the collection of cases from 1894 that I chose not to make public. Yet however noble in intent, the gesture turned out to be laughably feeble.

Periodicals could not print enough about the story to satisfy the public. Newspapers constantly rehashed the details; magazines furnished long-winded biographies of the principals. So widespread were the accounts of the ugly business that one can understand why I had originally referred to the entailment case as "famous". In retrospect, I believe that "infamous" would have been the more appropriate adjective.

When I look at the three massive manuscript volumes which contain our work for the year 1894 I confess that it is very difficult for me, out of such a wealth of material, to select the cases which are most interesting in themselves and at the same time most conducive to a display of those peculiar powers for which my friend was famous . . . . The famous Smith-Mortimer succession case comes also within this period . . . .

Dr. John H. Watson – "The Adventure of the Golden Pince-Nez"

MX Publishing

 MX is the largest independent publisher of Sherlock Holmes books in the world with over 100 authors and more than 400 books in print.

The MX Book of New Sherlock Holmes Stories is the world's largest collection of new, traditional, Sherlock Holmes Stories with all royalties going to Stepping Stones School at Undershaw. More than 300 stories, a dozen volumes (with 4+ new volumes per year) and including contributions from some of the leading Sherlockian and mystery writers edited by David Marcum. Contributors include Lyndsay Faye, Lee Child, Jonathan Kellerman, Denis O Smith and over a hundred more.

"No historical material here. This is all new, and it's beyond impressive, in quantity and in consistent quality. Here are some — most — of the best, most dedicated Holmesian authors working today" Sherlock Holmes Society of London

Publishers Weekly has given the last seven volumes starred reviews:

"Marcum continues to amaze with the number of high-quality pastiches that he has selected"
Volume XII review

"This is an essential volume for Sherlock Holmes fans"
Volume XI review

"Marcum continues to find new Sherlock Holmes adventures of consistently high quality"
Volume X review

"Sherlockians will rejoice that more volumes are on the way"
Volume IX review

"The imagination of the contributors in coming up with variations on the volume's theme is matched by their ingenious resolutions"
Volume VIII review

"Sherlockians eager for faithful-to-the-canon plots and characters will be delighted"
Volume VII review

"This is a must-have for all Sherlockians"
Volume VI review

You can find all MX books at Amazon, Barnes and Noble, Book Depositorys and all good bookstores and direct from the publishers at www.sherlockholmesbooks.com

You can keep up with the latest news at www.facebook.com/BooksSherlockHolmes/